HAWKWOOD'S SWORD

Christian Cameron is a writer and military historian. He participates in re-enacting and experimental archaeology, teaches armoured fighting and historical swordsmanship, and takes his vacations with his family visiting battlefields, castles and cathedrals. He lives in Toronto and is busy writing his next novel.

HAWKWOOD'S SWORD

CHRISTIAN CAMERON

ORION

First published in Great Britain in 2021 by Orion Fiction,
an imprint of The Orion Publishing Group Ltd.,
Carmelite House, 50 Victoria Embankment
London EC4Y 0DZ

An Hachette UK Company

1 3 5 7 9 10 8 6 4 2

A CIP catalogue record for this book
is available from the British Library.

ISBN (Hardback) 978 1 4091 8025 8
ISBN (eBook) 978 1 4091 8027 2

Typeset by Deltatype Ltd, Birkenhead, Merseyside

Printed in Great Britain by Clays Ltd, Elcograf, S.p.A.

www.orionbooks.co.uk

For Nancy

Queen of re-enacting, Goddess of Teaching, cancer survivor, and the reader I think of when I write William Gold!

PROLOGUE

Calais, 1381

The rain fell outside – a steady, soaking rain that discouraged exercise and recommended the woodsmoke smell, good beer and snug seating of the inn. The common room was packed with men-at-arms and archers, pages and servants.

The innkeeper glanced at Sir William Gold, who had just finished describing the 'Italian Wedding' and was sitting back, drinking deep from a jack of small beer. Chaucer and Froissart began to ask each other questions – Froissart clearly excited by what he had heard.

Sir William held up his jack, and Aemilie pushed herself away from the wall where she had listened all morning to the older knight's recital. She crossed to the bar, took a sandy, London-made pitcher off the shelf, poured it full from a cask on a trestle and then placed it between the three gentlemen.

Sir William smiled at her. 'I'm sure you're bored,' he said.

'It wasn't exactly a shower of blood,' Chaucer said to Sir William. He was speaking of the story Sir William had told the night before, of the wedding of Violante, daughter of the Count of Milan, Galeazzo Visconti, to the king of England's fourth son, Lionel, Duke of Clarence. 'I admit it had a nasty feel to it, but there was not *that* much blood. I don't think Clarence ever noticed it happen.'

Froissart leaned over. 'Was it really Lesparre?' he asked.

He had a five-fold wax tablet, an elegant piece framed in ebony, and he had covered all ten sheets of wax with notes.

'Yes,' Sir William said. He was still looking at the innkeeper's daughter.

'Bored?' she asked. 'Sir William, every one of us is waiting for you to continue.'

Froissart shook his head. 'Lesparre in Milan? How did I never meet him?'

Sir William took the pitcher and poured a third cup for Froissart and then, at a nod, for Chaucer.

'You really ought to give up the life of arms and write a romance,' Chaucer said. 'Your story is much better than the reality, even if it is just as sordid.'

'You flatter me,' Sir William said.

'I certainly didn't intend to.'

Chaucer smiled, as if to cover the insult, and Sir William began to laugh. Froissart turned his head away, as if he feared an explosion.

'Why don't you tell us what you saw?' Gold said.

Chaucer sat back. He looked out of the window at the steady rain.

'I don't suppose there's aught else today,' he said. 'No *sauvegardes*, no ships, and no sun.' He looked at Gold, and for the first time for hours his expression softened from a cynical disapproval to a smile of self-knowledge. 'William, I was besotted and you know it. I am not sure that I noted anything.'

'Besotted?' Froissart caught the word. 'With whom? The bride? She was very beautiful.'

Chaucer glanced at Froissart with something between contempt and pity.

'Not the bride, by God's mercy.'

'Italy,' Gold said.

'How well you know me,' Chaucer said simply. 'Boccaccio? Petrarca? I could barely see my knife to cut my food. It was like finding myself between the Archangel Michael and the Blessed Virgin at dinner.'

'And yet you talked constantly,' Gold said.

Froissart made a face.

Chaucer mimed taking a thrust in the gut. 'Unkind!'

'I can remember you, prosing away—'

'You are killing me,' Chaucer said.

'About time.' Gold smiled, but he seemed to mean it. 'You twist the knife often enough.'

Chaucer winced.

'I sat silent,' Froissart said. 'For my part, I was there to observe.'

'I ...' Chaucer began, and then his shoulders slumped.

'Master Chaucer needed the two most brilliant men of the age to know how intelligent he was,' Gold said quietly.

'Damnable and true,' Chaucer said.

'And they loved you anyway,' Gold said. 'So did Landini.'

Chaucer laughed. 'I don't suppose I ever had a greater shock than that all the literati of Italy knew you, William.'

'I've carried Petrarca's letters all over Europe,' Gold said.

'I remember when you took a letter to him from me in the year of the sack of Limoges.' Chaucer glanced at Froissart.

Froissart shrugged. 'The prince was a monster.'

'We're all monsters,' Chaucer said.

'The prince was ill, and the Duke of Lancaster behaved nobly,' Sir William said. 'It was scarcely a sack. To my shame, I've seen such. Limoges was merely—'

'Horrible? Shameful?' Chaucer spat.

'Brutal?' Froissart asked.

'War,' Gold said, his voice hard. 'War is terrible. Lancaster did what he could. Many of us did. In fact, the slur comes from the Pope.'

'You would say so,' Chaucer said.

An uneasy silence fell.

'Odd words from you, Chaucer.' Gold was angry. 'You're devoted to Lancaster.'

'And then you were with Hawkwood,' Froissart said carefully.

Gold sat back, drank some more beer, and glanced at Aemilie.

'Ah, messires, a great many things happened after the Italian Wedding. The worst year of my life, and no mistake.'

'You might as well tell us,' Chaucer said.

'I want to hear about your time with Hawkwood,' Froissart said.

'Very well,' Gold said with a grin. 'But be warned. It's a long time before I'll come back to Sir John ... and a lot of blood.'

PART I
SAVOY AND SPAIN

1368 – 1369

CHAPTER ONE

MILAN

May – June 1368

The morning after a great feast – you know how it is, gentles. Your head is hard and your legs are perhaps a little shaky. You've had too little sleep, and your stomach burns from all the wine. The day before, I'd fought in the lists. That evening had seen the wedding of Violante, daughter of the mighty count of Milan, to Lionel, Duke of Clarence, brother of the Prince of Wales and son of the king of England.

In my case I had bruises, wounds still fresh enough to bleed on our sheets, and a companion on a very narrow bed in the 'office', which was really just a passageway between the outer doors of a four-storey tower and the inner doors. You need to recall our arrangements before the wedding: the giant English Duke of Clarence and the Count of Savoy were sharing a tower in the Visconti palace. Richard Musard and I had seized it by *coup de main* from the steward, an excellent noble gentleman named Orgulafi.

And I'll remind you that I'd just faced a fight in the lists with hafted weapons, and then a feast that was in many ways equally dangerous. Despite the rain of blood and the terrible overtones to the festivities, I'd been in the state of euphoria a knight reaches with victory, and Emile was by my side, beautiful, thoughtful and powerful, drawing the attention of every man of blood, and every man and woman of wit.

Listen, and I will tell you a true, private thing. Neither my wife nor I led pure lives before we wed. And for that, it has always given me a sinful satisfaction to look a certain kind of man in the eye – the man who wants my wife – and I let my eyes say, 'Just try. Be my guest, if you think you are better than I.'

Because her scorn for the would-be suitors was always my reward. Courtly love is a dangerous game, and those who play for lust rather than love are often richly rewarded in scorn. As they should be.

Regardless, my lady stayed by me, both at the feast and as we moved through the streets with the revellers, drinking wine with a crowd of swordsmiths and then with our own archers – who, I discovered, were watching over us. Men beyond price. Witkin, of all people, was following us, mostly sober, with a staff, looking like a pilgrim – the best-armed pilgrim in Milan. Sam Bibbo handed me a cup of wine and told me where all of Camus's people were.

So when we'd wandered and drunk far too much, we felt perfectly safe making love in an open church, among the pillars. Ah, I'm making Messire Froissart blush, but truly, sir, I speak of my wedded wife, and we took delight in each other, which Aquinas says is no sin.

Emile laughed afterwards. 'I suppose the Comtesse d'Herblay is still a wanton,' she said.

I kissed her.

'A church, for God's love!' she said.

I laughed aloud. 'If priests did not want couples courting in churches, they shouldn't leave them unlocked all night.'

'Fie, sir, you are blasphemous,' she said.

'If I had had less wine, I'd make you a different argument,' I said, or something wittier.

She clutched me. 'By the Virgin, William, who would I be if I hadn't found you?'

'Just as true for both of us,' I said.

And as we swayed and stumbled down the nave in our outrageous finery, she stopped me. We kissed; I thought that was what she wanted. But she shook me off.

'I want to go on another pilgrimage,' she said. 'I want away from all this.'

I hesitated, even drunk.

She put her arms around me. 'The caravan from Jerusalem to Rhodes was the best time of my life,' she said.

'I have a company ...' I said.

'William! I am richer than any two rich lords. Appoint an acting captain and we'll pay him and them.'

Perhaps not the moment to explain that I was the leader, and they stayed with me for reasons. It always sounds so self-serving to say aloud, but *certes*, gentles, it is true, and every good knight knows it. Not with pride, but with humility. Men will willingly follow a good captain and will eagerly flee a bad one.

I managed to hold my tongue.

'Say we will go,' she said.

'Rome?' I asked.

'That cesspit?' she spat. 'Santiago.'

Spain!

I had never been to Spain. Chaucer here was there the year before, eh? With the prince, in '67. As you would hear, if only he'd tell the tale.

Any road, I can see through a brick wall in time, and she was right. Money was no longer any part of my life, except to spend it, which I confess was so remarkable that I oft-times forgot it. I kissed her again. Mayhap more than once.

'Santiago!' I said.

'Swear!' she said. 'After this bloodbath of emotions, I need something sweet and beautiful.'

I dragged her by the hand back into the church we'd just stumbled out of, and we went to the altar like a pair of penitents. And perhaps we were – a little sin can be good for the soul, if it leads to redemption, eh?

Very well, Chaucer, I'm a poor theologian. But we knelt before the altar in Milan and swore before God to go on Camino before the year was out.

We awoke to dusty mouths and aching heads on a narrow pallet of straw in the 'office', like any routier and his doxy. I was told in no uncertain terms by a pair of sober archers that I needed to clear the guardroom with my wife before the Duke of Clarence came through.

Let me turn aside here and say that Clarence was taller than me – almost as tall as a ceiling. He was always the tallest man in any room, and well built, with a heavy frame. He'd have been a terror to face in combat. He was also cheerful, the way big men often are; he was afraid of nothing, and had excellent manners. I had only known him a few days and already I was happy to oblige him.

So I ignored my doxy's complaints, but bundled her up in a linen sheet. I am not at my most gentle and chivalrous in such moments, and I suspect they still remember what I said, but Emile and I fled, and there was a certain amount of mockery. Marc-Antonio found me and put a cup of water in my hand and told me that the Count of Savoy desired my attendance on him as soon as I might be available, or some other flowery phrase, and there I was, my magical evening transformed into another working day, albeit enlivened by a hangover.

It was then that we discovered – pray remember we'd come in very late – that, of course, the bridal couple had come back to the tower, and Lady Violante had spent her wedding night in the safe apartments of her new husband, guarded, let me add, by Richard Musard and Fiore. The prince was up early, but his new wife lay in bed.

I mention these domestic details because, first, I think most of the city imagined that the bridal couple were in the palace proper, but they were not. We were still on the *qui vive* for some attack from the bishop's party.

I heard the count and his lady go down the stairs while I was 'indisposed', and I heard him enquire for me. Sam Bibbo had my back, and reported that I was 'inspecting the guard'.

Yes, well. Very exactly true.

I emerged from a garderobe to discover that one of the Lady Violante's women had found the Comtesse d'Herblay on the stairs and 'invited' her to visit her mistress.

I was there. This is complicated, and delicate, and I will not tell you all I know. Suffice it to say that I could tell from the tension in the Italian woman's face that something was wrong, and that she needed the support of a noble matron, which, of course, Emile did to perfection when she wasn't frowzy from lack of sleep and suffering from a headache of profound proportions.

I left her to it, and went down to the guardroom, where, amidst many offers of fat bacon and cups of hot spiced wine from my 'devoted' friends and archers, I was undressed by Marc-Antonio and prepared to attend the count.

'What's ...?' I asked.

Marc-Antonio read my stumbling mind perfectly. 'I think it is routine, My Lord. If I may be so bold ...'

'Go on,' I muttered, or perhaps 'gawg' or 'erg'.

'I believe all the great lords are simply counting heads and ensuring they are attended. The game of lords.'

Sam Bibbo hadn't had any more sleep than I had, but while I was still in braes he grabbed my hand as if I were a lass and dragged me down the stone steps to the yard. He proceeded to pour cold water from the bronze pump over my head and body for perhaps a minute, to the delight of a variety of cooks and children.

I sputtered, drank off a bucket of water, pissed it away, drank more, and felt much better, by God.

The Duke of Clarence came into the guardroom. His usually open face was hard, and he was in his underclothes without a cote-hardie or a doublet. He looked around. I could sense his anger.

'Sir Guillaume,' he said in Norman French.

His voice was loud, and cut through my head like a poleaxe. I did my best to bow. I was soaking wet, and on my third jack of water.

'My people are already engaged,' he said, ignoring my state. 'I would like an immediate audience with Messire Galeazzo. Will you arrange that for me?'

I made a reverence. It was easier than speaking coherently.

The duke didn't look like a man who'd spent a wedding night. He looked like a man who'd had no sleep and had been to hell.

I needed clothes, and sobriety, so I bowed again and passed him, heading for the stairs, abandoning Sam Bibbo to deal directly with an English prince. Not my most knightly act.

I remember passing two of Violante's maids on the stairs. I was effectively naked, and there was a good deal of giggling. I bowed to them and my head didn't pound, and quickly enough after, I was fully dressed in emerald-green hose and a golden yellow cote-hardie with hanging sleeves. I put on my chain and a hat, and Marc-Antonio gave me a purse with a dagger on the belt – not de Charny's.

Bibbo came with me as my attendant. He looked at me as soon as we started to cross the great yard.

'The duke's in a right state,' he said.

'I noticed,' I answered.

'Nay, listen to me. He's angry, and he said a thing or two ...' Sam glanced at me. 'He thinks Violante has been ...' He looked away. Very tough men can be very shy about other people's troubles. Sam, for all he could kill men with a bow or his hands, was in his heart a protective older brother. 'Ill-used,' he said, so quietly that the loud gossip of a pair of servants almost drowned him out.

'Sweet Christ,' I said, or something equally blasphemous. Not that I hadn't already suspected.

I tried to adjust my wine-sodden mind to the idea while also thinking about guarding our party, and what the Bishop of Cambrai's next move might be. Even after the wedding, I had to imagine he might strike again, and I needed somebody. The streets and even the internal yards of the palazzo were packed, and we knew our opponents still meant business.

'Where is Savoy?' I asked Bibbo.

I took for granted that he knew where to find the count, nor was I disappointed.

'They call it the "Blue Room",' he said. 'In the wing across the main yard. I have Ewan out at the drawbridge watching.' He smiled his quiet smile. 'You heard the thing I just said?'

'Aye, Sam,' I agreed. 'I'm just not sure what to do about it.'

'I'm not the plotter here—' Sam said.

'Jesu, I'm a plotter?' I snapped.

'More 'an me,' Bibbo said. He leant close. 'I don't think the duke should be allowed to speak … directly … to Messire Galeazzo. There could be blood.'

'Jesu,' I said again. 'Thanks, Sam. Where would I be without you?'

'Dead? Or cooking someone's food?' Bibbo laughed. 'Ye're a fine cook, as I have every reason to remember,' he added. We both laughed, and then he said, with rare severity, 'You coaxed me through the pestilence. I don't forget. But this is serious. Killing serious.'

We walked along the outside of the palace proper, which formed as two long buildings connected at one end, with a magnificent garden in the middle. We crossed the garden, bowing to our right and left. Every single functionary of the palace was as well or better dressed than I, and Bibbo, in his severe green pourpoint, looked like a monk. A military monk.

My relations with the Green Count had changed profoundly, as you've no doubt remarked. Far from keeping me waiting, he smiled as I entered his presence in one of the palace halls, and his wife allowed me to kiss her hand, as did his sister, who sat with them. A servant gave us pickled figs, which I devoured, and little saffron-covered sweetmeats from the East, which, to my shame, I also devoured.

However, Lady Bianca, the count's sister and the wife of Galeazzo Visconti, lord of Milan, smiled at my greed, and commented that at least I was bold enough to eat. Lady Bonne, the count's wife and the sister of the king of France, stared at her hands and twisted a scarf, betraying her unease.

'Your people were brilliant yesterday,' he said.

'Your people, My Lord,' I said.

That made him smile like the sun.

'By God,' he said. 'You give good service, Sir William, and you and Richard have become pillars to me. Now I seek your counsel.'

His wife smiled at me, and his sister looked away.

'Monsieur Richard,' Lady Bonne called to the page who often attended to the count. He'd survived the plague and some other incidents, but that's his story, not mine. He was fourteen or fifteen, pretty as a girl, and ready to be someone's squire. As you'll hear, presently.

He came up, gave me a good bow, and knelt by his mistress.

'Take the other chamber people and go outside,' she said, and gave him a gold florin.

Uh-oh.

I assumed, of course, that this was about Clarence. Or rather, Violante.

When the chamber was empty, the count stood and walked to the windows, which looked out over the courtyard where Fiore was practising.

'I am contemplating a step,' he said. 'It will have ... ramifications.'

'Just tell him,' Lady Bianca said.

Count Amadeus glanced at me. 'Join me,' he said, waving me to his window.

He handed me a parchment.

I glanced at it. It was a will, a legal testament by the Prince of Achaea's father, Giacomo, barring him from the inheritance. I think I have mentioned the prince – an ally of our enemy, the Bishop of Cambrai known as Robert of Geneva, and an obstacle to the ambitions of my friend Nerio. Among other things. In the testament, Giacomo clearly and unequivocally left everything to his young wife and her children. He completely disinherited his eldest son – that is, Prince Filippo – for reasons which he spelt out in no uncertain terms.

As soon as I touched it, I knew it wasn't the original, even though it had the requisite seals. I ran my hand over the beautiful milky vellum, and then looked carefully at the signature.

'It's not real,' I said.

Bianca laughed aloud.

Count Amadeus glared at her.

'I told him, and so did Montjoie,' Lady Bonne said.

Montjoie was the countess's knight.

'We have the original,' Amadeus said. 'It says all this.'

'It says it in a muddled language that no one could understand,' Bianca said.

'It is nonetheless my brother's will,' Amadeus challenged her.

'No one will believe you,' his wife rejoined.

Oh, *par Dieu*, gentles. Hell is where you have a hangover and your lord and his lady want you to take sides in a family argument. And my very slow wits were also comprehending that they didn't know about Clarence.

'He wants to present it today,' Bianca said.

'Against our wishes,' Bonne said.

Well, no one hires me to be a counsellor.

'I agree with you, ladies,' I said, making a full reverence.

'You agree with the women against your lawful lord?' Amadeus snapped.

'My Lord, if you don't want my opinion, don't ask!' I shot back.

Bonne laughed aloud. 'I wish all my brother's courtiers were like you,' she said. 'You remind me of du Guesclin.'

'Indeed, My Lady, he is my friend,' I said.

Bonne turned her head. 'Tell me a little of this, sir. How does an English knight come to be friends with a French knight?'

I was standing, so I bowed again. She was the king of France's sister, after all.

'I took him prisoner, and then later he took me, and then we were friends,' I said.

Even the Green Count managed a laugh, and I saw how skilfully Lady Bonne had moved us around the count's anger. Women – some women – are very skilled at this, because, I suspect, they are not encouraged to punch people or draw daggers when annoyed. A good knight might learn some things from such a lady.

'And poor Boucicault, who died last year, was also friends with this knight,' the count said. 'They're all friends.' He shrugged. 'So, messire, tell me *why* I should not reveal this thing?'

I tried not to shrug. Everyone but Bonne was on edge.

'My Lord, it would only serve to put a damper on the wedding festivities, which certain forces already seek to effect,' I said. 'And it might humiliate the Visconti.'

I was gathering my courage to mention Clarence. It struck me, suddenly, that if I wasn't quick enough, he might act on his own. Clarence was big, bluff, and not a deep thinker. And like any good knight, I think he was deeply protective of his lady from the moment he saw her. Various nightmare scenarios came to mind.

'Exactly!' Lady Bianca said. 'My husband is ready to react to any slight. Believe me.'

'Against that, if the document were examined, any clerk would say that the signature was in the same ink as the document . . .' I shrugged. I couldn't help myself.

'Damn it to hell!' the count swore. 'I want to be rid of this bad vassal.'

I nodded. 'My Lord, when the wedding is over and we are safe in our own lands, publish it,' I said.

'Exactly what Musard said,' the Green Count muttered.

'How is your countess?' asked Lady Bonne.

'Attending the new bride, Your Grace,' I said.

'Ah,' she said in her pure French. 'I cannot imagine a more perfect friend for a new bride than your wife.'

Was that a sting in the tail? I wondered if it was a reference to her wanton reputation, except that she smiled at me.

'Please ask her to attend me when the duchess can spare her.'

I bowed. Gritted my teeth.

'The Duke of Clarence is seeking an audience with Messire Galeazzo,' I said carefully. 'About matters relating to his new wife.'

I looked at Bonne.

The count's sister, Bianca, wife to Galeazzo, had a pale complexion – but all remaining colour left her face.

'Blessed Virgin,' she said quietly.

The count looked at me.

'My Lord, if you accept my advice, the duke would not meet with Messire Galeazzo today.'

Or maybe ever again.

Lady Bonne put a hand on my arm.

'Is ... *this* what your lady ... is talking to my daughter, Violante ...?'

I bowed. And said nothing. You may all think me a coward, but I didn't *know* anything. Add to that – my wife grew up with them. I was, by comparison, a hedge knight. I didn't know ... anything. I didn't know what the queen of France's opinions were on ... anything. Or those of the sister of the Count of Savoy, wed to the most dangerous man in Europe. I didn't know if they liked my wife or not, and I didn't know what they all thought of Violante, or Clarence, or the wedding ... It was all as far beyond me as the stars in the celestial dome, and I *still* had a crushing hangover.

Lady Bianca smiled. It was a very particular smile, one that a woman of immense power and excellent training used.

'I will see to this. Perhaps I need to have a little chat with my cousins,' she said with a cheerfulness that only a person of immense will could have summoned.

She stood, I bowed, and she and Lady Bonne swept out.

Young Richard, assuming the private audience to be over, allowed a host of servants in; they were cleaning up the breakfast and taking down the tables.

As much to cover the silence as anything else, I said, 'My Lord, what is your will concerning my company? They are serving the Visconti at your expense.'

It seemed as good a time as any to ask, and my intention was to give him time to cover his thoughts. He had shock writ large on his face.

He glanced at me. 'Sometimes I think you have a pact with the Devil, you can so clearly read my mind. In Venice once ... Never mind. They are fine just as they are, for now. I will want you in attendance on me for the next few weeks.' He looked after his wife and sister as they swept out. Shook his head. 'This is bad,' he murmured.

'I will appoint an acting captain,' I said, a little too loud. 'Another very small matter,' I added. 'My wife wishes me to ask for your blessing. Last night we swore a vow of pilgrimage, to go on camino to Santiago.'

Amadeus looked at me. 'Are you dissatisfied with my lordship?' he asked.

'In no way, My Lord,' I said.

He raised his chin. 'Ah. Good, then. Yes, of course you may make a pilgrimage. I would request your attendance this summer, however. And I may need your full company, William. My nephew has hired not just Camus, but the Monk of Hecz. You know of him?'

'No,' I confessed.

'German. Apparently he's actually a monk, as well as a routier. He has a dark repute and a cursed record of success. His opponents die. Often in tragic accidents.'

The count looked at his two ladies, who were crossing the yard outside.

I bowed. 'My Lord, I think you are so well served by gentlemen that no poisoner or villain can get at you,' I said. 'But I will be happy to stay by your side all summer.'

'Good. I will be losing your friend Sir Richard very soon.'

That stopped me. 'My Lord?'

He nodded. 'The Duke of Clarence needs knights and attendants. He has asked for both of you. I cannot afford to lose you both. I am sending him Richard because I need your company if it comes to war with Filippo. Do I make myself clear?'

Well, there it was – the sheer arrogance of the Count of Savoy. I can be arrogant myself, of course – it takes one to know one. But how he could fail to see that he was going to alienate Richard by treating him like a chattel – Richard Musard, a knight of his own Order of the Black Swan!

Richard Musard, a former slave.

However, it is one thing to tell a great lord that his plan to use a forgery is badly considered, and another to tell him that he's being an arrogant sod. I held my tongue, and as soon as I was released, I went to find Richard, who was in a solar playing chess with a pretty woman from the household.

'I don't want to discuss it,' he said as I looked in.

'I want to know that this isn't between us,' I said, or something like it. 'And I need your help.'

He gave me a look that said it was, most definitely, between us.

'How could it be?' he said sweetly, and turned his back on me.

Well, there we were. I thought my day had gone as badly as it might have, and then I returned to our tower and found my wife sitting, half dressed and blank-faced, in a room shared by the other ladies.

I embraced her. She was stiff. Not interested in my embrace.

'My love?'

'I'm not really fond of men just now,' she snapped. 'Go and fight someone with a sword. Or something.'

I withdrew.

In the courtyard, Fiore was playing with a very long sword, snapping cuts in various directions.

'Care to practise?' he asked.

'Not particularly,' I said.

'Excellent,' he said. 'Practise anyway.'

'I'm injured,' I insisted.

'Mmmm,' he said, enigmatically.

So, as usual, I did what he wanted – picked up a wooden waster and did exercises until the wound under my cote began to bleed. Admittedly, by then I felt much better.

A little sword work is usually a miraculous cure, as even Fiore knew, and by the time I'd washed my wound and stretched a little and put on a clean shirt, my lady was fully dressed and of a better cheer.

'Can you tell me, love?' I asked.

'Perhaps later,' she said. 'A woman's crisis.'

'I have good news,' I said.

She looked at me. 'I would love to hear something good,' she said.

'Our lord gives us his blessing to go to Santiago in the autumn,' I said.

She kissed me quickly, without warmth.

'I will count the hours,' she said. 'Well done.'

'I am to spend the summer in direct attendance,' I said.

'Sir John Hawkwood will not love that,' she said. 'But I *might* come to accept it.'

She was recovering.

Thank God.

Let's say that a young woman needed an older woman's help. Let's leave it there.

Milan. I wanted out as soon as it could be managed. The pretty brick castle with its plastered walls and perfect symmetry was a maze of corridors and hid a chaos of politics, and I wanted to be out in the countryside, where the worst thing you'd encounter was a peasant spreading dung.

And wolves, bandits, routiers, and false monks, disease, starvation . . . *Par Dieu.*

That wasn't happening soon.

I took Sir John Hawkwood aside as soon as he made himself available.

'Sir John, my lord of Savoy has required my attendance for the summer,' I said.

Hawkwood glanced at me. 'Well, well,' he said.

'It may come to war, in Savoy,' I said.

I didn't think I was betraying a confidence. Hawkwood smiled his fox's smile. 'Oh, I know all about that,' he said. 'I worry that it will distract your count from our war with the Pope and the Holy Roman Emperor.'

'I share your worry,' I said.

'Of course, he wants all the lands of the Prince of Achaea,' Hawkwood said. 'A damn sight closer to home, and more valuable than anything that either the Pope or Milan can offer, which is very little this year.'

I nodded. 'But Milan is paying,' I said.

Hawkwood met my eye – a look as expressive as Lady Bonne's.

'Paying,' he said. 'Yes.'

Well, he said the word 'yes', but that was my first frisson that something was wrong between Hawkwood and the lords of Milan.

'My people will be paid directly by the count,' I said.

Hawkwood brightened.

'This is delicate, Sir John.'

'Lordy, William, I've known you since you were a cook. You are asking if I'll look after your little company and not feed them to the fire, and you have to know how happy I am to get thirty expert lances for no fee. Bernabò Visconti won't let me have two hundred lances, but this way I can go over my contract and he can't complain.'

Well, there you are. John Hawkwood was never a paragon of chivalry, but he was, in his bent way, absolutely honest. And he usually was a straight talker, although he could talk around a contract or an enemy if he had to.

'They'll need their own captain,' I said.

'Corporal,' Hawkwood said with a smile. 'I'm the only captain in my company.'

I shrugged. '*Bien sur.*'

'Who do you have in mind?' he asked.

'Gatelussi or l'Angars,' I said.

'L'Angars,' he said. 'Gatelussi is too much a prince, he has better connections than me. People might become confused as to who is in command. I have enough trouble with Antonio Visconti.'

Antonio was a veteran of the crusade in the East, a friend of both the count and Hawkwood, one of Lord Bernabò Visconti's dozens of illegitimate sons. He owed me money and a pair of warhorses.

'He's never given me the least uneasiness,' I said of Gatelussi – which, considering Visconti's debt ...

Hawkwood slapped my back.

'That's because you are a paladin,' he said. 'I'm merely a mercenary. L'Angars and I have climbed ladders together. He can lead and obey, too. And my other corporals know him.'

'I'll take Gatelussi with me, then,' I said.

Hawkwood nodded. 'Yes,' he said. 'I'd prefer that.'

I bowed, prepared to make my leave.

Hawkwood beckoned me. 'Another matter,' he said very quietly.

'At your service,' I said.

He handed me a slip of good parchment. Very expensive parchment. The kind used for the very best books of hours. White as snow, almost transparent. On one side, a continuous line of symbols, written quickly. Even a casual examination showed me that it was a code. At the base, an *S*.

'We took it off the man who made the bomb,' he said. 'And he died. In a cell, in the palace, surrounded by Visconti guards.' Perhaps I looked foolish. 'The bomb that your lad so ably threw into the well.'

I hadn't forgotten, only misplaced.

'Janet traced the sale of the sulphur to mix the powder. She's good at that sort of thing. We took the man with all his goods, and the Visconti seem to have murdered him.' Hawkwood gave me the slip of parchment. 'If you are protecting Savoy and Prince Lionel, I wanted you to know.'

I bowed, and went to tell Fiore.

And then I found l'Angars and told him the news.

'Me?' he asked. 'An officer?'

'Yes.'

'I'm not even a knight,' he said. 'I mean ... I call myself a knight. But I've never been knighted.'

'Lead the boys and girls through the summer and come back to me,' I said, 'and I'll see the Green Count knights you with his own hand.'

'I'd be just as happy if you did it yourself,' he grinned. He was delighted to have the command.

I was just leaving my temporary 'office' – a corner with two bunks in the guardroom – when Pierre Lapot bowed and gave me the sele of the day.

'Sir Pierre,' I said.

He smiled. 'My Lord, I'm here to ask for leave.'

'Leave?' I asked.

He nodded. 'My Lord, I am thinking of entering religious orders. Killing men with my sword has lost its savour. Father Angelo has found me a house that seems to me very ... well suited.'

'You don't want to go to the Hospital,' I asked.

He shrugged. 'Routiers with crosses,' he said.

He had reason to know. Lapot had every reason to know – he'd been with me since Jerusalem. And he'd been in the sack of Alexandria.

'Go, with my blessing,' I said. 'Where is this house?'

'Verona, of course, My Lord,' he said.

'Well, expect me whenever I come through. Will you be a priest?'

Pierre nodded, lowering his eyes. 'If that is God's will.'

I hugged him hard. I assumed I'd never see him again, except through the bars of an abbey grille, but I was wrong, as you'll hear.

I found Gatelussi in the courtyard, drinking with the Genoese ambassador. I took him aside and asked him to be my lieutenant for the summer in Savoy. He bowed.

'At your service,' he said, very much in Nerio's manner.

I then picked up Witkin as a bodyguard and went boldly – perhaps *too* boldly – to visit Florimont de Lesparre. He was in a palazzo not so far away – the same that was occupied by Camus and the Bishop of Cambrai. Many things are best done at a gallop or not at all. I walked out of the gates and over two streets without consulting anyone. I knocked, and was admitted by a terrified servant, and was introduced to a modern solar, where there was a fireplace with a very small fire, and Robert of Geneva, the Bishop of Cambrai.

He glanced up. For the first time in my life, I saw him surprised. He'd expected someone else.

I bowed. I'm polite.

'I asked to see Sir Florimont,' I said.

He looked at me, his bland face recovering.

'If you've come to gloat, you're very early,' he said. 'I will see all of you destroyed.'

'I'm really here to see Messire Florimont,' I said again.

'By now, Clarence must know what a poison pill he's married,' Geneva went on. He smiled, all but rubbing his hands with glee. 'Indeed ...'

Who knows what he was going to say? Camus stepped in from the far room.

He looked at me. But Geneva still held his leash. He was silent.

I bowed. 'A pity you chose not to meet me yourself,' I said. 'Were you indisposed?'

'Fuck yourself, Gold,' he said.

I nodded. 'I'm here to see Messire Lesparre.'

Geneva rang a bell and the terrified servant appeared.

'Show this routier out,' he said.

I smiled. 'If you send Camus out, who will protect you?' I said.

He turned, rings glittering on his pudgy fingers with the same hard shine his eyes had.

'Do you imagine you can threaten me?' he asked.

I had been through a great deal in the previous day and a half. I was too tired and too hung-over to feel the jolt of spirit that sometimes throws me off my best game. I didn't smile. I just nodded.

'I watched you turn craven in the face of Sir John Hawkwood,' I said. 'I suspect I could scare you just as well. *I am here to see Sir Florimont.*'

Camus stepped closer, but even with my arm in a sling and my shoulder wrapped in a mile of linen, I wasn't particularly afraid.

We all looked at each other for a bit. And then Cambrai summoned a servant, as if he hadn't a care in the world.

I was taken up a set of stairs, and there was Lesparre, lying on a bed. He was reading from a breviary, which raised him a little in my estimation.

I bowed. He rolled off his bed and returned my bow.

'I wanted to make sure you were recovering,' I said.

He smiled. 'You perform courtesy well enough, for a brigand,' he said.

I shrugged. 'Ah, monsieur, I'm not the one who brought a poisoned weapon to a chivalric contest.'

He had the good grace to look abashed; one of the few times I've seen it.

I bowed and took my leave.

Well, there was that done. I walked down the steps with my back burning worse than my shoulder, expecting a sword between my shoulder blades. But none came, and I turned the corner, picked up Witkin where he leant against a stable door, and went back to the palace.

Bibbo stopped me in the yard of our tower. News moves fast in a company.

'Lads an' lasses want to know who stays and who goes,' he said. 'An' how long we're apart.'

I nodded. Every eye in the yard was on us – and I didn't lie to Sam.

'Right, then,' I said. 'I'll take seven lances. Fiore, Gatelussi ... De la Motte. Grice. I won't take all the best men, so give me three young lances who can behave like gentles.'

Bibbo nodded.

'We'll be back together in two months at most.'

He nodded more sharply. 'Right then. Thankee, sir.'

I went back to Hawkwood and drank a cup of wine with him.

'Eventually I'll need them all back,' I said.

'You're paying,' he said. 'I leave in the morning, for the war.'

'Bibbo already knew that.'

'You're giving me Bibbo?' he asked.

I smiled. 'No,' I said. 'How would I get anything done?'

Hawkwood laughed his genuine laugh.

I shook his hand. It was the feast of Saint Willibald – a saint we celebrate in my part of England. See the mark in my book of hours? It would be two full years to the day before I saw Hawkwood again.

CHAPTER TWO

MILAN AND RIVOLI

June 1368

The next six days were as difficult as any I've ever known, as we all had to live packed into a tower at the back of the palace. Now, for those of you like Aemilie, who have lived their whole lives in a great inn, let me say that nobles are surprisingly used to being packed like salt mackerel into small rooms when they travel, even great nobles like the Count of Savoy and the Duke of Clarence.

But we had a single four-storey tower, which they still call the Torre di Bonna after the Countess of Savoy. In wartime, that tower might house twenty men. We had seventy men and twenty women; there was no privacy at almost any time, no water, two jakes ...

And there were people trying to kill us. Quite possibly, our host, the Count of Milan, and his son. Not to mention elements of the French embassy.

We had the routes to our church watched from above by archers on rooftops, something I'd learnt from Sabraham in the service of the order. And I went out in plain clothes with Bibbo and Gatelussi, and we paid for information and looked over our routes to and from our chapel every day and sometimes in the evening. And I'd learnt a fair amount by going directly to visit the enemy. The best defence ...

And we were actually the bait.

On our third day, someone bit. The truth was that we'd conduct our scouting while a dozen of our archers were already in place along our route – in windows, on roofs.

We went about our business with ostentatious stealth.

Our opponents bought it and swallowed the hook.

When I got back to the tower, there were two of Camus's men

bound and gagged, waiting my good pleasure, in the mud by the bronze pump. Ewan, who'd taken them, was not especially gentle, but they were alive and had no bones broken.

'They followed ye,' Ewan said. 'They're easy to spot in their French clothes.'

This from a barbarous Scot wearing expensive Italian clothes ...

'Shall I hand them over to the Visconti?' Bibbo asked.

I shook my head. 'No,' I said. 'Let's humiliate Camus a little.'

So that evening, when we went to Mass, we left the two, bound, naked, in the chapel. We went out; Robert of Geneva and his entourage swept in. I flashed the bishop a smile.

It was as good as a nun and an incontinent dwarf, as Sir John Chandos used to say.

We watched from the choir, where Sam and I lay in the choir stalls, as the Bishop of Cambrai ranted at Camus and Camus struck the helpless men. And later, when they left, we followed them, if only to hear them howl. After all, the bishop returned to his lodgings in the town to discover that thieves had stolen every one of his possessions, and rifled everything in his house.

Then he discovered that no one would loan him money.

I can be a bastard. With the power of the Count of Savoy and the name of Nerio Acciaioli on my lips, I could be a bastard with purpose. We also had four times as many men-at-arms as they had, and Lesparre and his retinue had left the city shortly after my visit.

We haunted them. I suppose we were expected to cower in our lair, fearing poison and betrayal, but perhaps Geneva never really understood the English. We went on the offensive. If any of ours met theirs in the street, they beat them. If they visited a shop to buy something, a pair of archers would go in and start dumping merchandise on the floor, until no merchant dared trade with them.

The Visconti turned a blind eye.

It probably reflects badly on me and my race, but my Englishmen revelled in this sort of thing, and the archers especially began to develop elaborate costumes and plans to fool Camus and his vagabonds. Their braes and shirts were all stolen at the laundry, for example, and then small boys laughed at them and called them 'bare-arse' in Italian.

Ah, Froissart, now you think me a bad knight. But remember, these men meant to harm my lord in the most cowardly ways, and we killed no one, nor destroyed much property. But we hounded Camus and his people out of Milan like revenants. Even when they left, some miscreant had painted 'bare-arse' on the rumps of all their horses in white paint.

I didn't go out to the gate to wave goodbye. I knew that Camus was a fearsome opponent, but I also felt that I had his measure, and once he and Prince Filippo were gone, we could relax and enjoy the city for two days.

We reckoned without the Bishop of Cambrai and his money.

I was shopping. I wasn't a complete fool; Witkin was somewhere behind me, and Ewan the Scot stood a few feet away, behind Stefanos, who was carrying my packages. Emile was on my arm, and I had no weapon but a small dagger, a pretty thing with a handle of white ivory.

A mendicant was begging his way through the market. In fact, there were a dozen beggars, all probably with licences – the Visconti taxed everything. It was an open-air market in one of Milan's overly clean and well-appointed squares by the Duomo, the great cathedral. It's a little old and dowdy now, and the Visconti are talking of erecting some fabulous new monument to their riches, but back in the year of Our Lord 1368, it was the old basilica, with a big paved square where all the merchants from a lowly wool dyer to the best swordsmith in Milan gathered, paying a stiff tax for the right to sell. Most of the world was there in Milan for the wedding, as you gentlemen will well remember, and the press in the market was worse than Smithfield on a feast day.

Emile wanted something in a deep, true blue, and we were looking at a remarkable piece of wool – English, of course, but dyed in Florence, fit for the Blessed Virgin herself, as the merchant didn't hesitate to tell us and everyone else in the crowd, over and over.

'We can buy anything we want,' Emile was insisting.

I had my eye on a riding sword that had too much gold on the hilt, but was otherwise perfect for court and city, even a city with footpads, if you take my meaning. And it was all set up in red and gold, as if the jeweller who'd finished the hilt had me in mind.

I walked us back to the swordsmith, or rather, the hilter and jeweller. He'd cast the crossguard in bronze and plated it in gold, and it was crisp and perfect; his casting was remarkable. But he hadn't made the beautiful blade nor made the scabbard, which was leather over wood, as pretty as a Bible cover with complex fretwork.

'Oh, you must have it,' my wife said. 'You'll need something like that for camino.'

Well, there's our lives in a nutshell – a sword to wear on pilgrimage.

She leant over to kiss me on the cheek, and the mendicant produced a dagger from the air and lunged at her. Not me. Her.

The dagger he had was long and wicked, a very long rondel. To keep it concealed he'd put it into his robes, and now he had to cross-draw it so that it came out with his arm across his body, blade down, hand up. He drew it back to plunge it in.

He was right next to her.

My right hand shot forward. My left shoulder was broken – I was still pretty banged up. But Fiore's training came to my rescue.

My left hand came up, catching the point of the long dagger, which gashed my hand, but it wasn't in Emile. My shoulder screamed, he screamed, and perhaps I screamed.

I had his knife wrist in my right hand, and my left hand, almost of its own volition, was twisting the dagger. I pivoted on the balls of my feet, wrenching his arm and pulling him off balance.

Ewan's staff caught him in the head and he went down, leaving me bleeding, with a dagger in my hands. Emile was gone – in her place stood Witkin. She was four paces back with Stefanos, who had his dagger in his hand.

The mendicant jabbered like a madman, which he proved to be. Sent by God, or so he claimed. The Visconti later executed him in one of their extraordinarily cruel rituals.

We bought the cloth and sword.

I failed to ask myself the obvious question – how do you get a madman to do your bidding?

That was a mistake, too.

The next morning, Count Amadeus formally presented Sir Richard Musard and his retinue, including two armed squires and two very English archers, to the Duke of Clarence, and Richard knelt and put his hands between the duke's hands. Clarence had about forty English knights and their lances, as well as some Gascons. Most of his people were lords from England, and they didn't willingly mix with my people. I'd had difficulties with Hereford on the trip from Paris, as you may recall, and relations between us were still cool at best.

Sir Richard was supposed to smooth all that over, but it was clear from the outset that the English lords viewed him as some sort of foreigner, and not as a proper Englishman. This had the effect of further alienating my people, as, let's face it, whatever petty difficulties Richard and I had, we went back a long way. Bibbo, for example, had little time for Humphrey de Bohun. The Earl of Hereford, as he was then called, had been at Alexandria and not been particularly distinguished there, and he resented me and made no secret of it. Set against that, I was struggling with Camus and Geneva. The earl was an irritant, not an enemy.

Clarence almost made up for all of it. Whatever his anger of the days after the wedding, he was not a man inclined to ill humour and he went out of his way to be pleasant. He made jokes, good jokes, with all of us, and he seemed to have a genuine inclination for Sam Bibbo, and even for me. He would take me aside just to whisper a joke, or a sally about Italians. He didn't detest them, but he did think them funny. Like his brothers and his father, he had the touch. He could banter away with the archers and the servants, and his lack of good Italian made him seem stiff and formal with Italians when, in fact, he could have been quite popular. Even as it was, Beppo took to him, and managed to make him laugh so hard, one day, that the duke had to sit on the stairs to hold his sides. Mind you, when the Duke of Clarence sat to laugh, he was still Beppo's height.

I'm sure that he was a fine lord in his own way, but it was Hereford and the other blue-bloods who set the tone of Clarence's household. And I'll bore you further by saying that I often refer to the Duke of Clarence as 'Prince Lionel' because that's what the Italians called him – a king's son must be a prince, of course. But in England and Ireland, he was the Duke of Clarence, all seven feet of him – one of the tallest men I ever knew. A good sword, and a fine lance. Not the deepest file, but I'll speak no more ill of him. He, at least, seemed to welcome Richard with the grace he deserved.

That evening, I went to Richard's bunk – remember, we're all cooped up in that damned tower. And that was a blessing. It's hard to remain distant from someone who you can watch taking a piss, if you pardon my frankness.

I sat on his bed.

'Richard,' I said.

He nodded. 'I know. You didn't seduce my own count, take my place in his affections, and supplant me.'

'I really didn't,' I said.

He nodded. 'I know. Bohun apparently hates you and besides, you have a company of lances that the count needs. But I don't *want* to serve Lionel. He has his own people.' He shrugged.

It was interesting that most of the prince's people were billeted elsewhere, and we'd done all the guarding. My feeling was that Hereford was too high and mighty to do his actual job.

'You are going to have to protect the duke,' I said, in English.

'From both Geneva and the Visconti,' Richard said. 'With my bare hands. While the *Frankesi* treat me like a foreigner.' He grimaced.

'I brought wine,' I said. 'I have a volunteer to help you. A pair of them.'

He looked interested.

'Peter Albin and Caterina,' I said. 'Caterina is a most excellent spy. Albin wants to return to England eventually. He is an excellent doctor, and was trained at both Oxford and Bologna.' That last was a bit of a stretch, but I knew my man.

'You don't need to tell me,' Musard said. 'Damn it, William. Would Albin really come with me?'

'Ask him yourself,' I said.

In fact, I'd done the ground work. And I'd just planted my own spy on Lionel's household.

For his own good.

Of course.

A week later, and we were heading for Rivoli, one of the Count of Savoy's principal residences, almost as rich as Pavia and with a beautiful castle – a warmer, friendlier brick. There we met Emile's retainers – my friend Sir Jason and his lances, Sir Bernard le Hardi and Sir Jean-François de Barre. They were Emile's own knights, but they had been to the Holy Land and back with my company, and we were old comrades. Joining them was an enormous relief to all of us, not least because Ewan and Bibbo could get some sleep.

We had travelled across Lombardy and into Piedmont with

hundreds of other lords and ladies, great and small, who'd attended the wedding of the century. As soon as we were out in the countryside, my wife and Lady Bonne led the ladies in putting chaplets of flowers in their hair, and it was a little like a painting in a book of hours. There was hawking, and games and cards. Emile had bought me a tiny chess set, and we played every night as she taught me to play better. We sang around campfires and drank the local wines, which were uniformly excellent.

'Pity the poor bastards servin' wi' Sir John,' Bibbo said. 'We're on a party, wi' flowers and wine, and they're in the mud at Borgoforte.'

We travelled with some of the French knights and their ladies. It was from them that we heard that there was real trouble brewing in the south and all the companies, the routiers, were gathering like vultures.

'You know that your Prince Edward took du Guesclin last year in Spain,' one gentleman said.

'I've heard it,' I said, 'although I find it hard to credit, even though I'm a loyal Englishman.'

The knight nodded. 'Well, then. He couldn't believe that his allies were as useless as they were. Your archers broke the Spanish levies in minutes, and yet it was a long fight. That's not my tale. What I want to say is that du Guesclin will be free – ransomed for a good deal more than you ransomed him.'

I nodded.

'The king will make him constable when it comes to war,' the man said.

'War?' I asked.

'How else?' my new friend answered. 'Your king holds half of France. Armagnac is ready to revolt at the prince's taxes in Gascony.'

I shook my head.

'Will I see you across the field?' he asked me.

I looked at the count and his lady, riding ahead of me.

'I doubt it,' I said. 'Perhaps you'll think less of me, but I have no particular love for Prince Edward, and you may remember why.'

'Oh, the tournament at Calais?' Le Clareaux, my new friend, bowed. He dismissed one of the darkest moments in my fighting life with a casual wave of his hand, like the great noble he was. 'He is a prince – above our cares and concerns.'

'The Count of Savoy is also a sovereign prince,' I said. 'I hold land

30

here of my own, and as my wife's consort. I hold no duty to the prince.'

Le Calreaux laughed. '*Par Dieu, monsieur! Nous avons fait de vous un gentilhomme francais!*'

And at that I bridled. And perhaps growled.

'Your Savoy is likely to be pulled into the war,' Le Clareaux said. 'If Savoy goes to war with England, where will you stand?'

'Sweet Christ,' I muttered.

I'm really only telling you this because it might seem as if my wife's riches and political power made my life a bed of roses, but nothing could have been further from the truth. The reality was the opposite, and it's true for any fighting man, even an archer or a page – the higher you climb, the more there is to fret about. I'd climbed high enough to have my loyalties divided. I held a barony on Outremer, on Lesvos, from Prince Gatelussi, and I held a knight's fee from Peter of Cyprus, and another in my own right from the Count of Savoy.

On the other hand, the life of arms also offers pleasures, and one of them was watching Fiore joust with the French knights every day as we travelled. Le Calreaux was the best of them. Both he and Fiore had enormous depth as masters of the art of arms, and so each seemed to be a different man every day, and neither could precisely take the other's measure. One would change the way he rode, and the other would change the crossing of the lances, and both of them would be puzzled by the result, and sometimes one would have an advantage and sometimes the other. I crossed lances with each in turn, and I was pleased to find that neither was utterly my master, but they were both better than I, which only made sense. Despite a gulf of wealth, both men had entered the life of arms as children, and both had ridden horses from birth. I had not.

Anyhow, it was a good week, and I've probably gone on too long, except that not everything is Hell come to earth, and many times were good times, though it almost makes me weep to remember.

And then we were at Rivoli. Emile and I were housed in the castle; the count was in his own lands and not being protected by hired lances, but by Sir Ogier and his own people, all the time. We all slept better, drank a little too much, and then spent a day or two stretching tired muscles in the yards, with Fiore barking at us. Then there was a feast for the French and they were gone, and the place seemed almost empty.

But before the French ambassadors left, the count read out the will of the former Prince of Achaea, his brother Giacomo. He did it at their farewell dinner, and if they were shocked, they hid their astonishment well, and at least pretended to be sympathetic.

Three days later, the Monk of Hecz struck, burning four villages in the valleys south of Chambéry. By then, all pretence of peace had blown away like old autumn leaves in a strong summer wind, and we were arming for war. The count didn't hire mercenaries, but instead summoned his vassals in the old way. His vassals were as good as the king of England's vassals – soldiers, all of them. Hundreds of them had been on crusade out east. We had some Genoese crossbowmen and even they were mounted, because, surprising as it may seem, war in the mountains is largely fought on horseback.

The next day at Rivoli, when I came in to attend my lord just after dawn, he waved his equerry out of the pavilion.

'I have a delicate matter for you, Sir Guglielmo,' he said.

It was delicate. By God, friends, that whole summer was 'delicate'. The paragon of chivalry, the Athlete of Christ, wanted me to ride to Vigone, a small castle and town in Filippo's trimmed-down holdings. It was the headquarters, according to a spy, of the Monk of Hecz, and probably the location of the prince and his 'army' of mercenaries.

Including Camus, of course.

He wanted me to offer Hecz money to desert his prince. Very Italian.

We looked at each other.

'You know these men,' the count said.

He meant that I had been a routier and I'd know how to talk to them, whereas he, a true nobleman, couldn't be seen to dirty his hands with such arrangements.

I probably nodded or bowed my head. I'd never heard of this Monk of Hecz before the wedding, and now I was supposed to suborn him.

The thing about obedience and service is that once you are fully entered in, it is very difficult to say 'no,' as we will explore more in this story. Perhaps I should have said 'no'.

We looked at each other. I wanted to say, 'You know what will happen to me if Camus takes me?'

And he wanted to say, 'What, Guglielmo, are you afraid?'

Well, I had the answer to this. I was afraid. I would rather have held a doorway against an army of Turks with bows, than ridden alone into Vigone.

That hour, I went to Emile, who was packing to move to Chambéry. She had an army of maids and a rather puzzled-looking Sir Bernard, who had an armful of white linens and was looking at the dark beams of the ceiling as if to proclaim his non-involvement.

I explained once the maids were gone.

She held out to me a parchment.

'Edouard sent a letter from Outremer,' she said. 'And a dried lemon from our tree. With cloves. Smell!'

I took a deep breath of the delightful scent.

'Keep it to remind you what goodness is, my love,' she said. 'Listen.' She sat on the rolled bed and shook her head. 'He's a fool. In this case, he still thinks all the routiers are greedy bandits—'

'Not so far wrong,' I said.

'But this won't wash.' She shook her head. 'Ah, sweet gentle Jesu and Maria the Virgin, I hate to see you go there.'

I started packing. I didn't want to take anyone – if this went badly, I didn't want a hostage. I wanted Fiore, but he was, for once, not there to watch my back. Or I his. He was with the count, both as a bodyguard and to provide training.

So I thought to go alone.

But Marc-Antonio would not hear of staying.

'So they pull all my fingers off?' he said. 'What will people say if you die and I'm here?'

Sam Bibbo also insisted.

'You need someone at your back who can do ... whatever has to be done,' he said in his quiet way.

'This is very dangerous,' I said.

Sam smiled. 'Sure,' he said.

Marc-Antonio nodded. 'My Lord, pardon me, but you are going about this all wrong.'

'I am?' I asked.

Marc-Antonio nodded. 'You need a herald, a squire, and at least six men-at-arms, and a banner,' he said. 'First, because this is in keeping with the pride of our lord, the Count of Savoy, and second, because it is very difficult to murder a herald, a lord, and twenty men.'

Bibbo looked at Marc-Antonio as if he'd never really seen him before.

I blinked. 'But we're supposed to be *secret*.'

Marc-Antonio spread his hands. 'Did His Grace say "*secret*"?'

Well, well.

I ordered out my entire escort. Someone had prepared them; it took them less than an hour to appear, fully kitted, with grain sacks on their horses' rumps and one set of good clothes pressed in the leather *malles* on the cantles of their saddles. Francesco Gatelussi carried my banner, and Marc-Antonio was dressed as the Green Count's herald.

The count came to a window of his palace and waved as I saluted him.

I explained to Gatelussi, who grinned.

'Of course Marc-Antonio is correct,' he said. 'These things are secret only in a very public way. An exchange of heralds on the eve of a war is perfectly correct.'

Marc-Antonio grinned. I'd seen that grin on him at the moment when a young woman gave him an overfamiliar smile – a wolf's grin.

'I have the count's cartel of defiance,' he said. 'It's genuine.'

So much to learn.

We rode through a beautiful summer across Piedmont. It's only about twenty English miles from Rivoli to Vigone, but I chose to break my journey at Volvera. We had enough men to frighten the town, but we had correct *sauvegardes* and a herald, and we were escorted by town militia to an inn – a very nice inn, masters. God save us all; inns in the north of Italy are almost as fine as English inns, aye, and the food is oft-times better. I remember a good night and a surprisingly sound sleep, and a monk at the chapel who sang the Mass so beautifully I wondered if he was actually a man.

Regardless, we left early enough, and before the middle of the day we rode up to the barricades at Vigone. The militia on the gates sent for an officer while we sat on our horses and sweated. I remember the glare of the sun, and the feeling that we were being grilled under our armour.

And, because I list vanity under my worldly sins, let me add that I was wearing the Milanese harness that I'd received at the wedding

– very fancy, with all sorts of engraving and chasing and latten edging. Just arming in it made me think of Poitiers, and the cobbled-together harness, bits of ten different harnesses.

We sat and baked in the heat, and no one came to the gate. The crossbowmen there fidgeted nervously, as if we were demons from Hell.

Eventually, the portcullis behind the barriers opened. There were four mounted men – one with a standard, all black, with a skull. Under the skull it said 'Pariter es et in pulverem reverteris'.

'"Dust thou art, and to dust thou shall return",' said Gatelussi. He shrugged. 'I think the quotation is incorrect, but the meaning is clear.'

The standard was carried by a big, dark-haired man – Hungarian, I'd assume from his armour, which was mostly heavy maille.

Beside him was Camus, in his prince's gules and azure.

Between Camus and another knight – if one can call Camus a knight – was a big man in a tonsure. He wore a monk's robes over German plate and maille, and he was big – big enough that his horse was the size of an elephant. None of them wore helmets, so I slapped my visor up and rode forward.

'Ah, it's butt-boy!' Camus sang out.

I ignored him. The man in monk's robes did not. He turned.

'Unseemly,' he said.

Camus bridled. 'This man ...'

The Monk raised a hand for silence.

'Your credentials, please.'

He had an accent I couldn't place – German, or perhaps Hungarian.

I motioned to Gatelussi, who was acting as my squire, and he rode forward, all showy horsemanship, to present our passes and *sauvegardes*.

The 'monk' – if he really was a monk – handed them all, unexamined, to the man on his left. He looked familiar – another of the d'Albret by-blows, I suspected. He looked Gascon, or Navarrese.

He began to read the *sauvegarde*.

'I can't decide just what to do with you when I take you—' Camus began.

'Silence, now,' the Monk said.

His voice was wonderfully deep and full – almost magical in its intensity.

And just like that, Camus was silent.

'I gather you and my officer have some prior acquaintance?' the Monk said in his German-accented Italian.

'He is—'

'Silence!' the deep voice said. His authority was remarkable. 'I asked you, sir.' He indicated me.

'We have some acquaintance,' I said.

Camus writhed.

The Monk gave a mirthless smile.

'I see.'

The Gascon frowned.

'All correct,' he said, as if he very much wished our documents were forgeries.

The Monk nodded. 'So, sir knight, what brings you here? I must tell you that on the orders of my employer, I will not admit you to this town, even as ambassadors. Anything you have to say, you can say here at the barricades.'

I pointed to Marc-Antonio. He raised a scroll with a flourish, and proceeded to read aloud the Green Count's defiance and his declaration that the Prince of Achaea was a contumacious vassal, and that his vassals were herewith released from their feudal obligations.

A little silence fell. The crossbowmen at the barrier looked at each other.

'That's all?' the Monk asked. 'A piece of your chivalric theatre?'

I won't say I had his measure by then, but I had some idea what I was dealing with.

'Sir, you and your companions are serving a bad lord, a rebel against the authority of his own sovereign lord.' I bowed. 'My lord offers you release from a dangerous obligation, and furthermore offers to make sure your wages are paid in full.'

This was true, but it was a very, very nice way of saying, 'The Count of Savoy will pay you well to march away.'

'Danger is of little moment to me,' the Monk said. 'We all die, and after we die, we face our celestial judge. I fear none of that. And as for wages, sir, we are well paid by our prince, who I fancy is better prepared for this war than your master might think.'

'So go back and lie down for him, Gold, and tell him to fuck off,' Camus said.

'Again, I say you are unseemly,' the Monk said. 'Absent yourself. I detest empty posturing.'

I never thought that Camus would just obey, but he did – he turned his horse and slunk away. I watched him go, and I saw movement on the walls.

'Ware,' I said to my companions.

But instead of the bolt that I expected, a man leant out between the merlons of the gate wall to have a look. I didn't know his name, but I'd seen in him in France or Gascony – an English archer.

'Sam?' I said softly.

Bibbo was just by me, carrying my banner.

'Ned ... Ned something.'

'You have nothing to fear as long as you are engaged in lawful embassy,' the Monk said. 'Bide here, and I will prepare a proper answer for your lord, as he seems to relish these niceties. And be sure to tell him that I took his brother, Ogier, yesterday. The ransom will be one thousand ducats. I feel that the count should know that his men-at-arms didn't fight particularly well.' He didn't smile.

I knew Ogier. It had taken us time to become friends, but he was a good man, if somewhat blinded to the world by his fanatical devotion to his brother and the house of Savoy.

'Would you allow me to visit Ogier?' I asked.

'No,' the Monk said.

I shrugged. Enough playing nice. Time to be a routier and not so much a chivalrous knight.

'Well,' I said, 'I have no idea who you are, monk, but if you don't show me this man, I'll assume you're lying. Anyone can claim to take an important man. And while you are at it, please give me your style and titles, so I know how to address you.'

He looked at me for a long time.

'No,' he said. 'Titles are a worldly vanity. Lying is for children. I will neither share my titles nor will I lie.'

I looked at the Gascon.

'Are you a d'Albret?' I asked.

He smiled. '*Mais oui, Ser Guillaume. Par dieu!*'

'I thought you'd all be fighting in Spain,' I said.

Remember, I'd just heard the whole story of the campaign in Spain – the Black Prince's campaign – at the wedding. From Chaucer here.

The young Gascon laughed.

'The money is better here,' he said.

The Monk shook his head. 'This embassy is done. If you return tomorrow, I'll have an answer for you.'

I bowed in my saddle. 'Very well, *brother*,' I said, as I would to any monk who sung Mass. 'But I will warn you that if you actually have the count's brother, you had best provision yourself for a sharp siege.'

'I haven't seen anything from the count that would lead me to believe that his people would pose my Germans any threat,' he said.

I nodded. 'And here I thought you detested empty posturing,' I said. 'Also, I have a close friend who is a Latinist, if you'd like your banner corrected.'

Suddenly he drew himself up like an adder puffing.

'Don't pretend to learning you do not have. It ill becomes you.'

I smiled. 'Well, I can read Vegetius, slowly,' I said. 'Good day to you, now.'

I was particularly proud of the last bit. I wasn't shaking in my boots exactly, but there was something about the Monk of Hecz that was much more sinister than Camus's blustering and overt evil. On the other hand, I'd stung him with the accusation that his Latin was incorrect. And that made him both more human and very interesting, too.

'If you require us, we will spend the night at Virle,' I said over my shoulder.

Virle was four English miles away in the wrong direction.

Then we went back to our nice inn. Which wasn't at Virle.

That night, I sent Beppo, the Biriguccis' horrifying (but delightful) groom, and all our archers except Bibbo, off into the countryside. I purchased a pair of guides – that is, I did as Sir John Hawkwood taught, and offered a good deal of money, success only, for two local men (not just one) to guide my archers. And to help them vanish into the countryside. I didn't tell the guides that Beppo was himself Italian. And I sent Clario Birigucci, still recovering from his wound, to 'command'. To be honest, the scoundrel Beppo was in command, but he needed a mouthpiece.

Having been a routier, I know that perhaps the greatest failing of the mercenary companies is how small they are. A few hundred men can utterly overwhelm a town or fight a lord's vassals, but they cannot garrison every village and hamlet, nor really even patrol the countryside without placing themselves very much as risk. While we specialise in escalade, the assault of towns, that's because routiers tend to think in terms of roads and towns and castles – hold the strong places and you hold all.

I'd learnt differently in the East.

So I bought two reliable guides and sent my archers off to the west, to watch Vigone.

The next day I was at the gates a little after Terce, when monks pray at mid-morning.

There was no sign of Camus, but the Monk was there on his huge stallion, and so was young d'Albret.

'You may enter with one man,' he said. 'You will only come as far as the gatehouse. The count's brother will be there. You may not speak to him. You will not be armed. Do you agree to these conditions?'

I nodded. I dismounted and handed Stefanos my pretty gold-hilted riding sword. Gatelussi dismounted with me, and we clanked across the drawbridge in our sabatons. Close up, the Monk of Hecz was even larger than he had appeared before.

I had a good look at the gatehouse. Sadly, it was modern and well built, with no internal staircase. We had to go into the town and then through a door set in the wall and up a staircase set into the stone facade of the curtain by the gate. A tough nut, and not something amenable to an easy escalade. The stairs were stuffy and cramped. A pair of militiamen escorted us every step, but they left us at the upstairs door.

The Monk didn't accompany us. He was still sitting on his charger in the gate below. We clanked up into the first floor of the gatehouse, and there was Camus.

And Ogier.

Behind Ogier were two men-at-arms, both with drawn swords. Now, oddly, as I had my full harness and a dagger on my belt, I considered, however briefly, taking Camus then and there. Two ill-armed brigands in rusty maille with swords were no match for a knight in full harness. And I was sure I could take Camus.

But escape would have been very dicey indeed.

All that between two heartbeats. I noted that one of the men-at-arms was the English archer I'd seen the day before, and the other looked familiar too. Will. Will Cutter. I smiled at him and he winked.

Only then did I look at Ogier.

His eyes met mine, and I learnt what I had to. They'd been hard on him – he'd been beaten. But he was alive and unbroken.

Camus smiled. 'Are you friends, butt-boy? What shall I do to him that would excite you?'

'Ah, Camus,' I said. 'You bore me. But perhaps we will relieve you of Ogier, now that we know you have him. And I promise you, if you hurt him, it will be bad.'

'You don't threaten me, little Englishman.'

I nodded. 'If you hurt him,' I said, 'we will see. I suspect that you know that for all your bluster, the count's arm is both longer and stronger than your own.'

'As soon as I have your guts on my lance, Gold, I'm going elsewhere,' Camus said.

'I'm sure Hell will be happy to receive you,' I said. 'Good day.'

I bowed, having passed several reassurances to the prisoner without breaking my parole not to speak to him. I hadn't. I looked back at Ned, whatever his name was, and he winked too.

'You know that if you walk away from your rebel prince, the count will pay your wages,' I said to Camus.

In fact, I was talking to the two Englishmen. I spoke in French, but any archer in our armies could speak French.

'Fuck off!' Camus said. 'Then your little count wins. I want him to lose. And the Bishop of Cambrai wants him to lose. Or die.'

I nodded. I'd said what I needed to say; both Englishmen had responded with raised eyebrows.

Camus looked at Will Cutter. 'Escort these men to the gate,' he said.

On the stairs, I contrived to let Gatelussi go first. I had Cutter right behind me, naked sword in hand.

'One hundred gold florins if you help me recapture Sir Ogier,' I said in midland English. 'I'm at Volvera.'

I blurted it out – there was almost no time.

Death if he turned me in.

I went down three more steps. Gatelussi, who knew the score, put a hand on the long baselard he wore.

'Double it and we're your men,' Cutter said, also in English.

'Done,' I said, as the door at the base of the steps swung open.

I went out into the light, and there was the monk.

Just for a moment, I thought it was all revealed. But he leant down.

'Now you know I am not a liar,' he said. 'But you are, I think. I believe you swore not to speak.'

'I swore not to speak to Ogier,' I said.

He considered. 'You are very lawyer-like, for a knight,' he said.

I nodded. 'Perhaps,' I said.

I might have said, *You are very monk-like, for a routier.* But I kept my mouth shut. I was afraid my voice would shake.

All the militiamen were watching me as if I was their hope of Heaven. I got the impression that the mercenary garrison was none too popular, and the militia would like to have their two feudal lords stop fighting before some honest merchants and tanners got hurt.

The Monk snapped his fingers and his d'Albret squire handed me a scroll heavy with seals.

I led my little retinue back to Volvera.

Now, at this point I need to tell you a little about the conflict in which I was engaged. Froissart here doesn't know this at all. Chaucer, you probably know it all from your companions in the Duke of Clarence's household. Yes?

No?

Very well. It's a mare's nest of inheritance law and quibbles and naked greed. The Prince of Achaea – there are at least two, so this is Filippo – and the Green Count were cousins. Filippo's great-grandfather, Tommaso, Lord of Piedmont, was brother to Amadeus V, Lord of Savoy and the Green Count's grandfather. Tommaso's son, Filippo, the first of that name, married the Princess of Achaea, a Villehardouin, and thus his branch of the inheritance of the principality passed through her line into the Piedmontese line. Still awake?

Just nod along.

The problem is that, according to Italians – or at least Neapolitans and the Pope – the whole principality had been passed by the last Villehardouin prince to Charles of Anjou a century ago. That's why Nerio's father, the Seneschal of Naples, had administered most of the principality of Achaea for his mistress, Joanna of Naples, and then,

41

for all practical purposes, kept it for himself when she was betrayed by her own family.

So while Filippo enjoyed the name and coat of arms of the Prince of Achaea, his richest holdings were his towns in Piedmont. And these, his father Giacomo had held independently of the House of Savoy, but Giacomo had left the Count of Savoy as the guarantor of his will – a will that only my own Green Count had seen. And of course, old Giacomo was a lusty devil who'd remarried very late in his life, a very beautiful and much younger woman of impeccable birth, one Marguerite de Beaujeu. And the old prince had left her and her sons by him, everything, except five small towns.

Let's be precise here. Those five towns in Piedmont paid more taxes than five counties in England. The Prince of Achaea could have lived happily on the proceeds, and bought all the evil mercenaries he wanted. But he continued to protest to various courts that he had been dispossessed. In fact, he *had* been dispossessed. He claimed that young Marguerite, who was his own age, had seduced his father and used witchcraft to deprive him of his rights.

Sadly, I suspect that as Filippo was an extraordinarily difficult young man with some very ugly traits, Marguerite needed no witchcraft beyond her youth and her very solid practicality to undermine the original heir. And, of course, to even further complicate matters, she was *also* a descendant of both the Villhardouins and the Savoys – she *also* shared the same great-grandfather, and she was also a plotter. Did I mention beautiful? Of course she was beautiful.

And then there was my own lord, the Count of Savoy. I'd like to coat this in honey to make it easier to swallow, and I will allow that he is a great knight and a fine lord, but in this case, what he wanted was the whole of the Piedmont and its rich taxes in his own hand. The revolt, if you like, of the Prince of Achaea against him and his court gave him the perfect excuse to encroach on Piedmont and enrich himself. Remember that he'd spent almost ten years of his income on the war in the East and on the crusade.

In a very real way, it was a simple war of aggression conducted by my lord against a vassal foolish enough to break his law. When you add to this the fact that the prince had, more than once, attempted the count's assassination ... Well. No one is a spotless knight.

CHAPTER THREE

VIGONE AND SURROUNDING

Late June – Early July 1368

I left Francesco Gatelussi in command in Volvera. He complained that I was trapping him with responsibility when he was only a hundred miles or less from Genoa, his family home. As he was drinking wine in a grape arbour at the time, I didn't take his complaints too seriously.

I took my riding horse, Juniper, and rode hell for leather for the count, who was still camped outside Rivoli building his army.

I was escorted straight to his tent.

He was looking at a stack of pilgrim itineraries.

'I miss Richard Musard,' he said.

'My Lord, you should send for him,' I said.

He shook his head. 'That I cannot do,' he said. 'Your Duke of Clarence will need him. Now, what news? What's this of my brother?'

'My Lord, Ogier is taken by this Monk of Hecz, with some of his knights. These are bad men, My Lord – I saw Camus.'

I handed him the Monk of Hecz's reply to his summons. He broke the seals, read a few lines, and shook his head.

'How dare he? Who is this man?'

'I have no idea, My Lord. Some German mercenary. He thinks very highly of himself.'

'He accuses me of "unchivalrous behaviour" in sending you to suborn him.' He looked at me. 'You have done this badly, Sir Guglielmo.'

I nodded, trying to remember everything I knew about handling this difficult man. I, too, missed Richard. I knew, for example, that it was not my place to remind him that he had specifically sent me to the Monk of Hecz to suborn him.

So I tried a different tack.

'I believe that I might be able to recapture your brother,' I said. 'I will need fifty lances and some discretion.'

He looked down his nose at me. 'Surely we have just learnt that discretion is the very thing you lack?' he said.

Sometimes, he was a very difficult man.

Nonetheless, I took a deep breath. 'My Lord, I have done the best I can. This man is very loyal to his employer, and also believes himself to be very clever. For my part, I have met …' I glanced at him.

He raised an eyebrow.

'Some of my former comrades. I have reason to believe that with God's will we might have Ogier in our hands.'

He looked at his nails, as if he was concerned that they were dirty, and then he looked at me, and then at his book of hours and back at me.

'I am upset, messire. I apologise.' He shook his head. 'I am worried about Ogier.'

Also, you've been made to look bad.

I was tempted to make a joke. By God, an apology? The sky must have been falling on him.

'My Lord, you have nothing for which you need apologise. All I request is fifty lances for a few days … and … that you make it known that you are marching to lay siege to Vigone.'

'Make it known? But that was my thought – to march like lightning upon Vigone.'

'And yet …' I said, with a smile.

Sir William Gold, the duplicitous fox, that's me. I was pretending to be half Nerio and half Hawkwood.

I convinced the count to wait a few days.

And I managed to scoop up Fiore, whom I found in the yard, surrounded by the Green Count's squires.

'My friend, I need you for a few days,' I said.

'I am training these young men,' he said. He raised an eyebrow. 'They need me, I promise you.'

'And yet,' I said. 'I need you too. And there will be an adventure.'

He smiled. 'Ah, then.'

The squires looked at me as a saviour, I promise.

*

44

We sat for three days in a tavern in Volvera. My borrowed lances were all Savoyards, all gentlemen, and they weren't particularly good at either camping rough or hiding. And I couldn't have them discovered. Volvera is in the no-man's land between the count's holdings and the prince's.

So I purchased a monastery.

Well, perhaps I only rented it.

I rode into the courtyard with my official retinue and I was taken to the abbot. He was a gentleman of some years, from one of the older Piedmontese families, and seemed both pious and mild. I was encouraged when he said that he was a knight who had retired to a life of piety for his sins.

I asked him if he felt committed to a 'side' in the conflict between Savoy and Piedmont.

He raised both hands. 'Now God be with us,' he said. 'Between the count and the prince? Bah. The count is the better man, but the sin that besets both is pride, and in their pride, they will kill my people and ruin all these lands.'

I took my time and heard him out.

'I wonder if you would consider playing a small role in my negotiations,' I said.

I had my man. I didn't lie, precisely. That would be unchivalrous. And I didn't play the Knights of Saint John donat too much. I merely suggested that I would feel safer, as a negotiator, with my secret reserve of lances. I told him the truth about my fears concerning Camus.

And I offered him five hundred gold ducats.

He sat back.

'That is a hefty bribe, messire.'

I nodded.

'I worry that for that sum you will make me earn it.'

He looked at me over his steepled hands. No fool. Not even a little. I spread my hands as innocently as I could.

'Keeping fifty lances for a week is not cheap,' I said. 'Keeping them from going out or making mischief ...'

He gave me a long look.

I thought I'd misplayed, but after a moment as long as the Credo, he nodded.

'Half a thousand ducats will do a lot of good here,' he said. 'So would a lack of war.'

'I'll do what I can,' I said. 'Certainly no one will attack you this week.'

He shook his head.

Regardless, there we were in Volvera, drinking too much and telling stories. It rained and rained, and our horses were restless and ate too many beans. Fiore made the innkeeper clear all the firewood out of an old stable with a half-fallen-in roof, and we traded blows with wooden swords that we had time to make ourselves. Marc-Antonio took a blow that broke his thumb. Fiore explained to him how it was the fault of his hand position, and I just managed not to savage my friend for injuring one of my precious fighting men.

Every day that passed increased the odds that we would be reported to the Monk of Hecz, or his scouts would find my lances hidden in the monastery. And having chosen to hide, I could hardly go out and ride the roads and scout. The passivity wore on me, as did the waiting, which daily increased the chances of failure.

On the fifth day, we were a surly crew, and I was working myself up to call it off, when a damp crowd of fools in motley and other entertainers with two wagons passed the town gates. They offered the landlord a show for rooms, and he shook his head.

'No one here,' he said. 'You fools must know you're walking through a war.'

The lead fool was a proper minstrel, a big man with the kind of charm people pay money to see.

'You have this knight,' he said, pointing at men and then bowing, as if he'd done something rude. 'I'm sure this lord would like our entertainments.'

I shrugged, or said something derogatory.

But the man came over to me, bent his knee, and smiled a mouth full of teeth.

'Messire,' he said, 'I promise you an entertainment in the finest taste – good music, the best! Landini and Machaut and my own compositions. And news of the world.' He winked. 'News you would very much like to hear.'

'Where were you last, my friend?' I asked.

He nodded as if this was indeed a fine question. He was quite the amiable rogue.

46

'Vigone,' he said. 'A terrible place.'

I nodded to the landlord.

'I think we'll have them,' I said.

The landlord smiled a commercial smile.

'Will you pay, messire?'

'I'll split the cost with you,' I said.

And so that night, at least, passed very pleasantly. The theatrical pieces were either bawdy or religious – the actresses were all probably no better than they ought to be – but it was lively, and Fiore, for instance, was entranced. They did one piece that was remarkable, stolen entirely from Boccaccio, and it was as good or better than anything I'd seen in London.

Sir Benghi Birigucci, Clario's brother, got up to dance with one of the players, and then seized a lute and played. He played brilliantly – I had no idea he had it in him – and the impresario was as impressed as I. Bibbo also danced – who knew these men of blood were so capable? And soon we were all dancing, and the half a dozen players danced with us and taught us several new dances from the south. One brown young woman appealed to me a little too much, and I gave her a smile, squeezed her hand and went off to have wine and think of home, so to speak.

Then I waved the lead man over, poured him wine – good wine – and gave him five gold ducats.

'I knew you were a gentleman,' he said. 'Are you by any chance Guiglielmo le Coq?'

I nodded.

He nodded too. 'Really, there cannot be so many tall men with copper hair in all Italy,' he said. 'But in these matters it is best to be sure.' He took a folded parchment from his bosom and handed it to me. 'Marietta there could take an answer for you,' he said. 'For the right price.'

Marietta was my friend with the flashing dark eyes and tanned skin, as fit as a knight on his way to war. She'd just done a backflip so fast that her kirtle had no time to ride up her legs.

I do not like using women as spies, because of what happens to them when they are caught.

'She is the only one you can send?'

'She has a "friend" in Vigone,' he said.

'For your part,' I said, 'there is a monastery just up the road that would probably pay you twice this.' I really was learning to think like Hawkwood, as you'll see.

The note was from one of the Englishmen in Vigone. It was a straightforward note – a time, a date.

I went to bed – alone, let me hasten to add.

In the morning, I rode with the players to the monastery, ushered them all in, and saw Sir Maurizio, one of the best of the Savoyard lances, slam the gate closed.

I turned to the players' leader.

'You will be well paid for playing here,' I said. 'But none of you may leave. And your Marietta can take my answer. When she returns, you'll be paid and released.'

The man with all his teeth glowered at me. 'I don't respond well to threats,' he said.

I shrugged. 'If Marietta does her part, there will never have been a threat. What's your name?'

'Roberto. I compose music ...'

I nodded. 'And do a little spying, eh? Well, stay here. They'll pay well.'

I took Marietta into the abbey's barn. She was not afraid to meet my eye, although I suspect she expected a different game from the one we played. She flopped onto a thick pile of dry straw and smiled. The smile was a little more predatory than lascivious.

I handed her five gold florins and showed her fifteen more.

'All yours when you return,' I said.

'He'll just take it all,' Marietta said. She gave me a long look, and rubbed a gold piece on her kirtle.

I shrugged. 'I can't help that. Although if you want to follow my company, I can use a woman who can get in and out of towns.'

She smiled. When she smiled she looked like a cat.

'All these rich knights are your company?'

'I'm afraid not. These are much richer than my knights.'

She nodded. 'I will think on it while I walk to Vigone,' she said. Then she surprised me. She handed me back my five ducats. 'Anyone can take them from me,' she said. 'And no prostitute should have so much. Anyone would say that.' This was said without bitterness.

'I'll hold them for you,' I said. 'No parchment. Just a verbal message.

Say that "Yes, I agree." And I need to know where the convoy is going.'

'If I die, give it all to my mother,' she said. 'Swear on your cross.'

I swore.

She shivered for a moment. 'Very well,' she said. 'You are quick, Englishman. Don't let Roberto out of the walls or he will sell you to the Monk.'

Or has he already?

I couldn't help thinking that as I watched her. Later, riding back into Volvera, I passed her on the road, walking, singing and weaving a chaplet of wild roses. Very fetching. I passed her without a glance, because you never know when someone's watching. Another thing I learnt from Sabraham.

And then I sent Marc-Antonio to get the count.

The count's army marched the next morning at mid-Vespers, and by midday they were almost as far as Volvera.

The Monk must have had a watching post, because he acted immediately. He sent a messenger demanding reinforcements.

I know, because Beppo and his archers took the messenger and the message.

Before full night fell, Marietta strolled into the inn. I was sitting with Fiore and Beppo. Listen – Beppo is one of those men who is bigger than his class or his origin or his ugliness. His wit would commend him anywhere.

Marietta came in and the innkeeper made as if to send her back out. Good inns are intolerant of any strumpet who is not their own.

'Hey there,' Beppo said, catching my eye. 'That's my daughter.'

Even Fiore laughed. Perhaps you had to be there, but as Beppo looked more than a little like Satan come straight from a losing battle with Saint Michael, and Marietta looked a little too much like one of those ancient vases in Florence, with the perfect posture and the straight nose, there was nothing less likely than that she was his daughter.

But the innkeeper let her in.

She didn't sit. She crouched by our table.

'I am afraid,' she said. 'But I made it. He says dawn, the Moretta Road, and "For the love of God bring force".'

I nodded. She was crouching very low, as if hiding by the table.

49

'You will protect me?' she said. 'Men followed me today. I hid – I broke into a house ...'

She was rattled.

'Demoiselle, Messire Fiore is probably the best knight in the world,' I said.

'Probably?' Fiore asked. He raised an eyebrow. He never used to do that, but he learned it from Nerio.

'He will protect you,' I said.

'All night,' Beppo said. 'Ah, the torments you young, handsome men endure that I am spared.'

'I will certainly protect her for more than just the night,' Fiore said.

Beppo sighed, as if his very best wit was wasted on us.

I had my pilgrim itinerary and I had Beppo, and he had our two guides, whom he fetched. I called Gatelussi, and when he didn't come, I went to fetch him and found him gazing lustfully, or at least adoringly, at our spy.

'Where in God's name did you find such a creature?' he asked.

'Fiore, be so kind as to lock her in your room and come.'

Marietta looked at me. 'Messire promised I would be protected,' she said.

'I can bring her with me,' Fiore said.

'She will know all our plans,' I said.

She was a bold lass, and she made a face.

'Messire, what more do I need to know than dawn on a certain road?'

She made an excellent point.

I had the innkeeper bar the door and serve us wine, and Beppo fetched Benghi, and we went over the plan twice in detail.

'If we're caught on the road?' Fiore asked.

'We fight,' I said.

Fiore smiled. 'Splendid.'

'We have fifty lances,' I said. 'We can take anything that Filippo can throw at us.'

'The Monk has more than two hundred lances at Vigone,' Marietta said. 'My *friend* counted them when they mustered.'

I whistled. 'Two *hundred* lances?'

'Filippo must be made of gold,' I said.

'Or someone is helping him,' Gatelussi said.

I shook my head. 'Listen,' I said. 'The count will move south at dawn to invest Vigone. Unless the Monk is the boldest rascal in Italy, he won't dare denude his garrison.'

Beppo pointed at the itinerary. He couldn't read a word, but his memory was incredible.

'None, Castagnole, Virle,' he said, naming the villages on our route.

We were riding half a circle around Vigone, leaving a few good English miles between us and our enemies.

Both the guides nodded.

'One hour,' I said.

We rode through the total darkness of night on the Piedmontese plain. The villages are unlit – farmers go to bed when the sun goes down. A few hamlets had bars across their roads. Barking dogs and terrified householders beset us every few miles.

Otherwise, we moved fast, riding through the cool darkness down lanes lined with whispering poplars or shaded by old oaks. I moved up and down my column. Gatelussi was at the back, and Maurizio at the front, with Fiore, Marietta, and our guides. More than a hundred and fifty horsemen, moving through the night.

It was like any other night march. Horses went lame; men fell out, sick or injured. Leaving the monastery, one luckless archer hit his head on a stone post and had to be taken back inside. And night is full of delays. As I said, some villages had barred gates, and others had streets so narrow that only one man could ride through at a time, and twice our guides lost their way.

This is one of the most difficult moments in command – when your foreign guide tells you he is lost. Is he lying? Is he working for the enemy? Is he actually lost?

Try to ride your home valley at night. Please, take all the time you want, and tell me you don't miss a turn or two in the dark.

It takes time and thought to know whether a man is lying or scared. A scared man lying looks very like a scared man being afraid to tell the truth. Hawkwood says always hire two guides and keep them separate.

Regardless. We went about ten English miles in the full dark of the moon – twice that, I suspect, when measured over ground. But we clattered into Moretta, a town well south of Vigone on the road to Fossano, about half Lauds, when the sun is still far away but there's

51

the first tinge of grey in the sky, and suddenly you *can* see your hand in front of your face.

My guides were visibly relieved.

It was a cold, damp summer morning, with a heavy fog everywhere. Some of the intense darkness of the night was explained as the sun rose and we still couldn't see much more than a long bowshot.

Marc-Antonio brought me the mayor of the little town, and I told him to keep his people indoors. I put Sir Maurizio and his lances behind the town, in two squadrons behind the two good woodlots that were closer to the road. There wasn't time to do more, and I was lucky those woodlots were so close – in the fog, I could have missed them altogether.

Beppo took a dozen archers and vanished into the fog.

I sat on Juniper, fully armed, in the tiny town square, and waited.

An hour passed.

And another.

The sun was coming up somewhere. Juniper was unhappy, as there was no food and she'd polished off all the flowers growing up the front of the mayor's house.

Well after Prime – I know, we could hear the bells from the Franciscan house – the sun appeared. The fog, which had been as dense as a cloud, was suddenly burning away.

Now, I'd cursed the fog, but the sudden new reality was that once the fog burnt off, I was ten miles deep in enemy country with no food and no remounts. The fog had guaranteed my retreat.

I cursed, no doubt, but the die was cast, and I slapped Juniper's neck ...

Beppo dashed into the square, the hoof beats of his palfrey like harbingers of doom.

'Twenty lances, *Bosso*! Less than a mile.'

'Stay on them, Beppo,' I called, and dismounted. Juniper was the finest riding horse in the world, but for fighting, I had Gabriel. I handed Juniper's reins to Stefanos and collected Gabriel's, mounted and turned my horse to face the road.

The leader of the enemy convoy was a tall German in dark armour. He halted when he saw twenty of my lances blocking his road south.

The two forces were about a hundred paces apart, and my lances were between the two woodlots – dismounted, with spears.

Fiore rode forward and ordered the German to surrender.

He snarled some insults, but he was no fool. Already his reaguard was turning to ride back into the village.

No plan is ever perfect. Sir Francesco had taken too long going around his patch of woods. In fact, there was a deep drainage ditch none of us had seen.

So while my blocking force was in place, my hammer was not.

Luckily, I had Sam Bibbo. He had twenty archers with him, and they dismounted like lightning, a handful of the younger archers taking the horses.

Bibbo didn't wait for my order. He drew and loosed, his shaft killing a horse and dropping the rider on the road even as the whole convoy milled in confusion. The commander roared orders in German, but men panic when there is an enemy behind them.

A dozen more shafts dropped into the convoy. By then I'd ridden up to the archers with Marc-Antonio and both the Birigucci boys, and although we were just four armoured men, we had a big banner.

'Throw down your weapons or you will all be killed!' I roared.

Bibbo called, 'Nock!'

It was 1368. Every knight in Europe knew the sound of a master-archer's orders by 1368.

As if on some mummer's cue, Beppo led his scouts out of the trees on the road that the roaring German knight was trying to get his men to take. In fact, Beppo had four Italian-speaking archers, two guides and a beautiful young woman. But to a panicked knight, more and more enemies came out of the shadows and fog all around him.

They began to throw down their lances.

Which was just as well, because Gatelussi still hadn't managed to take his position. As it proved, he had to give up on the ditch, turn around, and ride back to the road for longer than it would take a bad priest to say the paternoster.

The German knight called his men-at-arms cowards, and I told them to dismount and stand by their horses.

I could see Ogier. He was by the German knight, his reins being held by a different man.

I rode out towards the enemy commander with Marc-Antonio at my stirrup. Fiore was coming forward too, on horseback.

The German commander couched his lance and rode for Fiore.

That was quick. Fiore dropped him like a sack of oats.

I rode past. 'Drop your weapons!' I ordered.

The man holding Ogier's reins didn't comply. Instead, he raised his sword.

I rode right at him. It is one thing to claim you'll kill a prisoner, and another thing to do it, and yet another to know, for certain, that when you kill that prisoner, you are yourself a dead man. He hesitated, and then turned his sword to point at me.

No one else was moving.

I deceived his point, Gabriel perfectly collected under me, and my thrust went right through the maille under his arm. Gabriel was already turning, as my knees told him to, and I had Ogier's reins in my left hand and we were gone, through the gap left by the German knight.

Only then did they react. They shouted, and one man came after me.

Then, and only then, did Gatelussi emerge from the last of the fog behind me, but he settled the deal. Even the man behind me reined in, just in time to receive the butt of my banner in the head from Marc-Antonio.

We took them all – twenty German knights and as many lesser men-at-arms. And Ogier, of course.

I took all their armour and weapons and loaded them on their warhorses, and then sent them back the way we'd come, guarded by Maurizio's lances. I noted that William Cutter was there, an archer in one of their lances, and I had him stripped like the rest.

'I'm English, Sir William!' he said. He sounded very convincingly desperate.

I reined in and looked at him.

I pointed to Mike Burn.

'Watch this lout like a hawk,' I told him. 'The English are the most dangerous.'

And in the confusion as our people rounded up the prisoners, young Marietta rode over to me.

'Messire,' she said. 'Please. Don't point. You see the man in the black jupon?'

Indeed, there was a young man-at-arms in a good helmet and a heavy, padded jupon covered in black wool, over maille. Old-fashioned armour, but still good enough to get a man hired.

'I see him,' I said.

He was angry because Ewan was stripping him of his armour.

'Please ride aside,' she said. 'I cannot let him see me.'

I led her horse into the stand of woods. There were insects, but it was cooler.

'He is ...' Marietta shook her head. 'I have a friend in Vigone,' she began.

'I know,' I said, probably with a leer.

'This is a very bad man. A very dangerous man. He uses poisons. He was an apothecary.'

'He looks to me like a badly armoured man-at-arms,' I said.

She shook her head. 'No, no, messire! He is a man-witch, a very dangerous man!'

I didn't dismiss her. But she was a peasant girl, too pretty for her own good, and this bearded ruffian was no worse than all the other hired killers, as far as I could see.

We went with them, of course, but I armed Ogier and put him on the best warhorse, and we were the vanguard – ready to ride out the moment we scented trouble.

And because no plan is ever really perfect, the count decided not to move forward from his camp north of Volvera. So while we rode along dusty Italian lanes in the bright sun, confident in our safety because the count would be moving into position at Vigone, in fact, we were naked to our enemies, moving at a snail's pace, the sun reflecting off our armour and visible for miles.

I could see Vigone off to the west – they could no doubt see me. And so, about sext, as the bells rang in Virle ahead of us, I saw the flash of armed men.

'Beppo!' I called.

The villain rode up.

'I need to turn east. Get your guides to take us east.'

Beppo talked to the guides and came back.

'There's a lane running east from Virle.'

I looked at Virle, and at the flash of armour or spear points towards Vigone. Close.

'Let's go,' I said.

I gathered all my mounted archers and eight of Maurizio's Savoyard lances and we rode straight for Virle at a gallop, pounding into the town and dismounting across the road where it passed between two stone barns as it turned west for Vigone.

Perhaps two minutes later, a troop of mounted crossbowmen appeared on the road.

The archers loosed and three men and horses went down, and the crossbowmen loosed back and rode for it. They dismounted out of sight, and I sent Mike Burn and Ewan and a handful of the better woodsmen into the town to try and catch them when they came to outflank us, which they no doubt would.

But before there was any more than a desultory exchange of missiles at a very long range, my column came up the road and turned east, led by Fiore. As soon as he had made the turn, he handed over to Maurizio and joined me at my barricade. I didn't know then, but was told later, that some of the German mercenaries had begun to walk very slowly. Fiore rode up to one, put his sword to the man's back, and prodded him hard enough to draw blood.

With their captain hanging head-down over a horse, still deeply unconscious from Fiore's blow, they didn't have much spirit. Sir Maurizio and his Savoyards, with their usual love for routiers, kept them moving with a will. Walking is no joy at the best of times, in the Italian sun. Walking in arming clothes after surrendering must have been a misery.

Fortunes of war.

They turned the corner behind my position and began to march away.

Virle is a maze of brick walls, and the flat fields outside the town are hedged like French fields or English ones, so that it was very difficult for our pursuers to get around my little force on the road.

After perhaps half an hour, they came at us on the road – twenty lances, well led by a determined man on a black horse. They burst from cover and charged.

The black horse didn't live to reach its stride. Unarmoured horses are very vulnerable to archery.

The horse fell, and the two knights behind went down in a tangle, and the others had to rein in. Our archers flayed them – close range, mounted men, an almost stationary target. The survivors broke, and Marc-Antonio and I ran forward with the Birigucci brothers and took three more prisoners as they lay stunned by their dead horses. We dragged them back behind our barricade, which by then was two big farm wagons turned on their sides, with some barrels to fill the lane.

'Boss? Some big bastards coming into the town from the north!' Beppo appeared from nowhere, as was his wont.

'I thought you were with the column?' I asked.

'And miss a bold, chivalrous *empris?*' he asked.

I took my friends and rode off down the road to the left that ran north, and suddenly we were in the midst of a dozen men-at-arms.

I was tired, and I'd made a mistake, waiting too long, and I was almost taken. I dropped my first opponent but the rest pressed up behind, and we were fighting in a walled lane with little place to do anything, and I had to fight with a dagger. I put my next blow into a man's horse just in front of the saddle and he went down, but a dozen hands were reaching for me. If Gabriel had been any the less a horse, I'd have been done right there. As it was, we backed along the alley, fighting and then retreating, for what seemed like forever. Gabriel was doing all the work, moving, pounding away with his hooves, biting with his teeth, as I did my best to stay on and used the dagger like a pick to pull men from the saddle.

The Germans weren't very good at wrestling on horseback. Fiore was. He dropped men, and at one point he rolled a horse by turning its head. But still we lost ground.

Eventually, we had retreated to the edge of the central square, which in Virle was quite large. As the two brick walls of the lane fell away, the Biriguccis and Marc-Antonio could get into action, and suddenly it became clear that there were *more of us than there were of them.* This is what happens when you fight in the confines of a helmet – I had grown too accustomed to being outnumbered. When Marc-Antonio passed me and roared my war cry, I was at first puzzled, but the Biriguccis followed him and suddenly the remaining German knights were turning ...

I recovered de Charny's dagger, which I had left in one of my opponents, to my shame.

I rode back to the barricade.

'Anything?' I asked.

Bibbo shrugged. 'No one visits,' he said. 'No one even stops by.'

I didn't have time to ponder Sam Bibbo's rare assay at humour.

'Time to go. Get the horses – on my word, gallop.'

'Break contact?' Bibbo asked.

'Exactly,' I said.

Before a monk could have read the lesson, the archers were mounted and gone, and I was riding clear of Virle with my eight lances. It was not a great battle – not even a great deed of arms. But I'm told the Monk of Hecz was very angry.

And, as it proved, I had his son – the man on the black horse.

Late that afternoon, we trotted into the count's camp. Despite our two fights and twenty-four hours in the saddle, Bibbo demanded that we halt the column so that men could buckle their armour and wipe away the dust, so that we entered the count's camp looking like victorious professionals. Men came out to the roadside to wave at us and cheer us, and the count came out from his emerald silk pavilion to embrace his half-brother.

And then he embraced me.

'I will not soon forget this,' he said.

I waved to Sir Maurizio.

'I know this brave knight needs no introduction by me,' I said in the flowery language of the count's court, 'but he and his knights have given sterling service and without them nothing would have been achieved.'

'You took twenty knights?' he asked.

'Twenty-four, I think,' Fiore said. 'A most refreshing change from training squires.'

The count's army withdrew west without burning anything and set its camp at Buriasco, and the count went to the palace at Pinerolo to hold court. I accompanied the count, and Ogier took command of the camp. The count sent a proper embassy to Prince Filippo, demanding that he end his 'rebellion' and submit.

I'm passing over too many important things. Listen, back when we were all at Milan, Filippo asked the Duke of Clarence to be the arbiter of the quarrel, and Lionel, with one eye on his long-term relations with the Green Count, told Filippo that he was a bad vassal and should appear before a tribunal of his peers. Filippo was increasingly hemmed in, just as my lord intended.

I was especially careful with the count's food, as I was sure that assassination was Filippo's only remaining weapon.

I was wrong.

Again.

Some time in that week, the Monk of Hecz handed his correspondence with the count over to his paymaster, Prince Filippo, and the prince became enraged. He wrote a long denunciation, claiming that the count was a liar, a false lord, and challenging him once again to a duel of fifty champions on a side, to be fought before Galeazzo of Milan.

I was present when the count read Filippo's response. I expected him to explode – in fact, I think I even crouched slightly.

One of the count's officers, Pierre de Murs, a knight who was also a legal expert, looked at me. I didn't know de Murs as well as I knew some of the other officers, but I knew he was a solid thinker – conservative, but well informed.

His eyes told me that he, too, was waiting for the explosion.

Instead, there was a heavy silence, which grew more awkward as it lengthened.

Finally de Murs shook his head.

'Your Grace has no need to answer this man's foolish insults, much less to meet him in combat. He is no knight – he has tried to use defamation and assassins to bring you down.' De Murs looked at me for support.

'He tried to challenge you before,' I said. 'I believe we were to fight in the presence of the Emperor.'

'The Emperor is still in camp at Borgoforte,' Amadeus said. His voice was quite calm. 'As my knights were recently in action against him, I doubt that this is a good moment to invoke his arbitration.'

This was the count at his best. I smiled.

The count shrugged. 'Do any of us believe that Filippo can defeat me in a contest of arms?'

'No,' I said.

It was no flattery. Of all the great lords I've known, only Amadeus and Prince Edward of Aquitaine truly practised the life of arms all his life. He was fit, and thanks to Fiore, he was also brilliantly well trained.

'I can choose from hundreds of veteran knights every one of whom brings a full harness of the most modern, and Filippo must hire Germans,' he said. 'With a little luck, one of us will kill him, and the matter is resolved.'

There you have it, friends. I have heard the count's decision to accept the challenge criticised, as, I'm told, Filippo would have collapsed anyway. But the truth was that the little war in Piedmont was a boil that could fester. Every so often we'd look over our shoulders at the vast Imperial army at Borgoforte, and wonder if the Prince of Achaea had the diplomatic skills to drag the Emperor in. None of us wanted northern Italy devastated the way France had been devastated.

At any rate, three heralds and Sir Pierre de Murs wrote the count's answer to the challenge. I delivered it with Sir Pierre at my side. By then, the Prince of Achaea was reduced to the lands around Vigone – he didn't hold much more than that.

I had ten lances and a pair of heralds at my back. I'd seen Camus recently enough, and I wasn't afraid, or perhaps I thought that I was just the right amount of afraid. Either way, I entered the old bishop's palace at Vigone and was escorted straight to the prince.

He looked different – better filled-out, in arming clothes of velvet and leather, sweat-stained. He had been practising.

I had a very particular role to act out for the count, and I did it with some relish. I read out the proclamation by which the count released the Prince of Achaea from his feudal obligation to his superior, so that he could legally fight the Green Count in the lists.

Filippo rose to his feet – remember, he was very tall – sputtering with anger.

'I have never been his vassal!' he spat. 'This is a lie, like his other lies!'

I didn't shrug or answer.

The world is a very complicated place, messires. The truth, and I would not like to hear this repeated, is that Filippo had much right on his side. But that truth was complicated. Filippo was one of those men whose reach exceeds his grasp, whose abilities are not what he imagines them to be. He consistently overreached, and he enlisted unsavoury allies and used foul means. The result was that, regardless of the justice of his case, no one would stand up for him.

The Green Count's role was more complicated. He desired to see himself as fair, but he hated Filippo and was not interested in anything but total victory. Even then, in late June, all of those around him knew that one of the reasons he wanted the combat of fifty in a mêlée was that Filippo would be killed, and the problem solved forever, for Filippo alive would poison Savoy for years to come. Or so the count saw it.

In romances, someone is very good, and others are very bad. In Italy, some were mostly good, and others sometimes bad. It could make life difficult for a knight who desired to be just.

When Filippo was done ranting, he threw the baton he held in his hand to the floor.

'I will kill him,' he promised. 'And then I will have what is mine.'

There was nothing to be said to that.

As I withdrew, I was seized by four armoured men. I was not in harness – I was an ambassador. It only goes to show how wrong you are when you allow yourself to believe that everything is safe. I was not, as it turned out, sufficiently afraid.

They took the emperor's sword and de Charny's dagger, and landed a few stout blows, so that when they dragged me before the Monk of Hecz, I was not at my best.

'So,' he said. 'I want my son back.'

I had been forced to kneel, and I couldn't see very well.

'You could just pay his ransom—'

A spear shaft struck me across the shoulders.

'You took my son by foul means, and you will restore him immediately. Or my men will break your bones.' He smiled. 'After which, perhaps I should let Camus have you.'

'You are attacking an ambassador,' I said.

He shrugged. 'You know that men like ourselves are of no account to the great lords. If I brutalise you, perhaps the Green Count will remember that in a year, and perhaps not. Don't flatter yourself. I could behead you and nothing would change.'

Sadly, I knew that he had a point.

'I fail to see,' I managed, 'how the means by which I took your son were foul.'

'My son is a brave knight,' he said. 'The best.'

'Your son attempted to attack a barricade held by English archers. On a horse.'

'He is brave.'

I shrugged. I was recovering a little, and I wasn't ready to just give in, although I confess I dreaded a lot of broken bones.

'Listen, Brother Monk,' I said. 'I'm a Knight of the Collar and a Knight of the Sword and a Donat of the Hospitallers. I don't think the count will yawn when he's told what you do to me. I think you are a German with no idea how war in Italy works, and I defy you. Break my bones, if you really are too cheap to pay your son's ransom.'

He fingered his huge black beard. 'You tempt me,' he said. 'You are very easy to hate.'

'Hate is surely a sin,' I said.

'This from you?' he asked.

Talking is better than being tortured.

'Monk, I have been to Rome, talked to the Pope, debated Filoque with Greek monks, gone on pilgrimage to Jerusalem, fought the Saracens and the Turks. I can't fathom why you imagine you are my superior in religion.'

The Monk looked at me for a long time.

'Release my son,' he said.

There comes a point in any argument where you can negotiate or fight. I was not in a position to fight. For all the tough talk, I was nothing *but* talk.

'Let me go,' I said.

'No, I'll hold you until I have him,' he said.

I shrugged. 'Then I have no reason to let him go. And I doubt my knights will release him when they know who has me.'

He ran his hand through his beard.

It's hard to sound tough when you are on your knees with a lump on your head, and a bigger man is sitting comfortably in a chair with two thugs at his back.

'You know your man, Filippo, is going to lose,' I said.

He laughed. 'I very much doubt it,' he said. 'Listen, William Gold. You are a great fool. Somehow you contrived to take my son and twenty of my men, and you have the effrontery to come in here as if your rank of ambassador entitles you to gloat.'

I was indeed feeling like a fool.

'Release me,' I said, 'and I will release your son. And then, when we meet in the lists, I will put you on your back and take *you*.'

'You are insane if you think you could defeat me in a fair combat,' he said.

'The last man to say that was Camus,' I said. 'But if you are so sure, then let me go.'

He laughed. 'You are a bold rogue. Is this how you made your way from cook's whore to knight? By threats and lawyer's tricks?'

'I find that a trifle high, coming from a monk with a son in armour,' I said.

Oh, aye, in the end, my tongue will be the end of me.

'You tax me with *my* sins?' he snapped.

'It seems better than correcting your Latin,' I said.

I had taken a wrong turn, and the spear shaft put me out.

They poured water on me and threw me in a dark place. I don't think Vigone had a dungeon proper, but the storeroom had an astonishing selection of insects, and wet wool seemed to attract them.

Camus waited until about four in the morning. Perhaps he waited until Matins were done; I don't know.

I'd like to say I was asleep, but I had a good notion of what was coming, and I was afraid. I prayed when I was able, but sometimes I was just cold, miserable and afraid.

I heard the sound of armoured feet ringing on the paving stones above, and then I heard Camus's laugh. He had six men with him, and they pulled me out of the cell. Camus abused me, whispering insults, running his hand down my chest, flicking my nose, slapping my face.

He was just warming up.

'I will have such fun,' he said warmly. 'All the insults avenged. All the things you have said – all the things other people have said. You know what I dream of?' he asked, his face so close to mine he could have kissed me.

I didn't even have a smart answer. I was, in fact, terrified.

'I dream of breaking you to my will and making you one of my men-at-arms, so that I can parade you in front of all these pious hypocrites,' he said. 'You are all just like me, and you all pretend to be better. This preening false monk ... another empty sack of meat and blood.'

Camus was mad – I thought his wits were gone. He was worse than before. And he hated me. In a court, or on a roadside, his insults are boring and his madness was like the madness of a dog who suffers the disease, but in a closed courtyard after a sleepless night, with six armed men around to do you harm, his madness was terrifying because you knew there would be no limit to his cruelty.

The only reason I didn't beg someone for my life was that there was no one to beg. I'd like to say that having been in this position before hardened me, but it did not. If being terribly beaten is bad, the recovery is worse, and I'd done it all, and my joints burnt like fire whenever the rain came.

So the sweetest sound I think I'd ever heard was Sir Pierre de Murs, and his outrage at finding the ambassador on his knees in the court-yard, being beaten by men-at-arms.

Sir Pierre showed a kind of courage that is beyond price. He walked straight in among them, seized one man's spear and threw it across the courtyard.

'You,' he said to Camus. 'Get you gone.'

Camus smiled. 'Perhaps I can find you a place in my entertain-ment.'

'A l'arme!' de Murs roared. A door opened and slammed. He roared again. He'd taken a sword, or he had his own. 'Attack me, you cur. See what you get.'

Running feet. I was near unconscious by then, and didn't really understand what happened, but someone dragged me away.

I spent the night in de Murs' room, expecting them to retake us at any moment – I knew that four of the monk's men-at-arms were outside our door. But when his squire had done his best to make me presentable and Marc-Antonio had re-stitched a doublet to go over my swollen left arm, we went – bravely, let me add – to face the Prince of Achaea.

He affected to be amazed and appalled at what had been done to me.

'This is the hatred that my cousin of Savoy incites,' he said. 'But I am sorry for it.'

He handed me my sword and dagger, and then an equerry gave me a purse of gold.

For the first time, I hated him. It was irrational – princes paid people off all the time. My cheeks were puffy, my jaw felt badly hinged, and my eyes were squeezed shut.

I still managed to toss the purse back.

'Your Grace, I hope …' I had to take a breath. 'I very much hope to see you in the lists.'

We were allowed to ride away.

As a coda, Marietta later told us that there had been a tremendous argument between the Monk and Camus, and the Monk had won. Of course he was afraid for his son. The whole thing was a piece of idiocy. I only mention this because another man's foolishness can kill you, and not everyone reckons the odds as we do.

CHAPTER FOUR

SAVOY AND PIEDMONT

July – August 1368

The next month passed in a chivalric whirlwind as my bruises healed and my left arm returned to its duty. The count spent almost every minute either fighting with Fiore or organising his team. As a side note, I witnessed one of these sessions, and saw Fiore teaching the count a very subtle throw against an armoured man, and I was hurt the way a boy is when he sees his girl walk out with another. He'd never taught me that throw.

The count appointed five captains to make preparations, of whom I had the honour to be one. We did everything, from counting the available baggage wagons at Rivoli, to ordering that the count's magnificent emerald-green pavilions that had travelled all the way to Bulgaria and back were finally shipped from Venice across war-torn Milan to reach us in time for the tournament. The count spared no expense to prepare for the fight. Men were armed at his expense, and our 'bands' within the team received different colours, and we were expected to have horse barding and surcoats to match our colour, so that we could easily find our own in combat.

By early July we were practising as a team. The count sent four of his best knights back to Vigone to make arrangements for the fight, and with four Piedmontese knights, they agreed on a location, at Savigliano, deep in the prince's territory, and on the size and shape of the lists. The count hired hundreds of workmen to build stands and level the lists.

The date for the fight was set for the fifteenth day of August.

On the twenty-first day of July, the Duke of Milan sent a cartel demanding that the fight be suspended and threatening to use force to prevent the two men from meeting. We judged this an empty threat – no matter how powerful the Visconti might be, their entire force was in the field at Borgoforte, facing the Emperor. Our preparations continued.

I don't remember those weeks very well. I was in a dark place. Camus had broken something in me, or perhaps broken something open, and I had a great deal of trouble sleeping.

I was afraid again.

It wasn't that I was particularly afraid of Camus. All of you who have faced the arrow storm and the mêlée know that you can grow accustomed to them, but under that is the fear we try to hide from ourselves and our companions – the fear of death, of humiliation, of failure. And you know that when you are happy – when you have companions, love, fame – you forget those fears.

And you all know that when you are tired and hungry, fear comes faster.

Kneeling in the courtyard waiting for an ugly death had reawakened the dark beast. I make no excuse – I live by the sword, and the beast comes with it.

But to my shame ... By gods, gentles, this is more like confession than recitation, but Chaucer, here, loves to hear of my sins. To my shame, I lay with Marietta. And not once, but many times – I took her the way a drunkard drinks wine. The night after we returned, I found her sitting open-eyed by the hearth of an inn in Rivoli.

'You said I could find a place as a *bonne amie* with your compagnia,' she said. 'I followed you.'

Well, well. One thing led to another.

And I could add adultery to my list of sins. But she kept the darkness away, and she was, in every way, a delight. In her body I found courage – aye, I took her like a drug.

Nothing is simple. And I am, at times, a bad man and a sinner.

It was Fiore who confronted me. I was coming down the steps from my loft in my inn and he took me aside under the stairs.

'You are not training,' he said.

He sounded as shrewish with me as he often did with Nerio, and my resentment was immediate.

'I train a great deal compared to—'

'To whom?' Fiore said. 'We are about to perform the art of arms before the whole world and you, the leader of a *banda*, are so busy tupping your little witch that you can't bring your arse down to the tourney ground.'

I probably drew myself up and I know I was angry. What makes you more angry than hearing the truth from a close friend? Nothing, I promise you.

'Keep a civil tongue in your head.'

'Do you think that no one knows?' he asked. 'Do you think Emile will enjoy hearing about your whore in Rivoli from some jealous courtier? Guglielmo, you have made a variety of enemies in your rise to fortune – not great, powerful people, but petty little men. Don't you think a herd of them will trample a path to her door?'

Now that made me sick to my stomach.

I hadn't even thought . . .

It's hard to believe, now, sitting here, how little thought I gave to my little sin. To Marietta, to Emile, to my own peace of mind. But then, this is also the effect of fear – it is like rust on a sword, ruining everything. Spreading slowly in your scabbard, working on the hilt, the quillons, the blade, the edge, the point – so subtle that you can't feel it – and then one day, you can't even draw your sword. Or it breaks in your hand.

Looking back, I also know that I was losing touch with the knight I wanted to be. This may make no sense to you, but when I was in the midst of my compagnia, none of this would have happened. But I was curiously alone – a lord of Savoy, and not really a lord. A captain, but not of my own people, with whom I'd have closer ties. And being alone, even with Marc-Antonio and Stefano and Bibbo, was poison for me.

'And the example you make for Marc-Antonio,' Fiore said in disgust. 'I thought we were showing him the path to knighthood. He has too much of the pimp in him at the best of times, and I don't think he needs a whoremaster as a—'

I hit him.

Or to be honest, I tried to hit him, and he passed my arm off with a block and then tossed me ungently into the stairs.

'Really?' he asked.

So that afternoon, I went to the horse lines and purchased a good roncey. I bought a used lady's saddle from the same dealer. And I sent Marietta to the compagnia with a note to Janet, and I sent Sam Bibbo to escort her.

Fiore wasn't speaking to me.

It was a week until the fight at Savigliano.

That day or the next, the location of the fight was changed to Fossano. This was agreed between the principals – I can only guess why it was moved. I rode all the way to Fossano with Marc-Antonio to help Pierre de Murs to mark the new lists, which were huge, and then we rode all the way back. De Murs was becoming my favourite of the count's inner council – brave and thoughtful, and incredibly well read for a knight. He'd read Aristotle and Vegetius and ... Well, to be fair, he'd read everything I'd ever read and hundreds of other works besides. Other knights twitted him for being a 'scholar', but I borrowed books.

I do remember sitting down to write Emile a letter, and failing.

Peter Albin's wife, Caterina, contrived to send me a detailed message about the Duke of Clarence. It had nothing very specific in it – I add this detail merely so you know that I was trying to keep an eye on my English prince.

I sent Caterina a carefully drafted note by a military messenger, and then tried to write to Emile again, sitting on the bed where Marietta and I had enjoyed ourselves.

I drank too much. And I went to the fields with Fiore and he hit me a great deal.

And that was our only communication. He would not speak to me. I tried to apologise, and he simply walked away.

I went to church many times. For several days I prayed the whole breviary.

And then, at last, we packed our tournament armour, prepared our warhorses, and rode to do battle.

I am perhaps dwelling too much on those dark weeks. No one likes a tale of torment, self-inflicted or not. But another aspect of those weeks that seemed to add to my burdens was that, from the moment I led the rescue of Sir Ogier, my life with the count entered a new phase. Servants smiled to see me and I was always taken straight to the count. He pressed small signs of his favour on me – a gold pendant, an earring, a dagger. One day, when, by chance, we both wore our Tartar kaftans, bought in Constantinople, he laughed and said that we might be brothers, which may sound like a commonplace, but great lords do not usually refer to former cooks' apprentices as brothers.

It added to the air of unreality, and somehow it added to my darkness. I was at a height of fame and reputation, and I felt hollow and false. No, Froissart, here's the rub – I *was* hollow and false.

We rode south through the end of summer. Nights were already brisk, hence the kaftans. The days were magnificent, and the wheat was ripe and a deep, rich gold, lining the roads. I should have been happy.

Instead I was scared. Afraid to face all my fears. And eager, too – eager to fight them. I didn't eat well, and I desperately wanted Fiore's forgiveness, and I wanted Emile's as well. And as I rode, I thought of Emile, and her distaste at her own infidelities and promiscuity. I knew in the pit of my gut that my dalliance would cost her in blame and self-loathing and memory.

And I was a commander of ten Savoyard knights, and I was no use to them whatsoever, lost in my own black thoughts.

We were south of Vilne when we encountered the Duke of Clarence. I happened to be leading our advance guard, about forty lances and some archers. We were not precisely at war or at peace, and as we were still protecting the count every minute, it made sense to conduct our march across the prince's domains as if we were marching to war.

Clarence's force was well formed – almost two hundred lances, a mixture of his English men-at-arms and the feudal knights of his Italian towns, which were, I promise you, both rich and full of armed men. Whatever I may believe of the Visconti, they had given their English prince a rich dowry and some very good towns. In fact, I sometimes think that all the trouble that was to come might have been avoided if the dowry had not been so large.

I met Richard Musard on an open road lined with poplars. I knew his banner at a distance and he knew mine, and we rode up to each other and embraced – the best thing that had happened to me for days. Indeed, I almost blurted it all out to him. Behind him, the tall duke, on one of the biggest warhorses I've ever seen, waved in his casual way. He was an easy prince to love.

Richard returned my armoured embrace. Then he leant back and waved at his squire, a Savoyard gentleman, not so young, named Jean d'Entremonts.

'Leave us some space, Jean,' he called out.

So I turned to Marc-Antonio.

'Take our lances back down the road a piece,' I said.

Marc-Antonio snapped some orders and I recall wondering if I sounded so tyrannical when I gave orders.

Richard looked both ways.

'My lord is here to prevent this fight. The Visconti have made it clear that this is not in their interests, nor in Clarence's.'

'Oh, sweet Jesu,' I moaned, or something equally blasphemous. 'The count will explode.'

Richard looked at me and shook his head. His horse fretted under him. My Juniper turned almost a full circle as I showed my own anxiety.

'William,' Richard said. He paused. 'I wouldn't say this to any other man. But ...' He looked around. 'I will predict that the count will perhaps feign indignation for an hour. He never intended to fight.'

'What?' I asked.

'He sent a message to his sister asking the Visconti to intervene,' Richard said. 'I enjoyed serving him, but can we both agree that he is a prince first and a knight second? He wants his rebellious vassal dealt with. In fact, Filippo is virtually out of money and allies. Unless he summons the Emperor.'

I pulled at my beard. 'He's trained every day. He has spent a fortune on tents and horses ...'

'He needs to keep the appearance of being willing to fight, William.'

By the Cross of Christ, I get angry all over again. I could have been with Emile, innocent of adultery, sane in my head. This was all posturing?

There's no anger like anger directed at someone else when that anger relieves you of responsibility. Of course all my own actions were my own faults. But the count was wasting everyone's time, and that gave me an excuse. Or so it seems to me now.

I shook my helmeted head.

'Don't be too hard on him,' Richard said. 'Imagine what Filippo's revolt is costing him.'

'By the Cross,' I muttered. 'It's better with Hawkwood.'

Richard frowned. 'No,' he said. 'You're forgetting how it is when you are a routier.'

Well, he perhaps had me there. It had been five years since I'd been such.

I turned and rode back. It was my unfortunate role to inform the count that the Duke of Clarence lay on our march with a small army and the Visconti banners, and that the Duke of Milan forbade the meeting in arms.

Now, as this is a private place and I'm exposing men's sins, let me say that I believe he was genuinely angry. In fact, all of us can be two men. I loved Emile and yet sought to lie with Marietta, for example. I believe that the count, in his person as a knight of some renown, truly intended to fight the Prince of Achaea, while the Count of Savoy, independent ruler of a principality, schemed to cause Achaea's downfall without a fight. Men are complicated.

Let me add that Pierre de Murs looked relieved. Personal combat means a risk of death, and let's be fair – the death of the Green Count would have shattered Savoy. And for what? A thoughtless, witless prince with lice?

And yet ...

Bah, never mind. The count spoke some unkind words to me, somehow implying that I must be responsible for this turn of events.

I was angry enough myself.

'Would Your Grace prefer if the roads ahead of him were not scouted?' I spat. 'Or does His Grace imagine that I demanded that the Duke of Clarence come to detain him?'

The military courtiers – we were all on horseback, in armour, in the broiling sun – all sat silently.

'Take yourself from my presence, Sir William,' the count said, 'and do not return until I ask for you.'

'Very well, Your Grace,' I said. 'Who would you prefer to handle the advance guard?'

Later, de Murs said that it was my tone that snapped him.

'None of your affair! Be gone!'

I rode in the back of the column with my lances. Gatelussi looked secretly amused, and Marc-Antonio began to tell the story at the count's expense and I stopped him. Look here; I had behaved foolishly. I remember when I was new to the count and I used to bridle each time Musard gentled him, but as I became accustomed to him, I realised that anyone, even John Hawkwood – nay, even Fra Peter Mortimer – placed in high command, needs some handling because of the pressures they bear. This is the way of the world.

'Well, I'm a fool,' I said to Gatelussi.

'I'm glad I got to see it, though,' Francesco said. 'Mother of God, it was all I could do not to laugh.'

'But I was wrong.'

'Oh, of course,' Gatelussi said with an Italian smile.

So I missed the actual meeting between the count and the Duke of Clarence. I gather that there was a little ice at first, but that the count quickly thawed, and all was cousinly friendship.

I assumed we'd turn back, but that's not what we did, and that's when I realised how very right Richard Musard had been. Look, let me remind you that before we had even reached Milan from Rome the year before, my lord count was deeply concerned that the Visconti would side with Achaea. Yes? And initially, it appeared that Gian Galeazzo might do just that – Italian politics is as bad as the Scottish border – but in fact, the Visconti had some reason to want to weaken the power of Savoy on their north-eastern borders.

But now, a year later, it became obvious that the Visconti had turned fully to face the other direction. Perhaps the most revealing moment was when my old friend Antonio Visconti rode up to me and clasped my hand.

'You've taken service with Clarence?' I asked.

He smiled the Visconti viper smile.

'Never,' he said. 'I'm making sure that my uncle's money is spent well. And avoiding ... certain other conflicts. You understand?'

And there it was. Antonio was 'family', and the family had decided to back the count. That meant that the count now had carte blanche.

'Other conflicts?' I asked. I was still smarting.

'I was told that you know ... that there were ... *issues* that ... shall we say, caused the Duke of Clarence some concern?' Antonio smiled his crooked smile.

And my wife called Rome a cesspit.

We rode together to the lists at Fossano.

*

The prince's men camped with us – they'd brought their own beautiful pavilions. The count had arranged for a market, supplied by local farmers. We had fifty lances, as required by the agreement of the contest, but the Duke of Clarence had two hundred lances, with archers and armed squires – more men, I suspect, than Filippo could field without stripping all his garrisons. Clarence was there to 'keep the peace', but his bias was obvious.

At any rate, the fifteenth day of August dawned and there was no dust cloud. Indeed, it appeared that Filippo was simply not coming. Then, fairly late in the day, a herald in the full colours of the Prince of Achaea arrived, bearing the Villehardouin arms – which was itself a bit of a slight to the count – and accompanied by the Bourc Camus, escorted by six well-appointed lances. They didn't pause at the barriers, but trotted straight into the lists; a pretty display, for all I loathed them.

The herald was none other than the young d'Albret knight. Now I need to make another of my little trips off the main road of my story. For as long as I'd been a fighting man, the d'Albrets had been a famous family of Gascon routiers – noble routiers, but routiers nonetheless. They were, for the most part, pro-English, except that those of us who knew them well knew them to be mostly pro-d'Albret, if you take my meaning. But just about this time, the d'Albrets were beginning to slip from the Black Prince's duchy of Aquitaine and look for new lordship. That's an entirely different story, but it is worth remarking that young d'Albret was serving the Prince of Achaea, who was defying the authority of Milan that was allied to the king of England. Do you have all that? Because in the year of Our Lord 1368, a knight had to think about all of these things.

So young d'Albret, magnificently mounted, trotted his horse to the centre of the lists, took a scroll from his purse, and read it aloud. In it, the Prince of Achaea referred to the count as a coward, who hid behind his sister's skirts.

'By arriving at the lists with a greater number of knights than is permitted, the count reveals his intention of treachery! Therefore Prince Filippo declines the opportunity to be murdered, and will remain in his castles. The truce attendant on this meeting of arms is hereby renounced, and the prince bids the count defiance and may God judge the right.'

I was, at the time, fully armed. I glanced at Marc-Antonio, who was also armed, and when I knew he was with me, I trotted out into the lists. I didn't ask permission.

Camus saw me coming. But he didn't lower his lance – instead, he raised his visor.

And smiled.

'I won't fight you, William,' he said with a terrible smile.

'We are both here,' I said.

He shook his head. 'I will not allow my own desire to humiliate you to overcome my own lord's refusal to participate. This has become a farce – your cowardly lord will not have the satisfaction—'

'You call the count a coward?' I spat. 'How many times did you try to kill him in Venice?'

D'Albret reached out a hand for my bridle.

'This is not a parley,' he said.

'If it's a state of war,' I spat, 'then I'm within my rights to cut you down.'

'You wouldn't dare!' Camus shouted, but d'Albret pulled away.

But his men-at-arms closed in on me, and I was alone in the middle of the lists.

I put my hand on my sword.

Camus shook his helmeted head, waving his men-at-arms back.

'Tell your yellow count that if he touches a hair on my lord's head, we'll see to it that he and his friends die like the cowards they are,' Camus said. 'And tell your so-called Duke of Clarence that he's a turncoat in the pay of a turncoat.'

'I will say no such thing,' I spat.

Camus turned away.

'Turn and face me!' I roared at him.

I stood in my stirrups to yell at him. Unbeknownst to me, half a hundred Savoyard men-at-arms were coming out into the lists at my back.

'I would be afraid you'd cheat!' Camus said with a laugh. 'Gentlemen don't fight cooks. Don't worry, William the cook! Degradation and humiliation are coming for you.'

He turned, already covered by his men, and rode away.

Richard Musard took my bridle, and Pierre de Murs escorted me to the count. He was livid, his face red.

'How dare you?' he roared at me. 'I gave you no leave to bandy words with that false herald! Now the so-called Prince of Achaea can pretend—'

I interrupted him. 'I have a writ allowing me to make private war on the Bourc Camus,' I said coldly. 'Signed by you, Your Grace. My enemy was there in the lists.'

The count turned his back on me.

It was a long ride to Savigliano.

I relive those days too often. I felt that I had failed as a knight – I should have just cut at Camus and provoked the fight. I still think so. I had a clear case – he was not covered by any protection. And he was evil.

And some people I loved would still be alive.

All my sins. Marietta, Camus, and then Fiore. Because as soon as we left Fossano, Fiore collected his lance and rode away without a goodbye. He hadn't spoken to me since I had attempted to hit him – and now he was gone. My last connection to my friends rode away without a backward glance.

Fiore is a difficult man – a difficult friend. I had hurt him, and he hid it expertly. He felt betrayed. But there were other issues at stake and I wasn't aware of them, and when he rode away, I felt isolated in a way that I had not been since I was an apprentice in London, scared of my uncle.

The next day, I was summoned by the count's chancellor, who told me, in no uncertain terms, that the count wanted young Edouard, Emile's son, to return from Lesvos, where he was a page in the service of Prince Gatelussi.

'The count requires his homage for his lands, and would like him to be in his own service, as quickly as possible.' The chancellor shrugged. 'That is all.'

And that is how fast the wheel of fortune can turn. Two weeks before, I'd been one of the count's favourites – I'd saved his bastard brother, whom he loved.

Now, the summoning of young Edouard indicated that I was to be dismissed entirely. Because if the count accepted Edouard's homage, I was, almost by definition, a person of no importance.

However, from Savigliano to Genoa was only a five-day trip – over mountains, it is true, but nothing so difficult. I was too angry and hurt to argue. I was in a mood to burn everything I loved to the ground, and if you have never been in this sort of mood, you are lucky.

I summoned young Francesco Gatelussi, and asked him, or perhaps ordered him, to take our lances and sail to Lesvos, there to fetch Edouard.

Francesco gave me an odd look.

'Guglielmo,' he said, because we were friends and I didn't expect to be 'my lord'ed all the time, even when I was in a mood. 'If I return to my father's palace, I will not be coming back here.'

I nodded. 'I know. But I have had you more than a year.' And some of my anger dissipated as I thought of that year. 'You are a fine knight, Francesco, and you are ready to be a captain of lances, or lead your father's galleys.'

He nodded. He looked away, out of the window of our tavern.

'I'm not really ready to leave yet.' He looked at me. 'But it is time. I've been thinking so since ...' He looked me in the eye. 'Since you passed me over and put l'Angars in command of the compagnia.'

I shrugged. 'You were my choice,' I said. 'Hawkwood said you were too rich and too well connected.'

'Uh,' Gatelussi said. 'Well. I'm not so very fond of your Giovanni Acudo either.' He nodded. 'I was your choice?' he asked.

'You were,' I said.

'Damn,' Gatelussi said. 'I have fretted about that for these two months.'

We embraced. And as a leader, you have to watch these things. I did what Hawkwood wanted ... and Gatelussi paid in his gut. A lesson for me.

I informed the chancellor that I was sending my best knight to fetch Lord Edouard. He didn't even reply to my note.

The next day, the count summoned the Prince of Achaea to appear at Savigliano. We were still with the Duke of Clarence – that is, he and his army were 'visiting' Savigliano.

The count's position was unassailable. He could muster thousands of men, and the Prince of Achaea was apparently out of money. And out of allies.

Two days later, while I drank too much in an inn, Filippo, Prince of Achaea, rode into Savigliano, attended by a handful of knights. In effect, he came to surrender.

As soon as I heard, I sent a note to Pierre de Murs asking that he represent to the count that, as the threat of war had passed, I'd like to return to my wife and estates.

When I received no reply, I decided to take matters into my own hands. I sobered up – I'd spent a good part of the last three days drunk. I hadn't gone to Mass, hadn't shaved, and I was in a sad way. So I sobered up, as I say, and bathed, and put on good clothes. I'm not quite sure what my actual intention was. I was in a strange way, and perhaps I thought to provoke the count into dismissing me. Or perhaps all I intended was to beg Pierre de Murs to intercede for me. I was convinced that more than anything, I needed to see Emile, confess, and see if I could begin to redeem myself.

It wasn't far enough to the palace to justify riding, so I walked through the streets, attended only by Stefanos. I haven't mentioned him much – he became very quiet after the death of his brother. But he'd become an expert page, and his French was as good as his Italian. I'd even heard him swear in English with my archers.

Any road, we walked up through the town to the castle, where I was admitted with a smile by the guards, all archers of the count's retinue. I crossed the outer yard to the bailey, only to find that the gates to the inner courtyard were blocked by half a hundred ladies and gentlemen summoned to court. The count was choosing his jurors for the trial of Prince Filippo, although it wasn't, technically, a trial. Rather, there were to be six judges to examine the facts and make a final declaration regarding the prince's charges and his inheritance.

In time of war, there would have been no other way into the inner court. But things were relaxed – the war was apparently over. Everyone was in court clothes, including me.

'On me,' I said to Stefanos.

We turned away from the brilliantly dressed throng and walked around to the right, where the kitchen block was. The kitchens appear to be a separate wing, but they have a tunnel connecting them to the main hall, and I knew I could get directly to the count.

No one in the kitchens was especially surprised to see courtiers walk through. For my part, I was appalled at the lack of guards, and for the first time for two weeks I realised that as I was out of favour, and Fiore had ridden away, the count was not being guarded the way we'd guarded him before.

No one challenged us in all the great chaos of the kitchens. And when I say kitchens, I mean six great fireplaces each large enough to roast an ox, with huge long tables crowded with workers – chefs like lords, giving orders, and dozens of boys and girls carrying and fetching, and servers, both noble and non-noble, standing against the walls or pouring wine. Not quite the chaos of a battlefield, but very difficult to control.

Nor did I know Savigliano well.

I saw a man push past a page, a very young page. Something about him was wrong – and this is very difficult to explain, except that all the men and women, boys and girls in those kitchens fit together like cogs in a great clock. If you were to stop and watch them for a moment, you'd see them nod to each other, flirt, scowl, play a prank, or open a cabinet. The connections were there to see.

This man had no connection. He didn't look around. He didn't see the pretty cook stripped to her shift turning one of the fire cranks, nor the boy stealing an apple. He had no social regard for the superior status of the pages ...

Well, I can't say I saw him immediately. I merely noted that he was different and somehow wrong. Then he was gone.

I admit that I was more interested in the young cook in nothing but a sweat-stained shift. I was contemplating combining gluttony and lust ...

Stefanos grabbed my hand.

'That man!' he said in Greek.

'What man?' I asked in Italian.

'He's the man!' Stefanos said.

He mastered himself. We had to move for a boy with a huge tray, and then he shook his head.

I knew which man he meant. I'd just connected the man's thin black beard ...

To Marietta's black-clad man-at-arms. The one she claimed was a man-witch. An apothecary.

In a kitchen.

In the *count's kitchen*.

'I saw that man!' Stefanos said. 'The night my brother died!' He looked at me, all but pleading for me to believe him.

'Follow him,' I said to Stefanos.

The boy obeyed immediately.

I turned to where two noble pages were taking trays, prepared trays, full of delicacies – tiny birds and bits of fruit and pastry. I knew young Roger.

'Messire,' I said.

He smiled to be addressed as a lord.

'Ser Guglielmo,' he said.

'I need you to hold this food right here. It is for the count?' I asked.

'Of course,' he said.

'Do not serve him. On my honour.'

'As you command, My Lord,' he said.

I went into the tunnel. I moved as fast as courtesy allowed, slipping past encumbered pages. My black mood fell away.

Sadly, I could also see how foolish I'd truly been. In my self-created private hell, I'd forgotten to protect the count. Not that the count himself didn't bear most of the blame.

I moved faster. I began to order people out of my way, and as I'm more than six feet in my hose, people generally do get out of my way.

I burst out of the long tunnel and up the steps, which were completely unguarded. In heartbeats I was in the great hall of the castle. Heads turned. I'd made a stir.

The Prince of Achaea was sitting comfortably at a table on his own dais, surrounded by his courtiers – a pair of notaries, young d'Albret, and the Monk of Hecz's son.

At the other end of the hall, the count sat. He was wearing a magnificent emerald-green gown of brocade covered in embroidery and pearls, and a great bag hat that must have had three ells of silk. He looked like a king.

He looked up, and his eyes met mine. Pierre de Murs stood at his elbow with a tray of sweetmeats. Closer to me, and also looking at me, was Sir Ogier. He was almost as magnificent as his brother, but wore a long sword.

In one heartbeat, I forced myself to abandon my foolish anger, my self-punishment, my black mood. I pasted a smile on my face and advanced on the count's table. I made every attempt to radiate courtesy and subservience. I inclined my head.

But I didn't go to the count. Instead, I went to Sir Ogier.

'My friend, you should not be here,' he said, but his smile for me was genuine.

'Messire, I most urgently need a moment with you in private,' I said.

'Not possible,' Ogier said.

'Life and death for your brother,' I said.

Ogier stiffened.

I had to risk it. I leant close. 'We need to go back to close protection. I fear poison. Immediately, Ogier. Please stop the count from eating those sweetmeats.'

Ogier looked at me. Then, in one stride, he was at his brother's elbow. He took the tray from the surprised page and took the cup from his brother's hand. He gave them to me.

I swept out with them, back to the kitchens. Almost no one knew me, but I managed to get myself obeyed. I summoned a cook.

To young Roger, I said, 'Where's the taster? And the dogs?'

Roger paled. 'We haven't used a taster or dogs since Rivoli,' he said. 'The count said they no longer mattered.'

'Hold all the food here. Get wine, yourself, and serve the count with your own hands.'

I didn't have enough hands to arrange all this, but Ogier appeared.

'The cat is fully among the pigeons,' he said. 'My brother wants to know—'

'I'll explain in ten minutes,' I said. 'Please humour me. Get me a mongrel.'

A very cute young dog was brought, frisky and full of life.

Bah. I've killed good men, too. I hardened my heart and gave the dog some of the wine. He lapped it up. I'd already sniffed it and it smelt fine, and indeed, the puppy showed no ill effects.

He was a smart young dog. He ate one of the little birds, and then he sniffed the second and made a whimpering noise.

I picked it up with fire tongs and smelt it. It was a tiny songbird. The others were stuffed with spiced meat or fish.

This one smelt like metal. No wonder the pup refused.

Also, all the other tiny birds were quail. This one was a songbird, even smaller, and the plucking hadn't been as thorough, although I'd never have noticed if it had been on a silver plate.

I showed it to Ogier.

'There's a man,' I said. 'It's a long story. I think he's an assassin. My page is trying to follow him. I saw him leaving the kitchen.' I pointed at the doors. 'No guards, no tasters.'

Ogier winced. 'He hates all that,' I said.

'He'll hate being dead more,' I said.

Guards came. We detained all the cooks and cooks' helpers, and we questioned them. Stefanos returned. He'd never caught up with the man, but he'd found a silversmith's apprentice who'd seen him, and we had his cote-hardie where he'd dropped it in an alley, as the silversmith pointed out.

Pierre de Murs came, saw the poisoned songbird, and left.

I was sweltering in my best gown over my tightest cote-hardie, and I'd stripped off the gown and handed it to the half-naked cook's apprentice to hold. None of the staff seemed guilty, although whenever you question people you learn things you don't want to know – everyone is guilty of something. Regardless, in an hour we were reasonably sure that the black-bearded man didn't have an accomplice, although there were two adolescents about whom I was unsure.

Ogier came and went. Now we had guards on the doors, although they were dressed as cooks' helpers with smocks over their maille.

I took the two head cooks aside. In my opinion, it would be virtually impossible to suborn one of the count's personal cooks. I knew them both from Savoy; Alonzo had been on crusade.

'Remember Milan?' I asked.

They both winced.

'Milanese rules,' I said. 'Everything is tasted. Everything is tested.'

'I need to hear this from the count,' Alonzo said.

'No, you don't,' Ogier said. 'You heard it from me.'

Alonzo shrugged. 'He said it was all over,' he said.

'He's not the best judge,' I said.

Ogier and I put half the songbird on a plate with some cheese in the stable.

I sent for Marc-Antonio and Gatelussi and all my archers. By the will of God, they had been delayed a day in leaving for Genoa by some sick horses.

As he is one, young Francesco can pass for any kind of prince himself. I asked him to dress for court and he appeared in five hundred gold florins' worth of fabric and jewellery. Ogier walked him into the negotiations and he stood by the count. We put a long sword at his feet on the floor, where it couldn't be seen.

Just about Vespers, the two principals rose from their tables. The Prince of Achaea withdrew to his house in the town, which was well fortified, and the count withdrew to chapel. We all heard Evensong – and immediately after Evensong, young Roger took me by the hand and led me to a very small room with a heavy tapestry, where I waited for a long time in near darkness.

'Sir Guglielmo?' a voice called.

I stepped through the tapestry to find the count with his bastard brother.

Ogier smiled. 'I brought him dinner,' he said, flourishing our tin from the stable. On it was a large, very dead rat.

The count turned and glanced at me.

I bowed.

The silence lengthened.

'Your Grace ...' I began.

He interrupted me. 'I have not been myself these weeks,' he said.

'Your Grace, I was rude to you, my own lord,' I said.

He nodded. 'Yes,' he said. 'Your timing is terrible, messire. Nonetheless, your care for us is constant.'

'My Lord, I did not attend—'

He raised a hand dismissively. 'We are all mortal men, and in God's hands,' he said. 'Please return to our direct attendance, and see to our protection.' He pointed at the rat. His hand was shaking. 'Ogier says this was on a plate intended for me.'

'Yes, Your Grace,' I said. 'One of the prince's creatures threatened ... you and others.'

The count nodded. 'Yes, I gather that Filippo now holds Clarence as his enemy. He's a fool.' He looked at me, his eyes sharp. 'In fact, I must tell you, it makes no sense. If Clarence is to live here, he has no reason to incur Achaea's enmity. Nor should my useless cousin be attacking him.'

I nodded. I wasn't sure if I was dismissed or not. But I could see the issue. Why, exactly, would Filippo try to kill Clarence?

He nodded. 'Some of my councillors have ... questioned ... my path on this matter. And I have not told everyone all I know; Sir

Pierre de Murs does not know that Achaea tried to kill me in Venice. But this man is a canker and I need quit of him.'

'Will the treaty draw his fangs?' I asked.

The count looked at Ogier and then at me.

Ogier said, 'Tell him.'

The count was silent.

Ogier shook his head. 'Amadeus,' he said, using the count's first name, which hardly anyone ever did. 'I would sleep better if Sir Guglielmo was ... with us.'

The count looked out of a narrow window and played with his sword hilt.

Ogier put a hand on his brother's shoulder.

'Camus,' he said.

The count turned. 'I agree,' he said. 'Don't pester me so, Ogier.'

Ogier smiled. 'Of course, My Lord.'

The count glanced at me. 'If the Prince of Achaea does not sign the submission, we are going to take him.'

I looked at him, then at Ogier. 'You understand the threat Camus made, My Lord?'

'I do,' the count said. 'I'm above his threats, don't you think?'

I bowed. 'No,' I said. 'Those of us who serve you have to take his threats seriously.'

He was silent for a moment.

'*Eh bien,*' he said. 'There's another threat – we have reason to believe that Filippo intends to send a feudal submission to the Emperor.'

Ah, now we were in it. The Emperor was less than two hundred English miles away to the east, with the largest army in Europe. It was *unlikely* that he would march all the way to us and become involved in Filippo's dispute.

Unlikely, but if he did, the result would be devastating.

'Guglielmo, could such a messenger be ... stopped?' the count asked.

And there it was.

'Yes,' I said. 'I'd—'

'Don't tell me how,' the count said. 'My conscience is none too light as it is.'

'My Lord, I will need my people. I will not be able to send for Edouard d'Herblay.'

He looked at me.

'Yes,' he said.

That was all.

'So I'm not going to Genoa,' Gatelussi said. He smiled. 'You look better.'

I probably smiled. I was better.

'I need you to go back to Volvera. Take Beppo and the lads and watch the roads east.'

I explained about the prince and his messenger.

Gatelussi shook his head in wonderment. 'You want me to pluck a single messenger out of the air?' he asked.

'We need to get Marietta back,' I said. 'I'll send Marc-Antonio to Hawkwood.'

But Beppo dismissed the idea of fetching Marietta.

'Beppo knows her people in Vigone now,' he said. 'Beppo might just favour them with a visit.'

Any time I employed Beppo, I wondered if I was going to pay in Purgatory. It wasn't just his looks, which were terrible. It was his whole point of view, as if good and evil were just about the same to him, and everything was a game.

I was tempted to use the count's line and say, 'Just don't tell me what you intend.'

'Go with God,' I said.

'The Devil is usually more reliable for poor Beppo,' he said with a bitter smile.

I sent Marc-Antonio to Hawkwood anyway. Not for Marietta, though. I was that wise.

That evening, the count's men searched the town with hunting dogs who'd been given the assassin's discarded clothes. A little after Matins they found a house that seemed to be the hidey-hole, and they surrounded it, but the man was gone and the house was empty.

But that afternoon, I went through the house myself. Huntsmen are sharp, but I thought I might be looking for different things.

And indeed, there was a smell in the kitchens that I knew but couldn't place. I followed my cook's nose to the oven, and in the oven I found that if the assassin was good at killing people, he was bad at building fires. He'd tried to burn a lot of parchment. Little twists of parchment. That was the smell – the smell of burnt parchment. I knew it from my days with monks as a boy.

Most of the little scraps were mere black twists.

Several had writing – lines of symbols in what looked like vermilion ink. Like the scrap that Hawkwood had given me, back in Milan. Including the letter *S*.

There was also a piece of almost unburnt parchment on which someone with good, trained handwriting – almost perfect Gothic letters better by far than my own – had written out a few lines and then ... abandoned the attempt? Changed his mind? No code.

Just Italian.

Lo scherzo e che verremo pagati due volte.

'The joke is, we'll be paid twice.'

I sat in an empty kitchen on a comfortable oak stool and tried to imagine why Filippo employed an assassin ... who was in contact with Milan? Who worked for the Visconti?

Did we have this all wrong?

In the morning, Prince Filippo was gone.

Before Vespers that evening, a messenger came from the prince, saying that he'd only return to the 'negotiations' if he had a *sauvegarde* promising that he was immune from any form of redress or prosecution.

The count was beside himself with anger, and it was patently obvious that we had a traitor in our councils. At the same time, Ogier and I both knew that the problem of a messenger going to the Emperor was just as pressing, and so, very early the next morning, I rode out with Marc-Antonio and covered the thirty miles to Volvera in a single day. We rode across the prince's territory, and we moved fast.

Francesco Gatelussi had taken a different tavern in Volvera, and before full dark we were ensconced. I rode out and checked his watch posts – one man-at-arms and one archer at four different crossroads. Gospel Mark and Ewan and Lazarus the Greek were all in place. All of them had made themselves snug in various ways, and their men-at-arms were there only for muscle – the Birigucci brothers and de la Motte.

Beppo didn't come on time. In fact, he wasn't back before I went to bed, and he wasn't there in the morning. By Nones, the Biriguccis themselves were worried.

'If he's taken ...' Clario shook his head.

Benghi growled, 'We'll take him back.'

Before full dark Richard Musard came in, followed by his squire. He handed me a note. It was unsigned.

> A sauvegarde *has been issued to the prince. He will be very dangerous now.*
> *Do what you can.*

Richard took me aside.

'It's bad,' he said. 'The count is distrustful of everyone.'

I nodded.

'Do you remember Florimont de Lesparre?' Richard asked.

'A month ago I was stabbing him with a pole-arm,' I reminded him, and he shook his head.

'Damme,' he said. 'I'm getting old. He's recovering, and now he's trying to get a position with the Duke of Clarence. He's around all the time.'

'And he's a Gascon, and mad as a March hare,' I said.

'Exactly,' he said. 'And he knows young d'Albret.'

'You think he's the spy?' I asked quietly.

'Spy?' Richard all but spat the word. 'Lesparre is too self-important to be a spy. He's the centre of God's creation. But he might give information to an enemy to further his own ambitions.'

I had crossed paths with Lesparre a few times. He was no Camus – he was merely a man who thought he was Lancelot come to earth.

'We may have lost Beppo,' I said. Since Richard didn't know him, I just shrugged. 'One of my people. He went into Vigone.'

'That was rash,' Richard said.

I handed him wine.

An hour later, using his retinue, we doubled the watch posts and added a backstop at Carignano, well to the east. Abusing the count's authority to a ridiculous extent, I sent messages to the various bridges and fords over the Po to hold any armed traveller.

I never went to sleep that night. Richard and I played dice, and then cards. We drank, and then stopped drinking. After Matins, I rode out alone and visited two watch posts. Clario shook his head and demanded vengeance for Beppo.

'He's too smart to be taken,' I assured Clario, although I had my own fears.

'As long as the Prince of Achaea is alive and has the backing of the Bishop of Cambrai,' Richard said, 'the count will have to have his food tasted.'

I nodded.

'I'm getting too old for this crap,' Richard said.

'How's Clarence as a lord?' I asked.

'Surprisingly good,' Richard admitted. 'He granted me a manor in England, William.'

I congratulated him.

'In fact, I'm considering a visit. Perhaps I'll retire and be a gentleman farmer.'

'The duke must need you,' I said. 'Surely the Green Count still needs you.'

Richard made a face. 'He's changing,' he said. 'The crusade, and then this ...'

I'd seen it too. 'I saw it happen in Venice,' I said. 'And again when the Pope refused to entertain any thought of the Union.'

'Yes. He's been ... hurt. And ignored. And now he's going to strike for his own survival.' Richard shook his head. 'It's too bad. The world needs paladins, and then treats them like dirt.'

Then we sat in silence so long that the man who was serving us wine fell asleep and started to snore.

'If Beppo isn't back by dark tomorrow,' I said, 'I'm going to try and get into Vigone.'

Richard's teeth flashed in the darkness.

'For someone's servant?' he asked.

'Beppo is a very good man,' I said. Actually, I wondered if anyone had ever said that about him before. 'Regardless, he knows too much to leave him in their hands.'

'This is a dirty business. In some ways, worse than running a whorehouse,' Richard said.

He hated to refer to his ugly past, so that meant he was disturbed in his spirit.

The hours of night crawled by. I wished I had Marietta for a variety of reasons – most of all to make a contact inside the city. Or so I told myself. Men are very good at rationalizing sin, or at least, I am.

At dawn, I went with Gatelussi and Musard and our squires, and we rode down to our watch posts with archers to relieve the men who'd lain awake all night. But we all knew that the peasants knew where we were. Anyone with good scouts and a few silvers to buy information could avoid us.

We changed our watch posts, and then, almost without discussion, we turned our horses down the road to Vigone. In the east, the sun was just rising – another beautiful day, with a hint of chill coming down from the mountains. We rode almost to the very gates of the prince's city of Vigone, and then turned around and rode back in defeated silence.

We stabled our horses. I left Juniper saddled for my next patrol and gave her extra oats as compensation, and then the three of us went in.

Beppo was sitting at our table with a pitcher of wine.

'Ah, gentles,' he said. To men, he bowed. '*Illustrio*,' he said, his ugly face giving away nothing.

'You're late,' I said, although I wanted to embrace him.

'Ah, *Illustrio*, Beppo had some little difficulties. A damsel to rescue from her maidenhead, and some wine pleading to be drunk, and a scoundrel worse than Beppo who desired to be killed for everyone's good.' The rogue grinned.

I couldn't help myself. I threw my arms around him.

'Bah,' he said. 'You will hug me harder when you see what Beppo has for you.'

'But the messenger?' I asked.

'Gone three days ago,' Beppo said with a smug satisfaction that might have turned the stomach of a weaker man. 'Hecz's son. He left before we went to have our little tournament.'

Of course. I felt a fool.

'Now the fat is in the fire.'

Beppo smiled, the very cat who's already eaten the cream.

'Perhaps. Or perhaps Beppo has moved the pan for the good count. Beppo is, you know, not such a very good man.'

'Out with it!' I said.

Beppo shook his head. 'No, *Illustrio*. Even for Beppo this is a mighty stroke. Beppo might wish to savour it a little while.'

Well, there are more heroes in the world than just my friends. Froissart, you will never tell tales of the Beppos of the world, but Chaucer here might, and Boccaccio would have loved him.

Anyway, I poured him more wine and he sat back.

'Beppo met with Marietta's friend,' he said. 'Beppo persuaded him, despite lacking some of her "talents", that he was best served by serving you, *Illustrio*.' He shrugged. 'Sadly, the false dog sold Beppo to Camus.'

I froze.

Beppo smiled his evil smile. 'What choice did Beppo have?' he said. 'Poor Beppo. He sold you to Camus.'

Richard put his hand on his sword.

Beppo shrugged. 'Sadly, Beppo is no gentleman, no good *cavaliere*. Sometimes Beppo lies – indeed, sometimes it's difficult for him to tell the truth. Especially when men are beating poor Beppo with their fists.'

He was marked. His face wasn't bad, or perhaps under his heavy brow and bulging cheeks it was difficult to say where he might be bruised – but I could see from the way he sat that he'd been hurt.

'When you look like Beppo,' he said simply, 'people beat you. And you grow adept at telling lies. And sticking to them. Eh?'

Not for the first time, I wondered what kind of life the man had led.

'Camus believes that everyone is as ... *excited* by pain as he is,' Beppo went on. 'Beppo told him some lies and he rode off towards Rivoli.'

'Thank God,' I said.

'You missed Beppo, *Illustrio*?'

'Like a long-lost, if slightly ugly, brother,' I said.

'Slightly ugly?' Beppo asked. 'Is this a compliment or an insult?' He smiled.

'You are, just now, quite beautiful, even if your news is terrible.'

'Ah, Beppo's beauty is about to increase sharply, by Satan and all his fallen angels. Listen. Almost no one saving you, *Illustrio*, and Messire Clario, has ever suspected Beppo of having much in the way of brains.

And so with Camus, who discussed quite a few of his master's plans in front of stupid Beppo.'

Richard nodded grimly. 'He's always been a braggart.'

'Never the best course,' Beppo agreed. 'Having ordered Beppo beaten and then put to the question, he then accepted stupid Beppo's conversion as if he were God and we were on the very road to Damascus, and proceeded to issue orders while Beppo was still strapped to a very hard chair. And when he was done, Messire d'Albret also issued some orders concerning the prince, which were very interesting. They concerned a most important document, a *sauvegarde* issued to the good Prince of Achaea by the Count of Savoy, that very legalistically and in a very fine manner offers the prince every legal protection.'

Richard nodded. 'Yes,' he said. 'We had no choice but to issue it. Now the very best we can hope is some sort of temporary truce. God. War with the Emperor?'

I poured Beppo more wine. As the sun rose outside and the light in the tavern grew, I could see better and better how badly he'd been beaten.

'And after some pompous crap,' Beppo went on, 'young d'Albret asks Camus if poor unlucky Beppo was to be killed, and Camus mouths one of his pious remarks about Satan placing Beppo in his hands and his having a tool to ruin everything you love.' Beppo spread his hands. 'Camus believes he knows Beppo. Beppo may have told him some lies about your constant mistreatment of poor Beppo. And your various sins. That one hates you, boss. And when a man is torturing Beppo, Beppo is quite adept at making up what the torturer wants to hear.'

'By the risen Christ,' Richard said. 'I'm sorry.'

'Bah! Beppo has had as bad, and worse, many times. Beppo has a devil's face. Men hate Beppo for existing.'

My sense was that Camus had hurt Beppo badly – not just on the surface of his skin. But he hadn't broken.

'However you parse it, messires, Camus said unlucky Beppo was not to be killed, and so d'Albret ordered the poor wretch released and given work. Beppo curried horses, naturally. And the next day, this morning, Beppo tacked up a dozen horses for the Prince of Achaea and his entourage, riding to meet your Green Count.'

'Of course you did.'

'For Beppo, the depth of the irony of astonishing good looks is the ease with which people trust poor Beppo, as if, given that Beppo's face comes from a devil of Hell, Beppo must be trustworthy.' He shrugged, and it hurt. 'So the prince comes to the stable and gives a string of orders to Camus, who is commanding his escort. Camus takes the *sauvegarde* and puts it in a little bag on his saddle pommel.'

Beppo glanced around. And dropped a heavy sealed parchment on the table.

'And here it is.'

'Good Christ!' Richard said.

Beppo allowed himself a sly smile. 'Beppo is not a good man,' he said. 'But Beppo is very loyal indeed to those who treat Beppo like a man and not some beast.'

I went over and gave him a hug. He tried to escape me – then, after I put my arms around him, he sagged for a moment.

'Beppo will weep,' he said.

'We need to ride,' I said. 'Beppo, I'm leaving you here with the Birigucci boys and the archers. Gatelussi is in charge – advise him.'

Beppo nodded. 'Gatelussi is a nice boy.'

'How can I reward you?' I asked him.

He shrugged. 'A dozen willing virgins?' he drawled. 'Maybe just another pitcher of wine. It never screams and runs, except down my throat.'

It occurred to me as I rode south that Beppo might need to go to Lesvos. And stay there.

Six hours later, I entered the hall at Savigliano through the kitchens. There were guards everywhere, and I was passed forward from post to post in a way that I found satisfying. I also cadged a berry tart on my way through, ate it in two bites, dipped my hands into someone's rose-water, and then borrowed a cook's towel – to wipe my face and clean my hands. Finally, I took a silver tray from a rack of them, and put two cups of wine on it.

Then I went through the tunnel and up the steps to the great hall.

The Prince of Achaea was at his table. He raised his head and looked at me without interest. At his side, Camus stiffened. D'Albret raised an eyebrow.

I looked down the hall, to the dais on which the Duke of Clarence sat. He had Lady Violante on his right hand and he was chatting with her – a Titan conversing with a tiny fairy. But she was the happiest I'd ever seen her, her small, perfect face beaming with delight. Caterina and Peter Albin said they were very happy together.

Florimont Lesparre was standing quite close to both of them, behind the thrones. He looked at me – indeed, he might have been said to have glared.

My own lord, the Count of Savoy, was off to the right, at another table. He had advocates and notaries around him, and a vast number of scrolls and folios on the table. Despite that, he looked the most serious and the least pleased of the three great lords.

For those who wonder, I had given a great deal of thought to my actions. I knew that what I was about to do was at best, underhanded.

Let's be plain with each other. Beppo had stolen the prince's *sauvegarde*. The *sauvegarde* was the written guarantee that he would not be brought to trial for any felonies committed in the county of Savoy – it said so.

But *sauvegardes* are magic scrolls. They only protect the bearer if he is bearing them. That's the law.

And the Prince of Achaea and his thugs were bad, bad men. I feel it only fair to remind you – he'd tried to kill the count in Venice, and then in Tuscany and later in France. He was blind to chivalry, and he had killed my page Demetrios with poison and his actions had led to the death of at least three Savoyard knights.

I mean what I have said about things like using torture and killing innocents. If you do these things, you are what you hate.

But a knight is also a judge. And I had judged Achaea and found him to be a dishonourable arse who needed to be put down like the mad dog he was. When he sent to the Emperor, after offering to swear fealty to the king of France, he indicated that there were no legal rules that bound him. When he used poison to try and kill the count, he showed that no rules bound him at all.

So I feel that I acted as was best for all. Except Achaea.

And I confess that I was perfectly aware that I was helping Nerio as well.

I walked along the wall, where the servants waited, and approached the count's table from behind. I spoke briefly to Sir Ogier and handed him a food tray. I didn't want anyone who was not one of ours to know what I was handing to the count, so I had placed the *sauvegarde* flat on a silver tray and set a pair of wine cups atop it.

As I say, I handed Ogier the tray, and he bowed.

'What?' he mouthed.

'Read it,' I said. 'And act.'

I turned. I walked down the hall, again along the wall where the servants congregated. Achaea never saw me, and Camus was ignoring me, his eyes on closer threats.

I went down the tunnel to the kitchen, and found Roger.

'I need a room here,' I said. 'I need to be able to watch the count at all times. Also, I need to know that every damned thing he eats or drinks is tasted.'

Roger bowed. 'My Lord, I taste everything. The dog has everything first, but he won't eat greens and sweets.'

'Get a dog that will eat sweets and greens,' I said. 'There's dogs enough running feral in the streets. I'm not joking. Get the count's huntsman to round up a dozen.'

'I can do it, My Lord,' Roger said proudly.

I put a hand on the boy's shoulder.

'Roger,' I said, using his baptismal name, 'I plan to dance at your knighting – mayhap even put my sword on your shoulder or the spurs on your feet. *You will not live to see that if you taste all the food first.*'

'I'm not afraid,' he said

By God, gentles, that boy was not afraid. And he was perfectly willing to give his life for his count. This is not some devoted peasant – this is the first son of one of the great lords of Savoy, who had a life of riches and power ahead of him if he didn't swallow a bellyful of *arsenico*.

Courage comes in many forms. Women bear children, and who praises them for it? And pages taste food. Doctors and nuns tend to people with plague. Listen, my friends – when I go forward into the arrow fire in my harness, with Gabriel between my legs and a fine sword in my hand, what are the odds that some lucky bastard will put me down? Not that high, I promise you. Good armour, good horse, good skills ...

Face the black plague, or the poison of an enemy, alone, with no friends, no banner, no bright light of chivalry. Ah, friends, my apologies for so much moralising. Let's get back to the main road of the story.

Richard Musard had his baggage moved back into the small palace. It was like old times – the two of us were living in a barren loft, directly under the beams of the slate roof. Our little space, hardly a 'room', reminded me of Anne's quarters above the inn in Avignon. I unrolled my blankets and laid out my spare clothes and put on a clean shirt, while Richard found us two very serious maids to iron our good clothes. Then, as soon as he was presentable, he washed his face and hands and prepared to attend the Duke of Clarence ... and the count.

'Watch Lesparre,' I begged.

'I will. But I will watch everyone.'

We clasped hands, quickly, and then we ran in different directions – both of us wearing maille under our doublets, both wearing the longest daggers we owned.

When I went into the kitchens, I could tell something was happening – the guards were very alert, and all the kitchen staff were together at one end.

I took an apple off a pile and turned to the cook's apprentice who had been so nearly naked the day before.

'What's happening?'

She curtsied.

By the risen Lord, I hope you always understand when I tell these little titbits that it still amuses me when anyone, much less kitchen staff, see me as a lord, because while I recognise that I am a good knight and a fine blade, I'm also still a cook's boy in my heart.

'They have *just* arrested the Prince of Achaea,' she said.

I smiled more broadly.

I passed up the stairs into the hall. I saw Richard, close by the Duke of Clarence, and a dozen of the count's men-at-arms surrounding d'Albret and Camus.

I came up behind Ogier, who had his sword drawn.

'How did you get that?' Ogier asked.

I smiled. 'I have no idea what you are talking about,' I said. 'Are we taking Camus?'

'Only to evict him from the palace,' Ogier said.

Savoy himself was on his feet, looking at the proceedings like a bird of prey watching a stumbling lamb. He had not hesitated, I noted. Given the *sauvegarde*, he'd struck.

I didn't want to catch his eye. Indeed, I was wishing I'd thought of a way to take Camus at the same time.

'I want to see every man Achaea has with him,' I said.

I was thinking of the hooded man who'd tried poison the week before.

Ogier nodded. His naked sword was in his hand, and together we walked to where a dozen men in full armour were surrounding the Prince of Achaea.

'You cannot do this!' Achaea was shouting. 'You accursed coward! You bastard! I have a *sauvegarde*!'

Savoy was perfectly polite. 'You are being arrested on charges of felony and high treason. You will have a trial.'

'You gave me a *sauvegarde*!' Achaea shrieked.

'You should produce it, then,' Savoy said. 'Otherwise, you are an attainted traitor riding abroad. Come, cousin! You cannot tell me that you lost such an important document as you claim to have? A magical *sauvegarde* protecting you from prosecution for treason? After you offered the king of France your submission as a vassal?'

'This is unfair! Unfair! You cannot act in this way! There are laws!'

'There are laws, cousin,' Savoy said. 'And we will follow them. Tomorrow you will confront your accusers in open court – the court of the county, with nine trained jurors.'

'Accusers?' he spat. 'Who would dare?'

'Princess Marguerite,' Savoy said.

'That whore?' Achaea roared.

'Calm yourself, cousin, or you will die of apoplexy right here.'

Savoy was utterly master of the situation. He'd chosen his path – if the morality of it concerned him, there was no shadow on him.

'Who else would dare?' Achaea ranted.

'I will myself,' Savoy said.

'You ... You bastard! It's all fixed, all a sham! A lie, like all your other lies ...'

I found it curious that Achaea, who had used assassins and poison against us for over a year, was suddenly so very outraged to have the tables turned. But I wasn't watching him. I was watching Camus, who was not ranting. He was calm – almost smiling. I knew him so well. I knew when he looked smug, and I knew that this calm meant he still felt that he was in the saddle.

I realised that I needed to prick his composure – not out of some vengeance, but because I needed a glimpse into what he had planned.

I moved up next to him and he turned his head.

'Pity about the *sauvegarde*,' I said.

His eyes met mine and locked like two sharp blades biting into each other at the first cross.

'That was clever, Gold,' he said.

Worrisome. Camus was easier to deal with when he thought himself invincible, and harder when he was rational.

'I think you may need new employment,' I said.

He smiled. 'The Bishop of Cambrai has never stopped paying me,' he said. 'I offer that for nothing. You imagine that I work for Achaea?' He laughed. He put his thumbs in his belt, hands in sight, a threat to no one.

'It's good that someone will pay you,' I said. 'Given your record.'

That got him.

'I hate it that people think *you* are a good knight,' he said.

Achaea was shouting at the Duke of Clarence behind us. In fact, Clarence had just told Savoy that he would be the judge of the prince's case.

'I think ...' I said, glancing at Lesparre and Musard, who were close together. 'I think that it is not so much that I am so good, as that you are so bad. Or perhaps just so unsuccessful. It might be your tactics—'

'Fuck you, Gold. Fuck you.' I had him. His eyes had lost their flinty shine and the rage was written on him. 'We will kill them all, Gold, and you and your paramour Musard can't stop us all. And when I'm sitting on your dunghill, see if you can crow then, *Coq*!'

I turned to the Savoyard man-at-arms by my side.

'Sir Amadeus,' I said.

'Sir Guglielmo,' he nodded.

'See that this man is kept in isolation ...'

'You can't hold me!'

'... and if anything happens to the count ...'

'*You cannot hold me!*'

'... kill him,' I said. 'Or call me and I'll do it.'

I wonder what would have happened if my orders had been followed. Camus had given me much to think on, and think I did, standing

on the battlements and looking towards Chambéry. I wanted Emile.
I wanted to go and throw myself on her mercy and confess my sin. I
wanted ...

Bah, never mind. I spent the time thinking about Camus, and
Robert of Geneva, Bishop of Cambrai. I won't say that I solved
anything, but I took the evidence available to me and arrived at a
workable theory.

That evening Count Amadeus summoned me.

'Ah, Sir Guglielmo,' he said.

He waved me to a seat. He was cutting a pear with a silver knife,
and he gave me half.

It was sticky but delicious.

He watched me eat it.

'You were poor as a child?' he asked.

I nodded. 'Yes, My Lord,' I said.

'Interesting,' he said. 'Your manners are excellent – a year with me
and you have the polish of a born gentleman.'

Mostly due to Emile.

It was odd how easily he annoyed me, given how devoted I was
becoming to him and his cause.

'I have released Camus and d'Albret,' he said. 'Clarence ordered
it. They are to collect evidence for the prince and we are not to seem
partial.'

I blinked. 'Your Grace ...'

'Yes,' he said. 'I know that Camus is dangerous, and was the archi-
tect of several attempts on my person.'

'With careful questioning,' I said, 'he would probably reveal himself
in court. He's mad as a March hare – he might even brag.'

The count winced. 'I do not want to charge Achaea with attempted
murder,' he said. 'That can be very messy. It would also make public
some things I would rather keep private.'

I thought that he was wrong, even foolish, but it was not my place
to say so. So I nodded.

'Camus told me today that he didn't work for Achaea,' I said. Roger
brought me wine. 'That he worked for the Bishop of Cambrai. Robert
of Geneva.'

The count sipped his wine. 'I don't think that makes a difference,'
he said.

'My Lord, I don't know what limitations your cousin Robert might have,' I said. 'But what if he intends both of you to die?'

Savoy turned and looked at me with a griffon's eye or an eagle's. He was very still for a long time.

'My sons are young,' he admitted.

'My Lord,' I said, 'when Robert of Geneva arranged for the prince to offer his vassalage to the king of France, he showed his hand. He is offering Savoy to the king of France, intact, in exchange for at least a cardinal's hat, and perhaps ...' I shrugged. '... in time, the papacy.'

The count sucked in a long breath. He set his wine cup down sharply.

'Sir Guglielmo,' he said slowly. 'I do not wish this to be discussed with anyone.'

He was angry.

I probably blinked, or shrugged.

'I'm sorry if I have angered you, My Lord,' I said.

He shook his head. 'Damn it!' he spat. He was not a man given to even the gentlest profanity or blasphemy. 'Damn it to Hell!' he said again. 'I am afraid that you are correct.'

'He does not control everything,' I said. 'The king of France, is, according to Musard and some of your knights, warming to the idea of war with England. France will not have armies to seize your fortresses if they are facing the Prince of Wales in Aquitaine.'

He closed his eyes. 'Yes,' he said. 'I gather that the king of France has ransomed du Guesclin for twenty thousand gold ducats.'

I laughed.

'This is amusing?' the count said.

'I ransomed him for a hundred, once upon a time,' I said. 'My Lord, I very strongly wish to visit my lady wife. May I ask ...?'

'You have the charge of my person,' he said. 'We will ride for Chambéry in a few days and you can see your countess.'

I had to accept that. But it was cool in late August, near the mountains, and I shivered.

CHAPTER FIVE

LOMBARDY, PIEDMONT, SAVOY

Autumn 1368

I spent the next week riding back and forth between my outposts north of Vigone and the count's palace at Savigliano. We – that is, those of us who knew exactly what game we were playing – still wanted to intercept any messenger from the Emperor to the Prince of Achaea.

Off to the east, Hawkwood and Bernabò were still facing the Emperor. But the Emperor was, like most princes, having trouble paying his people, and Bernabò was not – so there was a deadlock that benefited Milan and drove the Pope to anger. Albornoz's papal troops were mutinous for lack of funds.

North of us, the fighting season was coming to a close, and France and England were still not at war. In fact, it appeared to us that the Milanese–English alliance, as represented by Violante and the Duke of Clarence, had been accepted by the king of France. He was manoeuvring to undermine the Prince of Wales in his relations with his Gascon vassals, but that was life in France.

On the twenty-sixth day of September, a cold, wet day, the trial of the Prince of Achaea began at Rivoli. Young Princess Marguerite, the stepmother of Achaea, and a few years younger than he, appeared on the first day with a list of grievances that was quite stunning, and even damning – or unbelievable, if you didn't know Achaea. In fact, it struck me that it was incredible that she was still alive. Why hadn't he poisoned her?

The princess was small, very pretty, and full of the spirit that can make a man a great knight, or a woman a great lady. She was possessed of the charisma of a lioness and the energy as well, and she was determined that her son would inherit.

In the interest of honesty, let me add that she was perhaps as danger-ous as Achaea herself. I doubt that anything would have stopped her in her drive to have her children succeed to their estates. But what puzzled Achaea was obvious to me – people *liked* her. She was charm-ing and direct. She remembered people and places and details – she never forgot a birthday – and all of her close retainers adored her.

While she was quite pretty, as I have said, her attraction was in no way that of a wanton. She was more ... a force of nature.

I wished I had Sir Jason or Sir Bernard.

The more I thought about that, the more I realised that they were three days' travel away. I did what I should have done weeks before. I wrote to Emile, a letter full of love, and asked that she come to the count's court at Rivoli and bring her knights. It was clear to me that, whatever the count might say, we were not going to Chambéry until the affair of the Prince of Achaea was over.

Just after the prince was taken to court, I had a letter from Hawkwood, via Sam Bibbo, who returned to me with Marc-Antonio – and Fiore.

I did not know how alone I had felt until Fiore clasped my hands.

'I was angry,' he said with his usual bluntness. 'I went home. Now I am back.'

Marc-Antonio was full of the news of the camp and much of the political gossip I've mentioned in the last few moments. From Hawkwood and Marc-Antonio, we learnt much about the Prince of Wales and the war in Spain.

Bibbo just drank wine and shook his head. I ran down all the events of the last few weeks, and put him in the rotation of men guarding the count directly. But after some thought, I loaned him to Richard Musard, who was now working just as hard to guard the Duke of Clarence.

Somewhere in the midst of all that – and my recollection may be faulty because it was a terrible, busy time, and I was jumping at shadows and also desperate for my wife to join me so that I could confess and move on – Gatelussi sent for me. I rode south to our little inn, where he produced an unliveried man – a gentleman from one of the northern Italian families that provide so many retainers to the warring states. He was an Orgulafi, like Milan's steward. And he was very angry.

'By what right do you seize an imperial messenger on the roads?' he asked.

Gatelussi shrugged.

'You are a messenger from the Emperor?' I asked.

'Yes!' the man spat.

'And to whom are you going?' I asked.

'Prince Filippo of Achaea!' he said.

'I will take you to him myself,' I said.

We rode to Rivoli before the gates closed, on a chilly evening. I sent a note to Sir Ogier, and he and the count met us as we waited in the anterooms to the Prince of Achaea's tower, which was also his prison. Both were soberly dressed.

A few minutes later, Florimont Lesparre joined us with Richard Musard. Lesparre glanced at me. He frowned.

There are times when a little grace is better than a great deal of bluster. I crossed the anteroom to him.

'I hope you are recovered,' I said. 'I think the next time we meet ...'

He looked down his nose at me.

But I persevered. 'I wanted you to be sure,' I said carefully, 'that I knew you had nothing to do with your tampered weapon.'

Lesparre, being the man he was, rolled my words over in his head, looking for an insult.

'I would never—' he began.

'I know, messire.'

There – he'd once called my wife names and called the king of Cyprus a coward, but I was polite, and he bowed.

'For my part,' he said, 'I found the proceedings very irregular and ... regrettable.'

I suspect that's as close to an apology as men like Lesparre come.

Then, as if we were old companions, he bent down close to me.

'Why are we here?' he asked.

'You will see presently,' I said. 'I do not wish to spoil my lord's plan.'

The prince's equerry was d'Albret. He opened the door to the anteroom.

'I am directed to enquire why these estimable gentles are forcing themselves on my master in prison.' D'Albret was deliberately impertinent. No one does this better than Gascons.

I bowed. 'There is a messenger for your prince. I assumed that you would wish to see him. My lord makes the stipulation, as this no doubt will impact on his case in court, that he be present when the messenger is presented, and free to read any message. Lesparre and Musard are here for the Duke of Clarence, to see that everything is fair.'

'Fair!' spat Achaea from the doorway. 'Nothing is fair. Who is this supposed messenger?'

'I am not a *supposed* messenger,' Orgulafi said. He was very like a little hawk, and his feathers were ruffled. 'I am a herald to the Emperor! I have my baton of office right here, and a reply to your message to my lord.'

Achaea's head snapped back as if a viper had tried to strike him.

'A messenger from the Emperor?' he said.

D'Albret put his hand on Achaea's. 'My lord cannot receive you, messire, as he has never sent a message to the Emperor. You have replied to a provocation from this *gentleman*.' He pointed at the count.

'Provocation?' the messenger asked. 'With all the seals of your *comte*?'

He reached into his satchel and pulled out a scroll tube.

'I will not receive this forgery!' Achaea said.

I probably grinned.

An hour later, the Duke of Clarence had proof positive that Achaea had committed high treason against the count with the Emperor.

After that, it should all have been easy.

And some time that same day, Sir Jean-François came in with his squire and a pair of archers, from my lady, with the news that her party were on their way from Chambéry and would arrive in a few days. As soon as he'd seen to his horse and we'd shared an embrace, I sent him – a local man, who spoke Savoyard French and Savoyard Italian – to Princess Marguerite's captain, to try and bring her under my net of protective guards and tasters. My people had lost Camus in the countryside. We hadn't seen the dark-haired assassin, and we were growing increasingly frantic. In fact, I'd allowed Gatelussi no rest, even when he'd picked up the Imperial messenger, and probably no thanks either.

Having Fiore present made all the difference. It was not just that I could trust him. I knew he could defeat any physical assassination attempt, and I further knew that his intelligence and powers of observation would make the count safe. Fiore freed me to take a more active role in finding the prince's agents.

If they weren't a figment of my imagination.

I spent a lot of time praying, I fully admit it. And for the first time in a long time, I felt constantly that I was over my head – that I was doing work that I didn't understand, responding to threats that I couldn't really imagine or plan for. My sleep was fitful and my dreams were dark. I don't imagine that I was looking forward to seeing Emile and telling her.

Almost everything about that week is lost to me, except the pivotal events. I ran about, I probably irritated all my own retinue and the count's people as well, and I had nothing to show for it. Princess Marguerite did condescend to accept our help, and her captain moved her into apartments close to the count's the same day that Marguerite and the prince confronted each other in court. He accused her, formally, of witchcraft, and demanded an ecclesiastical trial. She accused him of a list of crimes, including attempted murder.

The count, with an appearance of impartiality, bound both of them to appear to answer their charges.

I was not present, but it was a day full of drama, and I correctly predicted that the prince would summon the Bishop of Cambrai to lead his prosecution of Princess Marguerite for witchcraft.

That afternoon, I was invited to join the count. In the hallway outside the council chamber, I found Richard Musard with Master Albin and Caterina. She curtsied and he bowed, and Richard and I embraced.

I looked at Albin.

He shrugged. 'I have been replaced on a pretext,' he said bitterly.

Richard gave me a look that I found difficult to interpret.

'I thought you two were going to England?' I asked.

Caterina smiled. 'I think instead we are going to Venice,' she said. 'A ... patron ... of mine might find my husband a place.'

Albin nodded to me. 'Thanks for trying to get me a place in England,' he said.

I took a small parchment out of the wax tablet that I habitually kept in my purse when I was at court and, using a side table as a desk, I wrote Carlo Zeno a note, and another to the Corners in Chioggia, requesting both to find Maestro Albin a place in Venice, for my sake and for his own. Richard watched me.

I handed the two notes to Albin and bowed. They both bowed and went down the hall with an equerry – I assumed they'd just met with the count, but he hadn't been mentioned.

Richard looked at me. 'Clarence is being very difficult,' he said quietly. 'And someone arranged to replace his English doctor with a Milanese doctor.' He nodded after them. 'I'm glad you can do something for them. I feel so powerless.'

'Not good,' I said. 'Talk after.'

And we entered the council chamber together, he in the Duke of Clarence's livery, and I, by some irony, in the count's. There was Sir Ogier, the count's half-brother, and Pierre de Murs, whom I realised I was now regarding as a friend. There were enough candles burning to light a High Mass, and the count was silent as we entered.

When we were seated and had wine, de Murs outlined the various cases against the prince, civil and felonious, from a legal point of view. He then proceeded to outline the prince's likely case against Marguerite.

'Not much of a case,' Richard Musard said. He leant back, probably more comfortable with the count than I was.

'Until the Church politics start. The poor woman will be a pawn between the unionists and the anti-unionists.' De Murs shrugged.

I had a hard time seeing Princess Marguerite as a 'poor woman'. She was of the nobility of Savoy – ruthless, very stubborn, charismatic. And rich. Like my wife, if it comes to that.

I remember shaking my head.

'Can you imagine a man who'd prosecute his own cousin for witchcraft?' I asked.

'He's murdered at least one of his brothers,' the count said, as if it was a commonplace.

I sat back. I hadn't known.

'Emile says he used to pull the wings off flies,' I said.

Richard's eyebrows shot up.

'Emile would know,' the count said. 'I deeply regret that in childhood I found his torment of her ... comic. A jape. It is only in adulthood that I see him as the monster he is.'

I had never heard the count speak so broadly – so vehemently.

Richard leant forward. 'But despite the bishop, the prince will be convicted.'

De Murs sat back with a hiss of disgust. 'And then he appeals everything to his new liege lord, the king of France.'

'Perhaps also to the Emperor,' I put in, as much to show that I was listening as because I really understood it all.

But the count glanced at me as if I'd said something very wise indeed.

'Exactly.'

The count then turned and stared out of one of the great mullioned windows. Despite all that happened that week, I remember that moment precisely. He got up, walked to a window, and a servant hurried to swing it open. He stood for a long moment, silhouetted against the darkness, his pale skin lit by the candles. He looked like a military saint.

Then he turned and walked back to the table.

'I am going to describe a course of action,' he said. 'First, I request, with some regret, that each of you swear not to discuss this for ten years.'

I swore. We all did. Richard met my eyes again – I'm not sure what he was trying to tell me, even now. I assume he already knew the count's plans. And it was thirteen years ago. Everyone knows now.

He held up a hand and ticked off points on his fingers.

'I go from this room to my own chambers, and put on working clothes. I go to the Prince of Achaea's chamber, offer him a sword, and fight him to the death. We dispose of the body and disclaim responsibility.'

I think that, had you had a sharp knife, you could have cut a slice off the air of the chamber and eaten it. It was that thick.

De Murs nodded slowly. I was surprised – he was a very legalistic man.

'You would be within your rights,' he said. 'High treason is a demesne crime. You can be the sole judge, and trial by combat is allowed.'

I looked back and forth.

'If it is to be a trial by combat,' I said, 'let it be in the yard, with witnesses.'

They all looked at me, even Musard.

The count nodded. 'If I kill him, it is over,' he said. 'If he kills me ...'

I nodded. 'I'll kill him.' I meant it.

'Isn't that a trifle unchivalrous?' Ogier asked.

'Chivalry is for those who use chivalry, or for the defenceless,' I said.

Richard leant forward. 'Then do it tomorrow. I want every defence in place for my lord the Duke of Clarence. We know they will strike if their precious prince dies.'

I shook my head. 'They strike either way.'

The count nodded. 'Tomorrow, then,' he said. 'I will send you, Guglielmo, to him. Now. Inform him we fight at dawn. As this is a judicial duel before witnesses, inform him that he will be allowed an arming coat, no maille, and chamois gloves. He may choose either an arming sword and buckler, or a long sword.'

I rose and bowed.

I went directly to the prince's tower, spoke to the two men-at-arms guarding the door, and passed inside.

There I found d'Albret. We exchanged bows.

'I would like to speak directly to the Prince of Achaea,' I said.

He nodded. Let me add that the prince was not alone – he had a slattern, a pair of pages, a squire, four of his own men-at-arms and Lord d'Albret.

'I'll ask him,' he said.

In almost no time, the prince came in – just as tall as ever, and just as ungainly.

'Who are you?' he asked, although he'd met me a dozen times.

'Your Grace, I am Sir William Gold,' I said.

'Christ, the insults never stop. My cousin has noblemen in his train, but he sends me a routier.'

I bowed. 'Your Grace, I bring you the count's cartel. He will fight you, tomorrow, in the yard.'

'I decline,' Achaea snapped.

I nodded. 'This is not a formal challenge, Your Grace. This is a mediation, if that is the correct term, of your charge of high treason. If you decline to fight, you will be executed. Tomorrow.'

'Murder!' Achaea said.

I said nothing.

D'Albret looked at me with wide eyes.

'You can't be serious!' he said.

'Dawn,' I said. 'The prince has the choice of an arming sword and buckler, or a long sword. Or a swift death.'

Achaea shook his head. 'No. I don't believe it. This is another trick – another sham. You cannot just kill me. I am the Prince of Achaea.'

I decided that I should speak. 'Your Grace, I have just come from a meeting of the count's councillors where they decided that very thing. Your crime of high treason is obvious to all.'

'Lies!' Achaea said.

It was remarkable, in that as far as I could tell, and I am a good judge of men, he actually believed what he was saying.

'Your Grace,' I said gently, 'you and your … agents have made repeated attempts on the count's life. These are crimes of high treason. I was personally present for several of them. Monsieur d'Albret here has heard you plan them.'

D'Albret moved as if he'd been struck by lightning.

'Further, you sent to the king of France and the Emperor offering your vassalage if they would help you replace the count,' I said.

'No!' Achaea said. 'No! Just manoeuvres!'

'The count has all your correspondence now,' I said gently. 'I recommend you fight.'

The prince went through the door to his chambers and slammed it.

D'Albret glanced at me. 'What happens to me?' he asked.

'I'll see you free,' I said. That may seem odd to you, but despite some underhanded actions, d'Albret had, for the most part, simply been a loyal man-at-arms to his prince. 'You wouldn't like to tell me where Camus is hiding?'

D'Albret shook his head. 'On my honour, I don't know,' he said. 'Also on my honour, if I did, I wouldn't tell you.' Then he said, with a sideways glance, 'If my feudal bond were dissolved, I might feel differently.'

Look, you may say this was a lawyer's quibble. But you have to have rules. I rather liked d'Albret. He had rules.

'I'll keep that in mind,' I said.

I bowed, and so did he.

I left the prince's tower and went back across the brick courtyard. I stopped and exchanged a few words with d'Entremonts, the princess's captain – a wide, short man with a forked beard who had certainly seen some actions. I have no idea what he said because what followed robbed me of my wits for a bit.

I was going to the count's chamber when I met Count Amadeus and Sir Bernard on the spiral stairs.

I could see that something was wrong, but honestly, so much was wrong that I assumed that the count was worried by the duel.

'It is done,' I said.

He waved a hand.

Sir Bernard put a hand on my shoulder.

'It is bad,' he said. 'Bad news. A messenger from the countess.'

I knew, then, what he was going to say. That Emile knew all about my stupid affair with Marietta.

'Your daughter Isabelle is dead,' he said.

I didn't even understand his words at first. It was not the bad news I was expecting.

'Isabelle!' I said. 'Gracious God – why?'

Bernard blinked. 'I am sorry, Guillaume. And Emile—'

'Oh, Christ!' I said.

The count turned his head away.

'She is very sick ...' Bernard said.

'Christ!' I said. 'Poison?'

But Bernard had not lived as I had lived for two weeks.

'Plague,' he said, as if poison was an absurd possibility.

Plague. The ultimate killer, but not everyone died, and God has mercy on poor sinners.

'She is still alive?'

'Eight hours ago ...' Sir Bernard said. 'She asked for you.'

I was already heading down the stairs. I didn't ask the count's permission – indeed, I left him to fight the Prince of Achaea in the morning without a qualm. I didn't pack. I didn't summon Marc-Antonio.

I ran to the stables and got my riding saddle on Juniper, my riding horse, and also took my spare Arab, Olive.

I mounted, and rode, in my court clothes.

*

There are so many horrors and ironies. She was just at Oulx – forty English miles away up the pass to France. I set out in late afternoon, and I rode into the night. It's cold in the Alps, and colder in October.

I have no great tale to tell. No bandits attacked me, no monks accosted me, and there was not an avalanche nor a county fair nor a cavalcade of imperial knights.

I rode for hours. Somewhere in the high pass, I changed horses and rode Olive, and we went on, mile after mile. It's difficult to ride at night – there is no light, and I had rocky ground and unbridged streams to cross. Good horses make all the difference.

We rode on. Miles and miles of moonlit gravel and stone, grass like pools of waving darkness by the road. Steep-roofed cottages close by the road, and nary a light – sometimes you smell the animals in the barn before you see the house.

Lots of time to pray, and think of all my sins, and pray again.

About Matins, I rode into Oulx. The village was asleep and I hadn't asked Bernard where they were, but I knew the town a little and I hammered on the castle gate. The gate was locked because of the possibility of open war with Achaea – his vassals had attacked farms quite close.

A sleepy soldier opened the gate.

'The Comtesse d'Herblay?' I asked.

'Oh, gracious God, monsieur!' he said. 'She is dying.'

'Not dead,' I said with desperate hope.

'No, My Lord.'

'Take me.'

The man wrapped a scarf over his face and led me to the chapel.

'All of them ...' he said. 'With the pestilence.'

He turned away hurriedly. I couldn't blame him. I had seen how people behaved at the Lazaretto in Venice and I was scared of the plague, too. But I was salted – my parents had died of it and my sister and I had lived. You know that my sister is a famous nun and healer.

I opened the door to the chapel and went in.

The stench hit me immediately, and the darkness. The stench was not death, but all the bodily functions that accompany plague – pustules, seepage, faeces.

It was dark in the chapel. People groaned, or cried out, but I couldn't see them. It was cold and damp.

It was hell.

The windows didn't let in enough light to see even to take a step, and I had to pause, take my purse off my belt, find my flint and steel and the nub of a taper, and get it alight.

The light revealed twenty people lying on the chapel floor. In the wavering shadows of my one taper, they seemed to flicker on the cold floor like damned souls in agony. Christ, I was scared and angry and not entirely in the real world.

And it was squalid beyond anyone's imagining. Filthy, with clean altars and fine candlesticks just to hand.

I lit a dozen candles, and I found Emile. She lay with Richard on her breast. She was alive, but very late in the disease, and my son was alive and angry, red, crying and filthy.

Sir Jason lay by her. His buboes had already burst. He lay in a torpor, unable even to open his eyes. Emile's household lay around her as if they were casualties on a battlefield – Roland against the Moors, a desperate last stand of innocents against the Life Thief. There were both of her nobly born lady's maids, dead, their fingers entwined and black from the pest, their mouths locked in grimaces of pain. There was her steward in a path of dried filth. Servants, a groom. There was Sister Marie with swellings all over her body. There was Sister Catherine, dead.

All our people.

I plucked Richard from Emile. There was Isabelle, unburied, grey-white in death, lying by an altar; there was Magdalene, Emile's first child.

You may think me stone-hearted, but the chapel was a battlefield, and we – we who fight – we don't mourn on the field. Later, perhaps. For me, sometimes it is a year later, or even more. I looked at Isabelle, saw that she was obviously dead, and moved on to see if anyone could be saved. As you do in a desperate fight.

Magdalene was alive. I thought her dead, but she was ten years old, and she awoke and knew me instantly – threw her arms around me and burst into tears.

'Oh, Mama! Mama! Mama is dying!' she wept, the little mite.

All I could think was that she was the same age my sister had been when our mother died.

'I need you to take care of Richard,' I said. 'Find some cloths and we'll clean him.'

It's the battlefield. You act – you don't let yourself think. That chapel was the worst battlefield of my life. In truth, gentles, I have trouble telling this, and by God, I had trouble believing that there was a God.

But I found clean swaddling cloths in the dead lady's baskets, and little Magdalene and I cleaned Richard and washed him with water from the font, and he stopped crying. He was hungry, but clean – he knew someone loved him. I have a little experience of babies.

'Find him food,' I said.

Magdalene looked at me in the candlelight.

'He can't *eat* anything,' she said. 'He needs Mama!'

I had not forgotten Emile. I went back to her, and her face was covered in black spots, as if the fingertips of death had brushed her face. Her armpits and thighs were hugely swollen with buboes.

Albin swore that lancing the buboes increased the odds of a person surviving. Let me tell you of my cowardice, gentles.

I ...

I knelt with my rondel dagger in my hand, looking at the evil swelling in her right armpit.

I couldn't do it.

I, who have killed men in their dozens.

I couldn't cut her.

Oh, sweet Christ. Let it go, friends. I cannot ...

There. More wine.

So ... I got her head up and trickled some water into her mouth. I cleaned her as best I could, and then Jason. I went to deal with others, and every time I went back to her, I thought, 'Get your courage up, knight. Peter Albin is the best doctor you ever knew. Do it.'

And then I'd go and clean another.

Finally, as the light began to grow outside the windows, I faced my fear. I put my rondel away and took the eating knife from my scabbard. I stropped it, and heated it in a candle, because I'd seen Albin do those things.

Then I pricked the bubo under her left arm because it was the biggest – gravid like a pregnant rat. I pricked it too softly. She moaned.

Christ. I could just pass over this, could I not? Froissart, even you cannot want to hear this.

It took me three tries to drive it in far enough to release the foul pus.

Her eyelids fluttered.

'Emile!' I said.

Suddenly the tears that I'd kept back came into my eyes and everything blurred, and all I could see was my fear. I could smell the stink, and I knew she'd hate it, and I had our little lemon pomade still in my purse. I took it out and pressed it to her nose and she groaned. Her head turned towards it.

I left it on her rolled cloak under her head. Then I slit open her shift and opened the bubo on her thigh. Even in my terror and revulsion, I found it remarkable that one side of her body was so much more swollen than the other side, as if only half of her was infected.

At the second gush of pus, I heard her cough. I pressed the wound until I had all the yellow-black stuff out and only blood emerged, and then I moved to kneel by her head.

Her eyes were open.

'Oh,' she said.

Her left hand had the little lemon.

'Our lemon tree,' she said. 'So good.'

Then she died.

I lost a week. Maybe more.

I can tell you what happened. I tried to save the children and Sir Jason, and the groom who was still alive, and no one helped me. And to be fair, I wouldn't have wanted them to. I was happy, if happy is the word, that Jean-François and Bernard were safe in Rivoli. I was numb, and for perhaps a whole day I kept going back to Emile's corpse to see if I was wrong.

I was not wrong.

Magdalene was apparently immune. Richard, the poor wee lad, went through the whole process, from the first spots to swellings. I watched him dying.

But he was certainly my son, because he fought it all the way.

The people of the castle brought us food and pushed it through the door, every day. So that day, when the guard came, I called out.

'Do you have people in the town who have survived the plague?' I asked.

He was going to walk away. I put my sword around his neck.

'I need a nursemaid, one with milk,' I said. 'Send me a girl who survived the plague and I'll pay her in gold.'

I let him go and was ashamed that I'd threatened him. But he must have been a good man. He rode to the next village and fetched us Rosa, a young woman who'd just had a baby. And had survived the plague in '51, when she was two or three.

She took Richard and put him to her breast without even asking about wages. I'll pay her until I die.

Let's be brief.

Richard lived.

Somewhere in that week I cleaned my knife and did to Sister Marie what I'd done to my wife. It was doubly odd – my wife's body I knew well, but it seemed a sacrilege to expose Sister Marie's naked flesh. I did it anyway – all six of the huge swellings. I collected the pus and burnt the rags.

Marie recovered.

Emile was still dead. On the third day, she stank – all the corpses stank.

I buried them myself. Little Isabelle, who'd never really known life and yet had been so cheerful. Emile, who was the world, not just to me but to most of her people. Never again would we make love beneath the lemon tree. Never again would I unlace her kirtle, nor listen as she explained household accounting, nor watch her fight her own fears and emerge victorious. Never to see her comb out her hair, or the way she would stretch on waking in the morning, or her delight in a berry tart with cream, a fat cat, a donkey by the road.

Never.

Never.

Forty miles to the east, the Prince of Achaea was dead, too. I wasn't there and neither was Richard, but I gather it was squalid and does no credit to anyone except perhaps Fiore. The prince begged for mercy, standing bareheaded in his arming coat with a long sword in his hands, and then ranted against the count. Fiore says that when the word was given to commence, at first he spread his hands and begged for forgiveness *again*. When the count, disdaining to kill him in cold blood, sent for the headsman, he leapt to his feet and went forward with his sword held in front of him, and that the count played him as Fiore had taught him – a rising cover from the *garde* Fiore calls '*Vera Croce*' that swept his blade aside, a thrust into his chest ...

The thrust revealed that the prince was wearing maille under his gambeson.

He wounded the count, a cut to the thigh, and the Green Count thrust him through the throat, maille and all.

I wasn't there. But it was quick, and the count, at least, behaved like a knight. I am still not ... happy in my heart about the proceeding. But I am not, thank God, the ruler of a state.

I had become a gravedigger.

I buried them all, one by one. My hands grew new calluses, and so did my heart. I admit it, Chaucer – I cursed God.

I cursed God.

What is knighthood? Nothing.

Perhaps, I thought, perhaps Camus is right. Sacks of meat, filled with blood and pus. Camus forgot the pus.

I am disgusting you. But this is my story. Ah, Aemilie, you are weeping. Well might you weep. My Emile was everything that a woman should be – I will never be the same without her. My Isabelle was a child, innocent as a lamb. Her death didn't really affect me at the time, but you will hear later ...

I buried seventeen people. Sometimes I buried five in a day. I dug them all their own holes because exhaustion was my only refuge. There wasn't enough wine to keep me drunk, really.

I dug and dug. I felt as if I was digging myself a path to Hell, one grave at a time.

I dreamed of men I'd killed, battlefield horrors, sacked towns and plague corpses.

I terrified poor Rosa, who was an honest girl, and any wits I had were saved for Magdalene.

I'm telling this badly. After about nine days, it was clear Richard and Sister Marie were going to live.

Sister Marie opened her eyes and said something that wasn't from the Bible. All of her fevered ranting had been lengthy quotes from scripture.

Now she said, 'My back hurts.'

And the next day, she said, 'William!'

'Sister Marie,' I said.

She blinked. 'I'm not dead,' she said.

'No,' I said.

She looked around. I'd made new beds for the survivors – Sister Marie, the groom Gautier, and my two children. All of them had pallets of clean straw every day. By their lights, the castle folk were caring for us.

Marie looked around.

'My lady?' she asked.

I wept. 'Dead,' I said.

She, who had almost died, held my hand.

On the tenth day, it was clear that the contagion was over. I was allowed to open the chapel. I've left out that two people in the castle, not our people, got the plague, and were placed in the chapel, and they also died. The local people were very cautious, but they never blamed us, for which I bless them. Now. At the time I cursed them more than once.

I tried to pay for our food and a priest, wrapped in a scarf, turned away my money.

I burnt incense in the chapel for him, and together we swept and cleaned it, and he burnt his own altar trimmings and all his altar linens.

And the castle's people had cared for Juniper and Olive and all Emile's horses, so that we had a tiny party and thirty expensive horses, and Gautier, scarcely able to walk, was not going to be able to handle so many. It was only then that I sent a boy riding down to Rivoli.

The next afternoon, my first in the relative freedom of the court-yard, I was desperate for work. I had too much time to think. Ten days had not softened the blow at all. Emile was still dead every time I paused, and I was not friend to God, but Sister Marie had begun to wrestle with me for my soul.

Marc-Antonio rode into the yard. He'd been weeping – indeed, he had tears in his eyes as he dismounted.

And he did not hesitate to throw his arms around me, plague or no plague. We stood there for too long.

And then he said, 'The Duke of Clarence is dead of poison.'

*

I got them all to Rivoli, but all the praise belongs to Marc-Antonio. Oh, sure enough, he was fresh, and I was at the end of my strength – but he never shirked, and then, in my moment of utter darkness, he simply stepped forward and acted. He carried Sister Marie to her mule and put her on it, and he got us across streams and he didn't force conversation on me. I had stupid rages. Magdalene, being a child, was recovering, and I heard her laugh at some jape and in my foolishness, I roared at her to have respect for her mother, and I made her cry.

He got us to Rivoli, and there the good regard of the count became like manna from Heaven. We were given a house in Rivoli, and servants from the count's train – all men and women who had survived the plague, and they were tender.

The count has never mentioned to me that I'd deserted him on the night he went to risk his life against Achaea. Never.

I had one night, weeping with Jean-François and Bernard. Jason was as heavy a loss to them as Emile.

And even in the state I was in, I knew what must happen now.

'You will go to Lesvos and fetch Lord Edouard,' I said. 'He must know, and then he must come and take his mother's lands.' I paused. 'His lands, now.'

Bernard winced. But then he nodded.

'Yes,' he said.

'We must think of these things,' Jean-François said.

'He will need a ruling council until he achieves his majority,' Bernard said.

I shook my head. I had already made up my mind, and I'd scarcely had two thoughts altogether.

'Not for me,' I said.

Bernard looked hurt. 'Why not you?' he said. 'You were my lady's true lord.'

I nodded. 'I don't think I could do it,' I said.

'We will help you,' Bernard said.

I almost screamed at him. I didn't mean that I didn't have a head for figures – Emile had taught me all about her estates. I meant that I was not sure I could wake in her beds, talk to her servants, and see her in every corner.

Listen, some men drown grief in wine, and some between the thighs of women.

I didn't love wine enough, and I'd discovered somewhere that women were also people with their own problems.

What I wanted was a war. What Hawkwood called a 'good fat war'.

I wanted to hit something over and over.

Instead, I listened to rumours. With Caterina and Albin gone from the Duke of Clarence's retinue in Alba, I heard nothing from that quarter directly, but rumour had it that Lord Bohun was blaming the Milanese for the duke's poisoning. I was listless, but I knew this was important, and I asked Beppo to ride south to Asti and 'have a look'. I told him to listen to what was said in taverns, and he laughed.

'Beppo is being paid to drink in taverns,' he said. 'Maybe there is a God.'

Even through the fog of my sorrow, Beppo made me laugh.

And then the count summoned me.

If he was afraid of the plague, he gave no sign. Instead, he took my hand, and then pressed me in a gentle embrace.

A good lord.

'Clarence was poisoned,' he said.

I nodded. I admit that I barely remember any of this. But my world was coming back into focus, a little at a time. It was as if I'd taken a bad wound – or a blow to the head.

Really just a blow to the heart.

He nodded. 'Sir Guglielmo,' he said. 'I realise that you have taken a terrible loss. But I need you and your friends now.'

He was wearing a black ribbon on his arm.

I didn't ask, then. But, believe it or not, it was for Achaea.

I merely bowed.

He swirled wine in his cup.

'This is all so unpleasant and grim,' he said. 'I am sorry the Comtesse d'Herblay has died. But I would like to keep you in my service.'

I nodded.

'I have a fine village near Chambéry that I would like to give you as a barony.'

It meant nothing to me.

Perhaps I muttered some thanks.

He nodded. 'I want this to be clear to you, Guglielmo. Because now I must beg you to send for your stepson.'

I bowed again. 'Sir Bernard and I have already arranged it,' I said.

He breathed a sigh of relief.

This is the real life of lordship, friends. He had faced a major war among his vassals, and he needed every holding to be secure. The Prince of Achaea had scared him. I'm sorry to say it, but he was a different man afterwards – not as generous, nor as chivalrous. Still a fine man and a good lord, but some of the boyish openness ... aye, and arrogance too, was gone.

He needed Edouard safe and under his tutelage – loyal, and available. Remember, he, and not I, was my wife's heir. I was merely the consort. I was lucky to be considered at all.

That, too, is the way of great lords and ladies.

Even in my cocoon of mourning, I understood completely.

And the barony for me? Because he needed to keep me, but he didn't want me on that boy's council any more than I wanted it. He would keep Edouard's wardship for himself.

As I say, this is the way of lordship, but just at that moment, I was sharply reminded that without Emile as my wife, I was once again no one. A self-made hedge-knight.

I may have felt a little disgust, but it did not stop me from putting my hands between his and swearing fealty for my town of Les Marches. It was a fief that Emile's family had held of the count, without ownership; now it was truly mine.

I went back to guarding the count. For twelve days, my outposts had functioned without me, because Bibbo, Fiore and Gatelussi all knew their business. With Beppo, they'd recruited guides and worked their way through the countryside. They'd found one of Camus's men-at-arms – one of the broken young men who'd been with him for ten years. He died fighting and wouldn't be taken alive.

Everyone was on edge – the count, the princess, the countess – all my people. We missed Emile. I'm happy, in an odd way, to say that Fiore and Gatelussi were almost as broken-hearted as I was myself, and Fiore took me aside as soon as he saw me.

'She was a great woman,' he said.

I burst into tears. I was like that for weeks – it took almost nothing to set me off.

And then *Fiore wept, too.*

'I suppose I'll never be married now,' he said later.

I was numb to other people's needs. I'm sorry to dwell on this, but it was like when the petard exploded at Corinth – it took us days to recover our hearing, and similarly, I was not there for my people and they forgave me. This is why people need friends. Friendship buys tolerance, aye, and forgiveness.

But Fiore's comment went through the cocoon. I remembered the slim girl in the golden kirtle. She was wrapped up in the time when I was happy, on Lesvos, with my love. And that was the right thing of which to remind me.

'We'll make it work,' I said.

'Really?' Fiore asked.

I looked at him. In some ways, Fiore is a very complicated man indeed – in other ways, of almost childlike simplicity. When I tried to strike him, I betrayed his notions of friendship. He was not Richard Musard. Richard and I had done each other injuries and injustices and somehow stayed friends. In Fiore's mind, a blow was a sign of enmity.

But when I said I'd try and do what Emile was intending, to make his marriage, he believed me. And trust was restored.

Just like that.

A tiny ray of light entered my own darkness. It wasn't much. But I began to realise that there was still a world.

And now we come to the little black cross.

I redeployed my lances around Volvera. But most specifically, I wanted to search Vigone. Listen, gentles, my military mind seems to function even when I am drunk, filled with lust, or lost to sorrow. Vigone was still held by the Monk of Hecz, but with Achaea dead, there was no further point to the standoff, and he no longer had an employer.

Fiore, Gatelussi and I assumed that the black-bearded assassin had poisoned the Duke of Clarence. I wanted to see Richard and hear any details he could provide, but until I had them, I had to assume that Black-Beard and Camus were at large in the no-man's land between Clarence's holdings around Alba, fifty miles south of us, and Volvera, and my money was on Vigone, which had been their headquarters since spring.

The count had ordered d'Albret held. I went to see the Gascon.

'You said I'd be freed,' d'Albret said.

'I've been busy,' I said.

D'Albret was a devil, but he was still a man in his heart.

'Your wife died,' he said. 'I'm sorry.' He shook his head and looked away.

We sat in silence.

'Easier to release you if you'd help us,' I said.

'You and Musard must be the only two people in the world who aren't afraid of Camus and Geneva,' he said.

He actually looked around before he said it, as if speaking against that pair of Satan's spawn was a crime.

I nodded. 'Camus is mostly talk,' I said.

'That's just not true,' he said.

I just sat in silence. It wasn't a threat, and yet he finally reacted, folding his arms across his chest and shaking his head.

He sighed. 'I really don't know much,' he said. 'Camus's people were all in Vigone, I'll tell you that much. And he meant to kill all of you – the Duke of Clarence, the Count of Savoy, the Princess Marguerite. Galeazzo of Milan, too, I think. He's quite mad.'

'That's why Geneva likes him,' I said.

He leant forward. 'I'll tell you one thing,' he said quietly. 'But only when I'm on a horse with the reins in my hand and an open gate in front of me.'

I nodded.

I got him a good horse. I made sure they packed all his kit and his armour, and I found him a good mule.

'You really are an honourable man,' d'Albret said. He actually had the reins in his hand.

'Where will you go?' I asked.

'Home,' he said. 'In the spring, we'll be fighting in Aquitaine. I think my father will stay loyal to the Prince of Wales. Either way, my duty is at home.'

'I thought your clan supported Armagnac?' I asked.

He smiled. 'It's complicated,' he admitted. 'Listen, here's my say, and may it help you. There's a house in Vigone – a tall house with bad, peeling red-brown paint. It's called "the House of the Pelicans". That's where Camus kept his pets – the poisoner and the false monk—'

'False monk?'

'Christ, Guillaume, he has a dozen of these people, every one of them as mad and broken as he is himself. I went once – it was like a madhouse. That was when ... never mind. It was all a game for a while, and then ...'

I nodded. 'Then suddenly you knew you were no longer Galahad or Lancelot,' I said.

He nodded. 'I was with Mordred,' he said.

I shrugged. 'Yes,' I said. 'You are free to go.' I went and took his hand. 'Can I give you a bit of advice?'

He shrugged. 'As you have certainly won this round, I'm willing to listen.'

I nodded. 'Be a better knight,' I said. 'It's always worth it in the end. And I say this because I have been a bad knight, and I know.'

A number of emotions crossed his face – anger, guilt, shame ... hope.

He waved.

That night I took a new offer to the Monk of Hecz. He had more than a hundred lances – a bigger company than Sir John Hawkwood. His principal was dead, and no one was going to pay his people.

I was admitted to the gates of the town with considerably less cere-mony than the last time, but he met us again, on horseback, outside the drawbridge.

The Monk was still in a plain brown robe over heavy armour.

We bowed cautiously. I had that odd feeling of having done all this before, as if I was locked in some tale of King Arthur and it was my role to go around in a circle. Perhaps I'd awaken and Emile would still be alive, somewhere in the West Country of Lombardy.

That's the real reason I couldn't rule her lands. I knew that if I rode away, I could pretend, for a long time, that she was alive in Chambéry and I was ...

Christ, I still cry.

Bah, never mind. Back to the Monk of Hecz.

'Well, sir knight?' he asked.

I held out a scroll. 'The count offers to cover your wages through today, if you will pass over the town and march. And a *sauvegarde* anywhere across the count's lands.'

The Monk frowned. 'And if I said I did not trust the count's *sau-vegarde*?' he asked.

I shrugged. I did not need to feign indifference. I didn't care if I lived or died. I didn't need to care about this man or his mercenaries. I had the curious feeling that if I could provoke someone to a fight, I might find something in life worth staying for. For the first time since I had hair under my arms, women held no interest for me whatsoever.

'What if I said I wanted a *sauvegarde* signed by the lord of Milan?' he said.

I shook my head. 'Then I'd leave you here to rot,' I said.

That seemed to surprise him.

'Is this a negotiation or not?' he demanded.

I shook my head again. 'Not that I'm aware of,' I said. 'My lord made you an offer. Take it and leave, or refuse it and starve. And end up as prisoners.'

He shook his head. 'I refuse.'

'Fine,' I allowed, and turned my horse.

An hour later his page caught me up, and the Germans surrendered Vigone for their wages. Possibly my most successful negotiation ever. Some irony there.

The next morning, before dawn, Fiore, Gatelussi, Marc-Antonio, de la Motte and I, with all our people, were gathered around the House of the Pelicans in Vigone. Most of our archers had hunting crossbows because they're better for house fighting than a longbow.

We went in through both doors and some of the ground-floor windows, all together on a horn blast.

Fighting in a house is not like any other kind of fighting. And, in the clarity of retrospect, we didn't take enough time to learn what we were facing.

We expected a dozen people, and there were thirty people in that house. It wasn't that grand – three storeys, brick and timber, with some glass windows and a big fireplace in the kitchen.

It was packed like a barracks. Men and women.

All quite mad. A military madhouse. A convent dedicated to Satan.

I went through a window. I was in full harness, with a long sword, an axe on my belt, a dagger. I climbed a barrel, sounded my horn, smashed in the hundred panes of the mullioned window and, for once, did not fall flat on my face.

I was in a downstairs room. It stank of too many people – there was an acrid reek of male sweat, and some other smell I didn't recognise – and unwashed dishes were everywhere.

There were at least a dozen men lying on filthy straw on the floor. I had taken the visor off my helmet so that I could see and hear a little, and I could hear my people coming through the kitchen door at the back and the front door. Gatelussi had planned to climb into the first-floor loggia with Alessio to back him.

We never imagined what a barrel of mackerel we were assaulting.

The men sleeping on the floor all heard the crash of my arrival. Like most men, they slept naked, and most had no weapons. I might have hesitated … The first thing I noticed was the overpowering smell of rotten meat, as if we were in a butcher's shop and the counters were never washed. Or on a battlefield.

They threw themselves at me. They were like a wave of rabid dogs – anger, rage, spittle. It might have been terrifying, except that I was a fully armoured man with a long sword.

The very horrifying thing was that I had to actually put them down. A thrust to the face was a kill, sure, but a thrust to the abdomen and they just kept coming. The third man, whom I thrust in the gut, reached out to grapple me, and I had to let my sword go.

But sabatons and knee-cops are weapons, and no matter how mad a man is, he cannot function with his privates shredded by steel. He fell away, and I couldn't free my sword, and so I got my dagger in my right hand and finished them.

Ugly. Worse, I still wasn't sure these men were guilty of *anything*. I was killing men who appeared to be insane. And insanity is a form of innocence, is it not?

Fiore came through the door from the kitchen, his sword dripping blood.

'*Manicomio*,' he said. Madhouse.

He seemed very upset – not his usual fighting purity.

Together we went into the front room. We could hear fighting upstairs. The front room was also full of men who were facing Marc-Antonio, as well as Bibbo and Gospel Mark and Ewan. There was a crash outside – a roar. A crossbow spat somewhere near me and a man shouted, but I had my hands full – two women with swords, and a man with what seemed to be a meat cleaver. It was, in fact, a huge hunting sword for opening game, and he wielded it with incredible strength.

I stepped back, unwilling even to risk a cross with the thing. His blow slammed into the door frame with the force of an axe blow, and I killed him while he tried to pull it free. Both women stabbed at me – one blow pinked me below my breastplate.

I turned, slammed my gauntleted hand into her face, and then killed her with the dagger.

Fiore kneed the second woman in the groin and then dropped her with a throw. She went for his feet and he kicked her savagely. But he didn't kill her.

'I hate fighting women,' he said. 'I can't kill her. God be with us.'

I don't kill unarmed women – nor men, if it comes to that. In fact, I've never done it. But a woman in arms is an enemy.

And still it stuck in my craw like a fishbone that won't go away.

Marc-Antonio and the archers had finished the rest of them, but Ewan was wounded, and there was blood *everywhere*. Perhaps I tell it badly. I have seldom known such savage fighting, because, like demons from Hell, every man and every woman of them had to be put down. Dead.

When the room was clear, I went up the narrow steps. I could hear Gatelussi fighting, and when I reached the top of the steps I was behind a dozen men. I still only had a dagger, but a good dagger is almost ideal for fighting in close confines.

I killed one man before he knew I was there. Then I used the corpse of a second as a shield while I killed a third, and then Fiore was there, a whirlwind of death and no women to impede his dance.

And then I was fighting Black-Beard. I knew him as he turned, saw that his sword work was competent even as he came at me.

But I got my dagger on his sword, using my plate-armoured forearm to help me deal with its length. I went to play close, and one of his companions hammered the top of my head with an iron rod. I stumbled back. Black-Beard thrust, and I missed my parry, but my breastplate was there. His blow skidded along my breastplate and went under my left arm, and my brain worked well enough that I collected his sword in an arm wrap, as Fiore teaches. I rotated my hips, turned on the balls of my feet, and then I had his sword and he looked stunned.

I wanted him as a prisoner, and Gatelussi and Fiore and Alessio were winnowing the madmen the way a patient farmer cuts wheat. I slammed the butt of my rondel dagger into his temple, and down he went.

And then we were looking at the steps to the second floor. It was a little like the scaling ladder at Corinth.

They looked at me.

So I went. And let me be honest – I wanted to go first. I wanted to keep killing. More than anything, I wanted Camus.

It was a house of madmen, but I was as mad as they.

Up I went.

There were no enemies on the top floor.

There was a flayed carcass – a woman who'd been patiently skinned. She was dead. Long dead. She hung from the ceiling like a decoration, like a rood cross in a church, arms and legs spread to make her body a pentagon, and her inners had been removed and most of her was ... dry ...

Good Christ.

Listen – I'd just buried fifteen people who had died of plague. Alone of the men on the stairs, I was virtually immune to this sort of thing, just then.

'Stop!' I called to Fiore.

I went up alone. There was an altar, or at least a fouled table at the head of the room, and benches, and some cups.

And skulls. Seven of them. Most had flesh still on them.

Camus had finally slipped over the edge from bad to mad. Or perhaps he'd always been over the edge. Perhaps this was not his first church to the lower powers – that's how I read it.

Father Pierre Thomas taught me that we have nothing to fear from the infernal powers – that we cannot be harmed by them unless we allow them to harm us through our own will. And that chapel to darkness offered nothing like the threat to my soul that a certain chapel at Oulx had offered. But the sheer weight of the blasphemy and horror implied wrenched at me. Things like this are not supposed to happen.

They'd left the woman's hair on her skull.

I need a moment.

I confess that it affected me more than I like to admit. I still see her in my dreams. I pray for her soul.

*

I searched the top floor – one long open room. I found no one. There were various blasphemies and an atrocity I won't mention.

I went back to the stairs.

'Basement,' I said. 'It will be horrible.'

I wanted Camus.

'Search everything,' I said. 'Every chest, every leather bag.'

The archers hardly needed an excuse to loot. Nor the men-at-arms, come to that. But men – hard men – crossed themselves every time they looked up.

He was here, somewhere. The madhouse had a leader. He had brought these people together.

We pounded down through the charnel house, our heavy footsteps making the whole house shake. The archers were angry because Ewan was hurt, and we went into the kitchen and saw what Fiore had done coming in. Then we went down the steps to the basement, Gatelussi in the lead because he'd been last on the steps up, and that made him first going down.

'Oh, God save us,' he said as he reached the brick floor below.

The area under the house was an abattoir – men hung on meat hooks from the beams, and there were piles of offal.

There was no Camus.

We went through the house again. My people opened every chest, every crate, every wardrobe. I stopped Gospel Mark from killing the wounded – I wanted them all questioned.

We'd cleaned the Augean Stable, but Camus was gone.

I went outside when Marc-Antonio called my name, and only then did I understand the shouts I had heard in the first moments of the action.

My first thought was for my horses. They were gone – Olive and Juniper.

Stefanos lay curled in the street, dying of a thrust through the abdomen.

I cursed.

Marc-Antonio had been hit in the early fighting. He had a bad cut to his right wrist, and another to his cheek that had laid his face open to the teeth, but he was still functioning, as you do when you are used to taking wounds. He knelt by the boy, taking his last confession. My squire was weeping.

In that moment, I knew how Lucifer fell.

In that moment, it was all too much for my equilibrium. I cannot describe it better.

How can God allow these things? Camus had escaped and killed an innocent boy. Emile had died of plague, and Camus was free to murder and rape and torture.

I didn't stop even to take the dying hand of my page.

I leapt, fully armed, onto the back of Marc-Antonio's riding horse, gathered the reins of his spare, and I was off. Camus had, at best, a fifteen-minute head start. He might have been stopped at the gate – we held the gates of Vigone.

I rode to the 'Milan' gate and they had allowed him to go. They were Savoyard men-at-arms and none of them knew Camus, and he always had Satan's luck. I took the time to run up to the top of the wall. In armour. After fighting.

There was a speck, riding at a gallop, out on the main road heading north.

Have you ever noticed just how quickly a person can vanish in a few minutes? Have you ever turned aside in a shop, and then turned back to find your wife or your squire has vanished into the streets?

That dot riding north was the last glimpse I had of Camus for days.

But I had become a madman. I wanted revenge, perhaps for the first time since I'd been tangling with the squires when I was a cook's boy. Oh, Father Pierre Thomas taught us the worthlessness of revenge – that the best revenge was no revenge. That revenge was a tool for weak minds.

My mind was weak. I felt that I had lost everything – that Camus was killing everything I loved, just as he had threatened. Even Emile, perhaps. It was not rational – nothing was rational.

I rode north. I changed horses. I didn't stop at Rivoli even to collect clothes or arms or a retinue, but went north after his rumour – here, at a tavern, where they'd remember him; there, on the road, a bit of brass with my spur-rondel badge off Juniper's fancy harness.

It was terrible, that chase. At first it was a horse race – and I had the deep pain of realising four hours in that my enemy had Juniper, the best riding horse I'd ever owned. He rode her to death. She died well north of Rivoli, just a few miles from where Emile had died, and he left her on the road and mounted Olive, leaving my saddle on my dead horse.

I loved that horse. She had saved my life more than once, and she was cheerful. And she'd been with me since Outremer. I dismounted. I think I even kissed the dead horse. Then I took the saddle and tack off her and left it at an inn high on the pass, and I rode on. By then, I was six hours behind him, and I hadn't slept for two nights.

Two days later I passed Les Marches, my own holding. I collected clothes and money and ate a meal while my terrified steward, a man I'd met only once, collected horses for me. I had left four of the best Arabs to start a stud the previous winter at one of Emile's farms, and an efficient steward had sent them here already. I took a mare, and an older, steadier riding horse that had been Emile's, wrote a note to the count and another to Marc-Antonio, drank a cup of wine . . .

And rode on.

CHAPTER SIX

SOUTHERN FRANCE AND ARMAGNAC

Autumn 1368

I lost Camus completely after Chambéry. My rage was subsiding, and perhaps a little sense wriggled in, but the weight of my failure fell on me like five coats of maille, and I could not face turning back. It is difficult to explain to you, now, in the cold light of day. But at the time, when I rode into the village of Saint-Christophe west of Chambéry and no one had seen anyone like Camus ...

All I could think was that I'd failed everyone. And that, in fact, I had nothing to go back to.

I realise that this sounds impossible to you, unless you, like me, have experienced despair. It is difficult to describe despair to those who have never felt it, nor would I wish it on you.

I will not wallow in my sin, for despair is surely a sin. It is a self-indulgence, like other sins. What is lust, but greed for the body of another with no regard to their soul? What is gluttony, but greed for food or fine clothes with no regard to how you get them or what effect that has on yourself or others? And so despair, the desire for self-destruction – the ultimate pride, as you are refusing to recognise the gift of life from God, and you are spurning God's grace.

Like Lucifer.

And that was me, at Saint-Christophe. In that dark hour, I would rather have *died* than ridden back to Rivoli to tell the count that I had failed to kill Camus.

Today, I know that the count scarcely cared what happened to Camus. The truth was that *no one* cared about the mad routier, except perhaps Richard Musard. And if I had had another friend by me – someone like Marc-Antonio or Fiore ...

I could never have sunk so far, nor acted so foolishly.

The only antidote for despair is friends.

But, I was alone.

At Le Chambon I found a trace of him – pure luck, or God's hand. I stopped to get grain for my horses and I met a pedlar who'd been robbed. I gave him a few soldi and he gave me a blessing and told me that he was the lucky one, as a routier had killed two other pedlars with whom he'd been travelling. In ten sentences I knew he'd been robbed by Camus. He said Camus had tied him up and thrown him over a horse, but that the horse had bolted. He was still shaken. He said that the ride across country, slung over the back of a packhorse, had been the most terrifying thing that had ever happened to him. I didn't tell him how lucky he was.

I did pray with him. And then I was away, riding south. I found the spot where the pedlars had been robbed. Two tiny villages later, I got a report of the man himself, at Rosières.

West of Rosières was no longer Savoy, and I passed a toll and a guardhouse there and had another odd experience. The local lord collected tolls for himself, but as I was crossing into France, a man-at-arms asked me for a *sauvegarde*. I was still on Marc-Antonio's horse, having the others behind me as spares. At his saddle bow, alongside a little fighting axe, was a leather case that proved to hold the documents that the Green Count's secretary had issued to him for his ride to Hawkwood and the main army back in August. So it was that I entered France as Marc-Antonio Corner, Squire, of Venice. And damned lucky I did, too.

Regardless, I led a strange life. I was alone, with no squire and no page and two horses for which I had to care. I was in wild country – wild twice over, because not only was it broken and mountainous, but the English and the routiers and the French and the Jacques had all burnt their way through, so that the towns had become villages and the villages hamlets. The plague had hit hard before war came – there weren't enough people left to maintain the farms, much less the inns.

So I rode through a wilderness. And it was much the same wilderness I had crossed with Fra Peter Mortimer back in '59, when I was learning to be a moral man and also learning to do the work of being a squire, and here I was again with two horses needing food.

Every day was much the same. I would ride from the moment there was enough light to see the trail, until when it was starting towards full dark. I needed an hour of light to make camp and cut firewood, which I did with a light axe that was, providentially, at Marc-Antonio's saddle bow. It was a fighting axe, but it cut wood well and had a keen edge.

I had a light crossbow – something of Emile's father, my steward led me to believe, a pretty thing set with bone and ivory, which I had picked up at Les Marches with some thought of shooting Camus. In fact, I gradually spent the blunt bolts, all of them headed in horn plugs, on shooting birds and rabbits for my food.

When I found people, I paid hard coin for wine and grain for my horses.

But as soon as I found Camus's trail again, I found dead people. He didn't pay for what he took, and he liked to kill. So several times I'd ride into a farmyard and find a man dead and a woman keening. The worst was high in the mountains, where a hard-working family had scraped out a good farm of olive trees and grape arbours across a hillside.

He'd killed them all – man, wife, two sons.

It all began to seem as if it was my fault. If I'd killed him ... I could think, as I rode alone, of all the opportunities I had had to kill Camus, and how often I had declined for various reasons, all of which, while looking at dead children, seemed specious. What value is reputation and law, when you look at a dead family of peasants you might have saved with a casual dagger thrust?

But I knew I was still on him. And I was not going to give up. Killing Camus had become the whole definition of my existence.

And I had to be careful, too. I was painfully aware that if the man doubled back, I would be easy to ambush, and as I began to awaken to something beyond revenge and despair, I also became a little more cautious, watching the hills above my track and asking every pedlar and farmer for news. It was as well I did, because somewhere in the middle of the high ground north of Montpellier, as I rode down a red and gold valley, a crossbow bolt struck my saddle – a good shot at the distance he tried.

Again, looking back, it was a foolish thing for Camus to do. He squandered a day-long lead to wait for me, and he'd killed his greatest asset, the good horses. Had he simply turned north, or stopped killing peasants, I'd have lost him after Chambéry.

Instead, his hatred choked him, and he lay on a rock, high above my leafy autumn pass, and tried to kill me with a crossbow.

How did he even know I was after him?

I'll never know. Maybe Satan whispered in his ear.

Camus wasn't utterly a fool. His rock was unreachable from my horse, being forty paces above the road, and he slipped down it on the back side, mounted a horse, and vanished over the ridge, and I was three hours reaching that rock because of the way the road twisted in the mountains.

But spirit is everything. I had never chased a man so far, but I'd hunted animals with various princes and with Emile. I can only say that there is a sharp difference between the rumour of your quarry and the hope of a success, and the sudden sighting of the stag, the chamois, or ... Camus. Now I knew he was there.

That night I made a cold camp near Varaire. I watched the hills for his campfire, but perhaps he, too, sat all night with a cocked crossbow in his hand, waiting for his enemy. And I slept, in the end, my hood up and my head slumped painfully forward over the stock of my bow.

I woke late and cursed. The sun was already rising, and my muscles were stiff and painful. It was cold. Autumn was going to give way to winter, and my wife was dead, my page was dead, my horses were dead, and suddenly, on a stony hillside high above the red and gold leaves of the valley below, I wondered what in God's name I was doing and felt a fool. It was as if I was waking from a terrible nightmare – or perhaps I was just cold, hungry and miserable, and the misery served to awaken my inner strength.

Regardless, that morning I prayed for the first time in weeks.

My beard was long and my body unwashed, and I was riding my clothes to pieces. I'd left my harness at Les Marches and wore only a coat of maille over a good arming doublet. Everything I owned was dirty.

I considered, then, giving up the chase.

A very different encounter changed my mind.

It is easy to say that God works in mysterious ways – I often hear the phrase from the most impious people. But it applies here. I rode down my little mountain and found the road, and we – that is, my horses and I – began working our way along a road so bad that it was more like a track.

I saw someone moving ahead of me. In the mountains, quite frequently, you see someone ahead of you. They can be quite close, at a bend of the road, or across a gorge, and yet, in France and in Spain, they may be a whole day ahead. This was assuredly not Camus, because it looked like a man on foot, clothed in grey.

But it took me all day to catch him up. I came up with him at dusk, and stayed on the track longer than I might have otherwise, just to catch him.

He proved, in the last light of the sun, to be a pilgrim in a grey robe. Now, pilgrims are no uncommon sight on the roads of France, but this was a big, capable man with a bit of a hobble to his walk. He proved to be a knight who'd taken a bad wound and sworn to walk to Santiago de Compostela if he recovered, and he was fulfilling his vow.

And he'd met Camus.

'He came for me,' the pilgrim said, when I asked him.

By that time, we were sharing a little fire. I had half a rabbit, and he had some carrots and a beet. And some bread, two days old, and best of all, half a pilgrim bottle of wine.

'Aye,' he said in good Norman French. 'He tried to kill me.' The old knight showed me his staff. 'I dissuaded him,' he said with a wry smile, and I loved him. He was the first sane human being with whom I'd exchanged more than fifteen words in half a month. We talked long into the night.

And from him I got the notion of going to Saint James. Santiago. I'd been to Rome and to Jerusalem – it was really the only major pilgrimage left to me. And you might recall that Emile and I had discussed it – indeed, we'd made the vow together.

I could retrieve my vow, and more. I had much to repent, and by then, my foolishness – my *insanity* – had been laid bare to me. I was three quarters of the way across France to Spain, and I was chasing a dangerous madman alone. He was obviously running for home in Gascony.

I renewed my vow that night, by the side of the road, at a little wooden statue of the Blessed Virgin, and the next day I rode on, saner, and more conscious of God's grace. Which is not to say that I was without sin, as you'll hear. But the despair dropped away. Not all at once, and it returned in bouts like an ague. By the risen Christ, it still returns sometimes, and I feel it as keenly as when I looked at Emile's body, or Stephanos's.

But I was my own master and I was determined to finish Camus, albeit in a calmer mien. Revenge is rage and anger. But a knight carries justice in his scabbard. Justice is never angry or personal.

I prayed, and rode on.

It was a long climb from Varaire into Armagnac – everything seemed to be uphill, and then more uphill. My horses were tired. I was tired. I hadn't really been eating well – a single cup of wine with my pilgrim friend put me to sleep.

Armagnac is rugged, and the people are poor, proud, and vastly overtaxed by their ambitious lord. Of course, I hate him. He was a traitor even by the loose standards of the sixties, and if it hadn't been for him, we would never have lost so much of Gascony.

Armagnac was a great lord over a county at least as large as the Green Count's Savoy. Like him, he saw his county as an independent nation. But Armagnac, at least the greater Armagnac, was composed of three great counties – Armagnac proper, Foix, and Albret. All of them were part of the ancient kingdom of Aquitaine. All of them came to England with the Treaty of Brétigny in '60.

Armagnac had mostly supported the king of France before Crécy, but thereafter was ours, and although we're not to his part of the story yet, you need to know that he commanded the Prince of Wales's rearguard in the Spanish War. He also spent most of the fifties in a losing war with the Count of Foix, another near-independent count who preferred hunting to war and yet seemed to be very, very good at the former. In the end, the Count of Foix took him in battle and set his ransom very high – as far as I know, he's still paying. Or rather, his peasants are still paying.

So while I was watching the marriage of Prince Lionel to Violante of the Visconti, Armagnac was creating a fallacious case against the Prince of Wales and taking it to the king of France – not in any way different, let me add, from what the Prince of Achaea did to the Count of Savoy. In case you have no head for politics, or just weren't listening, the new king of France was very fond of using his law courts to annex his neighbours, which was as well, because he was not much of a fighter, as I think I've also mentioned. Wince all you like, Froissart – I saw his back fairly frequently in the fifties, and he hasn't changed.

I offer all this because, while I was vaguely aware that Armagnac was acting like a typical angry Gascon, I had no idea how poisonous relations between Armagnac, Albret, and the prince had become by the late autumn of '69. I rode into the county from the south and east, on small tracks, following Camus, and as the tracks became a Roman road with inns, I saw that I was garnering a fair amount of attention. On the other hand, I speak Gascon French like a native and I still had some hard currency from Italy. I got an excellent dinner at an inn, drank the local brandy and enjoyed it far too much, and rode out the next day with my horses better rested than they'd been for weeks, and better fed.

The bedbugs were terrible in that inn, though, like a plague of locusts that sucked blood – fat and evil. I moved to the stable to sleep and had a better rest. No part of the story, but by God, gentles, an inn infested with bedbugs can be a curse.

I was late on the road, but by noon I knew that Camus was less than a day ahead of me. I pressed on across the magnificent valley of the Garonne and up the steep slope to Laurac.

Laurac had a small castle, very old, and a toll gate, and at the toll gate were a dozen slovenly men-at-arms. I paid them no mind, rode up, and offered the toll-keeper, a toothless veteran, my silver penny.

One of the men-at-arms called out, '*Heya!*' in that Spanish-French you hear in the south.

I waved a salute.

He came forward, swagger in every inch of his posture. He wore a dirty arming coat and a haubergeon of scales so old that I wondered if it had been Roman. His sword hilt was iron, brown with rust, and his horse, apparently a charger, was not much bigger than my riding horse.

'Who are you, then?' he asked without even a pretence of gentility.

I was instantly on my guard. Listen, I'd been on the road a month. It was cold, and I'd been riding through various debatable lands, and the only harm offered me had been a crossbow bolt from Camus. On the other hand, I was on the watch all the time, and I certainly knew a dozen mounted men were watching me. I just didn't think I had anything to fear.

But something in his body gave away that this was bad.

I backed my riding horse.

'I mean no trouble, gentlemen,' I said in good Gascon French.

'Let's see a *sauvegarde*,' he said.

It chanced that I had one, as you may recall, issued for Marc-Antonio.

It said I was a squire of the Green Count's, on his business, and that I was born in Venice.

I handed it over. A little deception does no harm, and having given it into his hands, I backed my horse again. His companions wanted to crowd in around me, but I wasn't willing to let them.

The man looked up. He had huge mustachios, and a vanity to match, but now he was puzzled.

'Italian?' he asked.

'Venetian,' I corrected him.

'Let's hear you talk some Italian, then,' he said.

I quoted some Boccaccio for him. I really don't speak any Veneziano, but then, who outside the Veneto does?

He frowned.

'Take him anyway,' said another man.

They looked worse than routiers, and I cursed myself for my in-attention.

'I'll take his horse,' said a third.

'Gentlemen,' I said, and drew my sword, 'you will not have any part of me.'

Mustachios shook his head. 'Don't be a fool,' he said.

He pointed at the toll gate, where two men appeared with crossbows. And I was taken.

They stripped me. The Emperor's sword, my spurs of gold, my belt, my purse, all my money, two horses, Marc-Antonio's axe and all his tack. Gone. Curiously, after some argument, they left me my donat's ring, despite the large red stone and the gold.

That wasn't the half of it. They were men-at-arms of the Comte d'Armagnac, and they had orders to take me – me being Sir William Gold, notorious English routier. Camus wasn't completely lost to madness – he'd whispered in someone's ear.

But Marc-Antonio's *sauvegarde* saved me. Not from capture and ransom – just from worse.

I rode a day with my captors, who were a surly, vain lot of

blasphemers much given to bragging. I watched one dirty excuse for a man-at-arms claim that the Emperor's sword was poorly sharpened and take a stone to it, as if he'd 'fix' the edge that way – something any peasant who'd sharpened a sickle could have set him straight on, but he was a fool. Two of them had what they imagined to be a knife fight. Each cut the other's hand in a blazing display of military ineptitude, and the rest congratulated them on their 'bravery'. I felt triply a fool because after a day with them I began to assume I could have put the lot of them down.

Bah, perhaps not. A good knight can face two inept men, but three are very difficult. Fiore used to say that the best fighter will fall to four determined children.

We rode into the castle at Condom, the Château de Mothes, where the Comte d'Armagnac was staying. I didn't see him. I was merely re-lieved of my belongings by bored and greedy guards, and taken, bound in iron, to a cell that sat like a damp toad deep beneath the donjon.

I demanded to see the Comte, and the return of my *sauvegarde*. In fact, I made a number of demands that were unheeded, and by the next day, my fears were choking me. I had received neither food nor water, and I began to dread the appearance of Camus. I was astute enough to know that he must have arranged for me to be taken – he was, after all, home, or near enough. It seemed all too possible that I would be handed over to him.

The next day, filthy and blinking, I was brought into a whitewashed room where the Comte d'Armagnac sat on a wooden seat very like a throne, with two armoured men by him. Neither was one of my captors, and both wore good harness.

Filthy has advantages. I didn't stand as straight as I might have, and my hair was lank and brown, not copper red.

I bowed.

He looked at me. In Italian, he said, 'State your name.'

I nodded. 'Marc-Antonio Corner,' I said proudly.

He sighed. 'This says you are a squire of the Count of Savoy,' he said.

'I have that honour,' I said.

He nodded. 'Are you worth a ransom?' he asked.

'Yes,' I said. 'But by what right did these men take me? My lord count is in no way in conflict with Your Grace.'

Armagnac turned to the man with him. 'He must be what he says. No peasant could pretend to manners like this.'

The other man made a face. 'He *could* be Venetian,' the man admitted.

He sounded Genoese. He had a beak like an eagle and fat mustachios, too – I assumed this was an Armagnac affectation.

Armagnac frowned.

'Just kill him,' said the Genoese. 'Some squire from Venice – too far. No one will look for him.'

'What are you worth?' asked the other man.

I won't say he was kind – that would be too much. But he was businesslike.

'A hundred ducats, gold,' I said with waning confidence.

Sir William Gold was worth two *thousand* gold ducats. Should I say so?

Armagnac spread his hands.

I bowed again. 'My Lords, I won't threaten. I won't tell you how powerful my father is, because I am from the family of Chioggia and not the Venetian Cornari. But why kill me?' I tried to be brave and smile.

The businesslike man in armour nodded. 'Why indeed, My Lord? I think we've made an error, but not a great one, and we'll ransom this young man to his father and be a little richer for it.'

Armagnac looked at me. 'The Bourc Camus,' he said aloud.

I was looking at the businesslike man-at-arms, and I didn't blink.

'But this Coq d'Or fellow also serves the Count of Savoy,' Armagnac said. 'Do you know Le Coq d'Or?' he asked me.

'My Lord, he is the captain of my lord's knights,' I said.

'Jesus, that's not what Camus said, either.' Armagnac let loose a long string of profanity.

'Why were you riding in our lands?' Businesslike asked.

I shook my head. 'I was on my lord's orders,' I said.

'You can do better than that,' Armagnac spat.

I bowed. 'I hope that if I was one of Your Grace's men-at-arms, I would say the same,' I said.

Armagnac shrugged. 'You are a bold rascal. Very well, put him somewhere and write to his father, and the Count of Savoy. Get three hundred.'

'I will be beggared!' I said. 'Your Grace! They took my horses and all my arms—'

'Don't make me regret keeping you alive, little squire of Venice,' Armagnac said. 'Christ, he stinks. Who in all the hells thought this was some great knight?'

Businesslike came and ordered me out of the room. I followed him, and he turned.

'I'm Sir Tancred,' he said. 'I'll see you well housed. Listen, my lord is a touchy bastard at the best of times, and this is not a good time. Don't try him.'

I nodded.

'Give me one straight answer,' he said.

I looked at him. If he was a bad man, he was a fine actor. I'd looked in his eyes and I thought I knew the type – a straight arrow. They're the same from the steppe to Cairo to Rome to ... Armagnac.

'Yes, My Lord.'

'Are you hunting Camus?' he asked.

'Yes,' I said.

He nodded. 'Care to tell me the crime?' he asked.

'Murder,' I said. 'And he tried to kill the Count of Savoy.'

He whistled. 'Well, that puts a little bit of a different complexion on it,' he said. 'I see. And this Coq d'Or—'

'I think my lord asked for one question,' I said.

He smiled. He was no fool, and he had a fine sense of honour.

'Follow me.'

He led me out of the castle, which I found incredible. We went up a steep street to a big house with an enclosed courtyard, not entirely unlike a house in Venice or Chioggia. He bargained with the owner for a few sentences in rapid Occitan, and nodded to me.

'The widow demands you have a bath. She wants three gold louis a month for your keep, and that includes her own table for food.'

'My Lord, the bastards took all my money ...'

He nodded. 'And you'll never see any of it again,' he agreed. 'So best think of the widow when you write to your father for your ransom.'

The next day, cleaner and better fed, I wrote to my 'father' in Chioggia, requesting five hundred gold ducats to pay my ransom and refit myself. I wrote another to the Count of Savoy, in my character as Marc-Antonio, and hoped that someone would read it and put two and two together, so to speak.

The widow, whose name was Marie, was a gentlewoman of perhaps sixty years, who boarded visiting gentlemen and ransoms. She had excellent manners and her cook was good, and if it had not been for my lingering despair and my anger at being captured and my fear that Camus would take me any moment, I might have enjoyed my stay with her. She had a dozen ageing servants, a couple of young grooms, two big men with clubs who I suppose were intended as my guards, and a big house for all of them. Her man had died in Armagnac's endless wars, and she was quite capable of carrying on alone.

But Camus was around somewhere, and I was all too aware that as a tall man with red hair, I was very vulnerable to a few words in description. The ruse that I was Marc-Antonio couldn't last.

I had to run.

I did have one thing on my side, or perhaps two. The first was that Armagnac desperately needed money – so desperately that my three hundred ducats, which any other prince would have assigned to someone he wanted to favour, was going straight into his own coffers. Second, he was deep in treasonous negotiations with the king of France, and he had no time for small fry like Camus.

Evil often defeats itself. I don't *know* what happened, but a combination of observation, gossip and tales from Sir Tancred suggest that Camus was just too *mad* for anyone to want him around. Too odd. Too ... evil. I gather he cooled his heels in anterooms demanding to see the Comte d'Armagnac, and was not admitted, and caused a fuss or two. Patience was never his best suit.

Meanwhile, I was afraid. But eating well. There was a good deal of chicken, and some game, and fish. The wines were nothing on Italian wines, but the food ...

I began to feel like a whole man. The race across France had cost me in body and soul, and so in the courtyard of that house I did my exercises. I started teaching the two grooms to fight.

I started thinking about Emile. About Isabelle. About ... about our lives. Did I ever act the part of father? Or family?

Time to think is the enemy of sin, I promise you.

*

One day, Sir Tancred visited me. He found me in the yard, one groom nursing a split thumb, the other practising at an impromptu pell.

I was showing them how to counter-cut into a cut.

Sir Tancred listened attentively and then demanded that I show him, and an hour later he was covered in sweat.

'You're no squire,' he said quietly.

I bowed. 'So kind, sir knight,' I said in my halting Occitan.

He told me that Camus was asking after me – the squire, that is.

I felt as if I might throw up.

I have often discounted Camus. I have beaten him, even humiliated him. But I knew damned well that if he took me alive, it would be very bad.

Tancred nodded. 'Well, the count is too busy to see him, and I have told no one where you are guested.' He looked at me for a long time. 'Do you know what this town has?' he asked.

I shrugged. 'Brandy?' I asked.

'Pilgrims,' he said. 'A great many pilgrims.'

He looked at me for so long that I *had* to understand that he was telling me to run. And hide among the pilgrims.

Here's the thing. I hadn't even been taken legally – the Count of Savoy was not in a state of war with the Comte d'Armagnac, so he had no right to seize me. They'd stolen my horse and arms ...

The Emperor's sword.

Gone forever.

At the same time, I wanted money, and I'd been mostly wealthy for so long that I had forgotten how to be poor. I was thinking in terms of a horse, a sword, clothes ...

I was foolish. My life and sanity were on the line, and I was balking at a few gold coins.

So I didn't run. Like a fool, I sat in the widow's house and ate.

Christmas came and went. I attended Mass quite regularly with the widow and her household, and most days I heard Mass and either Matins or some other hours. Sometimes we prayed in her house, and there were two priests who came quite regularly.

But for Christmas her daughter came, another widow, also Marie – this time Marie-Claire. She was tall and had forbidding dark eyebrows, and a heavy face, but a rich laugh, and she brought a joy to the house that it lacked. She was forty or so, and had borne three children alive. Her husband, like the widow's, had died fighting Foix in the fifties.

Marie-Claire and I were almost instant friends. We played chess, and there was a little flirtation. Flirting is as natural as breathing – I could mourn my wife and flirt with Marie-Claire. She was quite athletic, too, as I discovered when she invited me to hunt and loaned me a horse.

On Epiphany, Sir Tancred came, and he was courtly to Marie-Claire – it was plain they knew each other right well. We dined with a priest, and then Tancred took me by the hand.

'Listen,' he said. 'Camus is back. He was gone for a few weeks, but now he's about, and he's got one of the d'Albret lordlings with him. D'Albret has my lord's ear.'

If he'd chilled me before, now his words seemed to go straight to my spine. I flinched and he saw it.

'A nudge is as good as a wink to a blind man, and perhaps better,' he said.

I bowed, and he bowed in return and was gone into the night.

I sat up late in the spare solar, plotting. I was trying to imagine how to start. The rest was easy. The two men with clubs had become my friends – Antoine and Raoul. They were probably dangerous, but I'd spent hours training them and they thought of me as their teacher. I knew I could walk out of the door any time – I went to Mass, after all. But it stuck in my craw to actually rob a pilgrim. And I had to assume that the first few days would be rough – damned difficult, really, with the count's people looking for me.

And early January is a miserable time to be a pilgrim. Even in the south, it rains all the time, and it's cold enough to kill.

I was contemplating all of this when Marie-Claire came in. She smiled, in her demure way, and lit two candles.

'Messire is sitting in the dark,' she said.

I smiled. 'I'm thinking,' I said.

'I was sure that I smelt something burning,' she said. We both laughed.

She settled into a chair.

'I cannot sleep,' she confessed.

She picked up her embroidery from a bag she kept there and began to sew.

I couldn't exactly ask her to leave me alone to plot my escape, so I said something like that I was sure she'd enjoyed Sir Tancred's visit.

'A fine man,' she said. 'We've been friends since childhood.'

She spoke a little about her childhood. It's always interesting to listen to people, especially when they tell of the past. Through her eyes, I saw the widow as a young woman with a son and a daughter, making ends meet in a tiny castle in the mountains and waiting for a husband who never came home.

It's not my story, but everyone has a story, and I saw the widow and her strength and silence in a new way.

The next day, Marie-Claire went back to her little manor, and I began to sit in the front of the house and watch the street while I considered escape. But just after Marie-Claire left us, one of the widow's priests grew sick, and died, and two days later, I had it too.

I lost a full month. It wasn't plague – it was a fever, and it was bad enough. I was merely a little ill for two days, and then I have no memory until I awoke and it was night, and the widow's daughter was sitting by my pallet. I was on the floor in a storeroom in the dark.

I must have asked where I was. Marie-Claire bent over.

'You're safe here,' she said.

And then I was gone again.

As soon as I was capable of moving, even though I was so weak that walking made my head spin, the grooms threw me onto a horse, and Marie-Claire led me on a nightmare trip. I know now that we went only about three English miles, but we did this while I was still sick, in the dark, in mountains, and I dreamt I was riding across hell with Dante's Beatrice. None of it made much sense.

Camus had come with a writ from the Comte d'Armagnac.

The widow, may God bless and keep her, had been forewarned by Sir Tancred. She showed Camus my sheets and told him I'd died of the fever. By then, five hundred of the town's people were dead, and Camus apparently swore a great deal, ripped the room apart, and left.

I was already lying on the floor of the storeroom, shivering.

*

Marie-Claire lived with a dozen servants in a fine small house of stone. She had a manor, a whole knight's fee, and she spent most of her time outdoors, riding. She knew the name of every peasant on her lands, and she brought them food, laid up preserves, gathered wild herbs and dried them herself – in effect, she never stopped working. I was just one of her many projects, and as I recovered she gave me tasks and I did them. Most of them were no more strenuous than separating the best oregano, or sorting her embroidery thread by colour. She praised me extravagantly for that.

'The things I don't ever get to do,' she said warmly, and pressed my hand.

I recovered for a month, and one day she had me out picking oregano with her on a hillside. I was leaning well out over a cliff-face to get some unblossomed flowers, and she was steadying me, and when I got them, she kissed me. The kiss went from cousinly to explosive too fast for either of us to resist or even, I think, fully comprehend.

There had never been more than the lightest touch of flirtation to our conversation, and I would most definitely have placed Marie-Claire among women who were beyond the needs of the flesh, and yet, there we were, lying on some very uncomfortable, rocky ground, naked as children, having made love so abruptly that it bordered on violence.

She began to laugh.

I have said her laugh was infectious. I laughed, too. It was sweet and absurd.

I put a hand on her. 'Could we do that better?' I asked.

She laughed harder.

The next day, she sat on the edge of my bed.

'You need to go,' she said.

She had a pilgrim's gown, a scrip, and a staff laid out for me.

I smiled at her. 'That bad?' I asked.

She made me feel alive, and old sinner that I am, I felt ... better. Not healed, but ... alive.

She looked at me, under her heavy eyebrows. '*Eh bien*,' she said. 'Listen, *monsieur*. I want you gone before I can't let you go. Also, servants talk. Also ...' She stretched. 'Also, I am twice your age and you won't stay anyway.'

I shook my head. 'Perhaps you have ten years on me,' I said.

She kissed me. 'Or fifteen or more. In fact, I am old enough to know where all this goes and how babies happen and everything.'

'Babies?' I said, possibly with a shock.

'Don't you know?' she asked lightly. 'When a man—'

I pushed her away, laughing ruefully. I had children, far away. And men-at-arms, a whole company. Also far away.

But she was right. And despite having started with a little sin, my heart rose at the notion of going to Santiago.

More war, you say, Froissart?

Listen, you lot. This is my story, and I will have leave to tell it as I would. And even though it ends on a battlefield in Italy, it started with the death of the Prince of Achaea and I'll tell it my own way. There will be battles enough.

The next morning, very early, I walked down through her little village, dressed as a pilgrim. It was mid-March. Already the valleys were green, although it was cold and wet on the hillsides higher up, and I was soaked to the skin before my first day was done.

Walking.

It had been years since I had just walked. By my estimation, and supported by the report of two priests who had both made the whole trip, I had several hundred English miles to walk from Condom, across the south of France and then right across the top of Spain.

The first day, I walked to Montréal-du-Gers. I discovered that Marie-Claire had filled my scrip with food – wonderful food, and a flask of her own brandy, and a twist of vellum in with a bunch of oregano, with a note.

'When I cook with this year's, I'll think of you.'

I laughed.

There were also two precious gifts, or perhaps three. A flask of excellent brandy, as I mentioned – beautiful glass, that I still have, a string of prayer beads that I put on my belt, and best of all, a tiny, precious book of hours. Not a fancy one at all – just a plain-written forty pages with the psalms and the breviary a pilgrim would use.

I might have cried a little.

I walked.

*

146

Walking is remarkable. It is slower than riding a horse and more intimate with the landscape, and you meet everyone. Late on the first day, as I approached Montréal-du-Gers, I met a knight and a squire riding the other way. I gave them a greeting, and they waved and wished me a '*buon camino*' and I walked on.

Only an hour later did I consider that I might have met Sir Tancred, or even Camus.

I consoled myself that men mostly see what they expect to see.

That night was my first night in an *albergue*, one of the hostels maintained by churches and monasteries. Now, the very best of them are run by my order, the Hospitallers, as I have no doubt said before. I am sure you'll think me biased, but I promise you they are the best. But the other orders run adequate hostels.

My first was perhaps twice the size of a peasant's house, with twenty beds, all stripped to the ropes, and clean straw. When I arrived, I was invited to change shoes for sandals, and to help with the work of making dinner, and then, with a dozen other men and two women, we stuffed the mattresses with clean straw donated by the local farmers for our comfort. We shared a dinner of soup and bread, and the women went to their own beds, separated by a strong door, and I collapsed. I, a knight who fights and trains all the time, fell into a deep sleep and awoke to the ache of muscles I had perhaps never fully known that I had. I rose with the other men before the sun rose.

I ate an egg and stale bread, then we gathered in the chilly air outside the *albergue* and started walking. Eventually my muscles warmed and I felt better. Later still, I stopped at a roadside cross and prayed. For Emile. For Isabelle. For the men I'd killed.

I had lots of praying to do.

And then I walked some more.

It took me almost ten days to harden my legs. I'm a fit man – I'm a knight. But I ride. I do not walk. Indeed, I understood by the end of the third day why the indulgence and the remission of sins was so much greater for those who walked than for those who rode. The rider is above his companions. The man on foot has humility forced upon him.

And I'd been very sick. My sickness had put me down almost a month, and now, as I walked across Armagnac, I felt my illness falling away, but I was still weak, and all my companions of the first night were far ahead by the time I'd walked a week. And I stopped at almost every church to pray, and the land was studded with churches. And crosses, and crude wooden statues to the Blessed Virgin, and fine stone statues, too.

But the humility ... I was reminded, every day, of my lowly status by men – aye, and women – who demanded that I clear the road so they could ride by – a rich merchant, a high-born lady and her retinue, a pair of routiers ...

And another kind of humility. Almost everywhere, people would wish me a good camino. Several times, peasants came from their fields to the road to bow to me or touch their caps, and more than once I was asked for a blessing. A pilgrim is a kind of holy figure, and I began to think of myself as such, not with pride, but humility. One night – I think it was perhaps the fourth or fifth – I was sitting in the yard of my hostel, and praying. I had my small book of hours open, and I was saying my evening office.

A woman sat down opposite me. She was swathed in fabric, but then, most pilgrims were. She had on a wimple and a heavy gown.

'May I pray with you, Brother?' she asked in Gascon French, and I agreed. She was very halting in her Latin, and after we finished, she prayed alone, and later she brought me a cup of wine.

'I haven't prayed and meant it since my boys died,' she said.

I nodded. What do you say to something as profound and serious as that?

'Thank you, Brother,' she said. She touched my hand. 'You reminded me of God's love.'

Christ risen, is there more humility to be had on this earth than a good woman telling you that you brought her to mind of our Saviour? Is the feeling of being unworthy part of the learning of humility?

Strange days. And walking, alone, for the most part. Watching the countryside, covered in dust, burnt brown even under my straw hat.

Or walking with other pilgrims, chattering about anything from local politics to funny stories. I was three days with a good group, around Éauze, and we all told stories. I told them of the tournament at Didymoteichon, and a woman told a brilliant story about a Moorish prince in Spain. And another day, I walked with two men who'd served in Spain with the Prince of Wales, and I heard the whole campaign, from the dark beginnings to the Battle at Nájera where the prince won a great victory. How I wish I had been there!

By the time we were walking the last days to Saint-Jean-Pied-de-Port, I was more relaxed than I had been in ten years of war. I had forgotten Camus. I had forgotten the Green Count, and my company, and war. I had not forgotten sin – I had not forgotten my wife, for whom I prayed every day, nor Isabelle, our daughter. But I didn't think of them in torment. I was finding that humility has its own releases.

There is nothing more healing, my friends. Just walk. Walk far, and hard, with new friends along the way and a cup of wine in the evening. Or two, or six, eh?

We were, I think, two days from reaching Saint-Jean, climbing into the foothills of the Pyrenees, which towered over us on the left. For days they never seemed to get closer, and then suddenly they were right beside us. We were coming into the mountains again and leaving the flat of Pau behind us, but my legs were hard and fifteen miles a day or more was no longer any effort.

I was alone, as I often was, cutting occasionally at a roadside weed with my staff, praying and thinking about many things.

I heard hoof beats behind me and as I was on a humped road, as ancient as Rome or older, I only moved to the margin.

I glanced back.

Six mounted men-at-arms, all in black and white.

With Camus.

The ground from Saint-Sever is no longer flat, but I was on the main road through the rolling hills. The nearest cover was a stand of trees five hundred paces away. Even the stone wall along the road was too low for hiding.

I blinked, hardened my heart, and prayed. I turned back towards Saint-Jean and began to walk, swinging my staff.

It probably sounds simple, or foolish.

It took all my courage, and even then, my insides turned to water as the hoof beats grew, and my knees were weak. Just try turning your back on a terrible enemy and walking away. I knew it was the right answer, but the actual execution took everything I had, and two weeks' worth of calm vanished in ten steps, and my hands trembled.

And I knew that they might kill me just for being there. Camus killed pilgrims – he'd killed one in Italy.

On the other hand, I was not alone on the road. There were pilgrims ahead and behind. Even as I glanced back, Camus drew even with two monks, and ahead of me was a group of a dozen.

He passed the monks.

The hoof beats grew louder, with the rattle of harness and the clop of heavy horses. They weren't moving fast, that much was sure.

He *had* to be looking for me. And he'd know I was a pilgrim. And he knew me well.

On the other hand, I was stooped over and as skinny as a rail, and I hadn't had a proper bath for two weeks.

I made myself keep walking.

Camus was in the lead, and I heard his horse come up. A horse, walking, is not much faster than a man walking briskly. It seemed to take forever for him to draw abreast.

He was talking to one of his men-at-arms.

'Can you imagine so much hypocrisy packed into one path?' he asked. 'Hundreds, nay, thousands of liars, fornicators and killers, all pretending repentance for their petty little sins, and imagining that the pain in their feet exculpates their murders and adulteries. Imagining that there is a god, and that their invisible sky god cares a whit, in his power, for their powerlessness. What a fucking lie! If there was a god with so much power, then he's an evil bastard more like me than like them, catering to his whims and treating them like the cattle they are.'

He glanced back. He was now ten paces ahead of me, and he only glanced to see the reaction of his men.

'And Satan supposedly fell from Heaven for telling this sky god the truth!' Camus barked, and he laughed. 'Left to myself, I'd set up a toll booth on this cursed road and make them pay in blood for daring to imagine that redemption exists. The arrogance of the meat.'

Blessed Virgin, I prayed. Blessed Virgin, I said to her, get me through this hour and I will repent and I will dedicate to you an altar and one hundred candles.

What a creature Camus was, and what an amalgam of horror. Who made him that?

I confess that I have a theory. Regardless, after he rode past, I had to stop and shake. And I had to get off the road. Eventually, assuming he was looking for me, he'd come back, and facing me, he'd know me. If he hadn't been in mid-tirade against religion, he'd probably have picked me up anyway, the way we know a friend two streets away by the manner of their walking.

But God works in mysterious ways.

The moment they were out of sight, I turned and crossed the fields to my right. It was very open, and I was visible on that hillside to every other pilgrim on the road. I felt exposed, but then I might have been a shy man going to relieve myself.

A mile to the north, I came across another road – this one just a farm track – and I followed it. My breathing had slowed, and I was clear-headed enough to reflect.

First, on what had made Camus who he was. A life of making war is not, I promise you, the most conducive to reflection and philosophy, but he had been bent, if not broken, when I met him in my teens.

How is such a monster made?

Terrible parents? I always assumed that I had had a terrible childhood. My parents died, my uncle was a horror.

On the farm track above Saint-Jean-Pied-de-Port, I considered that perhaps there were worse childhoods. Father Pierre Thomas and the Franciscans denied that any human being could be cursed by God – that, they said, was heresy. And their reasoning made sense to me.

The other thing that I thought was that Camus had been blinded by his sense of my pride. He was looking for me – Sir William Gold. A knight, on a courser.

He wasn't even looking at the poor dusty pilgrims, with their dirty feet and their sweat.

I'm sure that there's a lesson there – perhaps a whole set of lessons.

I kept walking. It was a long day, and I made it longer with my detour. I came into Saint-Jean with the last of the light on the following day, still alive, undiscovered, and possibly even humble.

There are a dozen hostels and *albergues* in Saint-Jean. My order maintains one, but it was full and I didn't want to show my donat's ring. Now, in an *albergue*, it's quite close, which is a nice way of saying that twenty to fifty unwashed men and women can give the place a certain smell, even if monks and nuns wash it with all their holy fervour and might. And on that April evening, it was warm enough that most of the pilgrims were outside in the streets, sitting on benches outside their *albergues* or paying the ridiculous prices for some very mediocre wine at the little taverns and wine shops.

I had been to three hostels and the Hospitaller gate, and was moving cautiously toward the next when a voice behind me said, 'Sir Guillaume?'

And another, a deep Gascon voice, said, 'Will Gold?'

I turned, drawing my dagger and getting my back into the wall. I had my staff in my right hand and my dagger in my left, and a wall at my back. I wasn't going easily.

At the same time that my dagger came into my hand, I was thinking that the first voice, the northern French voice, had been a woman's – that Camus hated and even feared women …

The street behind me was clearing. The violence of my turn and draw had panicked a dozen people. Pilgrims vanished up narrow side-alleys. A brave nun stood her ground with an old monk behind her.

'Guillaume?' the nun asked again.

I was looking at the monk, who had his staff in Fiore's posture that we call '*Finestre*'.

It was Pierre Lapot. His narrow, ferrety face was smooth-shaven, and he was less thin than when I'd last seen him.

And the nun was Sister Marie, whom I'd last seen at the deadly chapel of Oulx.

We embraced a dozen times, exclaiming 'How come you're here?' and '*D'ou viens-tu?*' and a dozen other questions.

'Camus is after me,' I said when the first delightful shock was done.

'God and his saints be with us,' Marie said.

Lapot nodded. 'A bad man,' he said. 'But then I have also been a bad man.'

'Never as bad as Camus,' I said.

We moved to a backstreet and I bought wine for the three of us.

Their story was quickly told. Both had vowed to make the camino. Pierre had started from Milan in the summer, when he left the Company – his abbot had made it a condition of his taking vows, having heard his confession.

Sister Marie had started from Chambéry in October, and on her fifth day on the road she had found Lapot sick to death in a mountain hostel.

'I nursed him,' she said. 'And did all of the abbey's Latin letters, as well.' She smiled. 'The abbot condescended to find my Latin acceptable.'

Lapot smiled with half his mouth, the way he did when he was considering killing someone, back in his fighting days.

'He was a right bastard,' Lapot agreed. 'Although a life of obedience is going to require me to obey such.'

They'd been walking together since Savoy.

I told them a little of my pursuit of Camus, but Marie only asked me how I felt about Emile.

'I cursed God,' I said. 'You were there.'

Sister Marie is a severe-faced woman of about forty or forty-five. She had been the papal legate's Latin secretary, and then she had been a sort of tutor to our children. She was one of the few people that Father Pierre Thomas, the papal legate and saint, had consulted on various issues.

She is also, you may remember, a skilled swordswoman, with a writ from Cardinal Talleyrand to teach nuns the use of the sword and the buckler for their own defence.

And Lapot had been with me since Jerusalem, and even before – a deadly lance, a skilled sword, and a man who had been a routier with some success. A Gascon, like Camus, except that the life of arms and violence had sent him in a very different direction, so that by the time the Company returned to Italy, he was ready to enter holy orders.

'I cursed God,' I said again.

Marie nodded and put a hand on mine.

'We all do, one time or another,' she said. 'Christ did not come to earth because we were already saved. But the opposite.'

Lapot raised an eyebrow. 'Where did you see Camus last?' he asked with devastating practicality.

'Yesterday, on the main road from Tarbes,' I said.

Lapot looked at Marie. And then at me.

'You should walk with us,' Marie said. 'Are you ... truly a pilgrim?'

I nodded. 'It is not just a disguise. I vowed it with Emile.'

'Then come with us,' Lapot said.

I looked at them. 'Three staffs against ten swords? All I'm doing is dragging you into a bad man's revenge.'

Marie shrugged. 'You need to have a little more faith in God, monsieur. What are the chances that we three would meet in these mountains?'

Lapot smiled. 'We should have been gone this morning, but my feet hurt and her donkey looked so forlorn ...'

We all laughed.

Sister Marie was very serious, though.

'Listen,' she said. 'There are dozens of ways to go on from here. Most of the pilgrims cross here, over to Roncesvalles.'

'What?' I asked. 'Roland's Roncesvalles?'

'The very same,' Marie said. 'But there are other ways.'

Lapot nodded. 'We were told in Italy that the coast road is worse,' he said, 'but the people are better and the inns much cheaper.'

'And if Camus is really hunting you,' she said, 'he's not likely to look on the coast road. He'll be down on the plains with ten thousand pilgrims.'

So, they led me to their *albergue* off the main road, and I slept soundly despite the snores of fifty tired men.

In the morning, we rose in darkness and Sister Marie retrieved her mule from a communal stable at the Franciscan house.

She was gone for a long time, and Lapot and I both fretted. After half an hour, the sun began to rise on the cold mist of the early morning, and all the rest of the pilgrims set off. There were nearly seventy men and women in our hostel, and all of them were going over the great pass to Roncesvalles.

I was preparing to go and look for her when she came around the corner.

'I saw Camus,' she said. 'He's one street away. We're going.'

I admit, I had the temptation to get it over with – the knight's temptation to commit to combat.

Sister Marie looked at me steadily.

Listen, this may make no sense to you. I see you already looking pained, Chaucer. But I thought of it as a test of my resolve to *be* a pilgrim. Jesus has no time for revenge.

The donkey was packed, and we were ready.

'I wish I had a sword,' I said. I admit it – I'm both men, or several men.

Marie shrugged. 'I have one,' she said. 'Is this your plan? To go back and fight Camus in the midst of a pilgrimage of God?'

'He's pursuing me!' I said.

We were already walking, going west, not south. We were virtually alone. It was very early, and the sound of horses' hooves clipping along a cobbled street came to us from lower in the town.

'You are responsible for your own actions,' Marie said, sounding remarkably like my sister.

The mist was thick, and houses emerged out of it in the odd, other-worldly early morning light. Suddenly we were climbing sharply, and the track switched back and we could look down on the town, not so far below. Some *albergues* had oil lamps lit in the fog, and I could smell woodsmoke and grilling sausage.

We turned around and went west, and in less than a mile we were among trees, and then the track turned and we climbed again, and the town was lost behind us, and with it, I hoped, Camus as well.

And if you wonder that I had gone from pursuing him to him pursuing me, well, the irony was not lost on me.

But *certes*, gentles, I had two good friends by me after a long drought, and I was happy. Maybe Sister Marie helped me make the right decision, but let me tell you this – I am no more than the sum of my friends. I need them.

We walked, up and up through old oak, the leaves soft under our lightly shod feet, and we were not afraid. Indeed, Sister Marie and Lapot began to teach me pilgrim songs and a hymn, and we all sang together.

PART II
CAMINO
Spring 1369

CHAPTER ONE

NORTHERN SPAIN

Spring 1369

If the walk from Tarbes had hardened my legs, the climb out of
Saint-Jean was a forge and my legs were hardening from iron to
steel. And the worst of it was that I didn't know that the first day's
climb was merely a presage of weeks to come.

Most pilgrims walk over the ancient road through the pass of
Roncesvalles and down onto the plains of Spain – a long walk,
but mainly flat after the first days. Instead, we took the older road.
Older, because when pilgrims began to flood the shrine at Santiago,
the plains were still in the hands of the Moors. But the hills to the
north, or the mountains, to be clear, had never fallen to the Moors.
The Basques and the Asturians had never been conquered, and so the
oldest pilgrim road lay over the mountains and next to the sea. A few
pilgrims took the old road – although the wine was not cheap, there
were usually *albergues*. The Hospital – that is, the Knights of Saint
John – maintained a dozen inns and hospitals along the way.

We climbed into Navarre. You know that I have no love for the
king of Navarre, who betrayed nearly everyone in the fifties, including
his own cause and the poor Jacques. More recently, he'd hosted the
Prince of Wales and sworn his allegiance and then, suddenly, wandered across the border to France and been 'captured' by his cousin
the king of France – a legalistic betrayal. The prince had triumphed
in Spain despite Navarre's efforts to undermine him, but now, as we
traversed the high passes, I heard from other travellers how badly the
prince's entire effort in Spain was unravelling.

I know that you want me to hurry on to the story of brave deeds, but as usual, you have to know the players to keep score. The Prince of Wales, prompted by his father's notions of diplomacy, and mostly to keep England's coasts free of the very powerful navies of Castile and Aragon, had invaded Spain to make war on behalf of the rightful king, Pedro.

The problem was that we'd backed the wrong horse. We, the English, that is. Pedro had been driven from Spain by his half-brother, the illegitimate Enrique of Trastámara. And Pedro, our candidate, managed to combine arrogance, cruelty and thoughtlessness with an incredible level of faithlessness, so that once our prince had put him back on his throne, he virtually turned on us and refused to pay for the campaign. Prince Edward got sick and marched home, triumphant on the field of battle – you may have noted that he captured du Guesclin ...

But our prince was only master of the ground he walked on. He marched home, and Pedro wandered off into tyranny. He seemed to make a game of alienating his friends, as I heard at length from a middle-aged scholar in the mountains of Navarre – Michael des Roches, an English scholar of Oxford and Paris. As we were to become fast friends, I should mention that we were very much of a size, and he, like me, had a ginger beard and a full head of red-brown hair. He had no tonsure because he was no monk, but an itinerant scholar who travelled about, debating on points of theology and – even more shocking – philosophy. He was the first man I'd ever met who found Aristotle to be riddled with flaws, and I found talking to him something like talking to Fiore. Every time I thought I knew something, a great pit would yawn at my intellectual feet ...

But I get ahead of myself. When we first met Michael, he was sitting by a well near Tolosa, reading. Listen – you don't see a lot of pilgrims reading, unless, like me, they have a very small missal or a breviary. But he had one of Plato's dialogues in Latin. *Timaeus*, of which I had heard from both Petrarch and you, Chaucer.

Michael was not merely a cloud-dwelling scholar. He was passionately interested in the world, and it was from him that we got news of Spain, from Paris, where he had just been. According to Michael, Enrique of Trastámara had triumphed, and had King Pedro cornered in a castle in Castile called Montiel. And since Michael took dinner with us that night and then rose to continue his journey with us the next day, we benefited from his knowledge of languages. He spoke some Castilian Spanish, and some Galician, so that we could talk to returning pilgrims going the other way – and of course many were French, or even English.

That was the background to Spain in the early spring of 1369. We were walking into the end of a war. Every routier in the southern Mediterranean was rushing to du Guesclin's banner. It was my old friend and enemy who was again leading Enrique of Trastámara's army, and his army was mostly routiers.

The immediate side-effect of the war in the south was that our twisting mountain path was utterly free of brigands. When the peasants spoke to us – which was not often, they being Basques and we being foreign – it was to tell us how remarkable it was that all the broken men had gone away.

'Like vultures to the smell of the corpse,' a nun told us with grim satisfaction.

And perhaps you feel that I should have stolen a horse and ridden south to save King Pedro. But I didn't, not least because Michael, who was as fair-minded a man as I've ever known, made it clear that the man was mad.

'I have only two good things to say about him,' des Roches said. 'He's a good scholar, or so men say, and he's kind to the Jews. His half-brother kills Jews wherever he finds them.'

'God be with them,' Sister Marie said, crossing herself. 'They both sound bad.'

'They are,' des Roches said.

Chaucer, I can see you want to protest – and sure, it's true that Pedro has been much maligned. I know that his willingness to use Moslem mercenaries had led to a blackening of his name, which seems odd, as the Pope, you may recall, hired Turks against us at Borgoforte until we lured them to our side ...

Regardless, the true reason that I didn't go rushing off on errantry is much simpler – I was quite genuinely on pilgrimage. A vow of pilgrimage is sacred, and it comes before any other vow, including fealty to one's lord. Pedro could go to Hell his own way. I was aiming at a higher reward, and as the miles rolled away under my feet, so, too, a great many other things fell away.

It is probably obvious to all of you that I'm a sinful man, but as I walked, it became clear to me that Marietta was the least of my sins.

In fact, as I walked, I began to consider my life as a courtier with the Green Count – the tangle of alliances and social commitment, the constant desire for recognition and reward, the striving for honour …

What is this but pride?

The fighting, the use of violence to solve almost every trouble, the endless training to violence, the sheer homicidal intent in the daily practice of the skills of knighthood …

What is this but murder?

The craving for land, anger and resentment at my lord's desire to have Edouard's homage, satisfaction at the grant of a manor and village of my own, the tents, the golden dagger, the horses won and lost …

Greed.

And my pursuit of Camus – I've just told it. Selfish hatred. Cursing God.

I could list them all, because by the time I'd walked most of the way to Bilbao, and prayed with Marie and Lapot and des Roches, I'd visited my engagement with all seven of the deadly sins and most of the lesser ones.

Listen, friends. I'm no saint, and I do believe that the priests clip us too close, and think we should all be monks and nuns. I leave that aside. Nor was this the first time I'd had these thoughts. God knows, I've a dark side, and many a night I'd thrashed through my life as a routier or as a whoremaster and wondered all the dark things. Is there a God? Is there purpose? Are we all sacks of meat waiting for the maggots and worms?

But by the time we were eating oysters in Bilbao, I'd had more time to think than perhaps I'd ever had in my life. And thinking, despite its poor repute among some of the fighting *ordo*, is not to be despised. I was not made like Lapot. I was not ready to give up the world, and as a pilgrim, I was capable every day of listening with delight to Sister Marie and des Roches discussing the impact of pagan philosophy on early Christianity, or ideas of the Trinity and the theology of the Godhead – of being deeply immersed in these ideas, and yet smiling at a pretty matron whose trim ankles under her kirtle suggest a fine figure. I can be both men in the same moment, and this, to me, is what des Roches's Plato might have been after in his *Timaeus*. Yes, I was reading it, with Marie giving me Latin lessons. Often the two of them spoke in Latin, and Lapot and I would stumble along. I think

I've said before that few things are more entertaining than watching a group of trained killers, belted knights, pretend that they understand a lesson from Fiore. Well, there was Lapot, on his way to priesthood, and me, trying to pretend to a level of Latin we absolutely didn't possess, so that we'd grunt and nod and smile as if either of us even knew which word in the long sentence had been the verb ...

But by the time we were approaching Oviedo, my Latin was improving by leaps and bounds. Sister Marie was my guide, but des Roches was almost as patient, and as their Latin discourse was unrelenting, both Lapot and I had to learn or be silent, and neither of us much fancied silence.

In the evenings, Lapot and I would sometimes slip away from all the scholarly discourse and have a cup or two of wine in a tavern. In the little fishing villages along the coast, the wine was excellent and cheap, and the fishermen there, all Basque, seemed to speak every language in the world. Back in Bilbao, when Sister Marie, who was not herself averse to a few cups of wine, had come with us and brought des Roches, we found a crew of a big, deep-water fishing boat – almost as big as a trading round ship. They were drinking good Spanish wine on the dock under the stern of their ship, and invited us to join them for Marie's blessing.

They all spoke English, having fished alongside Englishmen for most of their lives, and they told us about fishing far to the west. Des Roches tried to debate with them, until the older man, clearly the commander, laughed.

'Listen, scholar,' he said with good humour, 'you can tell me that I don't know what I'm saying all you like. But I'm the one with the ship. I've sailed hundreds of miles to the west – aye, more likely a thousand or more. Any fisherman who knows the ocean knows that past Iceland there's the best fishing on the face of God's creation – and land where we can dry our nets and salt our catch.'

I only knew Iceland as a name from the trader who'd provided the Emperor with a falcon to give to Peter of Cyprus. But I mentioned him, and the fishermen nodded.

Michael began to argue.

The fisherman shrugged. 'Have some more wine,' the older man said. 'I can't let you call me a liar, or I'd have to be angry.'

I tell this story because it made des Roches silent for more than a day, and in the end helped us be friends. I think perhaps he didn't want to appear small to Sister Marie, for whom he had an affection. So it was to me he 'confessed'.

'I have been a poor scholar,' he said. 'I want to walk back and tell the fishermen how sorry I am.'

'I suspect they're back at sea,' I said.

He shook his head. We were heading for Santander, right along the coast.

'I allowed my belief in Aristotle to blind me to the fact that they had actual, practical knowledge not in my books,' des Roches said.

'Because you don't believe that there's land in the far west?' I asked.

'It's hard to explain. Because ...' He frowned. 'Because if the ancients did not know a thing, it sets limits on what they knew, and that, in turn, sets limits on what we know.'

Lapot was showing Sister Marie a giant starfish.

'For my part,' I said, 'I have heard before of lands in the far west.'

Des Roches shook his head. 'Plato speaks of Atlantis as a vanished realm, a sunken island,' he said.

My Latin wasn't really good enough to comprehend everything Plato said, so I just smiled.

'I met a man who'd been captured by people in the far west. And then been let go.'

Des Roches shook his head. 'Bloody Aristotle,' he muttered.

We were walking along a beach west of Santander on a glorious, cold morning in March the first time I actually felt confident when speaking Latin to the educated pair. I had been listening since we'd left our cold *albergue* with a bowl of gruel and salt cod, and I was fairly sure I knew what they were saying. And I had struggled through most of a passage of *Timeaus*, and I knew that des Roches was still wondering aloud about lands in the far west.

I said, 'Isn't it true that even if Atlantis sank, there might be other lands of which Plato had never heard?'

Now, to be fair, that's the sentence I'd spent half an hour composing. Or rather, what I would like to have said.

Instead, des Roches, who was just ahead of me, turned. Without the least offence to his tone, he said, 'You're confusing the subjunctive with the optative.'

Sister Marie, on the other hand, said, 'William,' with genuine delight.

Ah, the life of chivalry.

As we walked, we were walking into true spring. The grass was already out in the valleys, but in the most remarkable contrast I've ever known, the upper slopes of every hill were still covered in snow. One day in early May, we walked up into the mountains and had to push our way through heavy snow, and then down into a magnificent valley with bright sunlight so hot that all of us stripped our hoods and rolled up our sleeves. I have never seen snow and broiling sun in the same day anywhere else.

We came down into Oviedo along a track so small that we were all almost certain that we'd lost our way. The trail, for I won't call it a road, wound between giant rocks with a few scrubby pines clinging to the sides, and sometimes vanished in a carpet of dead leaves, so narrow between the rocks that our donkey had to have his panniers removed to fit through, and Michael made a joke about rich men and the eye of the needle.

The trouble was that the donkey took the removal of his panniers as a sign that the cold, wet work day had come to an end, and he was very unhappy at being loaded again on a windswept hillside.

But eventually we came to the top of a very steep pass, and saw the valley of the Nalón river ... or the Nora. I honestly can't remember which.

Regardless, we started down, relieved that even if we weren't on the 'right' path, we were at least on a path. It was a terrible day, with rain squalls off the Atlantic Ocean hitting us periodically between brief moments of chilly sunshine. High up on the mountainside, we were sometimes *above* the rain clouds that were pouring on the valleys, and we'd have the unpleasant experience of walking down through the rain cloud into the driving rain. We were all wet through, cold, and very late because of the narrow track over the pass, and because the donkey was making it clear that he had had enough of carrying our bags.

That donkey saved our lives.

About a third of the way down the steep slope, the donkey ripped his lead from Marie's capable hands and plunged off between two low spruce trees. I was behind the donkey and I followed, my face scratched by the low branches, and I discovered that the donkey was on a track and running.

He'd been fretting since we came to the first defile, now high above us, and Sister Marie later opined that he'd been stung by a bee.

That donkey had all our baggage, save the sausage in our scrips and the staffs in our hands, so the three of us ran down after him, leaving the trail, such as it was.

Our donkey was gone.

At first, Marie told us not to be concerned and she walked off, and I took her at her word and sat down. We were having a moment of sun, and I was content to be off my feet.

But after a quarter of an hour, Marie returned and we knew we had a real problem.

'Let's just follow its tracks,' Lapot said.

I probably looked surprised. Listen, I grew to manhood in London, not Cumbria. I couldn't track a new-shod horse on sand. Michael the scholar looked as thunderstruck as I.

Lapot put his head near the ground, like a hound taking the scent, and then walked off down the little farm track. We passed some sheepfolds and a low byre, and then the ruins of a house.

'Listen,' Marie said suddenly.

Back on the main 'road', there were metallic hoof beats – shod horses clambering over the rocks. We were well off – a third of a league or more – and the bands of drifting cloud obscured our view, but that was not our unshod donkey.

'Stop moving,' I said.

'Tired of being fucking wet ...' came as clear as day through the clouds and across the scrubby furze of the hillside. The voice was Gascon French, and Lapot and I looked at each other and crouched lower.

Grunts. A yip, as if someone was trying to encourage a horse. A low song of voices, and the tinny rattle of horse tack and harness. Armed men on steel-shod horses. I couldn't be sure it was Camus, but ...

'Climb, nag!' spat an angry voice.

They were coming *up* the trail from Oviedo.

But close as the voices sounded, I couldn't see them and they couldn't see me.

'Follow the donkey,' I said quietly, and Lapot went off along the farm track.

Des Roches glanced at me.

'Is there something I need to know?' he asked.

He was both earnest and calm – an easy man to like in a tight spot.

'There's a man trying to kill me,' I said. 'It's very personal. I suspect that's him, over there on the road. We'll just do our best to avoid him, now.'

Des Roches nodded. His eyebrows shot up. He considered for a moment, and then nodded.

'*Eh bien*,' he said.

And that was all. We walked east, almost directly away from Oviedo. Now, in addition to being cold and wet and possibly hunted for our lives and having lost all our baggage, we were going the wrong way.

'Perfect,' Lapot muttered, but he gave his 'I've seen worse' smile and we moved on. The one advantage of the narrow trail was that it was silent – mostly leaf mould underfoot, some mud ...

After a mile or more, we emerged into a fog-shrouded field that sloped sharply away to the east, like a cliff of grass. Somewhere above us there was a sun, but we could not see more than a bowshot.

And there was our donkey, well down the alpine meadow, eating dandelions.

We made our way down the meadow. Sister Marie slipped and fell on the damp grass and cursed – one of the very few times I can remember hearing her curse, using a phrase I was quite surprised that she knew, a coarse term that the *bonnes amies* used. When she got up, her heavy wool gown was soaked and she looked at me.

'I'm thinking we may eat donkey tonight,' she said.

I'd given her a hand up. She made a face.

'Mock me at your peril,' she said.

I turned my head away and we slipped down the hill, leaning on our pilgrim staffs. Closer in, Marie began to call softly to the donkey, who continued to eat dandelions – there was a blazing yellow carpet of them – merely turning to watch us with one broad yellow eye. He appeared to be saying, 'I see what you're doing there ...'

Even with Camus, or the possibility of Camus, somewhere behind me on the same mountainside, the donkey was as funny as any mountebank I've ever known. We'd stumble down the hill and he'd retreat down the meadow, a dozen dandelions hanging from his mouth. He was a sloppy eater and his bit, which was merely rope, was stained green and yellow.

Well, enough of that. When he ran out of dandelions, he just stopped. Lapot walked up to him and picked up his lead.

We'd come all the way to the bottom of the meadow.

'Sweet Jesus, Saviour,' I said.

The meadow rolled away into clouds above us. It was a long way up.

'To the Devil with that,' Lapot said. 'Let's see if there's a road along the river.'

Not that we could see the river. But we had seen it glittering at our feet, and we plunged through the line of trees at the bottom of the field of dandelions and entered into a very different kind of forest – old oaks, widely spread. The ground was damp, but the light rain barely penetrated the forest canopy, and the big trees cut off sound, so that we seemed to be in a different world. We turned back west and walked through the trees for a while, allowing ourselves to slip down the slope towards the hope of the river. It was growing dark.

We came to a little rill, just barely strong enough to cut itself a path through the trees. I dug a pool for it and we filled our pilgrim bottles.

'We should make camp,' I said.

Everyone agreed. We weren't lost, but we were possibly under threat and we didn't really know where we were.

Marie and Michael laid up a shelter of sticks and wet leaves while Lapot and I gathered firewood. It was all oak, and lay about in profligate abundance. No peasant had passed this way in many years – firewood is a commodity like anything else, and any wood like this near London would have been stripped bare. Not in Asturias, apparently.

We had a little sausage and some hard cheese, and we all shared around a good fire, and then, as soon as it was full dark, we pushed into the pile of old leaves and went to sleep. You might expect that we would keep a watch all night and such, but we were in the middle of woods and as we were virtually unarmed, I wasn't altogether sure that having a watch would accomplish much. Once the little fire winked out, Camus would need the Devil beside him to find us.

We slept.

And in the morning, we woke to another day of rain. Our shelter had kept us dry – indeed, Sister Marie had gone to sleep in her wet gown and woke up with it dry, because sleeping bodies have a good amount of heat. I have reason to know. But we had nothing to feed our beast, who was not very happy with us, and we had nothing to feed ourselves.

We went west again, and then down, and about midday, cold, wet, and hungry, we crossed a stone wall and, just like that, we were at the edge of a wide road, heavily gravelled. Just to our left was a broad two-arch bridge over the Nora, and we were virtually in the outworks of Oviedo.

Now, perhaps you think us over-bold, but I still didn't think that Camus would kill us in broad daylight in a major town. Or rather, I thought he might, but I thought it might take some effort on his part, as the people of Oviedo were very courteous to pilgrims. As we climbed towards the cathedral and the central *burgo*, I was given water, wine, a flower, and a small loaf of bread, and the streets were full of people. It was, as it turned out, the end of a market day. It was the feast of Saint Anastasius, or so a respectable matron told me while I split her sausage tart with des Roches. And as an aside, let me say that begging for alms – or rather, accepting alms from willing givers – was curiously satisfying and very humbling. This capable woman simply saw our gowns and approached us with pies.

'I have four that didn't sell,' she said. 'Christ have mercy on us all.'

Des Roches took half, and Sister Marie had the good manners to give the woman a blessing before we started eating. We stood in the magnificent square in front of the equally incredible cathedral, and ate good meat pie. Another man gave me a skin of wine. A priest came and introduced himself to Sister Marie, and we were taken inside the cathedral and given a tour before being sent to an *albergue* maintained by the knights of my order.

We never had to ask after Camus – it was a nine days' wonder in the whole town. A party of Gascon brigands had entered the *burgo* making blasphemous threats, and the men of the guilds had evicted them. At the Hospital, an ageing serving brother smiled at my donat's ring, and served us a fine dinner of sausage and white beans. We were the only pilgrims.

I can't remember his name, but he'd fought at Smyrna in '46 with De Charny, as a man-at-arms. We sat up far too late with Lapot, drinking wine and telling tales. In the end, I told him all my woes, and wrote letters to Gatelussi and to the Count of Savoy and he promised to see them sent.

'The lord in the argent and sable,' the serving brother said. 'A bad man, and a bad enemy.'

'Yes,' I said. 'The very spawn of Satan.'

The brother nodded. 'Aye. I saw him, sitting on his destrier, cursing God.' He shrugged. 'I was once as he is.'

So we prayed together, slightly drunk, and went to our pallets.

We all slept far too late the next day. I didn't rise until after Nones, which shocked me.

Our serving brother smiled at us like a beneficent saint.

'I have found you a small miracle,' he said. 'If you can be on your feet in an hour.'

The good man had found a big hay wagon headed south and west into the mountains, intended for San-Juan-de Villapanada, or some such – see here, I can't make it out because I wrote it in the dark. Aye, pilgrims are supposed to walk, but we rode in a dusty, dry, and very comfortable hay wagon. The farmer had sold all his fodder, but he had some loose straw and a dozen very old carpets in the bottom of the wagon. Our serving brother sent us off with our pilgrim bottles full of wine, and we shared with the farmer.

But our serving brother gave me another gift.

He handed me a good arming sword.

I tried to refuse it, but he shook his head.

'My superior said it was a little like sin for me to cling to it,' he said. 'But here you are, a volunteer of the order – threatened, and on your pilgrimage. Take it with good grace. I ask only that when you arrive at Santiago, you either leave it as an offering or give it to another man who needs a sword.'

I gave him the kiss of peace.

'You are truly a good man, Brother,' I said.

'Those who live by the sword will die by the sword,' he said. 'I was a very bad man, and now I am a bad man trying to be good.'

I girded the sword on my hip when I slipped off the wagon as we passed the little hamlet of Saint-Juan. The wagon never stopped. The farmer, who was a little drunk by then, merely waved, and his four patient horses clip-clopped away, turning back east as they climbed.

The other pilgrims, and there were more than twenty at the *alber-gue*, were none too fond of us. We'd cheated, taking the hay wagon. And further, my sword came in for some comment, as none of the other pilgrims had one.

My pilgrim flask was still full of good red wine. I handed it to a middle-aged man in a grey smock.

'Share with the others,' I said. 'We had trouble with bandits and we lost some time.'

Sister Marie nodded at me as she went to take care of her donkey, and Michael simply sat and put up his feet in the evening sun. But later, we all joined the *albergue*-keeper in fixing dinner – white beans and sausage again, but almost as delicious – and the keeper shared his own wine with us, and we were not sore-pressed. Indeed, looking down the valley from our height, I had reason to think we'd slipped Camus altogether. At Oviedo we'd joined one of the main pilgrim streams, and even the tiny hamlet in which we were staying boasted not one, but two pilgrim hostels. We'd crossed the wilderness and we were now in Asturias, with big mountains, yes, but a good road and farms. Camus could not really expect to find us ...

But, of course, I was afraid. But it was not part of my journey with God to be afraid, and I worked and prayed to put Camus *away*.

That night, Sister Marie led us in Vespers, or as we English say it, Evensong. Like my gift of wine, her prayers increased our popularity, so that, having arrived as lepers because of our hay wagon, we went to bed as respected members of pilgrim society.

I slept with my sword against the wall, ready to my hand. I can be two people.

In the morning, Michael des Roches was up and ready before even Lapot. We went outside into the cold morning air. Dawn was a line of grey-pink on the horizon, more a promise of dawn than the dawn itself, but it was light enough for me to see his face. The makings of a fine day.

'I'm no warrior,' he said. 'I'm not trained to fight, and I'm not sure I believe in it except *in extremis*.' He nodded at the sword I now wore at my waist.

'I understand,' I said, although in fact I'd seen that he kept a cool head in a crisis and was far more reliable a man than I'd expected from a clerk.

'I think I'll leave you here, much as I have enjoyed your company,' des Roches said. 'I'll go down the valley to the plains and follow another route.'

I nodded.

He shrugged. 'I feel that I'm deserting you,' he admitted. 'But in the face of some private vendetta, I feel that I have no place. I hope you understand.'

I was still considering my answers.

Lapot came out of the *albergue*, shouldering his blanket roll.

'Good morning,' he said, with more cheer than he'd ever employed as a mercenary.

Sister Marie came after him. We were the first people out of the place. Either we were the most veteran travellers, or perhaps we were just the lightest sleepers. A chorus of heavy snores came drifting out of the door until Marie closed it.

'Brother Michael wishes to part from us,' I said.

Marie nodded. 'I'll give him a blessing, then,' she said.

I shook my head. 'I can't let him go,' I said carefully.

Des Roches looked at me as if the worst of his fears had just been realised.

'You can't imagine that I'd betray you,' he said.

'I could imagine that, and a good deal worse,' I said. 'But that's not the issue at all.'

'His hair,' Marie said.

'And his height,' I said. 'Listen, Michael – you look too much like I look. You have my hair and my height. They'll take you and kill you in a very cruel way.'

'Blessed Virgin,' he said, crossing himself.

Marie nodded. 'I've been thinking about it,' she said.

Des Roches shook his head. 'Perhaps if ...'

'No,' I said. 'I'm sorry, but I can't let you go and be killed.'

'Surely as soon as these people see that I'm not you ...'

Marie put a hand on his arm in the growing light.

'Michael,' she said, 'you imagine that these are two routiers engaged in some sort of rough and tumble, perhaps over a woman, or gold.'

Des Roches made a face that, in effect, announced that was exactly what he thought.

'The Bourc Camus believes he is a knight of Satan,' she said. 'He *impaled* a pilgrim near Rome. He has killed men and women across Europe for no greater reason than to satisfy his lust for murder.'

'He attempted the murders of both the Cardinal Legate and the Green Count,' I said.

People were stirring in the *albergue* and this was not a public conversation.

'Good God,' Michael muttered. 'Why is he chasing us?'

I rather liked the use of the word 'us'.

'He wants to destroy me. Personally. He's lost any sense of proportion he ever had,' I said.

In fact, even as I said it, I had to ponder the sheer cost of his madness. Pursuing me along the Camino would cost money – money for horses and his men-at-arms.

And this led me to another thought – a thought about how he'd behaved in central France, killing farmers to take food. And his madhouse in Lombardy.

'Why?' Michael asked. 'Why destroy you?'

I knew what Michael was asking. He didn't really want to leave us. If he had, he'd have walked off into the dawn and been strung from a tree in a few miles, if Camus was about. But he didn't really want to leave us. He wanted to understand because that's the kind of man he was.

I raised an eyebrow. 'I've thwarted or defeated him half a dozen times now,' I said. 'But it is much more complicated than that. Walk with us and I'll explain.'

Sister Marie took the lead on the little road.

The road past the *albergue* and into the village was a spur of the old road we'd taken in the hay wagon. The little road ran west, downhill, and appeared to turn in the growing light.

Sister Marie stopped at the churchyard gate, looking both ways. I mention this only because determining our way was an everyday feature of life on our Camino, and, I suspect, the reason Camus took so long to locate us.

There were very few signs. We weren't on an obvious road. We were travelling a web of little paths and farm roads across a sparsely settled mountain range.

I waved at the main road.

Out on the road, where we'd dropped off the wagon, I thought I'd seen a cockleshell scratched into a fence post, and Lapot thought the same. But that was off to the east – the 'wrong' way.

Marie hadn't seen it, and in the early light, she looked disgusted, but we led her off to the left and down a steep incline to where we'd come off the hay wagon. There, in the new sunlight, was the cockleshell.

'That way,' Lapot said.

For a man of few words, he was seldom wrong about directions or any other practical matter.

Sister Marie made a face. Even I, who had supported the idea of coming this way, had to admit that it was counter-intuitive. The road appeared to turn back towards Oviedo.

But we trusted Lapot, and we followed him. The road curved a little and then straightened into a long, sharp, exhausting uphill.

'If this is the wrong way, we're all going to be very sad,' Michael said.

We puffed our way up the hill for the best part of half an hour.

At the top, the road turned west. A small farm drive departed the road to the east, and above us, at the very top of the steep slope, was a huge monastery. We were so early that only a handful of brothers were moving. One was driving sheep out into a pasture. Another was standing with his hands on his hips, watching us. A bell began to ring from the monastery chapel tower, sounding the call to prayer. It was just Prime, and we'd had a very early start.

The tonsured brother watching us gave a wave, and we waved back. He made a gesture in the air, probably a blessing, and turned to answer the call of the bell.

We all stopped. The hill had been steep and long, and we needed to breathe and adjust our straps.

The shepherd brother simply knelt in the pasture. He wasn't far from us, and we all knelt too. I said a few paternosters from habit, and a *Credo*, I expect. Sister Marie prayed silently, and Michael watched the brother with intense curiosity. Lapot prayed, his mumbled French low and growling, at my side.

It was a very beautiful moment.

Then the brother rose to his feet and came over to Marie. They exchanged a few words of Latin, and then she smiled.

'We are on the right road. He says we're in for a long day, and we should stay the night at the monastery of San Salvador de Cornellana on the Narcea river.'

174

He blessed us and Sister Marie blessed him. I still smile to think of these two devout people engaged in a sort of ritual duel of goodness. But eventually they stopped speaking Latin, and we turned west and started walking.

The countryside was breathtaking – the mountains high and some distant ones still capped in snow – and the trail wound down through fertile farm fields and then climbed a ridge to another incredible view out over the valleys below. Already, in the distance, we could make out what was probably the valley of the Narcea, but we had the oak highlands all to ourselves – a good road, but very lonely.

'Now, tell me why you and this evil man are locked in a combat,' Michael said.

I remember breathing the clear air of the hillside, admiring the sun on the new spring flowers, and feeling as if I was being given a vision of the Grail.

'I was a routier in France,' I said. 'So was Camus. I did many evil deeds, and I will not pretend that any difference between us was strictly a matter of degree. But ... my life was changed by Father Pierre Thomas—'

'The Franciscan?' des Roches asked, as if this was the first interesting thing that I'd said. 'I heard him debate in Paris. A brilliant man.'

'The very same,' Sister Marie said. 'I was one of his secretaries.'

Des Roches took this in. We walked a way.

'Father Pierre Thomas changed me,' I said. 'There were other men and women involved in the change – he didn't work any miracle—'

Marie laughed. 'So you say. I knew you then.'

'I joined the Hospital as a donat, and tried to change my life,' I said, hoping that I sounded humble, and not like a pious hypocrite. It all sounded thin, spoken rapidly on a long hillside in Spain.

'And then Camus hated you for your reformed life,' des Roches said. 'Yes, I have seen this before.'

'When I came back from the Holy Land,' I said.

'You were ...?'

'Jerusalem, Acre, Sydon, Tyre, and then Constantinople,' I said. 'And Alexandria.'

Michael smiled, but he sighed.

'I feel the worm of envy,' he said.

'Alexandria was Hell come to earth,' I said.

We all walked in silence for a bit. Lapot and I were probably reliving a little bit of our own vision of Hell.

'Anyhow,' I said, 'when I came back from the crusade, Camus was madder, if anything. Clean wode, and yet steeped in evil like good leather in a brew of oak gall.'

'How very pious you sound,' Marie said with a smile. 'Of course, William here pokes Camus the way boys will poke a wasps' nest. In fact, if one didn't know how very much better William is than his former self, you might think he took a joy in tormenting Camus and humiliating him.'

I glared at her. 'That's not true—'

'Did Camus ride out of Milan with his bare arse glowing in the sun?' she asked.

I was silent.

'So he really hates you,' Michael said.

'Oh yes,' I said.

A little before Sext, we came to the top of a ridge and looked down into the valley of the Narcea. Far below us, the line of the river shone in the spring sun. We could smell woodsmoke, see the great monastery of San Salvador laid out like a model across the river, and there was a fine stone bridge. We passed a slow-moving train of donkeys going down, and the bells of Sext rang out as we reached the bridge. There, I saw four monks fishing in the river, their horsehair lines wet and silvery in the bright sun. Even in the middle of the day they were catching trout, and half an hour later, over small beer, a tonsured monk talked to me about catching salmon in the spring and autumn.

They also told us that an armed party on horseback had passed the day before, presumably headed for the main pilgrim route at Léon.

It was only midday, and despite the evident hospitality of the good brothers, we chose to walk on towards Salas, where there was a local lord with a castle. But in the afternoon we were cautious, crossing open fields one at a time and climbing the high ridges with a sense of relief, because horses would be very difficult on the heights.

Sometime in mid-afternoon, I came to a conclusion. Or rather, I'd come to the conclusion almost instantly that morning, and spent all day examining it.

'I need to go after Camus,' I said.

Lapot raised an eyebrow and smiled his cautious smile.

Sister Marie sighed. 'I thought we'd discussed this,' she said. 'If you are not serious about your pilgrimage ...'

I shook my head. 'It's not that, *Bonne Soeur*. It is that I feel responsible for the damage he does. In Provence, he killed peasants when he could just have taken their food. He employs others of his stamp.'

Lapot nodded.

Marie made a sound very much like my mother's 'hmf'.

'Are you sure you are not justifying pride and murder?' she asked.

We walked for a while.

'I can't be on pilgrimage, my soul at peace with the Lord, while this man tries to kill people,' I said.

'Some of whom will be us,' Lapot said. 'I'm sorry, Sister, but I'm with William.'

Marie made a face.

'Let me add,' I said, 'that I don't believe he will expect us to turn on him.'

'Does that count as a moral justification?' Marie asked, and des Roches laughed.

'Perhaps it counts as a military justification,' I said. 'Better to finish him now than to face him on the road somewhere.'

Des Roches raised an eyebrow, his step firm.

'I like you,' he said. 'But I'm not convinced ...'

Lapot nodded. 'That's fine, lad,' he said. 'Leave it to us.'

That evening we slipped into Salas. We were cautious passing the castle until we saw the stables mostly empty. Michael unbent sufficiently to look into all three of the *albergues*, although I couldn't imagine Camus using one.

Salas was empty of enemies. Camus had to be criss-crossing the mountains, trying to catch me, but as I said, there are four or six or ten parallel routes to Santiago, and he no doubt had as much trouble finding us as we had finding the right paths. Or more.

And as he was on horseback, he was limited in his routes, whereas we had a good pilgrim itinerary, held by des Roches, and we were sticking to any route that threatened a good climb.

Of course, he had other options. Assuming he was willing to burn silver like firewood, he could recruit watchers. And, as if by some sort of eldritch association of ideas, I no sooner had this thought than I noticed a young, thin man with a scraggly blond beard and bad teeth watching me from the gateway of the castle.

I smiled at him and went into the *albergue* that Sister Marie had chosen.

Around Vespers, we all went out to the beautiful little church, and I noticed that Snaggle-Tooth never came into the church, but he was outside, and he wouldn't meet my eye.

That night, after we prayed, I read Michael's itinerary. I noted that after Salas came Tineo, at least if we wanted to stay on the high ground, and after Tineo a variety of choices.

The *albergue*-keeper was an old man who'd been to Santiago six times. He pointed at the little illumination of the name 'Tineo' with a small castle keep.

'Two ways,' he said. 'Not just one.'

With help from a French pilgrim and des Roches, we translated his advice, and Sister Marie wrote it in the margins of our itinerary. In short, he said that after Tineo you could have a short day and stop at Trones or the monastery at San Facundo, or a daring pilgrim could go all the way to Borres.

'A dangerous little town,' the *albergue*-keeper said. 'They are very wild people up there.'

I tried not to smile, as Salas was smaller than the town in which my parents had had their farm. In fact, except for the castle, Salas was smaller than many English manor farms.

The Frenchman made a little motion to indicate that he did not agree.

'There is a good *albergue* up in the mountains,' he said. 'Run by a Hospital brother. Good wine, and two little shelters lower down in case you get caught in the snow.'

'Snow?' Marie asked.

'It is a very hard route,' our keeper said. 'The longest climb on the whole Camino.'

He served us another wooden cup of wine and went to his own bed.

The Frenchman was dismissive. 'On a good day it is incredibly beautiful,' he said. 'Both of the other ways are much longer.'

I thanked him for his advice.

I thought it all over.

Sister Marie sat down next to me in the courtyard. Des Roches and Lapot were hanging our laundry, and that of another pilgrim who'd just come in.

'You want to take this high route,' she said.

'Yes,' I said.

'And you want to take Camus there,' she said.

I nodded. 'Steep trails and a Hospitaller *albergue*?' I said. 'Almost ideal.'

She let out a breath – very like a deep sigh.

'All right,' she said. 'I'm in. Camus tried to kill Father Pierre Thomas, and I am not capable of judging your inner devotions. Indeed, it would be a sin if I thought I was. I hope you do this for the reasons that you have said.'

'I hope so, too,' I said. 'I've been round and round.'

'And?'

'Why am I a knight, if not to rid the world of creatures like Camus?'

'Are you not arrogating to yourself the justice that is God's?' Marie asked.

I nodded. 'Yes,' I said. 'That's an important part of knighthood.'

'Be careful,' she said. 'If you are wrong, you not only commit murder, but you defy God's will.'

I nodded. 'You cannot convince me that killing Camus is a sin,' I said.

She gave a slight smile. But she didn't agree.

Another very early morning. We had stale bread and small beer, and we were away. But of course, I have forgotten the most important part.

I went out to collect Marie's donkey and there was a thick mist, which was not uncommon in the mornings. Snaggle-Tooth was already awake, sitting by the side of the barn that was shared by all three *albergues*, and I nodded to him and wished him a good morning as I passed.

'How far to Tineo?' I asked.

He mumbled something in Galician, and then in Spanish, about it being a day's journey.

I nodded. If Camus was off searching the southern route, it was unlikely that he'd be able to reach Tineo before us. Unlikely, but not impossible.

Back in the *albergue*, I asked the keeper if he knew the blond man with the bad teeth.

'Marcos?' the keeper laughed. 'A useless man. He won't work, and he's no man's friend.' He shook his head. 'My cousin, of course. I feed him.'

Well. No reason to make this too easy. Marcos would talk to his cousin and find that we'd been asking about the high route, the *Hospitales* route. Or he wouldn't.

Mostly what I remember of that day was that the farmers were manuring their fields, and every nook and cranny of Asturias smelt of cow manure. And the worst of it was coming down after our initial climb out of Salas, and we came to a little crossroads, where two little village trails come together. It was damp – ordinarily there was probably a puddle.

Today, it was a pool of liquid cow manure.

The face Sister Marie made as she kirtled up her gown to walk across was so funny that, for a mile, I forgot Camus altogether. She was barefoot in sandals, and I think she was more fastidious than she allowed us to know.

Women are more interesting than they often seem, to men. Perhaps I had too much time to think on Camino, but I was getting to know Sister Marie in a level of intimacy that was almost like marriage. Of course, she was older than I was, and yet as we walked I realised that forty, or thirty-nine, was not so very old. And I became interested in her, not as a bed-warmer or even as a Latin teacher. I had time to see how she was many people in one person. Teaching a Spanish peasant to use her staff as a weapon, she was all business. Reading prayers in an *albergue*, she was like a saint – and crossing ankle-deep manure, she was like an angry adolescent. Sometimes she was very much a woman, and sometimes not.

When you are a young man, all women are a bit of a mystery – older women even more mysterious, and also a little unnecessary, as they aren't interested in one thing that interests you. Nuns are worst of all, as they combine all that mystery and lack of interest with moral authority. And yet, here I was crossing Spain with a middle-aged nun, and she was very obviously a complicated mortal like the rest of us.

There, I've let slip my wisdom. I had seen Sister Marie be a bit of an imp before, but starting with caustic comments about the manure and the peasants and animals that had produced it, she was a little freer in her comments, and we all loved her better for it.

Regardless, we made it through the sea of manure and up the next ridge. When we came to a beautiful wild stream, both banks covered in flowers, she sat down and put her sandalled feet into the stream and dared me to comment.

I really only mention this to say that with veterans like Lapot and Sister Marie, you can laugh even when Camus is hunting you through the mountains of Asturias.

We came down into Tineo from the hills above, and we were very tired – it had been a long day. In fact, one of the things I remember best of that journey was how often the itinerary was inaccurate as to distance. It became a running jest – amusing, except for our feet. If Camus had caught me stumbling down the stony ridge above Tineo, he might have killed me and I wouldn't have cared much.

And after a day of wading through cow manure, you'd think we might have had some decent beef with our dinner, but for whatever reason the good farmers of Asturias were too much in love with their cattle to kill them. We were offered pork, and more pork – sausage, bacon, hocks, in soups, in stews – and never a shred of beef, although we walked through cattle all day. That evening we all drank too much, as if to make up for the rudeness of our host, who seemed to be the only man in Asturias who didn't like the very pilgrims on whom he waited. I did take the trouble to brag to him about the speed of our passage, and to mention that we'd make the next day a short day and go only to the next monastery.

And if you imagine that we should have been on watch for Camus, well, we should have. But we weren't. I was confident that he was south and east, and I was drunk on two cups of wine before I realised how foolish I'd been. I still wasn't exactly good at walking. I ended every day more tired than I expected, so a cup of wine or two would send me off.

We had smaller rooms that night. I shared with Sister Marie, and des Roches and Lapot shared the best room in the inn. You'd be hard put to decide who was more embarrassed – me or des Roches. But Sister Marie went and changed in another room and I did laundry, and by the time I'd finished our whites, she was snoring away softly and I was able to get into the clean white sheets without embarrassment. I was gone in moments.

Now, it would have served me right if Camus's greasy hand had clamped over my mouth in the night. But that's not how it played. In fact, in my arrogance, I was *almost* correct, as you'll see.

We awoke to an incredible level of bustle and activity for a cold, foggy morning in the mountains, and a most miraculous smell, and discovered that we'd overslept (how many errors can a captain compound?) and that the town's famous orange market was opening under our windows. The oranges of Tineo are as a big as a baby's head and tart like a perfect apple, and we each bought two on our way out of our *albergue*. Despite my many errors, I had got the clothes clean and hung them by the kitchen fire before I went to bed, so that we were all clean enough and bathed, and the smell of the oranges lingered in our noses as we climbed out of the town, heading south and west towards the monastery.

But once we passed the woods on the valley floor, we struck off across country, and climbed into the ridges above.

As we climbed, we first went out of the morning mists, allowing us to look back along the valley, and we could see for miles.

And there was the glitter of metal off to the east.

'Camus?' Lapot asked.

I shrugged. 'Half a dozen riders, with some armour,' I said.

Sister Marie stopped and looked back where I was stopped.

She shrugged.

'As God wills it,' I said.

She made a face.

We watched them, on and off, all day. They rode into Tineo as we came to the head of the valley, in mid-afternoon. And I watched with enormous satisfaction as they turned away, glittering in the afternoon sun, about half an hour later. They raised dust passing south and west, towards the monastery. We watched them go.

Des Roches smiled. 'You are a very clever man,' he said.

I winked at Lapot.

'Sometimes,' I said. 'Not last night, when we kept no watch.'

'God watches over fools, lovers and pilgrims,' Marie said, quite a bit more acerbically than I felt was needed.

'God also makes the cow manure,' I mentioned, and she flushed.

It was a good plan, and I'd laid my trap expertly. It was a pity that almost no part of it came off the way I'd planned, but then, given the size of Asturias and the complexity, it's probably some kind of miracle that we'd ever seen Camus at all.

CHAPTER TWO

HOSPITALES ROUTE, CAMINO DE SANTIAGO, SPAIN

May 1369

We walked down into Borres with tired feet and very high hearts. We'd seen Camus – and I was sure it was Camus – headed off to the south. He'd get to the monastery too late to ride here, at the base of the serious mountains.

Borres is a town so small that it didn't have a place in our itinerary until we wrote it in. About fifty houses huddle together on a mountainside, and every house has a barn built into it. The houses are *above* the barns, so that the heat of the beasts warms the peasants. There are cows on the hillsides, and the hills are so steep that the cows appear to have one pair of legs shorter than the other to allow them to move on the steep slopes.

The track runs up a long, narrow valley, with increasing herds on both sides, and then suddenly, the trail ends at a pilgrim fountain – really, an ancient cattle trough. But some thoughtful pilgrim had carved a message into the cattle trough, with arrows – to the left, 'beer' and to the right, 'bed'.

Now, the great fear of everyone on Camino is to get to some distant village and find that there is no room in the *albergue*. Then you either have to sleep under the stars, which is cold and wet even for old soldiers like me, or walk on another few leagues, and at Borres, you have to go all the way up to the top of the mountain to reach the Hospital – impossible in late afternoon. The mountain rose above us like a threat, its top covered in clouds. It was so high above us that it reminded me a little of Corinth, or Parnassus.

Sister Marie took Lapot and headed to the *albergue* – 'bed'. They went to secure us a place. Michael and I went to the left, towards 'beer', to secure food.

We climbed out of the little valley and passed half a dozen little houses atop their barns, all stone, and then a big tomcat sleeping on the back of a cow. He raised a sleepy head – it was hot in the afternoons – and gave a yawn.

We went up, through streets that smelt like barn stalls – cow and horse, with a touch of pig. There was hay in every barn, and some straw. They weren't rich, but neither were these people poor.

We were in the little town proper – narrow streets like Venice, with stone barn walls on either hand that rose, windowless, up to a second storey of wood. Up above us was a statue of the Virgin, and to the left I spotted a sign that had to be the inn, such as it was.

It proved to be the front room of a house, naturally, set above a barn. The front of the inn had once been a grain storage loft, and the 'common room' was smaller than many a monk's cell. The proprietress was serving her family an early supper, visible through a curtain of beads. She shouted a cheerful greeting in the local patois – at least, we assumed it was a greeting.

There was just one table. Michael and I sat down and waited a few minutes, our stomachs rumbling at the smell of the woman's food.

She emerged, a strong, practical-looking woman whose age did not erase the signs of a fine figure and a wicked sense of humour.

'Pilgrims?' she asked in good French.

'*Si, donna,*' Michael replied in Spanish.

She smiled. '*Bière, gentilhommes?*'

'*Oui,*' I said, and she laughed.

The beer was surprisingly good for a village smaller than many barns in England. I sat back against the wall, savouring the taste. Michael raised his jack and we grinned at each other. We'd both been in such a hurry to drink our beer that our hoods were still on.

That was the moment when the low outer door opened, and a man came in wearing a rusty haubergeon. He wore a sword, but he didn't have it in his hand.

It wasn't Camus. But it didn't really matter whether it was Camus or not.

I rose, flipping back my hood.

Rusty-Maille glanced at me and froze. Then he, very competently, went for a cross-body draw, putting his left hand out to stop me from closing.

'Stop, you idiots!' shouted the woman. Actually, I have no idea what she shouted, but I'm guessing it was to that effect.

Rusty-Maille turned to face me, his sword halfway out of his scabbard, his sword hand well back.

Des Roches shocked both of us by slamming his oak stool into the man's head.

He fell at my feet, out in one blow.

Des Roches looked at me. He shrugged.

'I decided you had to be a man of honour,' he said.

The woman looked at me.

I ignored her.

'You think he's alone?' des Roches asked, but I was already out on the grain storage balcony, looking down over the street. Just one horse. No accomplice.

Remember, friends – your opponents are never giants. That one man told me a great deal. Because he was alone, he told me that Camus was frustrated, and perhaps almost desperate. Of course, since we'd knocked him unconscious, we were sending Camus a positive report no matter what …

He must have broken his retinue into maybe four single riders? Keeping four or five men under his hand? So he'd reached the monastery west of Tineo, discovered we'd never gone that way, and sent his men out perhaps eight hours ago.

Or … Sweet Christ.

Michael and I spoke together, except he said 'Sister Marie' and I said 'Lapot'.

I put a piece of silver on the trestle table. The woman behind the bar was watching us, and her husband was behind with a cudgel.

'Bandits,' Michael said, with great presence of mind. 'They've been following us.'

'God and the Saints be with us,' the woman muttered.

The man looked unconvinced.

I knelt, took Rusty-Maille's sword belt and bound his wrists.

'Let's go,' I said. 'Tell the donna we'll be back.'

Michael said something in Spanish.

We were out of the door. It was a beautiful red-gold sunset, and we ran back past the tomcat and the cattle and the trough, and then more cautiously up the far hill. It was a perfect place for an ambush. We were coming up a steep incline on a rough trail with a few carved steps, and the sides of the gully were steep. We were, in effect, fish in a pond.

It had occurred to both of us that there must have been two men – and they'd split at the watering trough.

What hadn't occurred to either of us was that no one could have brought a horse this way. So we came out at the top of the gully to see a fine brick and stone *albergue*. Sister Marie was outside with the keeper, a local man, and he was helping her hang clothes on a line in the dying light.

I was about to call out when I heard the clip-clop of hooves on the road. Of course, until that moment I had no idea that there *was* a road – but in one sound I knew there was a different way of reaching Borres, and the second rider had no doubt gone around.

'Keep talking,' I said as I slipped past Marie. 'Michael, stand right there with your hood off.'

Red hair.

The second rider came up the road cautiously until he saw Michael. By then, I was in the trees that fringed the yard of the *albergue*. I had Marie's staff in my hand. Call me mad, but I was on Camino and I didn't want to kill.

He saw Michael, assumed he was seeing me, and froze. I guess that he couldn't decide between getting the reward for himself or going for help.

He never even glanced at me as I slid out from behind the tree and swung the staff. His horse didn't even start. The gelding flinched when his rider fell off, but I gentled him and got him under control, and Lapot, who was a very quick man, already had a dagger at the man's throat. I hadn't even seen him emerge from the *albergue*.

Lapot looked at me over the prostrate man.

'What took you so long?' he asked. 'And who the hell is this?'

'Michael and I stopped for a beer,' I said. 'And one of Camus's bravos came in.'

'And did you bring us beer?' Lapot asked.

This from a man on his way to becoming a monk, who was sitting with his knees on another man's arm, casually going through his purse.

'We ...' Michael sounded embarrassed.

Marie laughed. 'I don't know why I find you so funny, when it's so obvious that you have been such bad men,' she said.

The *albergue*-keeper looked as if all the demons of Hell had just emptied onto the road.

'We were attacked by bandits,' Michael said, again, or something like it, in Spanish. His Spanish was enough like Italian that I could sometimes follow it. 'They followed us.'

People don't like violence. The *albergue*-keeper was shocked at what had happened, and he wanted to run.

Sister Marie spoke to him very gently, in good Castilian Latin.

'What if Camus is out there in the darkness, waiting for his scouts?' Lapot asked.

'Fuck,' I said, or something similar.

Lapot raised an eyebrow, having finished his search.

'Nothing,' he said. 'Not even money.'

The scout did not have a convenient letter from Camus outlining his plans, or a juicy piece of incrimination, or even some sign of Satan worship. He had a good horn comb, a cheap brass ring, and a horn needle case that didn't even have any needles in it. He didn't have a maille shirt, either, but a filthy leather-covered haketon and a falchion so old it might have been a relic.

'A poor routier mounted on a good gelding,' Lapot said. 'We should kill him.'

'We're on Camino!' I said.

Lapot shrugged. 'I know. I mean, in a worldly, secular way, we should kill him. The *albergue* is empty. We can hole up here – it's quite defensible.'

I had the horse through all this conversation, and at some point I discovered that the thing pushing into my head from the saddle was the prod of a light crossbow.

'He has a crossbow,' I said.

'Better and better,' Lapot said.

He was right. I didn't fancy fleeing into the darkness on a cold, wet mountainside. Just because the afternoons were hot didn't mean the nights weren't as cold as a cold Hell.

I took the crossbow off the horse and tossed it to Lapot.

'I'd rather *know*,' I said, and swung into the saddle.

Marie was still chiding me as I turned the horse's head and trotted off into the gathering murk.

The road was narrow. I could smell the rich loam, manure, and oak tree smells coming off the farms. I could hear pigs, and a woman was clearly yelling at her useless man – that's a sound that seems to be international.

I liked the horse. Without being anything like a champion, he was a good animal, obedient, even trained. Not quite a real warhorse, but better than many plugs. As we rode, I loosened my Hospitaller's sword in the scabbard and used my knees to move my mount left and right. We could fight, as long as he wasn't shy.

You may think I'm a braggart, or too bold – mayhap a fool. But with a good sword and a decent horse, I assumed I was a match for any three men. I was willing to have a go at riding right into Camus's men-at-arms and killing him. And before you call me a fool, remember that we'd been followed for days. I was fed up.

And yes, it seems remarkable to me, now, that I thought to kill men so that I could go back to the contemplation of God.

As I rode out of Borres and then east along the switchbacks – east, west, east, west – night fell, and suddenly it was absolutely black, not just under the thick oak trees but out on the road. There were stars, but that was all.

I halted, listening. I'd come a long way – half a league, or perhaps more. I was out of Borres. I hadn't passed a farm for five minutes.

Wolves howled. You know that sound? It is chilling at the best of times.

The wolves were above me, on the mountain.

I'm not really a woodsman. But I am an old soldier. I sat on that horse, listening, for as long as a man might say two or three paternosters.

What I heard was a normal, healthy night. Birds – owls, especially. Wolves, chilling as they might be, and not so far away, so my horse raised and lowered a forefoot with a certain 'what are we doing here, boss?' sound.

No bandit moves on a mountainside in full darkness. You can die of a fall, or just break your ankle. And best of all, some of my opponents were on expensive horses, which meant that they wouldn't try following shepherds' paths.

It took me almost an hour to ride back the distance I'd come down in ten minutes. In full darkness, the road seemed incredibly narrow, and my good gelding was a little spooked and became a handful, trying to rub me off on walls and taking too bloody long to calm down, but finally I saw candlelight, heard pigs, and in a few minutes I was dismounting in the open yard of the *albergue* among all the clean, wet laundry.

'William!' Sister Marie said from the doorway. 'Do *not* do that again.'

'I had to be sure,' I said.

Lapot emerged from one of the upstairs windows – there were only four. I saw the curve of the crossbow's prod in his arms.

The *albergue* was built like a little castle – a nice arched doorway and a single window by it on the ground floor, one window on each face on the second floor. No kitchen, no jakes, no well.

Marie shook her head. 'This is not the pilgrimage I had planned,' she said with a certain spark, or perhaps snark.

'I'm sorry,' I said. I dismounted. 'Where are our prisoners?'

'On beds inside,' Marie said. 'They're waiting dinner for us over at the tavern. There are now a dozen other pilgrims.'

'Damnation!' I spat.

'Exactly,' Lapot said. He'd come down the steps.

We didn't have to discuss it. It was simple. If we were alone, we had no witnesses and no hostages. But with a dozen other latecomers, our private war would be very public.

'Blessed Virgin,' I muttered. I may have said something much worse.

'Trust in God,' Marie said. 'Listen – the two bravos are out. They're in pilgrim beds. They're tied, but under blankets. With a little luck, we're gone before they awake.'

I shook my head – I do not like living from moment to moment. Or counting on luck, or even on God's providence. In my experience, and I am a pious man, God tends to favour the side with the better horses, the superior food, and the better planning.

On the other hand, as I said to the rest of them while we walked to dinner, I'd wanted to lure Camus to the mountains, and now he was somewhere not too far away.

'We eat,' Lapot said. 'We go straight to bed, leaving one of us on watch. Four watches, two hours each by the church bells. We rise at Matins and we're gone up the mountain in the last of the night.'

'No one moves fast on a mountain in the dark,' I said.

Michael was surprisingly good at this.

'It won't matter,' he said. 'Once we're off the village streets, we're on the moon for all Camus will know.'

Well . . .

We went into dinner in the tiny tavern. There were now sixteen pilgrims, and I looked at them all with suspicion, but they all looked to me like the real thing. There was an English couple – merchants of London. The rest of them were all French, mostly from Aquitaine, and thus, at least technically, as English as I am. From them we got a good idea of how difficult the Prince of Wales's rule of Aquitaine had become. I had not known, until that night, that the Prince of Wales had declared himself to be in a state of war with the Comte d'Armagnac.

A horse-faced smith from the Dordogne shook his head.

'It'll be war as soon as the ground is soft,' he said. 'Back to the bad days of my youth. The king of France thinks he can defeat the prince and retake all the country round, and our Edward is old and ailing.'

Well. It may seem odd to hear a Frenchman say in French 'our Edward', but in fact a great many of the good people of Aquitaine had benefited from English rule.

One of the oddest aspects of Camino, and the hardest to explain, is that even with Camus's pursuit and all the attendant worry, Camino cuts you off from worldly things. You walk, you talk, you pray. The conversation in Borres woke me up to another world. I wasn't really just a pilgrim. I was a knight, with men-at-arms and responsibilities. And I was English, and if England was about to go to war, I might have a role to play.

Not very holy thoughts. But I had *not* been thinking them. I'd been thinking about violence, and eternity, and the Trinity, and the Virgin, and the Christ child.

It was all a bit of a shock, and I suspect this is how priests and nuns feel when we rude soldiers come to visit them. *Must we speak of profane matters?*

There were also two Dominicans – both priests. They were silent for a while, and then, when they discovered that Lapot intended to become a priest, they were . . . rude. Almost savage.

'You were a routier?' the smaller one asked in a drawl of poor French.

'I was,' Lapot said with genuine humility.

'Perhaps you should consider serving as a brother with one of the fighting orders,' the small, tonsured man said. He had a narrow face, thick eyebrows and bright eyes. His name was Domenico, of course.

'The priesthood is for those with a genuine calling,' the other man said. He was taller, wider – in fact, he seemed very well fed indeed. He was Père Bartolomeo. 'What you need is penance.'

Sister Marie glanced at the Dominicans in surprise.

'We all need penance, brother.'

'Father,' the Dominican said. He made a motion with his hand. 'I am your spiritual superior.'

Sister Marie, being older, wiser, and a veteran of many church spats, didn't even smile back. She looked down at the beads at her belt for a bit, and then went back to her food, which was *not pork*. It was a delicious, slightly spicy fish soup with a little pork sausage. The lady who ran the tavern was a magnificent cook. She had also decided, as women sometimes do, that I was 'all right', and she poured me a second helping with a smile. She'd also given Michael exact directions on how to cross the pass. The '*Hospitales*'.

Lapot was very slightly flushed.

'A former routier will do no credit to Christ,' Domenico said. 'But perhaps cleaning stables . . .'

The other pilgrims looked away.

Well. I wasn't under any vows. I smiled, leaning back.

But Michael beat me to it. 'That's a very dangerous path to take, is it not?' he asked.

The Dominicans looked at him.

'I mean,' Michael said, 'are you not arrogating to yourself the role of God in judging the worthiness of any man or woman to become a vessel of God's will?'

Père Bartolomeo shrugged. 'We are Dominicans,' he said. 'We know God.'

'Ah,' Michael said. 'I'd assumed you were Dominicans. If you didn't know God, it would all sound remarkably like hot air and arrogance.'

I laughed aloud. Now, perhaps that was ill-considered, but they were a pair of arses, and their attack on Lapot made me angry. Also, as I no doubt say too often, I'd learnt a great deal about the Church on crusade with Father Pierre Thomas. I knew a bad priest on sight, as it were. I still do – arrogant as that may sound.

Any road, some of the other pilgrims laughed with me.

Père Domenico got to his feet, his face flushed. He was going to pronounce something, I could tell.

I fixed him with my gaze. I don't do this often – it's not nice. But I know when I use it.

'You should be careful, Father,' I said.

He looked at me with contempt. 'Because you are a man of violence?' he asked. 'Because you would threaten me?'

'Because I know the Pope,' I said. 'Personally. And what you say is rank heresy.'

Silence fell over the whole table.

'You know the Pope?' Père Domenico asked.

'I had a private audience with him less than six months ago,' I said. I flashed my Hospitaller ring. 'And this worthy nun has a writ *from the Pope* in her scrip. Which I daresay is more than you have, *Father*.' I smiled.

Perhaps watching them fawn on us was revenge, but I'd have liked them better or thought more of them if they'd stayed arrogant.

Well. I'm a great follower of Aquinas, but give me Franciscans any day.

We woke very early, and we had the donkey loaded with our damp, cold laundry in no time. Lapot stood by with the crossbow, watching over us. We left by the road, so as to be as confusing as possible and to leave no tracks, and almost as soon as we started we realised that we were moving in thick fog.

'This isn't a fog,' Sister Marie insisted. 'We're inside a rain cloud.'

It wasn't merely dark. It was dark, cold, and very damp, and the lights in the homes of early rising farmers in Borres were like little halos in the dark cloud.

However, the cheerful woman at the tavern, who'd cooked us the delightful fish soup, had given us all the tools we required, and Michael led confidently into the darkness. In moments he turned at a tall stone pillar, and we were climbing away on a track no wider than my arm is long, but well-gravelled underfoot.

'I gave the horses to the taverner,' Lapot said behind me.

I had to smile. You cannot buy loyalty …

But sometimes you can rent it. Two good geldings?

'I warned them all about Camus,' I said.

'As did I,' Sister Marie said. 'I even warned the Dominicans.'

'You *are* a good person,' I said.

We walked into the clouds.

At first the incline was slow. We walked up and up, into the damp darkness, and the only sounds were our own and the donkey's. I was leading the donkey that morning, and I was comfortable enough, in good wool, but I was not hot. If anything, it was cold that threatened us when we stopped at a little church to break our fast. There wasn't much light – but we were walking through a sheet of grey mist, and the church appeared as if by magic. It had a deep porch lined in benches, almost like a knight's hall without walls. In Asturias, many churches are built like this, so that desperate pilgrims can sleep on the church porch.

We had bread and sausage and cheese, and Michael had had the foresight to buy a skin of wine, and it's just as well that we ate a hearty meal in the light of what came after.

While we were tidying up the crumbs, as Fra Peter Mortimer used to say, we heard the sound of horses.

In heartbeats, Lapot had the crossbow cocked, and I was standing with the sword in my hand. And to my near shock, Sister Marie had a short, broad sword in *her* hand and Michael des Roches had the routier's sword from our encounter in the tavern. Sister Marie also produced a buckler …

Well, well.

The horses didn't sound right for a troop of sell-swords, and indeed, as the fog brightened to a good, solid leaden grey, a farm cart pulled by two big horses appeared up the *other* lane. Four grey-clad pilgrims rolled out. They were clearly embarrassed to have been caught riding and not walking. They didn't meet our eyes, and by the time they'd paid their farmer, our weapons had vanished. Except Lapot's. He kept the crossbow spanned and aimed until the wagon was gone. The four pilgrims started off into the mist.

Michael watched them go.

Sister Marie made a face. 'God may excuse us defending ourselves against Camus,' she said. 'But I can't imagine God forgiving us for a massacre of innocent pilgrims we mistook for Camus's brigands.'

Lapot looked at me. 'I'm worried that every one of these poor people is in danger because of us.'

I nodded. 'We've done what we can,' I said as I put my bag back on my shoulder. 'He could be down on the main pilgrim route, but we've lured him here. Now he's on the least travelled of all the routes.'

Michael smiled. 'Besides,' he said, 'those four all just went the wrong way.'

In my flurry of spirit, I had missed that all four had walked off down the trail we'd just climbed. From Borres.

'Let's go,' I said.

I will never forget the *Hospitales* as long as I live. It's not just that it is hard – it is. Or beautiful – you'll hear. It is the closest I'll ever come to walking to Heaven. And the fog added to the mystery.

Of course, it also wrecked my plan.

By the time our lungs were working like forge-bellows, and our thighs burned as if molten lead and not blood ran through our limbs, we were probably half a league above the valley below, but we couldn't see any more than we'd seen at the little church. We walked and walked, and all we could see was the ground beneath our feet – gravel, shale, dirt, grass, then back to gravel.

Up and up.

We passed a cairn. We were veteran pilgrims by then, and cairns of stones marked the highest point, where pilgrims would leave a stone to cheer other travellers.

Lies. Or we were not the first *Hospitales* walkers to be caught in deep fog.

After the cairn, it was flat for a few hundred yards ... and then we were climbing again.

About Terce, we came to the first of the shelters – a low house, well built out of stone, with a dirt floor and good fireplace. No one had stayed the night. We had a drink of water, filled our bottles from the spring, and fed the donkey.

We couldn't see twenty paces. We couldn't hear anything.

Camus could be right behind us, and we wouldn't know. My whole plan had been based on having a long lead and time to watch him come, and now we were walking through a dense fog that killed sight and sound, too.

Let me add one important detail. On the *Hospitales* route, we did know one thing in our favour. Camus wasn't ahead of us, unless he had been lent wings by Satan. It was thirty miles to Berducedo on the other side of the mountains, at least by horse road. Our footpath was shorter, if much steeper. He wasn't going to get ahead of us.

Better yet, at the top of the pass, at the Hospitaller *albergue*, the path split in three, and each of the three came down a different route and ended in a different village on the Berducedo side.

Anyway, my hope had been to make Camus dismount and shed armour and follow us into the mountains, but the deeper we plodded into the fog, the more foolish that plan seemed. Why would he come up after us? Why not just wait? Further along the pilgrim road, all the paths started coming together. Lugo was a famous town – all the pilgrims coming back the other way praised it.

But on the other hand ...

If he was sending his men out in penny-packets, as I said, he was frustrated. And he was mad – wode. Not sane. There was no rational way to fully predict what he'd do, but I had a little hope that our handling of his bandits might spur him to recklessness.

Anyway, high up the *Hospitales*, it all seemed foolish, a plan made by a child. I've known the same feeling while waiting in ambush. Once you are committed to a plan, all of its many flaws become as clear as stars in the night sky.

'At least there's no manure,' I said.

We were standing under a handful of dripping trees. The rain cloud had started dripping rain, and we were tired and almost wet through, and very, very high in the air. It was much colder here – almost cold enough for snow.

Sister Marie kicked me. It was so unexpected that she actually clipped me hard and I almost fell, and Lapot laughed.

Michael looked at us all curiously.

'This madman is trying to kill us,' he said, 'and you are all laughing.'

Marie shrugged. 'People have tried to kill us before,' she said.

I was smiling, too.

I was still smiling when I heard the unmistakable sound of metal on stone in the fog, and swearing.

'Stop that, you sodomite!' said a voice.

'Fuck your mother!' spat another.

It's very nice when one's enemies choose to identify themselves. Another odd effect of Camino – there is very little swearing. The first day, perhaps, you curse God for every stubbed toe, but after seven or ten days ...

'Camus,' Lapot said.

We had a plan. And suddenly, we were actually going to put it into effect.

I pointed at the trail up. 'Go,' I said.

Marie knew her role. She took Michael and the donkey and headed off.

We waited in the dripping trees.

It took much longer than we expected. Sound carried very oddly in fog – sometimes blocked altogether, sometimes amplified. They must have been far below us, and we waited half an hour, in waves of anxiety, courage, fear, false cheer.

The fog was not breaking up. If anything, it was intensifying.

And then, suddenly we could hear them so clearly they appeared to be among us. I moved softly to the edge of what I assumed was a cliff beside me, just to be *certain* Camus was climbing around me, insane as that may sound, but when I looked back, there was a small, ferrety man with a blond beard and a maille aventail emerging from the fog. He had a crossbow in his hand, and he looked ...

Bored.

Then he was dead. Lapot waited until he was almost opposite me, and then shot him. It was a brilliant shot. I assume it went straight to the man's heart, as he fell without so much as a whimper.

As I have no doubt said too often, complex things are best done either with enormous caution or complete audacity. I stepped straight out of my cover and stripped the crossbow from his dead hands. The bolts were in a boiled-leather quiver in his belt, and the quiver itself was too hard to get. I took a handful, and stepped away. I must have kicked a stone.

'Marcos!' came a familiar voice.

Sweet Christ, he sounded bad. He sounded like two or three people in one mouth.

I looked at Lapot. We had a plan.

We began to retreat.

'Marcos!' Camus shouted.

We were backing up the trail. I motioned to Lapot and he went right up ahead of me, moving low to the ground and very quietly. He had been a very bad man – he knew how to do all the brigand things.

I waited, spanned my new weapon, and looked into the fog, having to refocus my eyes constantly.

I could hear people arguing in low whispers. Or I was hearing the very slight wet breeze in the trees.

Now we were past the dripping trees. Let me add that they were the last trees we had seen on the mountain. Lapot was going up a steep slope, and he scarcely dislodged a stone. I took a chance and moved fast, under the assumption that the trees and the fog might cover my movement.

I'll never know.

But in the timeless grey of the mountain fog, we caught Michael and Marie a little later. It was difficult to measure time in the fog.

'How can there be a cold wind,' Michael asked, 'that doesn't move the fog?'

'It's not fog,' Sister Marie insisted. 'It's a rain cloud.' She kept saying this with her patient pedantry.

'How many of them do we think they are?' Michael asked.

I shrugged. 'Eight.'

Lapot looked at me the way he sometimes did, as if he'd expected better of me.

'I heard six, and one of them is down,' he said.

We were speaking in a hush. We'd reached the second shelter, the big one, with a central hearth. People had slept there the night before, and the hearth was warm and smelt of woodsmoke. Our donkey was tired and fractious and thought that the shelter was home, and was clearly less than enthusiastic about leaving.

'Why would they follow us now?' Michael asked. 'If you ...' He looked at Lapot. 'If you *killed* one, won't the others ... hesitate?'

'Maybe,' Lapot said.

'Camus is more dangerous than ...' I shook my head. 'What I mean is, that they may feel that they have to press on, or he'll just kill them.'

'Sweet Christ, it's Satan himself you're describing,' Michael muttered.

Sister Marie took a deep breath. 'Ambush, or move?' she asked.

'We could wait all day, if they've already given up,' I said. 'We can't stay here. I didn't expect all the fog. I want to be able to *see*.'

Lapot made a face. 'I can just wait in the doorway here,' he said. 'Out of the wind.'

Marie settled it with a very pragmatic comment.

'If you wait, we all stay. We can't get broken up. That's a bad idea.'

Lapot nodded.

'But if I don't get this donkey walking in five minutes,' she said, 'he won't move again today.'

Lapot sighed.

My gut said we should keep moving. Our first ambush had been perfect – we'd broken contact. We couldn't hear a thing.

'Of course,' I said, just to be thinking aloud, 'we could double back and go after *them*.'

'I'd rather go up in fog than down,' Marie said, and she was right. Too right.

That settled that.

'Onward,' I said.

We went up. I can't do justice to how far *up* we went, but after the last shelter we were climbing with our hands and feet, and the donkey was very noisily complaining about the hard life it had. We went up a scree and shale slope so loudly that they no doubt heard us in the valley below.

And up.

The wind grew until it was blowing my warm wool gown right off my shoulders, and Sister Marie, who was not a large woman, was having some trouble clinging to the trail.

And *still* the fog didn't move. From time to time it would have an eddy, and a tail of deeper grey would lash us with rain.

And up.

My pack and blanket roll now weighed twice as much as when we'd started, because at least the outer layers were soaked through.

And up.

The sword at my hip weighed like sin.

And up.

The dead man's crossbow bit into my right shoulder like my fear of Hell.

And up.

And up, and up, and up. We passed a dozen cairns, until we began to quietly mock them when we came to them.

'What'd the poor buggers do?' Lapot asked. 'Turn around and go back?'

But at Terce, we came to the Hospital. A tiny *albergue* at the very top of the mountain pass, with my order's eight-pointed cross over the door in fine stonework.

There was no one there.

It wasn't really a bitter blow. But I had rather hoped for an old knight, or a veteran man-at-arms or serving brother put out to pasture here. Instead, we had a plain, clean room, neatly whitewashed, with a single good fresco of Christ's passion on the far wall, a low but very modern fireplace with an external chimney, and a single table with a jug of fresh water and another of wine. There was a good round of cheese on the table, and a note in good Latin that said 'Back by nightfall'.

We all had a cup of wine while Michael watched. The wind whistled.

I went out and prowled around while Sister Marie cut big wedges of the cheese.

'A long, knife-edge ridge,' I reported on my return.

We all ate a bite. The donkey's bit came off and he ate the scrubby, damp grass with gusto.

'One door, stone walls, firewood, water,' Lapot said. 'I say we wait here and finish it.'

'We're only halfway to Berducedo, if that's where we're going,' Marie said.

Michael shook his head. 'The slope,' he said. 'We'd never see them coming.'

It was true. The little *albergue* was perched on a tiny spot of flat ground at the head of the pass, and the trail up the last few paces was steep. A traveller emerging would appear almost at the door.

We went outside together, and stood or crouched silently for a long time – perhaps half an hour. Somewhere below us were cattle bells, and the cry of a hawk.

We waited again.

Finally, Marie made a sign, and we retreated into the shelter of the *albergue*.

'Let's go,' she said.

Even Lapot agreed. 'They've already given up,' he said. To me, he said, with real kindness, 'It was a good plan. We didn't expect the fog.'

We repacked the donkey, who was none too pleased that we were moving again, and we set out across the long, knife-edge ridge that I'd glimpsed to the west. To our credit, we didn't abandon caution, but it was lighter. We all felt the fog might break, and we moved faster.

The ridge was just a ribbon of path in the endless grey, and we walked on, Lapot in front, me in the middle, and Sister Marie and Michael behind. I had the mule again, and the walking was the easiest of the day – almost level, on a good gravel path. We made good time until the trail turned slightly, and we suddenly caught the full weight of the wind.

My heavy wool gown, which I wore unbuttoned over my shoulders for its warmth, blew off like a sail in a high wind when the grommets rip out of the corners. Only the neck buttons held, and thank God they did or twenty florins' worth of good English wool would have vanished into the grey.

Sister Marie almost went the same way. The wind caught her grey gown and she had to lean visibly to stay upright, and one gust caught her and threw her almost to the cliff. Despite that gust, most of the danger came when the wind *stopped*. The wind was so strong, and the cliffs on either side of us so steep, that when the wind flawed or fell, we'd stumble towards the cliff edges. Nothing could stop this – the wind was higher than any gale I've known at sea.

And then, even over the wind, I heard Sister Marie give a loud cry, but it was not alarm – more like joy. I turned . . .

The wind had finally parted the clouds.

It was as if the world was revealed at our feet. I have never in my life seen a sight so beautiful, so mystical, so like the revealed wisdom of God. Suddenly there was a ray of sunlight, and a flash of green and gold, and far, far below us I could see a stream running . . .

And then woods . . .

A tiny square that proved to be a house . . .

The valley below us was revealed a little bit at a time, as if just fresh from the hand of the Creator, and below us, the sun illuminated the world. We were a Roman mile above the valley, and everything was beautiful and new.

We prayed. What can I say? We all stood there in the wind and prayed, and drank it in. It was more beautiful than Emile, more beautiful than a breath of air when you've been drowning. I have never had a spiritual experience so utterly divine, and I stood there, transfixed, despite the wind.

But we are merely mortals, and eventually even the revealed wisdom of God palls. We shouldered our burdens and walked off into the wind.

An hour later, we were hungry, cold, and tired of the endless gusts. We used a tall bank of earth as a shelter, lay down on close-cropped grass – there were sheep and horses, even atop the ridge – and ate. Lapot kept watch behind us, and no one was more surprised than we were when a young man and a young woman we didn't know, wearing long pilgrim gowns, came up behind us on the trail.

Lapot hid the weapon. We offered them cheese and they took it, and they had not seen Camus or any armed bravos on the mountain. They'd started hours behind us, but they were young and very fit and they'd walked hard.

They were more lightly dressed than we. I loaned the woman my wool gown because her lips were white. They took a wedge of cheese and vanished down the trail.

By the time we were done eating, I could see all the way back to the little Hospital on the crest of the pass, almost two leagues behind us.

I shrugged. 'They turned back,' I said.

Lapot nodded.

In retrospect, it's obvious. Armour is no friend to a heavy climb. Crossbows and swords are useless tools on a mountainside. After we killed one of theirs, they had to fear the fog every step. And the risk was insane, seen from their side.

In fact, I'd made a poor plan, because *of course* they turned back after the first ambush.

Oh well. That meant that Camus was on the wrong side of the pass with dwindling daylight. And his men feared us.

'God's will,' I said.

Sister Marie sniffed.

Lapot looked down the long fall to the valley below, and then tossed the crossbow over the edge.

I admit, I carried the one I had another league, but when we came off the ridge and started down a terrifying steep path over shale, I tossed it and the bolts. I prayed, and let the weapon go.

I'd like to say that we were almost to Berducedo, but that's not how pilgrimage works, and in fact, we were still a solid five leagues from the pilgrim town. We walked down a long way, and then we started up again. It was hot, and we were climbing in late afternoon sun.

'Climbing?' Michael asked, as if it was my fault.

And at the top of our third ridge we came to a small village that was entirely abandoned. Abandoned by people, that is. Perhaps they had plague, or hard times, but there were a dozen stone houses with barns, very different from the houses in Borres, and there were no people. No bodies, no dead, no one.

But one dog.

You could tell immediately that he was a good boy. He was big – boar-hound big. And smart – he knew at once that I had sausage, and he was very eager to have a share of sausage. I cut him some and he followed me a way.

He was very friendly, aside from his threatening size. And his eagerness for sausage. He was better with Sister Marie than with me. She laughed, unafraid, and petted him and called him silly names.

We drank the rest of our water and looked at the well, but old soldiers don't drink from abandoned wells.

We started down the hill beyond the village, and the boar-hound followed us. He went by leaps and bounds, full of energy.

'That beast doesn't live off table scraps,' Lapot said.

Marie agreed. 'He'd starve pretty fast,' she said.

'He's used to people,' I said.

He bounded past, then came back and stuck his not inconsiderable nose into my side-bag, looking for sausage.

All the way down to the bottom of a lovely valley, and then up the far side through blossoming jasmine that smelt like a gateway to Heaven. The dog stayed with us, sometimes on the trail, sometimes crashing through brush to the right or left.

I thought of Beatrice, the courser in Italy who'd led me around Camus's ambush. But this dog, while very smart, didn't seem to want to take us anywhere – if anything, he wanted us to stop and play.

And he didn't run out of strength, while we were flagging. We came to yet another small town, this one well populated, and our big dog dashed down the main street in pursuit of a purely imaginary foe, and people got out of his way. I got us water at a town well, and I shared out the remaining food, including the dog in my sharing, and we were away. A cheerful older woman pointed at the next ridge.

'Berducedo,' she said.

We remained cautious. We went over the last ridge and through a long wood, and the wood was a perfect ambush spot, so we were very careful. The woods were old, and the trees enormous, and when our dog ran off to the left, we followed, donkey and all, off the trail and through the old trees like children in a fairy tale.

Heh. I'm having you on. Nothing happened. I want you to stay with me on all this, and understand that the tension never lets up when you are being hunted. You give your hunter supernatural skills, and I truly expected Camus around every bend, even though I'd willingly thrown away a perfectly good crossbow.

We walked into Berducedo, went directly to the best inn, and Lapot, who had won the foot-race of the last mile, had already put four silver coins on the counter and we had four brimming glasses of a strong, sweet, spiced wine.

The young couple were there. The man gave me back my wool gown, and we embraced. And then I went back to my friends, drank off my sweet wine, and was almost instantly drunk. But amazingly, the day had been so hard that I was sober again in time for Mass – my body just burnt it off.

We got all our clothes washed and hung them in the chilly air to dry. I won't try and explain the drunken contortions of four weary pilgrims in using a washtub and a hanging line, but I suspect we accorded some amusement to the other patrons, although they were none too sober themselves. There was no sign of the people we'd left in Borres, and as evening darkened towards night, and none of them came in, I began to worry about having left relative innocents with Camus on the Borres side. But after evening prayer at the beautiful little church, the English couple appeared, having faced no greater peril than a turned ankle on the down slope.

'I saw mounted men in haubergeons,' the man said. 'Coming down the road when we was going up. Perhaps late morning.'

'Mid-afternoon,' his wife said. 'And a nastier lot of blaspheming wretches I couldn't imagine.'

I looked at Lapot. 'Now he's two full days behind us.'

Sister Marie's face shone with her pleasure at worship and the effects of two glasses of sweet wine.

'Can we just forget this cursed sinner for a day, and be people of God?' she asked.

Lapot agreed with her outwardly. But when she went to bed, he sat by me and we shared another cup of wine.

'We could go back and get him,' he said. 'Surprise is worth a great deal.'

We drank the wine.

'I . . .' I paused. What I wanted to say was complicated and difficult and irrational.

I was petting the dog. He was wrapped around my feet. I'd had to pay a full human price for his dinner – that's how much he ate.

Lapot raised an eyebrow.

'I don't want to go back,' I said. 'I feel as if . . .' I shook my head. 'We're supposed to keep walking.'

'Because it's God's will?' Lapot asked.

I probably flushed with embarrassment. 'Yes,' I said.

He nodded. 'I agree. We are here to prove we are pilgrims, and not killers. So we keep walking forward, whatever happens.'

'We are killers,' I said.

Lapot shrugged. 'I count any man who attacks me as a suicide,' he said. He smiled slowly. 'I'm enjoying this,' he said.

I shook my head. I am not made as Lapot.

'I'm not,' I said.

Lapot shrugged. 'When I'm in holy orders, what will I do for excitement?'

We left Berducedo and our very comfortable inn in clean, dry clothes, our bellies full of food. We'd slept like babes, if perhaps slightly drunken babes.

I confess I've seldom felt better in my life.

Of course, our day started with an astoundingly steep climb, once again in fog. But it was a bright fog lit by the sun, and it burnt off like a proper fog, instead of lurking all day. We went up and up until Berducedo was a beautiful jewel set in the green velvet of the valley floor, and then we walked the ridge for a league or two until we came

205

to some fine farms, with big houses and bigger stone barns. We were in the richest part of Asturias, and we were welcomed by every passing peasant. It was clearly a market day somewhere – the roads were full.

A passing Jewish pedlar sold me a good needle and some thread and told us that he'd come up from Pradías.

I knew that name from my itinerary, and I asked him if he'd seen armed men on the roads.

'Oh, yes,' he said. He met my eye.

I gave him a silver coin, a Venetian soldo. He smiled at it and me.

'They asked me about red-haired pilgrims,' he said. 'Five men, all on warhorses. Three in armour. The *capitano* had dysentery and was shitting himself.'

'Sweet Christ,' I said.

The Jew shrugged. 'Yesterday they were at Pradías. I kept walking – I had to deliver something at Morentán. They probably awoke in Pradías.'

'How far?' I asked.

'For most men? A day's walk. For me?' The Jew grinned. Despite his enormous pack, he moved like a dancer. 'Half a day. They have horses, which will not help them.'

I gave him another soldo.

'If you see them again, hide,' I said. 'They are very bad men.'

'I have not lived this long on these roads without knowing a bad man when I see one,' he agreed.

'Meaning us,' Lapot muttered when the pedlar was gone.

'Perhaps,' I agreed. 'But Camus is not as far behind as I'd hoped. He must be riding horses to death.'

'He has dysentery,' Lapot said.

I nodded. 'Let's keep walking.'

Between Berducedo and Grandas de Salime, there is the deepest valley I have ever seen, anywhere in the world. My pilgrim itinerary described it, but we were utterly unprepared for the reality. We walked and walked on good trails and a road, and then went down across farm fields, and suddenly we were at the edge of a gorge. It fell away at our feet, and the bottom was so far below us that it didn't seem real.

Strangest of all, the far side was really not much more than a stone's throw away. It was as if God or Satan had cut a furrow in the earth.

The trail ran in endless sharp switchbacks. The slopes were covered in magnificent pines, as old as the earth, and the steep slopes were carpeted in pine needles that were as slippery as glass. There were huge pine cones everywhere, and as we walked, Michael and I began hitting them out into the endless space of the chasm with our pilgrim staffs, so that we could watch them fall away into nothing.

'Sometimes, William, you are like a child,' Marie said.

I grinned. 'Suffer the children ...' I said.

She laughed. And hit a pine cone into space.

'It is very satisfying,' she admitted.

We walked on. We watched our back trail, and when we stopped for lunch we made a very small fire and put it out the moment we had hot water. And I was sufficiently tired that I left my tinderbox sitting right there by the trail.

Well after midday we reached the bottom of the chasm, crossed a small bridge, and started up the far side. There were far more pilgrims than we'd seen any other day. We passed people all the time, and others passed us, with many a '*Buon Camino*' called out. It was a fine day without a hint of rain, and we climbed with a good will, stopped for a very good jack of beer at an inn with the royal arms of Aragon over the door, and then climbed away past an ancient mill. The chasm was now on our left hand, and we were almost to the top when we saw Camus.

It was the most remarkable thing.

He was less than a bowshot away. I could see him, plain as day, riding with his head down. He looked sick to me, even two hundred paces away. And one of his men came to the edge of the chasm, and looked down, and then they took his bridle ...

He was *right there*.

Lapot gripped my shoulder.

He was *right there*, but a whole day behind us – he was at the top of the far side of the chasm, and we were already up the near side. We were two hundred paces apart, and yet we were a day apart, and the cream of the jest was that he'd never get those horses down the switchbacks of the pine tree trail.

I was tempted to call out – to challenge him.

'If only I still had a crossbow,' Lapot spat.

Sister Marie shook her head. 'No,' she said. 'No more ambushes.

No more murder. We are pilgrims. Let him find redemption, or go to Hell, by his own will.'

I understood her meaning, but despite her holiness, for which I had great respect, I'd reached a decision of my own, and if I'd had a crossbow, I'd have put him down then and there and no regrets. If I'd hit him, which, to be honest, I beg leave to doubt.

But neither did I intend to quarrel with Sister Marie, who had become the captain of our *empris* to walk to Santiago. Hers was the motivating spirit. I would not cross her.

That night we stayed in a fine little house outside Grandas, and I cursed a great deal when I found that I'd lost my tinderbox, but we were otherwise safe. In fact, at Marie's insistence, we walked an extra two leagues and stayed on one of the alternative trails.

When we rose in the morning we walked still farther south, so that we'd skipped from the mountain route south to a more popular one, and that night we stayed in a huge *albergue* in Fonsagrada, complete with stables and a fine taverna. Our boar-hound was now one of us, and we called him 'Boy' and 'Good Boy' and many other nicknames, and he ate more sausage than an English archer.

At Fonsagrada we met forty pilgrims who were on the valley route, and after a fine evening of brilliant food and good wine, we walked away the next morning with an English knight and his lady, a Scottish matron and her daughter, and an Irishman from outside the pale in Ireland, who was also a scholar. The knight wore a sword and seemed to know his way around it, and the Irishman was big and capable. When we explained that we'd had 'trouble with bandits', the knight appeared more excited than hesitant, so we all went on together – first through deep woods, and then up another long ridge. But the ridge was to be among our last. The magnificent mountains of Asturias were giving way to plains, and we were walking out of the mountains. Now our path lay through woods and orchards, skirting farm fields, sometimes right along the edge of a stone wall, or between two tall walls.

It was hard to stay alert with so many good companions, and as we toiled along, we told stories and sang hymns and behaved like proper pilgrims. Sir Gregory and his lady, Tabitha, had shoes that were too tight for walking and the long day did them no favours. When we finally came down a long slope into our destination that night, he and his lady were hobbling. Even our irrepressible Irishman was slowing down.

Not our dog. He bounded about, and seemed, that day, to be focusing his efforts on Michael, and Michael, for his part, was throwing sticks and calling out and generally enjoying the dog's companionship. He was a wonderful dog, at least until you had to pay an innkeeper to feed him.

That night we purchased a big dinner in a fine inn, and had the best wine I can ever remember tasting, and Sir Gregory regaled the local farmers with his tales of fighting the French and the Spanish, and I added a few tales.

It was a splendid evening, at least until I saw Sir Gregory's feet. They were ... terrible. It looked as if he'd been tortured by infidels.

'Oh,' he said. 'It's nothing. I'll be fine tomorrow.'

Sister Marie and Michael had a conversation without me, and decided that we'd simply go slow and stay with the Englishman and his lady. So the next day we had an easy day on much flatter ground and grassy paths. The weather remained our friend, and while heavy clouds lowered all day to the south and west, we had no rain. Our short day cost me my calm – I was back to expecting the Bourc Camus at every turn of the road.

Otherwise, it was all so beautiful. I mean, our English were in real pain. Our Irishman was given to alternate moments of joy and flares of anger, and I was under tension like the string on a bow. But what of it? Never in my life had God been more evident, and I walked through the magnificent spring and early summer in the absolute assurance of Christ's love. Laugh if you want, Chaucer.

We walked into Lugo that afternoon, and it was another amazing sight, the cathedral's towers and cross clear in the air several miles away, and the magnificent round of its Roman walls visible as soon as we could see the cathedral. We crossed the river on a Roman bridge and then climbed up into the city, stopping for water and wine twice, so tired were we all. Our big dog had adopted the Irishman, and walked with him, at his heels, and sometimes in the way of his legs.

Sir Gregory found us a fine tavern, and we agreed to meet up for dinner. We were in several separate *albergues* because now we were on the main pilgrim road and everything was full. I shared with Michael and Sister Marie, and Lapot was with Stiofán of Leinster, the

Irishman, and our immediate need after a flagon of wine and a foot bath was to do laundry. I enquired along our street, and then all the way to one of the great Roman gates, and eventually a local sergeant told me with a leer that there was a house outside the walls that 'took care of pilgrims'.

And that is how, unwittingly, I took Sister Marie to a whorehouse. They did our laundry willingly enough, and I confess that I was sufficiently tired and blind that I didn't catch on immediately to what the house was for. It was a big wooden house with a new roof and solid doors, no hovel, and had its own well. A pretty thing too young for the trade served me wine, and they all stayed so far from Marie that it was as if I'd drawn a line around her.

And then, suddenly, I understood. Marie and I were talking about the Romans. She'd done an incredible amount of reading, and I'd at least read Vegetius by then, and we were speculating about the age of the walls.

I looked around for a second cup of wine. It was still light in the sky, and I wanted to ask my laundress if they'd have all our clothes dry in the morning ...

And I understood. These were not laundresses.

'Son of a ...' My curse died on my lips.

Sister Marie raised an eyebrow.

'I've led you into a brothel,' I said.

Marie shrugged. 'Not the first I've been in,' she said.

She got to her feet and walked off into the house.

I heard her talking, and then a rush of feet, and then more talking, low. I was brought another cup of wine, and an older woman assured me that my clothes would be ready at dawn. I had no idea what the woman said in Spanish, but her French was good enough that I gathered that they had a warm room to dry clothes.

I gave her a tip – a half-silver I had in my wallet.

She bit it and grinned. 'Thanks, m'lord,' she said with a curtsey, and she was gone, and the child returned.

'The good sister is saying evening prayers with my mother and her friends,' the child said very seriously. 'She begs your indulgence and says' – and here the girl switched languages to a very passable English – '*Run along and have some supper, William.*'

I walked out of the brothel well-enough pleased, and passed back through the gates of Lugo under the leers of my Spanish sergeant.

'Did you get your clothes washed?' he asked. 'Were the laundresses to your satisfaction?'

I gave him a slight smile. I was thinking of my own brothel, of Sister Marie praying with the girls, and how much I had to atone for. I was thinking those thoughts when I realised that somewhere under my red hair, my busy brain was not happy with the Spanish sergeant. He'd been ...

False. Something about him didn't ring true. The laugh? The facial expression?

Ahead of me, on Lugo's main street, two lamplighters were lighting cressets that were set in public sconces along the street. The town was so full of pilgrims that the streets were lit at night like London for a festival. I was less than a city block from the tavern where we were appointed to meet, and I realised, suddenly, that I was alone on a dark street in Lugo, the very town where I had predicted that Camus might go for me.

I still had the Hospitaller brother's sword by my side. I loosened it, looked back ...

And there they were. Two of them, on my side of the street, very close. In one glance I knew, and they knew, and they began to run at me.

A woman screamed.

I couldn't see Camus. I recognised only one assailant, but as the attack developed, I thought there were four of them. It's hard in the dark, but all four men made a swirl in the crowd of pilgrims.

I put my back to a big stone building and drew. Pilgrims scattered. An older woman screamed very close to me – the sight of my sword terrified her.

The two nearest our tavern were farthest from me. The two who had been behind me were closest.

Simple.

I charged the two behind me. I ran right at Big-Hat, who was closest. He didn't like that. I had my heavy wool coat, still wet from the *Hospitales* trail, over my right arm, and I flipped it at him. He stepped back, looking for his comrade, and I thrust at his face under the cloak with my hand protected. When you fight with an arming sword, protecting your sword hand is your first duty.

211

I'd slowed, and when he cut at my cloak and my offered leg, I yanked my left foot back. He cut empty air, and I leapt to my right and stabbed him in the head over the cloak, my thumb flat along the blade, my thrust passing over my own head and my outstretched left arm. My thrust went right through his left temple and he fell off my sword, stone dead. Whatever you may say about it, it was a beautiful thrust, and one that I'd practised over and over, all on my own. It is probably the only reason I remember the fight, because, in truth, I've never used it since.

Right there you have so many sins all together – for a pilgrim ... pride and murder, all together. But I digress.

His comrade turned and ran.

I whirled.

The fight was over. I didn't know why, but I discovered the reason in ten steps. Stiofán of Leinster had felled one of the brigands with a blow of his pilgrim staff, and when Sir Gregory drew his very long sword from under his gown, almost everyone on the street had run for it.

So the three of us were standing on the street. None of us were even breathing hard. Stiofán was looking at his stick, apparently worried he'd damaged it. Sir Gregory looked positively disappointed that he had nothing on which to use his beautiful sword.

Well, well.

My man was very dead. Stephen's was unconscious, and his breathing was bad.

'Sure, and I hit him too hard,' Stiofán said. He was completely unconcerned.

It was then that my friend the Spanish sergeant appeared with the night watch, twenty scrofulous-looking men-at-arms in rusting maille and unmatched surcoats.

'I'll be arresting you for murder,' he said, drawing his sword. 'Possession of forbidden weapons, felony assault ...'

I smiled. 'I'm a knight of the Hospital,' I said, showing my ring. 'And I have fifty witnesses that these men attacked me.'

Spanish Sergeant was rocked by the revelation that I was a knight of the Hospital.

'That's not—' he muttered in Spanish.

'Not what someone told you?' I asked in French.

While I was talking, Lapot came out of the tavern with Michael at his shoulder.

'I'm arresting you,' the sergeant said.

'No,' I said. 'I have a writ from the Pope. I killed a footpad. You can arrest this man here.'

I pointed to Stephen's victim. I didn't really have a writ from the Pope, but I didn't think Spanish Sergeant could read.

'I'm arresting you,' Spanish Sergeant said, but he didn't believe it himself.

'No,' I said gently.

I looked around. I had Stiofán and Gregory right behind me, Lapot was already circling to the left, and Michael had retrieved his staff. Lapot stopped and pointed a sword at the man nearest him.

'If you try and arrest us, a lot of you will die,' he said. He said it without bluster, his voice matter-of-fact. 'And we're innocent.'

We all looked at each other while the wind whipped the torches and the street stank of death and pine pitch.

And then the woman who'd screamed at me came out of the portico of the stone building. She was past childbearing age, with a strong face and a wimple of snowy white linen.

'This knight was attacked,' she said. 'I saw it all.'

Bless her, she gave Spanish Sergeant an excuse not to arrest us, and everyone backed down. For my part, my sword was clenched in my right fist so tightly that my fingers hurt.

But eventually we went and had dinner.

Lapot turned to me after the fish.

'He can't have more than four men left,' he said.

'Who's that?' Sir Gregory asked.

CHAPTER THREE

ON CAMINO, LUGO TO SANTIAGO

Late May 1369

Dinner was a trifle stiff. It's really not a good way to make friends, when you admit that someone is trying to kill you but you're the one with blood on your blade. Lady Tabitha was ... hesitant. Our Irishman seemed completely unconcerned, and was more interested in Sister Marie's whereabouts.

I did my best to explain just how mad and bad Camus was, and Lapot backed me, but I was all too conscious that we might sound like two sell-swords having a row with our employer.

Except that I had a donat's ring and was a respectable son of the Church. I even had the order's cross on my cote. And Sir Gregory had heard of me, which was fine, in its way.

We went out after dinner to hear Evensong, which was sung very badly by Spanish monks, and then we went for a walk on the ancient walls, which was lovely. I worried for Sister Marie, and left the others to go down to the house, where I found that she had already left. I didn't linger.

I considered it, though. I've never found that love of God and a woman's love were in conflict, and I had survived a fight and felt ...

Anyway, I went back to my *albergue* with no fresh sins committed, prayed a little, and went to sleep.

In the morning we went to Mass, all together, at the cathedral. It was a magnificent structure. The vestry alone, where pilgrims went to have their cartels signed, was larger than many a church in London. In one corner was an open trunk, full to the brim with silver chalices. I give you my word! There must have been more than one hundred.

While we were in the vestry, the oddest thing happened, occasioned by the cross on my cote. The bishop was about to say Mass, and he paused, looking at our party. He waved, and a monk approached us.

'Messire is religious?' he asked in passable Italian.

Gregory and I shared a glance. It was an odd question to ask a man who'd just taken Mass and was having his pilgrim cartel signed by a priest, but then, the Spanish are sometimes very odd – righteous, in a way.

'Yes,' I said.

The monk nodded and scurried back to his master.

The Bishop of Lugo – in full regalia, with a silk mitre on his head – came over to us, his magnificent chasuble brushing the floor. He had his gold and ivory staff in his hand, and he was wearing a thousand gold florins' worth of treasure. I admit it, the routier never dies in a man, and while I can love God, I sometimes tire of the riches of the Church.

He bent over and blessed me, which was kinder than most bishops. It was a long Latin blessing, and one I didn't know. Sister Marie looked shocked.

He then sprinkled all of us with holy water from a solid silver bucket with a solid silver asperge. I bowed, he inclined his head with a civil smile, and he was off, lead by a pair of thurifers.

In a moment, the vestry was empty, except for us. Lapot admitted later that even on his way to holy orders, the unguarded box of silver chalices tempted him.

An hour later and we were toiling up the long ridge beyond Lugo on the road to Santiago, our dog running after rabbits and then bounding back to us with his incredible energy.

'He thought you were a priest of the order,' Marie said with her barking laugh. 'He gave you the priest's blessing.'

Lapot snorted, and everyone had a good laugh, which proves, I suppose, how unlike a priest I am. But I'll say this for the bishop's blessing. Rain fell all around us the next days, and Camus was on the roads – but we never felt a drop of water, and our necks were our own. I have no other explanation as to why Camus couldn't find us, but we never saw him, although there was a rumour of some bad men-at-arms robbing pilgrims to the south.

At the same time, it became harder and harder to imagine that even Camus would try a massacre in front of so many witnesses. Past

Lugo, we were on one of the major pilgrim routes and we walked with dozens, and sometimes hundreds, of other men and women – merchants and beggars, cripples, lepers, most clothed in grey or brown. There were a few other men of arms, and once a knight of Calatrava rode by on a tired horse. The last day but one, forty Germans singing a hymn passed us, marching like soldiers. Later, we discovered that they were initiates in a German branch of the Dominicans.

And I lost a day there at the end. No idea what happened – a passing fever, a bad humour, or the curse of some poor devil – but I lost a day. I'm told I sang and walked faster, but I have no memory of that day at all.

And then, at last, we climbed another long, hard ridge. The ridges were lower in Galicia than in Asturias, but this one seemed to take forever. Sir Gregory was limping. My feet were swollen all the time, and I was weak from my fever. Sister Marie's feet were raw and her shoes ruined, and the Irishman's too. Really, only the scholar, Michael, seemed unaffected by the walking. Even our Good Boy, the dog, was moving slowly, favouring his right front paw.

I was talking to Lady Tabitha – probably going on a bit long about something – and she was trying to look interested. Or perhaps we were singing. The Irishman could sing, and he and Sister Marie had begun to make us learn hymns. Regardless, I was with Lady Tabitha, and Lapot, ahead of me, let out a gasp.

It wasn't Camus. It was Santiago. From the height we'd reached, we could see the city, and the cathedral. We laughed, hugged each other, and then sang a modest attempt at the *Te Deum*, and then we went on, lighter on our feet to know we were so close.

But Stiofán, the Irishman, had sharp eyes. We were coming down the ridge, and he pointed with his staff.

'Armed men on horses,' he said, pointing across the river. 'Damn me if I'm wrong.'

He wasn't wrong. They were five hundred paces distant and they hadn't seen us, and I had foot-weary people with me.

'We have to walk around,' I said. 'This gate is watched.'

'Perhaps they're all watched,' Stiofán said. 'Any road, no one's looking for me!'

I tugged at my own beard.

But Stiofán laughed. 'Just my way,' he said. 'I meant a jest.'

Sister Marie narrowed her eyes. 'No violence,' she said.

'I'm not starting it,' I said.

Lapot said nothing.

'We'll go to the north gate,' Marie said with authority.

Well, as I've said, this was one *empris* where I was neither the captain nor the corporal, so we followed her off to the right, which was north. We crossed the river at a ford that was both cold and wet, stopped to eat fresh bread in a bakery that was so warm it dried my boots, and then, at last, took our weary feet round to the north gate of the city.

There was one man in armour. He wore the sable and argent of Camus, and rode a miserable horse.

'He must be desperate,' Lapot said.

'If we drift apart,' Marie said, 'we should all pass him without comment. Put your hood up, William. You make friends quickly enough. Find someone else to walk with.'

'We'll all be alone ...' I said.

Marie put her hand through Boy's big leather collar.

'I won't be alone,' she said.

As it proved, it is possible to make friends in five hundred paces of walking, especially with joyous pilgrims at the very end of their road. I found myself with a dark-skinned man from Italy and a tall woman from Hungary. They knew each other, and by the time we were approaching the gates, I'd shared some wine from my pilgrim bottle and we were fast friends. Hanna, the Hungarian woman, was a great walker, having started far to the east and visited Vienna and Rome. When I mentioned Krakow, she grinned from ear to ear.

She was handsome enough that I wanted her to smile again, and suddenly I realised that I was in the streets of Santiago. The trickle of pilgrims had become a river, and the river a flood. Now we were walking slowly, pressing along like spearmen into a stiff fight. I looked back, and I could see Michael, and he gave me a wave. I had to assume we'd all made it into the holy city – I couldn't have left the side of my new African friend in that press for love nor money – and I shuffled along, shuffled along ...

The last five hundred paces up the hill took half the day, I swear. There were thousands of pilgrims. At every corner, more seemed to join the flood, until a man on his knees might have gone faster.

And then, suddenly, we came to the great square in front of the cathedral – or rather, the press ahead of me stumbled into the square, and we were moving faster.

It seems like a strange place to meet danger. But I could see the loom of the cathedral. My heart rose with joy. All around me, pilgrims, most of them people I'd never seen, were embracing, or calling out blessings. I turned to find Michael and the rest, and when I turned back ...

A child had fallen. She fell quite close to me and her mother screamed. My African friend tried to stop the crowd, but they were too excited by the proximity of the end of their quest, and they pressed forward. As soon as I understood, I threw myself behind him, and Hanna, who was, as I have said, tall and robust, joined me.

The three of us might as well have tried to stop the tide, or the wind.

The child was screaming. I think she'd been kicked, trodden on, already, and I knew what could happen. Men in armour died, trampled, in battles if they fell in the wrong spot, and this was the wrong spot. The crowd was beyond controlling, mad with eagerness to make it into the square. The child was doomed, and I suddenly realised that if I lost my balance I was doomed, too.

And yet ...

Can you save yourself when a child is dying?

Really?

I put my shoulder down and shouted my war shout, which shocked a few pilgrims and bought us a few breaths, although the ones who heard were pushed from behind. I skidded back, and I still didn't know exactly where the poor mite had fallen.

Then Michael appeared at my back, and he pushed like a veteran man-at-arms. And then Lady Tabitha, of all people, shouting for the crowd to stop. She had a high, clear voice.

Lapot was coming back from the square, and he's a big man.

A Frenchman understood, somehow, and he joined us, and we were holding the crowd. Lapot threw himself against the Frenchman's back.

Just for a moment, we held them, and Hanna reached down and plucked the little thing to her feet. She was hurt – weeping ... filthy ...

Alive.

The crush broke us like a spring torrent breaks a dam. Whatever fury we'd pent up for a moment, the crowd pushed us away like chaff, and I was slammed into an iron gate with enough force to leave the pattern on my back.

And then we were all swept along into the square, the Hungarian woman holding the little thing aloft. The square was much easier. The press was less, and in fact it was a different press, and I doubt that I have been embraced and kissed so many times in my whole life. But before we made it to the steps of the cathedral, the mother appeared, her face swollen and still weeping. She was incredulous that we had her child, and she took the poor thing and kissed it a hundred times, proclaiming that we were all saints and this was a miracle.

Hanna was a practical pilgrim, and she declined sainthood and gave the woman a drink of my wine to calm her. We made it to the steps, got into the free space next to them, and had a moment to look the child over. She was battered, but already recovering. I gave her a mouthful of wine, and Michael very cautiously tested her ribs and arms.

'I don't think there's anything broken,' he said.

'I've lost my man,' the mother said.

Hanna looked disgusted – perhaps at the woman's helplessness.

'What's he look like?' she asked, but we knew it was pointless, as every grey-robed pilgrim looks much the same as every other.

Sister Marie gave me a nod. 'We need lodgings,' she said. 'I'm going to see what I can do.'

She took Stiofán and set off into the crowd, and I stayed put with Michael, Lapot and my new friends.

There's no great tale to it. I only mention it as a moment where I was reminded that there are more ways to die than on the point of a bad man's sword. The crowd … A crowd of elated pilgrims was as dangerous as a river in spate. It had almost had the child, and it might have killed me or Lapot as well. It was a sobering thought, but the joy of the mother was palpable, and every pilgrim might want to end his pilgrimage with such an act – chivalry without even a sword.

I still had money, and I got a street-seller to bring us a skin of wine while we watched the child and the mother roamed the square, looking for her man.

The Hungarian woman shook her head.

'Maybe he's run off,' she said. 'It's what men do.'

I met her eye.

She grinned. 'All right, sometimes I run off myself,' she said. 'But a woman needs to know how to own herself.'

I was looking past her. I could see Camus, on a good horse, well off to the west, almost on the opposite side of the square. He was telling someone something. If I had to guess, he was trying to tell a pilgrim how foolish belief in God was.

I watched him.

'Friend of yours?' Hanna asked.

'Nope,' I answered. Trying to change the subject, I asked, 'What's your name?'

'Hanna,' she said.

The African offered a hand. 'Christopher,' he said.

I shook his hand. 'You're a long way from Aethiopia,' I said.

'What do you know of Aethiopia?' he asked.

So I admitted to having been at Alexandria, and he nodded.

'I'm from further south,' he said.

And we proceeded to discuss Africa like a pair of ancient geographers, in the square of Santiago.

'I want to go to church,' Hanna the Hungarian said. 'I want to take communion.'

Michael shook his head. He'd gone and fetched bread, which we were all eating in a mad rush. It was good bread, but exorbitantly expensive. The good merchants of Santiago, like those of Rome and Jerusalem, have had hundreds of years to perfect the art of fleecing jubilant pilgrims.

I looked at the press of pilgrims pouring into the square and shook my head.

'I'll wait for morning Mass tomorrow,' I said.

I felt dirty and tired, despite the elation at having rescued the little girl.

Still eating bread, our little group began to push our way around the periphery of the square. I was, I confess it, caught between two sinful thoughts – gluttony, in that I desperately wanted a meat pie of some sort, and perhaps a cup of wine, and an increasing awareness that Hanna was really quite attractive in her big, bluff, somewhat aggressive way.

Lapot caught my eye after I'd watched Hanna ahead of us, pushing through the crowd, her athletic figure showing under her pilgrim's gown. He smiled ruefully. I suspect my smile was the same.

'I'm not ready to be a priest,' Lapot admitted.

'Sin is easier than repentance,' I said, which is true, and also something that Father Pierre Thomas used to say all the time. I glanced back towards where Camus had been. He was gone.

Regardless of our various inclinations, we made our way to where the web of streets of the town proper opened off an elegant stone gate on the south side of the great square. I already regretted allowing Sister Marie to go off on her own. Free of the safety of the crowds, I realised how exposed we might be in the narrow streets, and I began to wonder how I'd ever find her. Santiago de Compostela had streets running in almost every direction from the cathedral, and if it wasn't as big as Paris, it was a good-sized town, full to bursting with the faithful making their way to the various shrines. I passed a dozen grimy men sitting on blankets, selling holy relics that they claimed to have brought from the Holy Land. I laughed aloud. Having been to Jerusalem and Athens and a dozen other pilgrim sites, I was used to the trade, and I could see at a glance that not one of these men had ever been to the Holy Sepulchre.

Marie pushed on, but my desire for wine and a meat pie overwhelmed my pointless lust, and I found a tavern in the second street off the square. Lapot and I sat, watching the street like two old soldiers, and got decent wine and hand pies.

I had perhaps two bites when Boy ran up to me, seized the pie from my tired hand, and ate it in one big dog bite.

'Woof,' he said.

I ordered another meat pie, took his collar, and let him pull me along to the corner, where I found Marie and Michael. They looked relatively clean, and had neither satchels nor staffs.

'God, I thought we'd lost you ...' Michael said.

'I saw Camus a horse length away,' Marie said. 'He takes the prayers right out of my mouth.'

Michael gave me a hug, which I confess surprised me, and then Marie wrapped me in an embrace as a priest walked by, shaking his head in disapproval.

I led them back to the little tavern, which, in truth, was more like a house with some tables in what had once been its downstairs room. We all sat down.

Christopher, the Aethiopian, came in and stood hesitantly by the door. I could see at a glance that he wasn't sure whether saving the child had created enough of a bond that he could sit with us.

Lapot grinned at him. 'Come on, then,' he said.

The dark man smiled, and I introduced him around the circle. The lady of the house came and served us with a good will – we filled her little basement.

'By Saint James,' Michael said. 'Every tavern in this city is packed to the rafters, and you find us this quiet spot ...'

I smiled. 'Soldiers have a few skills,' I said.

'We can find a good place to drink wine,' Lapot agreed.

'We made a nice find, too,' Marie said.

Two cups of wine and she had a fine flush to her face.

'I knew we'd find you here,' Sir Gregory said from the doorway. He laughed. 'Small, tucked away, good wine.'

His lady pushed past him and we expanded the circle again, so that now we had every seat in the small room. We had to introduce Christopher all over again, and then, when the dog barked, we found that Hanna had returned.

'Too packed for Mass,' she admitted.

She was abashed by the presence of a nun, and Marie didn't do much to put her at her ease, so that Hanna stood for a while against the wall. But I went and got her a stool, and put her between Christopher and Lapot.

'I've got us places at Mass tomorrow,' Marie said. She smiled around. 'And I have us a lodging.'

'Lodging?' I said. 'Where?'

She smiled.

Michael laughed. 'I had no idea how important my travelling companion was,' he allowed. 'She went to the archbishop's palace and handed over a letter from the Pope.'

Marie smiled. 'Not exactly a letter from the Pope,' she admitted.

'And we have a whole house! A whole house!' Michael said. 'It's as if a miracle was performed before my very eyes.'

'Can we take in two more strays?' I asked Marie in English.

She narrowed her eyes, but then nodded. 'I suppose. You are too generous, William.'

'I've never heard that accounted a sin,' I said.

'What are we going to do about Camus?' she asked.

The next morning was Trinity Sunday, the first Sunday after Pentecost. A major feast day. We awoke early, washed and dressed as neatly as our pilgrim clothes allowed and went directly to the great cathedral doors, but we needn't have gone to the effort. Sister Marie had worked her spiritual magic, and we were ushered into the cathedral by hushed servitors. We walked down the empty nave and were given space hard by the altar itself, just to the left, with the archbishop's staff and servants.

There was, of course, no place to sit, but we were so close to the sacred relics of the saint that we took turns, then and there, to go and visit the crypt. They hadn't even opened the great doors yet. Marie chatted to some Dominicans in Latin, and Sir Gregory did his best to follow along. I was introduced to the captain of the archbishop's guard, a taciturn Portuguese knight, Francesco d'Alvia. But in the time it takes a priest to elevate the host, Lapot made him laugh with a quip in French that was sufficiently anti-clerical to anger any monk, and d'Alvia took the two of us and Michael and led us to the crypt, and then showed us the back of the sanctuary.

'If the archbishop is presiding, I usually have guards here,' he said. 'There's Juan – the only man I have posted today.'

Juan was in full harness, standing with a long sword between his hands by the door to the crypt.

I didn't know many Spaniards or Portuguese back then, and so I did the usual English thing – I tried the only Spanish name I knew on my new friend.

'Do you know Juan de Heredia?' I asked.

'The Preceptor of the Order of Saint John?' he asked. 'Of course I do.'

'He initiated me into the order,' I said.

In a moment Francesco d'Avila was showing me his own donat's ring, and we were exchanging tales of caravans in the east when they opened the cathedral doors and the pilgrims came flooding in. There were thousands – the numbers were incredible, even after our experience in the great square the day before. They flooded into the church in an awestruck flood, faces upturned.

And the cathedral itself is magnificent. From the carvings over the doors to the design of the high altar, there are few buildings in Christendom to rival it. Every appointment is rich, so that to stand by the altar is almost to stand at the door of Heaven. In fact, to me, the Mass was not sung as well as I've heard elsewhere. The priest officiating could have used some practice with his music master, and the altar service left something to be desired. I'm sorry to carp, but I do like to see these things done well. Performance is not trivial – any soldier polishing his armour knows that.

For all that, taking communion with four thousand other Christians is a wonderful, uplifting thing, and the sheer sound of the responses roared like a furious wind through the aisles and nave, as if perhaps the Holy Spirit was visiting us in person. At the kiss of Peace, I embraced my friends, old and new. Sister Marie grinned at me and hugged me twice, and Lapot shook his head.

'Or perhaps I am ready to be a priest,' he said.

An hour later, we walked out of the side doors of the cathedral, bidding farewell to the captain and the Dominicans, and a pair of knights of the Order of Calatrava to whom Francesco had introduced me. Christopher and Hanna had accepted the captain's offer of a tour of the cathedral, and Lady Tabitha went with them.

Sir Gregory grinned as we walked down the steps.

'Wine?' he asked. 'Damn it, gentleman. I made my vow and I have fulfilled it. I think I can pay for some wine.'

'I want to change my clothes,' I said.

I had some notion that they wouldn't try so hard to fleece me if I was not dressed as a pilgrim. In truth, I had only one rather worn cote-hardie, and a second gown that was not grey and had the cross of my order on it.

Lapot nodded agreement, and since Sister Marie's miracle house was only a few steps from the cathedral, we all walked over together.

'I've a mind to go to the library,' Marie said. 'We have the house for a week. Will we stay?'

In truth, I had given no thought to my life after the moment of the Elevation of the Host. I had made a great pilgrimage, alternating between sinning and an elation of spirit. Now that I was changing from my pilgrim clothes, I felt a sudden loss of identity and purpose.

For so many days, I'd had a simple goal. I hadn't even *thought* about the world outside. I'd even ignored Camus, often, unless he was right there.

I shrugged. 'Time to think of that later,' I said.

I buckled a plain belt around my waist. I'd have to buy a knight's belt. One of the great advantages of pilgrim clothes is that they eliminate all badges of rank and social status, and now, if I was to be a secular man again, I would need to be a knight. Indeed, I had a suspicion that if I stayed a week, I'd be dining with Sir Francesco.

'Are you wearing a sword?' Lapot asked.

Camus was in town.

'Yes,' I said.

I may have said it pettishly. All things taken together, what I remember most is annoyance that Sister Marie and Lapot were forcing me to engage with the world, whether they knew it or not. I had been very content with the limited goals of pilgrimage – walk, pray, eat, sleep. Maybe a little wine if you are lucky. Avoid Camus. Simple.

So I turned back at the doorway and picked up the Hospitaller Brother's arming sword. It had its own narrow belt, like most good swords, and wearing it necessitated stripping my purse off my pilgrim belt and moving my dagger.

'I could have had a nap,' Sir Gregory called from the doorway. 'Look, the taverns are closing for the night ...' and other such witticisms.

I buckled it on, put a cap on my head and followed Lapot out of the door.

Our fine narrow house shared a loggia with all the other houses on the street, a long overhanging storey with deeply recessed archways so that pedestrians were fully protected from the elements. It all looked a little like Venice to me, except that there were no canals and the whole Holy City smelt strongly of urine, which may be a comment on the human condition.

Sister Marie stopped to make sure that our Boy stayed in the house. He wanted to be out on the streets, but his tendency to knock people down and the sheer volume of his meat diet was enough to discourage us from taking him to a tavern if we didn't have to.

'I'm for the library,' she said over her shoulder.

'Come and have a cup of wine!' I said.

She turned to me with a lovely smile. 'William,' she said in English. 'Think, please.'

I shrugged, aware that there was a commotion in the street, off to my right.

'I am a nun,' she said. 'I can't sit in a tavern in Santiago.'

It was true. For weeks we'd walked along, and the little taverns had also been the *albergues* – her presence had been natural.

Suddenly we were back in the world, and in the world, nuns and other decent women didn't go to taverns for any reason.

I sighed. Not for the first time, or the last, I felt a jolt, as if the end of my Camino was a loss like the death of a friend ...

'William Gold!' came a shout.

I knew that voice.

And it is also strange – perhaps a spiritual experience, perhaps just the odd, fey mood of the end of my pilgrimage. But when Camus shouted my name, many things came together, and some of them fell away.

I've heard men who've survived from very, very near the edge of death say that when you are about to die, many things become clear, and many other things become insignificant.

In one moment, I realised – not as William Gold, knight, but as William Gold, sinner – that I didn't give a damn about Camus. I've never been much for revenge – fighting is a profession, not some emotional mime. Hating Camus, fearing him ... all that fell away. Even the bravado of my last performance with him fell away.

Yet even as it fell away, I realised that he had to go down. He hurt people, killed, wrecked lives. I didn't need to hate him, or to want revenge. I just needed to drop him, for all his future victims.

I stepped away from Sister Marie. Behind me, I heard her unlock the door to our house.

I loosened my sword in its sheath and stepped out from under the loggia.

And there he was. He and four other men, mounted on tall horses. They were perhaps fifteen paces down the street.

'At last,' Camus said. 'Where have you been, you busy little hypocrite?'

'On pilgrimage,' I said.

'Why do you people lie to God so often?' Camus asked.

I could see that his blasphemy had almost no impact on the men-at-arms he had left.

I said nothing. I stood by one of the pillars that held up our archway. I knew what I was going to do – all my decisions were made.

'You know that I'm not just going to kill you,' Camus said. 'In fact, I can't yet imagine exactly what I'll do.' He pointed at the men either side of him. 'Take him.'

They all looked at him.

'Afraid to take me yourself?' I asked.

The four men-at-arms started forward.

Lapot stepped out from the arcade on the other side of the street. In one gliding step, he took a man's bridle, passed under the horse's head, and put a dagger into the man's thigh where his haubergeon didn't come down to his cuisse. He turned the horse so that the man's partner couldn't reach him with a sword cut, and the bravo fell, screaming, into the arcade on the far side.

Sister Marie emerged from one pillar, and Michael and Sir Gregory from another, in the silence between the man's screams.

Boy erupted from the house. His claws scratched along the stone – indeed, it's the sound I most remember in the moment before I charged Camus. I left the other three sergeants to my friends.

It is good – beautiful, even – to have friends in a fight. Real friends, people who you can trust. I never doubted that they could take four men-at-arms, despite the fact that we were all naked, by which I mean without armour, and they were all well armoured and on horses. Perhaps you want me to be afraid for them, but that is not what I felt.

I felt that particular joy.

I had perhaps ten running paces to reach Camus. From my first explosion off my pillar, I could see that he was surprised.

By my second step, I'd cross-drawn my arming sword and my rondel dagger was in my left hand, so that when Red-Turban, the left-hand bravo, cut at me, my sword and dagger made a nice cross of steel in the May sunshine. He turned his horse, but it wasn't all that well trained and it tried to pivot on its back feet, carrying him farther from me. While I may have failed to get him out of his high-backed saddle, he was unbalanced.

I kept going, flowing through his cut as his horse turned him towards the high arches along the right-hand side of the street. Blue-Corrazina, the nearest of the bravos on the right side of the street, put spurs to his roncey. The aggrieved horse burst forward at me, but I was low, going right at her, and she shied. Blue-Corrazina cut at me with a long war hammer, the kind of thing that the Turks and Moors use, but all he achieved was a ringing blow to my sword, which survived the experience. I was past him, too, and he had no room to turn.

And that left Camus, because Green-Feather, the outside man, was already fighting Sir Gregory, who had a very long sword in his hand and looked as if his hip and foot weren't bothering him at all.

Camus also put his prick-spurs to his mount, a much better horse than the others had. But he'd waited too long. He really wanted one of the others to take me.

Because Camus was afraid of me.

And so, as my seventh or eighth step rang on the cobbles, he was only pricking his charger, and the big horse did what any horse might do when surprised. He reared.

Now, I'd planned to kill his horse. I admit it – I was intending to charge the mount, spook it as I'd learnt to do from the order, and then run my sword through its head.

But when it reared, Camus had to fight for control ...

I passed to the left of the flailing hooves. The horse wasn't concentrating on me, but on the spurs.

I dropped my sword, got my right hand on his left ankle, and threw him from the saddle while he was wrestling for control.

Bless Fiore. I'd never have thought of that, years before.

Camus went down hard – it's a long way down from a rearing horse to cobbles. As soon as the charger was rid of his weight and the hated spurs, he turned. I pricked him in the withers with the point of my dagger, and he was off down the street.

I had time to collect my dropped sword, and to look over my friends.

Green-Feather was turning his horse, blood flowing from a cut on his face. Sir Gregory was standing, watching him. Blue-Corrazina was lying on the cobbles and Marie was standing over him with a sword. Red-Turban was apparently unhurt from his encounter with Lapot until I saw him slump, and blood flowing from the stump of his sword hand.

I watched Camus rise. It occurred to me to kill him while he rose. Make no mistake – I intended for him to be dead. But I couldn't make myself kill him that way.

Instead, I waited for him to rise and find his sword. It took him a surprising amount of time, and by then, Green-Feather was dead and Lapot and Marie had turned towards me. Michael had his dagger at Blue-Corrazina's throat.

Camus was hurt. I didn't care.

He had a fine, long sword. He was having trouble choosing a *garde* – he'd hit the stones hard.

It all should have been a little too much like murder, but that was not the will of God.

Camus stepped suddenly, and I was aware that some, at least, of his injury was feigned. He swung, a sharp, stiff blow. I covered crisply, stepping offline to my left as Fiore teaches, and my right wrist registered a shock as I rolled into my counter-cut.

The blade of my sword was gone.

That cut right through my new-found equanimity and ruined my momentary superiority.

I had a dagger, and I was facing a skilled madman with a long sword.

Camus was a bloody murderer, but he was not a fool. The moment he realised what had happened, he attacked, trying to overwhelm me, to break my *garde*. My dagger was a long one, a baselard with a heavy backbone, and I parried his first wrist cut and his second, both times passing backwards as he pursued me. I went in under the arcade and he paused, as his long sword would be disadvantaged by the stone pillars.

Only then did he look around.

The moment he turned his head, Sir Gregory threw me his sword. It was a good, English long sword with fine long quillons and a heavy fishtail at the pommel, and he threw it hilt-first along the arcade.

I caught it as if we'd practised the whole thing a dozen times. I went forward a step to catch it and followed the motion as if Saint Michael were leading me by the hand, going around the pillar of the arcade.

Camus turned, registered the long sword, and took a step back.

I tossed my dagger, underhand. It wasn't a strong throw. I thought perhaps to surprise him or draw a blow, and instead, the dagger hit him, point-first, in the groin.

Camus flinched, roared, and cut at me. I covered, rolling his blow off my blade like rain off a roof, passed forward with my left foot, slipped his blade and cut.

He covered most of it, but I landed enough to slam my edge into his armoured left arm. On reflex, I turned the blade and tried for his face. He stumbled back and I had the initiative and the balance, and as his shoulder hunched against my blow, I passed forward again, my right foot passing the left. I didn't quite land a fight-ending pommel strike. My pommel went into the side of his helmet when he ducked his head. Camus was good. He collected his weight, struggling to recover his balance, but he was in armour and I was using the weight of his armour against him. Once you start moving in any direction in armour, back or forward, it is difficult to stop.

He threw a blow. He shouldn't have been able to, but my pommel strike hadn't rattled him enough, even if it cost him some balance. His cut, one-handed, at waist level, almost got me. I raised my wrists, dropped my point over my shoulder – an odd parry and not one anyone had taught me.

I got cut, but I wasn't cut in half. I had to be aware that if I closed with him, all the advantage was his. A man in armour is deadly at close quarters.

But I was still a little ahead of him, even with his counter-cut, and I freed my point and went for his throat, passing my point straight over my head. He was still stumbling back. My left foot passed my right and went deep, and to hell with caution.

My point was short of his neck. He was backing that fast, trying to get his balance.

But he'd misjudged his back step, and for a second, even as my left foot passed behind his right, he was overextended, his weight change sloppy.

My left foot hooked his right and I pulled, my unarmoured foot feeling the steel of his sabaton and the ankle of his greave.

I dropped him. As his left foot came up, he had no reserve of balance to fight me, and he went down like a sail cut free from the yard.

He hit hard. As he fell away from me, I had a moment to see that my thrown dagger had really hurt him. Blood was pouring down his left leg.

He gathered his armoured feet away from me and made a weak cut at my feet.

I parried it. I was walking around him. He was trying to get on his feet.

You won't like this, Froissart.

I didn't let him up. I was done with him. I was done with hunting, and being hunted, with losing friends and servants, with fear, with triumph.

I was done with all of it.

'Gold!' he spat. 'I know things ...'

I stepped forward, a long pass with my right foot, so that I stepped on his blade where my parry held it.

'I can help you ...' he hissed.

Then, like the traitorous snake he was, he rolled, trying to pull the sword out from under my foot.

He failed. There, at the last, I think he knew he was done. He tried to raise his head, and met my eye.

'The Duke of Clarence ...' he said.

And then I passed my sword through his left eye, into his brain, and out the back, so that my borrowed sword made an ugly grating against the back of his helmet. For all the evil he'd done.

I watched the life pass out of his other eye.

From the moment he'd called my name, I'd known how this would go, if I won. And to be perfectly honest, barring the breaking of my arming sword, which must have been weakened by the blow from the war hammer, I'd expected to win. Camus's life didn't include Fiore, or the order, or all the training, or even the time and discipline to train. He was only a monster in imagination. He was just a bad, broken man.

'Sister Marie,' I called. 'Would you be so kind as to fetch Captain d'Avila?'

But I was puzzled as to why he'd died with Clarence's name on his lips.

And I wasn't willing to find out, and know something that might have forced me to leave him alive.

PART III

ENGLAND AND FRANCE

1369–1370

CHAPTER ONE

SANTIAGO AND LONDON

Summer 1369

Captain d'Avila was most obliging, as if a deadly duel with a foreign knight and his death was the sort of thing that could happen to any gentleman. A combination of Sister Marie's unflappable Latin eloquence, her letter from the Pope and my donat's ring disarmed the local authorities. You may call this corruption, but I call it justice. Camus had the reputation of a devil, and I had the reputation of a good knight.

However, Captain d'Avila did caution me, as you'll hear. In the meantime, the archbishop gave me a fairly harsh penance. He ordered me to spend some days on my knees in prayer for the soul of Camus, and he ordered me to go to Canterbury as a pilgrim. It was not so bad – he knew I was English. In fact, I had intended to work my way back to Chambéry and the count. That is, in as much as I had any thought at all.

I spent a few days on my knees in front of the Saint Michael's altar. If I haven't mentioned this before, I divide my adoration of saints between Saint Michael, the captain of the hosts of Heaven, and Saint Mary Magdalene, the reclaimed sinner – both of them represent aspects of my own life, eh?

I had a great deal of time to think about Camus as I prayed. It was no revelation to me that we were, in some ways, the same man. I knew that I'd had opportunities he'd never had – I'd had Fra Peter Mortimer, and Father Pierre Thomas, and Sister Marie. And Emile. And Fiore.

Really, I'd had a great many people. And he'd had the Bishop of Cambrai, peeling him apart, keeping the wounds fresh ... Using him as a murderer, encouraging his worst excesses. I thought of a certain house in Vigone.

Or hunting me on Camino. He'd snapped. He was no longer a bad man. He had become a madman. But Robert of Geneva had played a major role in making sure that he was bad, and mad.

I'm fairly certain these were not the thoughts the archbishop wanted me to have. And I've read enough theology to be wary of assigning blame. I killed Camus. But I didn't make him a monster. By the time I killed him, I don't think anything short of a direct visitation of Divine Grace would have changed him into a repentant sinner.

But I'd still killed him. While he lay, helpless, his sword trapped under my foot.

Here's something I've learnt about sin. The first person to whom you must confess is yourself – or God, if you like. I killed Camus while his sword was trapped under my foot. There. Let's not pretend, eh?

Once again, I was losing my friends. Sister Marie was going to Paris with Michael des Roches, and then on to Cologne to her home nunnery.

'I haven't seen them for six years,' she said. 'I've been to Jerusalem and Rome and Santiago. It's time I went home, before the world swallows me up.'

I fought tears, and turned to Lapot. He gave me a wry smile. We were sitting in our borrowed lodgings, comfortable around our own little hearth with our own wine, as if we were spending one more night in a tiny *albergue* in the mountains.

'I'm going back to the Company,' he said.

Marie nodded, as if this confirmed something for her.

'I don't have a true calling. Or rather, I think my calling is to be a knight, a good knight. Not a priest.' He shrugged.

Mind you, that was more words than Lapot spoke in a week, ordinarily.

We drank too much. One more time, I saw Marie with her face shining. One more time, I heard Lapot's dry humour. Des Roches, who hadn't been with us so long, didn't feel the same finality. He was walking to Paris with Marie.

He nodded to me. 'You know it's going to be war,' he said. 'France and Spain against England.'

I felt a thrill of panic. 'How soon?'

'Any day. That's what I heard at the scriptorium today.'

Michael was earning a little money copying for the cathedral. He had a magnificent hand, the sign of a truly educated man. In fact, there and then I asked Marie and Michael to each write a prayer for me in my little book. See? Here they are.

So I wrote out letters – one for the Green Count, one for l'Angars, another for Hawkwood. And I wrote to the king of France via du Guesclin, requesting a *sauvegarde*. I told all three to address my letters to the commanderie of the Knights of Saint John in Clerkenwell.

I was going to England.

None of my Italian banks had factors in Santiago, but I found a Jew at the base of the hill who did business with all three banks, and had known Nerio's father. He gave me a reasonable discount on a bill for a hundred ducats, and then an even better discount when I told him I was bound for England and would carry his letters. As it proved, and no surprise to me, he had dealing with the Bardi branch, Italian bankers in London who had offices within a minute's walk of the Priory of Clerkenwell.

So my scrip was full, and I had enough coins to be worth robbing. As it proved, Stiofán of Leinster was happy enough to walk to Finisterre and then take ship from Corunna. So although I had many partings, I had one good friend from my Camino to lighten my mood.

The next morning, Stiofán and I were dressed as pilgrims, Sister Marie in her habit, and Lapot was again a knight. We bid farewell to Sir Gregory and Lady Tabitha, and then we walked together to the great square in front of the cathedral, and Marie and I scandalised a generation of priests by embracing for a long time. Long enough to remember Father Pierre Thomas, Avignon, Alexandria, Jerusalem, Lesvos, Rome, Emile, and Camino.

'Be good, William,' she said.

I bent my head and she gave me a blessing. I'd rather have had her blessings than those of almost any consecrated person I've ever known.

I gave Lapot my letters and we embraced for almost as long.

'Will you come back to the Company?' Lapot asked.

'It's in the letters,' I said. 'I'll be back before the fighting season ends.'

He nodded. 'See you soon, then,' he said.

He went to lean against a corner of the cathedral. There was another person there.

I embraced Michael.

'I'll miss your wisdom and your sources of information,' I said.

He laughed. 'Perhaps I'll come and find you in Italy,' he said. 'Perhaps you'll need a notary.' He looked at Marie. 'I confess that Camino has had an unexpected effect – I find that adventure is as seductive as knowledge.'

I envied the three of them. They were together, at least to Paris.

But Stiofán and I bowed one more time, took our staffs, and began to walk down the hill towards the gates.

To my vague surprise, the dog followed me.

'We should buy some bread for the walk,' Stiofán said, in his matter-of-fact, on-to-the-next-thing way. Then he smiled. 'You usually feed him. That's what he knows.'

'He's a good boy,' I said, pulling his ears a little.

And he was right, of course. And we were walking.

Just at the gate to the square, Christopher the Aethiopian appeared. He, too, had a staff and a scrip.

'May I accompany you gentlemen?' he asked.

And then I knew whom I had seen with Lapot, leaning against the cathedral. Hanna, the Hungarian woman. Ah, people. No wonder Lapot was clinging to the world.

Stiofán smiled his acerbic smile.

'You going to feed him, too?' he asked.

Finisterre was magnificent – the end of the world, or so the ancients believed. Myself, I've been to Scotland and I used to be fairly certain that Iona, off Mull, is the true end of the world, although Stiofán assured me that Ireland is even farther west. And, of course, the man at the Krakow Fair who sold me a falcon had been to Iceland and Greenland and even farther west, so really, it's all nonsense, like so many other things men think.

It was beautiful, though.

Then we walked up the coast to Corunna, where the English wine ships come in all the time, unloading pilgrims from the Thames and picking up tuns of wine. Stiofán and I bought passage, including

Christopher. The shipmaster was suspicious of the dog, but we convinced him, and we all went aboard.

Having gone to sea on a glorious June day, we then were treated to nine days of brutal weather in the Bay of Biscay, blown almost into the coast of Aquitaine and Gascony and then back as the wild winds changed. I broke bones in my left hand working on the deck. So many of the sailors were injured that they asked passengers and pilgrims to lend a hand. The animals, equine and canine, were mad with fear, at first, and later lay still, as if waiting for death. Stiofán worked like a horse, and even injured I could cut and splice, and so, on day ten, we sighted Cornwall, or so the mates said. Then we had to beat, by which sailors mean going up and down the wind, all the way to Portsmouth, where we dropped our anchors, miles from the Thames or Canterbury, and yet completely thankful to be alive.

I had sworn to go to Canterbury as a pilgrim. Now that had been made a good deal more difficult, as I was more than a week's walk from Canterbury, but I shouldered my scrip and my staff.

'I'll come with you,' Stiofán offered.

'And I,' Christopher agreed.

It was a pleasant enough walk. Kent, in June, is very like paradise. We had a little light rain, and the smell of new hay, and a great many flowers. But the farther we walked, the more rain there was. In fact, as you'll all remember, the rain fell and fell, and in the end the harvest was terrible. But even before the bad harvest, there was a level of poverty I had never seen in England, and more loud discontent in wine shops and alehouses than I could remember. On the other hand, the English are an outspoken lot, like Venetians, and I hadn't been home for a long time. I'd forgotten how fractious an English yeoman could be.

Christopher was a wonder in most of the towns we passed after we left Portsmouth, where dark-skinned men and women were not so uncommon. And Stiofán's Irish accent was almost as alien. Men of Kent are not really fond of foreigners. But we were pilgrims, and we made our way, and as I had money, we paid for everything and never begged food as most pilgrims do. And the men of Kent are fond of dogs, so our good boy, whom we now called 'Pilgrim', was very popular. He would range ahead, or behind – sometimes out of sight for as much as an hour – but he always came back, and his behaviour inside an inn or a church was exemplary. He would sit by me, or on my left foot, for hours, if that's what was required. He'd been very well trained at some point.

So, after a good walk, a long bout of rain and three days lost while Stiofán and I had some sort of fever, we came at last to Canterbury. It reminded me of Santiago – which is to say, the taverns were excellent and very expensive. But my heart was rising, whether it was distance from the death of my wife, or the death of Camus, or both. Whether perhaps the smaller pilgrimage without a man trying to kill me was the more spiritual, or mayhap just the good company, for Stiofán and Christopher, while not sword-companions, were excellent company. Watching Pilgrim bound through the hay on a sunny afternoon raised my heart with joy. Regardless, when I rose from the Saint Michael chapel at the cathedral of Saint Thomas, I was light of heart and ready to live again. And my first order of business was to see my sister.

We walked to Whitstable, where I thought to buy the three of us passage up the Thames. I was negotiating with two different English shipmen when the Venetian galley, the yearly ship for London, entered the port. The capitano was not anyone I knew, but he was a friend of Carlo Zeno and he knew me, or knew of me, and he took the three of us aboard for nothing, and Pilgrim, who sat on the command deck as if he owned the place. Pilgrim's manners were so good that he didn't trouble the two ship's cats, who walked around him a few times and then decided to ignore him.

We talked about pilgrimages – he'd been to Santiago and Jerusalem – and about the coming war.

In fact, we agreed that war between England and France was insane.

'England has no money, and France has no money,' he said. 'So these two bankrupt states will now attempt to burn each other's peasants, thus destroying the capital that pays the taxes to pay off the bankruptcy, and some Italian will loan them both the money to do it. Your King Edward is lost between the thighs of his leman, and the king of France is a coward who will fight his battles from Paris.'

Michele Bembo, as my new Venetian acquaintance was called, knew more gossip than Michael des Roches, and that was quite something. I heard about King Edward's lover, Alice Perrers, and her various relatives now living at court. I heard more about the king of

France's ransom of my friend du Guesclin, and further about how bad the relations between the Prince of Wales, my Edward, and the king of England were.

'Your King Edward,' Michele Bembo kept saying, as if King Edward was my fault. 'He forced Prince Edward into a war with Spain that the prince didn't want, and then he forced Prince Edward into a corner with some of his Gascon vassals, and now he's going to make Prince Edward do his fighting for him, while he rubs his member against something much younger.' He shrugged. 'The king never forgave his son for capturing the king of France.'

'Ouch,' I said.

I admit that I'd heard it said, and even thought it, but never by someone as well informed as Michele Bembo, aristocrat and merchant of Venice.

'And King Edward won't want to leave his lovely Alice,' Bembo continued, 'so I'll predict that this war will be fought by Prince Edward and John of Lancaster against du Guesclin and some greasy Gascons – the d'Albrets. And no one will have any money. It will all be pretty ugly.'

'War is always ugly,' I said.

He shrugged. 'It's better when you have the money to do it well,' he said.

Which was both terrible, and true.

And then he said something that stayed with me a long time.

'Someday soon, Venice and Genoa will fight,' he said. 'We have all the money. And you will see a war. A *real* war.'

We landed in London, straight onto the docks, a privilege of the yearly Venetian galley. Sometimes there were two, or even three galleys, but everyone always called the event 'The Venetian galley', and they brought only the finest and most remarkable wares. Enamelled gold. Bolts of radiant silk brocades and velvets. Superb Greek wine from Monemvasia which we English call 'malmsey'. Ginger so fresh and hot that it can cut like a knife. True cinnamon. White sugar. Beautiful armours from Brescia, and swords to match.

I walked down a wide plank with a handrail, in a grey wool gown that had seen some hundreds of miles of wear. I had an old belt and a purse that might have seen work in Old Rome, and the shoes on my feet didn't even keep out mud. There was, you might say, more hole than shoe.

London is not a good place to be poor. So I took my friends directly to the Priory of Saint John in Clerkenwell, where I was received with open arms, thanks to God. My pilgrim's robe was completely natural there. I only got as far as the porter in the outer ward when Fra Peter Mortimer, whom I'd last seen, sick with grief, on a dock in Cyprus, was standing before me, my own height exactly, wearing the brown working habit of the order over boots with spurs. We embraced, and talked very fast. The upshot was that I got my two friends cells in the convent, and I was offered lodgings in the priory proper. That night I dined with the knights – a dozen men, and most of them men I knew from the Alexandria crusade. Fra Robert Hales headed the table and was kind enough to seat me by him.

The next day, wearing the habit of the order as if I was on Rhodes, I practised the art of arms with Fra Peter, despite my broken fingers, prayed in the chapel, confessed some very routine sins to the priest, and then, it still being early, I went to the Italian bankers with two parchment scrolls from Santiago. I had no trouble at all finding the Bardi; a youngish man called Antonio waited on me and he was tall enough to be a man-at-arms, and strong besides. He made a quip about early risers, but his demeanour changed when he was presented with the letters from Spain. I sat in his room under his house, and his servant served me mulled wine while I waited. He read the letters and then turned to me.

'How can I help you?' he asked.

'I'm looking to access money,' I said.

He nodded. 'I can make you a loan, but if you want your own money, I can only send you to the Italians. The Alberti—'

'I bank with the Alberti and the Acciaioli,' I said. Niccolò's death had virtually undone the Acciaioli banks, but the Alberti, the richest family in Florence, had seamlessly taken over. Or so it seemed to me, as a mere man-at-arms. I said it with confidence, but I was afraid – really afraid – that in the months that I had been gone, the Alberti had failed, or simply refused to cover the accounts of what had once been a rival bank.

'All the better,' Antonio agreed. 'Young Francesco Lona is their factor. I'm going to the Venetian galley – come, do me the favour of walking with me.'

Sadly, it really was a favour. A 'Lombard' in the streets of London was no great thing, but if people were feeling ugly – and friends, they were, just then – well, a Lombard walking with a man in the habit of the Order of Saint John was a great deal safer, or at least his purse was. I waited for him, and he made a thousand apologies as he gathered bits of money and pages of accounts, but eventually we walked south to the Temple. The great galley was docked just below the bar, almost at the bridge, and a whole market had sprung up there, with everything from the finest Byzantine samite to local meat pies. Sir Robert Hales, the English prior of my order, was there, seeing to it in person that the market had the proper licence and paid its taxes – that's how important the Venetian galley was to the elite London trade.

However, as Antonio had predicted, the Alberti factor had an exchange table going. And when Antonio introduced me, and vouched for me being who I said I was, the young factor rose, gave me a very deep bow.

'You are Messire Renerio's friend,' he said. 'Of course I know you. How may I be of service?'

It really is very satisfying to have a little fame and some good friends.

'I need money,' I said. 'My entire kit, harness and sword and all, were taken from me in Gascony.'

He nodded. He waved to a clerk.

'I think I have your entire account in the office,' he said. 'But unless you plan to buy the galley, here, I believe I can cover anything you care to spend. Indeed, I might suggest a few purchases that might make us both a little profit, if that doesn't offend. Messire Renerio says you are quite the canny merchant. What was it that you bought at such profit?' He asked this casually, but I could see he was testing me.

I really only offer this to show how they prove your *bona fides*. He really had heard about me from Renerio.

'Saffron,' I said with a laugh.

'Exactly,' he said, bowing to Antonio. 'My thanks, sir, as always.'

I did note that they exchanged small pieces of parchment. Lombards are forbidden certain forms of trade. So are Italians ... I should probably be outraged as an Englishman, but then, there really aren't any English banks, are there?

I followed young Lona back to his office, which was quite close. He flipped through a slim codex, and then located a smaller book, opened it and nodded.

'You are worth a little more than nine thousand ducats,' he said. 'I reckon that in shillings and pounds if you like, or florins.'

By then, I confess that I thought in Venetian currencies, or Genoese. In the Mediterranean, these were the standard coinages from Jerusalem to Aleppo.

But the number cut through me like a sword blade.

'Nine ... *thousand* ducats?' I asked.

'Hmm. Perhaps more. Those are Messire Frederico's accounts from our Bruges branch. It will take me a few weeks to update them if you need better numbers, but by the Virgin, My Lord, I can cover whatever you like on short-term credit.'

I was still wrestling with the amount.

'I hadn't expected to have so much money,' I admitted.

'Ah.'

Lona shrugged, as if he couldn't imagine a customer in such a predicament. Or, mayhap, indicating his unease at dealing with a customer who could hit him for such a huge sum.

It must have been the settlement of Emile's estate. And my ransoms, of course. I'd taken a couple that were good, back in the summer, fighting in northern Italy.

My head was spinning as if I'd taken too much wine.

'I have to sit down,' I muttered.

'I assure your lordship that I can cover any amount you care to spend,' Lona said, mistaking my unease. 'But a note of hand on our bank should be good anywhere in London, especially while the galley is here.'

Then we traded some political gossip. He said the same things about the coming war as I'd heard from Bembo on the galley – probably from the same source. He asked some questions about Spain, and told me how much the English feared Spanish raids on their coasts.

'The king of England will have to launch a pre-emptive raid into France,' he said. 'Or the French will come here.'

I confess that, as a veteran of Poitiers, I thought that sounded absurd.

'Any place we find the French, we beat them like a drum,' I said.

He shrugged, clearly not saying everything he thought.

'May I ask what your plans are, My Lord?' he asked.

'My plans?' I shrugged.

'You have a company in Italy, do you not?' he asked. 'And you serve with "Acudo", yes? He has just won a great victory at Cascina. An empty victory, but a victory.'

'Cascina?' I asked. 'We fought there years ago.'

'And now your "Acudo" has fought there again,' Lona said.

That caught my interest. Lona had a letter from a Milanese agent which he read aloud to me, an indication that, despite my pilgrim gown and worn-out shoes, I was a very important customer.

Hawkwood was fighting for Milan against the Church – the same sides, in effect, as they had been before. The Church's main army was fielded by Florence – no surprise there.

Hawkwood, like the old fox he was, lured the Florentines across a canal, collapsed their flanks, and took a lot of prisoners.

'Brilliant,' I said.

I wondered if any of my friends had been killed. I wondered what I was doing in England.

'Eh, I suppose,' my young Florentine said bitterly. 'My father says that we had another army in the field within two weeks, because we are *much* richer than the Milanese.'

'What kind of an army?' I asked.

I wasn't derisive, but I could picture the Florentines, desperate, hiring the riff-raff of . . .

'Lutz von Landau to command. Hugh Despenser and Richard Romsey and their companies. And you know that your friend Andrew Belmont is in France with his lances, serving the Prince of Wales? Your friend Acudo must be getting short of Englishmen.'

I was shocked. Hugh Despenser was an aristocrat, and also not a particularly reliable man. Further, he'd been deeply committed to Prince Lionel, and there was a rumour that he blamed Milan for Lionel's death. But Romsey and Belmont were important men in Hawkwood's companies, Andy had been around forever, and was absolutely competent, and Romsey was a rising star. If they had left Hawkwood . . .

Of course, I'd left Hawkwood, too.

Lona shrugged, curbing his Florentine patriotism.

'Regardless, Messire Acudo retreated into the north like a fox to his earth, and Landau retook San Miniato, which means that the campaign accomplished nothing.'

It's hard to explain how this felt. I had heard men speak about the world – Michael des Roches, for example, knew almost as much as Lona. But in that conversation, in a fine office in London in mid-June, my life came back to me. It was as if the Devil had stripped me of my pilgrim robes and forced me to look at all the kingdoms of the world.

I had lived for almost a year in a bubble of my own concerns – the death of my wife, the treason of the Prince of Achaea, the murder of Prince Lionel, Camus, capture, pilgrimage. But no man who serves in arms is disconnected from the world, and now the world was coming back.

'I suppose, if I may be so bold, My Lord, my question should have been, will you serve the king of England in his war with France? Or go back to Italy?'

I could tell that in this instance, he would sell this information, and I could understand why it was valuable. I also realised that I could turn this to my advantage.

'I'm not sure how I would serve the king,' I said. 'I'm not even sure I'm a vassal here.' I smiled. 'I owe service to the king of Cyprus and to the Count of Savoy. I don't owe service to the king of England.'

Lona nodded. 'England is in a sorry state for veterans,' he said. 'Sir John Chandos will have a command. Knolles is already in Normandy. The Duke of Lancaster is already in France with an army.'

'I am really only here to complete my vows and visit my sister,' I said.

Lona nodded.

'If you were interested in serving with Knolles, I could furnish an introduction,' he said cautiously. 'I am his banker. And he is running his command as a business. You could buy a share. A substantial share.'

I didn't say 'Never'. But I thought it. I am not a friend of Sir Robert Knolles, regardless of his reputation. Hawkwood's cold-blooded calculations I could appreciate – they included his men, his officers. Knolles was entirely selfish, or at least, that was his repute. And he was more of Camus's stamp than I could tolerate. As it turned out, my instincts were entirely accurate.

'And Lancaster,' Lona smiled. 'We're his banker, too.'

I enjoyed the afternoon, spending money like a rich mercenary.

I think the thing that I remember most is the prices. I was used to Italy. Armour from Brescia, the best in the world – except maybe armour from Bohemia – is much, much cheaper in Brescia than in London. Swords from Milan – much cheaper in Milan. And while English wool is far and away the best in the world, English tailors were making men long gowns with hanging sleeves, hopelessly out of date by Italian standards. And everything cost more than in Italy. Wine cost more, bread cost more, and swords were very dear.

It was difficult to get the attention of clerks when I wanted to buy something because I was so ill-dressed, but I am a popinjay and I had no interest in laying out money on 'English' clothes that I'd never wear in Italy. Fortune favoured me. I had just been ignored by two Italians young enough to be pages, who had, in effect, declined to sell me a magnificent pair of spurs in gold and enamel. I assume they thought I was a thief dressed as a pilgrim. But I found a young tailor, recently freed of his apprenticeship, by mistake. I bought a cup of wine from one of the casks coming off the Venetian galley, and jostled the young man's elbow. He was very tall and I was clumsy. We begged each other's pardon. I noted the Italian cut of his clothes and commented on them. He allowed that he'd made them himself, and went on to say that he was mostly visiting the Galley Market to see what the Italians were wearing.

He didn't have a shop. Indeed, he had to buy fabric and even some needles to start work on my clothes. Despite which, I had a feeling about him, and I was happy enough to try him, and to follow him patiently from shop to shop, buying thread, buying buttons, buying beautiful fabric.

I might have hesitated when I had to buy him shears. But I had already spent money, and he seemed absolutely confident. Shears are as expensive as good swords. I hadn't known that.

Before the sun set on a long London evening, he was making me a cote-hardie in the Milanese fashion, with a doublet to match, some hose, and a half-cloak. He cut with the same confidence that he spoke of fashion, and I stayed long enough to be certain I had chosen my man well. Then I walked out to find other items.

I regretted my beautiful knight's belt, taken by Armagnac's brigands, but I bought myself a good belt, mounted in silver, a new purse, and several pairs of boots. I didn't bother with armour. I had already decided to go back to Hawkwood. I'd buy armour in Italy, I assumed.

That evening, I collected news on my sister, who was at one of the priories, and I made plans to rent a horse and go and visit her. I listened to Sir Robert Hales's discourse on the state of the exchequer and England's chances in the war with France, and I misliked what I heard.

The next day, I met my young tailor and watched him work. It was high summer, late June. He'd sat up late, and he had four women making my shirts and braes. I fetched my new boots, purchased a nice leather trunk in which to store it all, and then, after a very pleasant exchange with the saddler who'd made the *malle*, I bought a riding saddle, bridle, and some other tack. His price was excellent, and in this, the English are at least as good as Italians, right down to the decorations, which were in this case, copper with some red enamel.

Then I walked around a little until I was standing outside my uncle's door. But I had no intention of visiting him. I merely stood outside, and then walked on, visiting the monks who'd protected me as a boy. The abbot of my youth had died. Brother Bartholomew, one of the more severe brothers, had been elected. I was still in my pilgrim gown, and he came down from his private solar to see me.

'Can we help you?' he asked. His smile seemed warmer than when I'd been younger. 'A bed and a good meal, young William?' He glanced at Pilgrim, who stood by me.

'No need, by your grace and the grace of Our Lord,' I said. 'In fact, I've brought a little donation. I have often thought of this place, and how you ... protected me.'

Indeed, Brother Bartholomew had beaten my uncle with his fists on one notable occasion.

He shook his head. 'Perhaps you should keep your donation for your own needs,' he said. 'There is no shame ...'

I realised that, as I had not yet collected my clothes or boots, I was sitting in the parlour in my holed boots and frayed pilgrim gown.

I laughed. 'Ah,' I said. 'Here, Holy Father.'

I counted out fifty ducats in gold on the table, the stone of my donat's ring flashing.

He began shaking his head in surprise as the first gold piece emerged from my old purse, and he didn't stop until I'd put the whole sum on the table.

'I'm just back from Santiago and Canterbury,' I said. 'I made a vow.'

'Now, glory be unto God,' the abbot said. 'Shall we say Masses for your uncle's soul?'

I was that tempted to say, 'No, let the bastard burn in Hell forever.' I formed the words in the base of my throat. I shook my head, but I was only shaking it at myself.

'I'd like fifty Masses for my uncle,' I said. 'And fifty more for a man called Camus.'

I confess that I didn't believe that either one deserved redemption. But let's leave that to God, eh?

'Camus?'

'A man I killed,' I said.

The abbot looked at me, and his eyes were wise.

'And now you feel remorse?' he asked.

I looked away. 'Yes,' I lied.

Because good men like the abbot have no idea what Camus was like. Or perhaps they do. The answer was 'No'. But Brother Bartholomew had once beaten my uncle to save me, and I wasn't going to burden him with Camus.

Never mind, then.

Next morning, I had a fine English breakfast of bacon, eggs, cheese and sausage with my tailor at an inn called the Blue Anchor near the docks. I paid him his price in hard currency for all his work, and then bought a riding cloak, used, at his suggestion. He was good company, and we walked back to the galley discussing Italian and French fashion. I picked up my new belt, new purse, boots, saddle and all, and hired boys to carry it all back to Clerkenwell. And at the galley I paid far too much for a good Brescian long sword. It had a broad guard and a beautiful blade and a faceted pommel like a big pointed jewel. It cost me a year's pay for a fully armoured man in Italy – four times what it would have cost in Venice. But Bembo appeared from the gangway and put the short staff he carried on the arm of the man selling, and suddenly the price fell a bit. Bembo gave me a smile.

'Now you look like a prosperous lord,' he said. 'Where did you find those clothes in England?'

I introduced my tailor – Gregory Fox. Venetian nobles are not too high and mighty to have wine with English tailors. I played with my sword for a bit, bought the pair of gold and enamel spurs that were worth more than most houses in London, and then, in a fit of expansiveness, bought a horse – a big, dark German horse, supposedly trained for war. In fact, he was not fully trained, but at the cost of renting horses in London, I had decided I might as well buy one and ship him to France.

I stabled the big horse at Clerkenwell and called him Percival. I sent my sister a note by a lay sister heading out to her priory, saying that I would come the next day but one, and I made plans to sail for Calais with a Thames merchant.

That night at dinner I broached my plans to Stiofán and Christopher.

'I'm for Dublin,' Stiofán said. 'London is too damned expensive.'

Christopher shrugged. 'I'm looking for employment,' he admitted.

'Can you fight?' I asked.

He shrugged. 'With anything,' he said.

'Take care of horses?' I asked.

He smiled. 'I grew up with horses,' he said.

'You're on.'

Christopher smiled knowingly.

I exchanged a long embrace with Stiofán of Leinster. He was a prosperous man, and said he intended to return to pilgrimage in a year, and perhaps go to Rome. I gave him various addresses in Savoy and Lombardy where he might reach me.

'You are not going to be easy to find,' he said acerbically. 'Don't you have a home?'

In fact, I realised that I didn't have a home. I had once, when Emile was alive.

'The Knights can always find me,' I said. 'There is a priory in Venice ...'

'Ah,' the Irishman said. 'Venice. I want to go to Venice.'

So, that's how we parted.

As it turned out, young Fox wanted to come to Italy as well. He put it to me diffidently enough. He was plain-spoken, although a little shy when anything but fashion was on offer. However, he made his proposal. He'd come with me as an archer, which he proved he was, like most London apprentices. His goal was to work in Italy as a tailor for a year or two, learn the patterns, and return in triumph to London.

It was a good plan. And what gentleman doesn't want a competent archer who is also a tailor? Especially one as fast as young Gregory.

I bought them both maille shirts and swords from the stores at Clerkenwell, and some used tack from my saddler in Cheapside. I'd never been to Buckland Priory, where Mary, my sister, was now housed. It was five days' ride from London, almost to Cornwall, which to a Londoner like me seemed an alien country – stranger, perhaps, than France or Italy.

Fra Peter Mortimer and I had several long conversations. Mostly we discussed the crusade, our parts in it, and the death of our beloved Father Pierre Thomas. We went to Mass together, said our rosaries together.

I knew what he had on his mind from the moment that I told him that Emile had died. So on my last night in Clerkenwell, with four good horses in the stable below and my two new 'grooms' cleaning and polishing tack and armour outside my cell, I sat with Fra Peter over wine, Pilgrim curled across both my feet under the table. I was waiting for Fra Peter to ask his question.

We talked of Cyprus.

'You know there's a rumour that King Peter is dead,' Fra Peter said.

'By God!' I suppose that I exclaimed, or something like it.

'Murdered by his brothers,' Mortimer said, and drank off his cup of wine.

'You believe it?' I asked.

He shrugged. 'Cyprus was a cesspool before we left,' he said bitterly. He'd had some wine – he was flushed. 'We are sworn to liberate the Holy Land, William, and yet I sometimes think that the Holy Land poisons everything it touches.'

I nodded.

He hesitated for a long time.

'I have not, perhaps, been ...' he began. He looked at me.

'I'm not really ready to become a Knight of the Order, Fra Peter,' I said.

There it was. I'd disappointed him in Jerusalem, and now that Emile was dead, he probably assumed I'd take the mantle of a Hospitaller.

He nodded. 'I should never allow myself to speak so bitterly of the Holy Land,' he said.

I shook my head. 'It's not that, Peter. But in the last two years, I've fought the Saracens for the order and for the Emperor, and for Nerio. Of the three, Nerio paid the best and has accomplished the most ...'

Fra Peter smiled. 'Indeed. A stable duchy in Romania. A new port being built at Corinth ...'

'Then I served the Green Count ...' I poured us both more wine. 'Listen, Peter. If you had asked me a year ago, I might have felt differently.' I shrugged. All I could see was the dead routiers hanging on the trees. 'Serving the Pope convinced me that there is absolutely no hope of retaking the Holy Land, in a way that fighting in the Holy Land never soured me.'

I told him about the failure of the Union of Churches. About the Pope's pride, and arrogance. About the Greek monks. The whole story.

In the end, he shook his head.

'We were so close,' he said.

I thought of Timurtash, and the Ottomanids.

'Perhaps,' I said.

It was very late when we found our pitcher of wine was empty.

'Will you come back to Clerkenwell?' Fra Peter asked.

'I'll be back in a week or two, after I see my sister,' I said.

Mortimer nodded. 'I'm for Avignon,' he said. 'But I can put it off for a week if I'd have company across France.'

That made me smile.

'Like old times,' I said.

The trip to Buckland took six days. June was giving way to July – the sun was too hot, but not as hot as in Romania or Cyprus or Crete or Lesvos. I was still absorbing the world, so to speak – wearing short clothes, riding a horse, receiving the visible signs of subordination, and sometimes fear, that an armed man on a horse gets in the countryside. We got badly lost one day, asked directions and got patently false information, and ... let's not dwell on all that. We reached Buckland on the evening of the sixth day, in late June. The priory smelt of new-cut hay, and as it was the longest day of the year, virtually all the monks and nuns were out in the fields, making sheaves.

I found Mary easily, as her hair is not much darker than mine, and she's the tallest woman in any crowd, and strong. I rode right up to her. A pair of sisters raised their forks cautiously, as if I might be some malefactor, but my sister threw her arms around me instantly.

The upshot of my arrival was that Christopher, who was very exotic in Somerset, and Gregory Fox, whose Italianate clothes were almost as foreign, found themselves learning to make neat hayricks under my sister's care.

'You are a farmer now, I find,' I said.

Mary laughed. I was stripped to my shirt and working, too. Believe it.

'When the plague passed ...' she said, and paused. 'Oh, William, I'm so sorry. We have all prayed for her soul, over and over, since I heard. She's on our "year's mind" now forever.'

I smiled, perhaps bitterly. 'Ain't it odd, sister,' I said, 'that we were salted young against plague, and it just keeps coming back to us?'

Mary nodded and kept on raking. 'Any road, since the plague passed, no one needs the nursing sisters. I've thought of going to the leper hospital – they nurse pilgrims. I'm no more afraid of leprosy than of plague.'

I got my cord around a good bit of hay and lifted it.

'Are you not?'

'If it is God's will that I contract leprosy, so be it,' she said.

I rocked the hay in my bundle and made another trip.

'I bought you a present,' I said.

'You always buy things,' she said. 'Just give the money to the poor and think of me. How long are you here?'

She looked at me and, just for a moment, there was another woman – a younger, more vulnerable woman.

Now, it's an odd thing. I am perfectly aware that I have a ... the Latin word is *persona*. I have a whole set of behaviours that I put on with some clothes, or armour. Emile used to call it 'The Great Knight', and she did not always mean this as a compliment, bless her. Nor is it fakery, I think. I merely act in the way that my soldiers and my peers would expect to have a great knight behave. Perhaps a little pompous ...

Never mind. What struck me, looking at my sister, is that all that strength, her aura of command, her fearlessness ... it was really her, but it was also a *persona*, like mine – something that she put on for much the same reason I donned mine. And perhaps the very best thing about Camino, now that I think of it, had been the setting aside of 'the Great Knight' for a few weeks.

Regardless, I looked at my sister and saw her as just my sister. Because I was there, she was letting go a little of her aura of command.

'The last time I visited, I saw you for an hour while your abbess watched us.'

'Prioress,' she corrected me. 'The order has prioresses and comanderixes.'

'I know,' I said.

We worked on for a while.

'Do these people ever eat?' Christopher asked plaintively.

Mary looked at me. 'We do,' she said mischievously. 'When all the work is done.'

The sun resolutely stayed in the sky, and our horses swished their tails at the omnipresent flies, and we worked our way down the fields, Mary and I chatting away.

'I gave the friars money for Masses,' I said finally. 'For our ... uncle.'

She nodded. She stood, put a hand in the small of her back, and leant on her hay rake.

'Good for you, William,' she said. 'As for me, I pray for him every day.'

She said it with a simplicity that went through me like a sword blow.

'I want him to burn in Hell,' I said.

She smiled. 'No one should burn in Hell,' she said. 'Hell is the triumph of evil and Satan. Jesus went there like a true knight, to harrow it and free the slaves. Why would you want anyone there?'

Well.

I was still digesting that piece of theology when we walked the horses into the priory stable. The sisters were chatty. Most of them were from very aristocratic families, as were most of the monks and the four brother-knights and the priest, and every one of them had been out in the fields, working like peasants.

The knights were all older men in their fifties and sixties. Many of the nuns were the same age, although they were a remarkably fit, hale congregation. I was introduced in the refectory, and I confess I forgot most of their names as fast as they were introduced. But Fra John Siward had fought at Smyrna with Geoffrey de Charny, and I certainly knew his name, and I was flattered that he knew mine. I even mentioned my friend from Camino who'd leant me a sword.

The prioress was an older woman, a Percy. On her black habit she wore a magnificent enamelled pin with her family coat of arms. She had not worked in the fields, but she was quick enough with thanks to those who had, and she had the touch of command that many religious leaders lack.

I was seated by her, and Fra John, by the gospel reader. Christopher and Gregory were well down the tables with the serving brothers, but they were well cared for and well fed.

My sister sat close to the head table, and I could see that the prioress leant heavily on her. That was interesting.

There was another guest, Nicholas de Dover, who was a knight of the Order of Saint Lazarus. Indeed, he claimed to be a Master of that order, and had a writ from the Pope ordering him to assume the position, and he told us a long, and to be honest, utterly dull tale of his court cases and demands. He monopolised dinner, and I can't say I thought much of him, as the prioress and Fra John both indicated, like courteous folk, that he should give way and let others speak.

Never mind. There are rude Englishmen, just like rude Spaniards – immune to our lack of interest. And of course, I'm never a bore myself, eh?

I confess that I used his lengthy description of a case before a canon court to talk quietly to my sister. After that, men and women separated for the night, which was a law among them. De Dover took me by the arm.

'You are a little rude,' he said. 'I was speaking of weighty matters of the common interest.'

I smiled and nodded. I don't provoke a fool, and de Dover had fool written all over him.

He shook my arm. My temper began to be engaged.

'We raise money for crusades, to fight the infidel. Raise your head out of the mire, and think of things bigger than yourself, sir.' He glowered at me.

Fra John was right behind me, and I had no interest in offending the old knight with my new-found views on crusade. So I nodded.

'I know a little of crusades, sir. Please release my arm.'

'Please apologise,' he said.

'I am sorry if I appeared rude,' I said.

He released my arm.

'Have you *been* on crusade?' I asked.

Fra John barked a laugh behind me.

'I have met many of the greatest crusaders,' he said. 'I have met the Green Count of Savoy in Rome, and Peter of Cyprus, too!'

I smiled. I was quite tempted to be pompous, but life has taught me that the de Dovers of the world learn nothing, so it's a waste of time to try to beat sense into them. I bowed.

When he was gone to a guest chamber, Fra John put a hand on my shoulder.

'You were very gentle with our guest.'

I shrugged. 'Tell me of Smyrna,' I said.

I had been dying to ask him all evening. De Dover was less than an insect on a man's collar by comparison. We sat up late, telling each other about other men's feats of arms.

In the morning we finished the haying before the rain came, to the utter delight of the prioress and the prior, too. There were two big houses, one for the men, another for the women, a handful of old knights, a first-rate horse farm where the old knights and the brother sergeants raised warhorses for the Holy Land, a dozen fish ponds, and farms. Mary took me on a ride around the farms. She chatted to all of the farmers and their wives, and we loaded our mounts with gifts of eggs, a ham, and a great deal of kale, most of which my charger ate before I could stop him.

Mary and I laughed a lot, cried a little, and generally had a fine day.

'Are you really thinking of going to the Lazars?' I asked.

She nodded.

'De Dover is an arse,' I said.

She shrugged. 'I'm bored,' she said.

Just for a moment, she sounded like Janet. It's not the first time

I realised how confining women's lives can be, but it was a powerful one. Here she was, at the summit of her ambitions – a full sister in the Order of Saint John, a hero, in a way, to the people of London, for her work in the plague. But that work had freed her to be something that women weren't, usually.

'I recommend a pilgrimage,' I said.

I found myself telling her all about Sister Marie.

She was interested, I could tell.

'Ride with me to Canterbury,' I said.

I could get a ship from there to France as easily as from London. And so, in a few hours, I convinced her.

Her prioress affected displeasure, but I think we could all tell that the old woman was so delighted that Mary wasn't leaving forever that she was happy to let her go to Canterbury. And as I was still a volunteer with the order, the old prioress gave me a sheaf of letters and accounts, some for Clerkenwell and four for Avignon or Rome. I was certainly capable of getting her accounts to the Grand Master on Rhodes, and I told her so.

'How do you come to know the Grand Master of the Order?' de Dover asked, his voice unctuous, as if the Grand Master might just walk in at any moment.

I smiled and bowed. Mary, like a good sister, laughed.

'My brother is a donat, Sir Nicholas,' she said, 'and served with the Grand Master at Alexandria.'

De Dover looked at me with sudden interest, the way some men look at a woman when her figure is revealed.

I ignored him to unwrap the present I had brought.

My present was a full Bible in a good Gothic minuscule, which I had picked up in London. It cost me quite a bit, but Fra Robert Hales had told us that Buckland lacked a full Bible, and that it was a trouble to him and to the priest. I presented it with my sister and was the hero of the hour.

The next morning, we rode away. It's not all war and pestilence, friends. My days in the fields of Somerset, and nights telling stories at the tables of the refectory, stay with me. If I ever overcome my enduring lust, I'll end my days there. I was happy. I may not have the fire in me to fight the Turks – I rather admire them, now. But I wouldn't mind ending my days telling lies about when I *was* fighting the Turks, eh?

Mary enjoyed the ride to London far too much, especially as we had good horses. She had discovered that she loved to ride, out in Buckland, and now she trotted and cantered in a way that might have been scandalous, except that there was no one to watch us. Three armed men and a nun and a big dog made for a great deal of courtesy on the road. Everyone could see we weren't brigands, and my sister, I now noticed, was a very attractive woman – dark brown hair with red highlights, green eyes, neatly set off by the black of her habit. Gentlemen bowed to her in all directions, because it's easier to be courteous when the object is attractive. Sadly.

In London, I took the liberty of buying her a good coral rosary and a pin – not as ornate as the prioress's pin, but a pretty thing with *Amor Vincit Omnia* on it. I gave it to Mary with a joke about her views on Hell, and she took it in kind.

Perhaps the best part of that time, for me, was how quickly we were brother and sister again. Mary was quicker of wit than she'd ever been in my uncle's house. Her deep goodness could not quench an impish sense of humour, and she had an annoying tendency to correct everyone around her with something that she'd learnt somewhere, and that I could tease her with.

I told Fra Peter of my intention to make another trip to Canterbury, and he took it in good part. My sister was a very popular woman in Clerkenwell.

I left Fra Peter assembling a whole party of pilgrims – easily done, as they tend to gather at Clerkenwell. My sister was chatting about herbs with the monk who kept the garden. Christopher and Gregory were practising sword cuts. I left Pilgrim with them, and slipped away.

I had one more visit to make in London.

I slipped out of the priory and walked briskly through the June evening to the Steadmans'. Really, it was only fourteen years since I'd lived around the corner – only ten years since I'd been back.

London was different, though. Richer – and poorer, too. The war, the long war with France, had hurt trade, but there were more houses, and more churches, but also more poor people, beggars on corners where there had never been beggars before. The Steadmans' house looked a little worse for wear. The whitewash on the plaster was dark with age and the corners needed repointing, and there was a broken pane of glass in the side window.

I'll be honest. I almost didn't go in. I debated it, and finally went. But I went to the back gate, slipped the latch boldly, and the kitchen door was open, as it always was.

'Just leave the cheese on the table,' Nan called out.

Guilds work long hours in summer. The guild laws prohibit them from working after sunset, but on the last day of June, which is what I remember it being, the sun lingers for a long time, and apprentices work forever, as I well remember. Her da' was a draper, and I could smell the wool, hear the hiss of an iron.

But it was Nan's voice. I felt as if I was being transported back in time fifteen years. I was visiting illicitly, as I often did after my own master released me.

I peered into the main room of the downstairs – almost like a squire's hall. There were three big tables on trestles down the centre of the room, and they were covered with bolts of wool. Nan was standing at one partially cleared table, a lit brazier at her feet throwing light up on her face. She was pressing the cloth, making it look perfect for a fair, or perhaps for the shop.

'I don't actually have a cheese,' I said.

She looked at me.

Just in that moment, my every good intention flew out of the window and into the street. There she stood, my first love. If she was a little stouter and her face had lines by her mouth, what of it? I was burnt almost brown ten times over.

Before I could think, I stood by her, my arm around her waist, and my mouth on hers.

After a minute, she pulled away, and put her head on my shoulder.

'Oh, William,' she said.

We had a long gossip, as Londoners say. I held the fabric for her and she pressed it. Her father had been unlucky – a ship lost to pirates with a fully paid cargo – and the last year had been bad. She was doing an apprentice's work, and not home as might have been expected, because her father needed her.

'The king ain't payin' his debts, and neither is anyone else,' Nan said. 'Da' is damn near broken, William, an' that's a fact.'

We kissed from time to time ... It took no effort, and yet we didn't seem to need to move to anything else, or perhaps we were our adolescent selves. She didn't mention her husband.

I had a brief fantasy of taking her to Italy.

Her father and mother came home from Evensong after about an hour by the bells. With her three children.

I smiled to meet them all – Mary and Elisabeth, the girls, and William, the boy.

Her father, the alderman, was bent by misfortune, but not broken. He grinned at me.

'I think I've forbidden you this house, young man?' he said archly, and then laughed and hugged me.

We chatted amiably about the state of trade, and the king's unpopularity and the unfairness of the taxation. I told them about my sister, and about Emile's death.

And finally Nan rose, smiled at me, and put a shawl around her younger daughter.

'I'd best get the mites home,' she said. 'Henry will worry.'

She kissed me on the lips, as old friends do, and walked out into the night.

'Henry?' I asked her mother.

'She remarried last year,' her mother said.

Another life I might have lived came and went in that moment. Alas.

In the morning, we left for Canterbury. Fra Peter had assembled a goodly party – a dozen or more pilgrims, all prosperous people on horseback, from almost every walk of life.

'Think of it as a very easy caravan,' Fra Peter said.

'Aren't you coming?' I asked.

'I have business for the order,' he said. 'I'll take a ship down the river and meet you.'

So I led them out of London – my sister, and Christopher, and Gregory and a dozen others. I can't remember them all, although there was a miller who was an angry ruffian, and a shipman who was never sober. And we sang songs and told tales. I told them about the taking of Corinth and the new Duke of Athens, and my sister told a little courtly romance, which surprised me, and then talked about the plague in London. Some of the stories were bawdy, but Mary shrieked with laughter anyway, and altogether it was as pleasant a trip as I can imagine.

I spent a good deal of time training my horse – or rather, the two of us training each other. Percival was a good horse, solid, dependable, with a surprising turn of speed. But he'd been trained for the joust and he liked straight lines, and I wanted him to be nimble and jump and turn. Nimble for a sixteen-hand German bred warhorse, I mean.

Mary, it proved, was game for anything on horseback, and we dashed about between stories, jumping low gates – or baulking at them, sometimes – and galloping along the ditches. If people were shocked to see a nun in a black habit jumping a three-pace wide ditch, back straight, head erect, no one said anything, even the miller.

'I just want this to go on forever,' Mary said on the last night. I told her about Santiago, and she allowed that perhaps she would take a pilgrimage every year or so.

'Just a chance to ...'

She didn't have to finish. A chance to be free.

'Will you be prioress?' I asked.

She shrugged. 'Not unless you become a great deal richer,' she said. 'Lady Anne covers any bill we can't pay ourselves. And honestly, good brother, being the daughter of a great lord ... it's an important part of who she is. She can command men. The knights might not take orders from such as we.' She looked at me. 'I suppose a great many knights take orders from you,' she said. 'I feel foolish.'

'I'm glad to know that you still feel foolish sometimes,' I said.

Any road, we said our prayers at Canterbury, and then I rode back with Mary as far as Rochester, where I left her in the care of the reeve, or perhaps vice versa, and I met Fra Peter and took ship for Calais. It was July of 1369, and I expected to find a *sauvegarde* to travel through France and to be with Hawkwood before the August campaigning was over.

CHAPTER TWO

CALAIS AND FRANCE

Summer and Autumn 1369

Crossing the channel is a chancy business, and that summer, in 1369, the same storms that dogged the English armies crawling across France dogged us. We left Rochester four times in a month. We heard of Queen Philippa's death when the church bells rang for her at Rochester while we were wind-bound, and we prayed for her.

At one point, the weather was so bad that Gregory Fox rode all the way back to London and gave some money to his mother and sister. He was still with us when we finally crossed the Channel in early September, a deeply frustrating and very expensive month. If you want to waste money, just sit in a dockside inn waiting for the weather to change, with five horses and a large dog.

We arrived in Calais and stayed at an inn that was in no way as good as this one. I won't say the name, so no one is embarrassed, but it was the sort of place where you can smell the jakes from the common room and the beer is a little flat and all the girls were scared ...

Listen, my friends. I do not love Calais. I admit that this fine inn is changing my spots, so to speak, but Calais is where I received the greatest humiliation of my chivalric life, when the prince refused to have me on his tournament team – the end of all my hopes. It had an odd feel to it in the autumn of '69. A feeling of defeat, only enhanced by the early rains and cold. I wanted to get through Calais as quickly as I could, and wriggle through France like a greased pig at a fair.

Aye. And when I went to the Knight-Commander, there were letters for me, but no *sauvegardes*. And none for Fra Peter.

I had a letter from John Hawkwood, telling me about Second Cascina and listing my wages and saying that de la Motte had been wounded but looked to recover. Sir John didn't order me to hurry, but something about the tone did suggest that he was short on lieutenants.

There was a note from de Murs that enclosed a scrap of parchment from the count. De Murs explained the sudden accession of money in my account. Emile had left me a sizeable money-fief and the count had approved it, and de Murs also confirmed my possession of two small but good estates. I had to read de Murs' letter three times – the part about Emile made me weep, and then there was a complex bit about Fiore and Bibbo. In the end, I discovered that quite a few people had been looking for me, and I'd missed them all, and then Sam Bibbo had ridden all the way to the Comte d'Armagnac in the count's livery, armed with both money and a warrant. I gathered that Sam was now serving the count directly. Well, he was a master archer, and such men don't usually wait around for knights errant to wander home. It amused me that they'd paid my ransom.

And there was a second note from de Murs, promising me a *sauvegarde* from the king of France. That note was more recent.

We were waiting. France was knee-deep in war that autumn, and I wasn't part of it. Calais was bustling with suppliers and the sort of vultures who hover near a war – pretend men-at-arms, and men who bought ransoms, and other men who bought and sold loot.

From one of them, I purchased both a young French knight whom I knew of slightly, and his armour. The young man was yet another d'Albret by-blow. He'd been taken in the fighting in the south, where the Prince of Wales was trying to face down du Guesclin. Everyone said the prince had no money and no men, but clearly he was doing well enough to take prisoners.

Regardless, I bought young d'Albret from the ransomer and sent him home to pay off his debt to me. I bought him cheap, and was very forgiving in my terms for his ransom. In fact, I suggested to him that he come and join my company in Italy, and bring a few Gascons with him.

Then I gave him no more thought. It was not even an expensive method of recruiting, and mostly what I wanted was his armour, which was new, Bohemian, pretty, and fitted me perfectly, because like me, the d'Albrets are all big men. I got a fine chain shirt from the Knight-Commander in a dice game, and *still* we had no *sauvegardes*.

Calais in wartime is, as you gentlemen will attest, very expensive indeed. I was not proposing to expend my dead wife's fortune on inns. In fact, by the second week in September, I'd made a number of decisions. First and foremost, that I was recruiting for my company, and would see if Sir John would let me have fifty lances. I wrote to him. I also wrote to the Pope. I still had a papal letter on me, and I showed it to Fra Peter and asked him if he thought we could use it as a *sauvegarde*.

'If we were French it would do,' he said. 'But we're English. We'd be taken immediately.'

I knew he was correct.

Meanwhile, the war dragged on. In Normandy, the Duke of Lancaster was apparently locked in a staring contest with the Duc de Bourgogne. Victualling convoys left almost every day – Calais probably had more wagons and carts than any other town in Europe. Burgundy's French army outnumbered Lancaster's by two to one, but the French were too aware of our superiority to come on.

I watched Christopher and Gregory at the butts, competing with the castle garrison. By the standards of English professionals in France, Gregory was an amateur – he was competent, but he was a tailor shooting for his own amusement. Christopher, on the other hand, was a fine archer – not, perhaps, a master like Bibbo or John the Turk. He did miss sometimes, but was capable of remarkable feats, especially at very long ranges, where he had some sort of genius for reading breezes. The garrison all called him 'the Moor', which he took in good part, after mentioning to me that his people had fought the Moors for the last five hundred years, which, of course, they had.

Fra Peter and I watched the roads for incoming heralds, and drank watered wine, and went to Mass. I was missing the whole fighting season in Italy.

One afternoon, as Christopher was fletching some light arrows, Gregory turned to me.

'I don't mean to offend,' he said slowly. He was never a chatty lad.

'Be my guest,' I said.

Gregory was watching as Christopher sliced a peacock whorl into fletchings. Christopher was much given to gambling, and seemed to win more than he lost. Somewhere in Calais, he'd found a peacock whorl.

'My lord, why don't we go and serve ... the prince?' he asked. 'Or the Duke of Lancaster?'

Christopher rolled his eyes, but said nothing.

I shrugged. 'Master Fox, war is a mistress not to be trifled with. I am English, I suppose, but I hold no land in England and have no contract to fight for her. My company is in Italy—'

Fra Peter barked a laugh. 'Sir William means that it would be foolish to be killed for nothing in France, when you can risk death for money in Italy.'

'And you're English, too!' Young Gregory was quite a patriot, at heart.

'When I took my vows as a Knight of the Order,' Fra Peter said, pointing at his habit, 'I left nationality behind me. I am a knight of God. Any conflict between Christian kings is abhorrent to me.'

Later, he swirled cheap wine in his cup.

'Well, that was a prime piece of hypocrisy,' he said.

'Gregory often forces my hand in conversation, too,' I admitted.

Fra Peter shrugged. 'I'd *like* to leave nationality behind me. The quarrels of the Christian princes are going to be the death of Christianity.'

I nodded. 'Especially since half the French Knights of the Order are in the field with du Guesclin or Bourgogne,' I said. 'Or so my friends the ransomers tell me.'

'How can you consort with such men?' Fra Peter said.

'Jesus consorted with tax collectors,' I said.

Fra Peter sighed. 'You used to just obey,' he said wistfully.

The rumour was that King Edward was coming in person. I thought that if the king came to Calais, I'd make my knee and see if he'd take me as a knight for the duration of the campaign. But I was damned if I was going to serve the garrison, although I'd begun to ride a few courses with the knights, and practise at a pell. I was bored, and inactivity was very expensive. I had Percival in fine condition, and although he really didn't want to turn very quickly, we'd reached an accommodation about speed and jumping. I began training in my new harness.

It was difficult to fill the time, even when I added some sword training of my two pages, or archers, to my schedule. I was drinking too much, thinking too much about Emile. Realising that I had virtually abandoned my lord, the Green Count, and my wife's children, who were in almost every sense mine.

I walked in from the tilt yard to have Christopher strip off my new armour, and he'd pinched me a ginger cake from the kitchens – he was a first-rate forager at all times. The smell hit me like a vision of home – the home I'd scarcely had. Emile made ginger cakes, or at least ordered them made, for Magdalene and Edouard.

My children had a succession of nurses and tutors and chaplains. If Emile had lived, we'd have walked to Santiago together without our children. I didn't feel a daily urge to be present with them.

But the ginger cake reminded me of my children like nothing else, and the smell was rich in my nostrils, and suddenly I just wanted to be at Chambéry.

A few days later, at least in my memory, the Earl of Warwick landed at Calais with a small army – about a thousand men-at-arms and another thousand archers. I watched them unload from Cinque Ports ships, and I wasn't overly fond of what I saw – bad horses and men-at-arms with poor armour. The archers were better. Most of them were arrayed men from the counties, and what they lacked in willingness they had in good supplies and good training. I wished I had Sam Bibbo or one of my English veterans to talk to them. Instead, I chatted with the Knight-Commander of the garrison and some of the officers of the array.

Sir John Burley was acting as Captain of Calais, and he was an easy man to like, big and strong and loud, but solid gold. He was also a cheaper and friendlier source of information than the ransomers, so I tended to go and drink with him every few days. He'd been at Poitiers and some other notable fights, and we swapped tales like old fishwives.

But Warwick, who was one of the king's 'old hands' from Crecy and whose name put fear into the French, a big, older man with dark hair shot with grey and a magnificent horse, didn't linger in the flesh-pots of Calais. He landed his people, rested his horses, and marched away into the French countryside. My sources among the ransomers said he was going to reinforce Lancaster, and that there would be a great battle, and most of the vultures left with the armies.

A week passed, and we *still* had no *sauvegardes*. I began to ride outside the walls, taking Percival on long rides over the muddy fields, and alternating with my new riding horse, a brisk and very young gelding of very uncertain ancestry who reminded me of the small Greek horses on the island of Lesvos – short and powerful. He was virtually untrained.

Christopher and I worked on him every day. The dark-skinned man had a fine hand with horses – gentle, firm, sure. I christened my gelding 'Frank', for various reasons, and Christopher and Frank and I passed a couple of pleasant days riding and walking around Calais. To the south, the great wood of Guisnes blocked the horizon. To the north and east, the land was mostly flat. One afternoon, in a weak and watery sunshine, Christopher and Gregory and I reined in where two ancient oaks marked the entrance to the road south, to Fiennes and Normandy. Somewhere down that road was Harfleur, and the fighting.

That night, I proposed to Fra Peter that we just chance it.

'I have no interest in spending a year or two as a prisoner,' Fra Peter said.

I nodded.

Early October. I'd wasted half a year, and I was impatient, and Fra Peter was beside himself. We had no way of knowing that Charles, the fifth of that name, king of France, was not issuing any *sauvegardes*. He wasn't playing by the old, chivalric rules.

Calais, on the other hand, remained full of the old rules. The king was coming, or not coming. There was a Spanish fleet in the channel. The Prince of Wales was victorious ... no, he was taken. And every day the guard was mounted, the bells rang, and no *sauvegardes* were issued.

Bloody hell, I was bored. I'm telling you all this so you understand how I came to make the decisions that I made.

Mostly, I was bored.

Rumour had it that the Bourgogne had retreated as soon as Warwick appeared, and Warwick and Lancaster had marched on Harfleur. Harfleur was a rich prize, and they were going to take it – a major blow to France, as it was one of the main French fleet bases and a good deal of the back and forth was about French and Spanish raids on the coast of England. It made sense – in fact, it was the first sound strategic thinking I'd heard from the English side.

I wrote a long letter to de Murs, asking if the count could procure me a *sauvegarde* or write one for me in his own hand. By then, I had some idea that the king of France wasn't using cartels or *sauvegardes*. Charles, the coward who'd fled from Poitiers, was fighting through proxies, and not taking the field in person, but he was making very sure that there was no news crossing France that was not approved by him.

In fact, when I went to Sir John Burley to send my letter, he shrugged.

'Not sure who will carry it,' he said. 'Sorry, Sir William, but unless the French send us another ransom party or a cartel, I have no way of sending a letter to your Count of Savoy.'

Frustrating.

It was the next morning that my frustration exploded, a little like a firestorm starting from a chance spark. I was asleep in my not-so-good inn, alone in a narrow bed that smelt a little of old mould, or perhaps bad cheese.

'Sir!' Sam Bibbo said. 'Sir!'

Except it wasn't Bibbo, of course. Nor Fiore. It was Christopher.

'Sir!' he said. 'Sir.'

I may have muttered some blasphemies. It was still dark outside. I poured some very cold water over my head, it being October, and drank off a cup of hot cider. Christopher was not just a good archer, but an excellent companion.

'Message from the castle,' he said.

There was a very cold-looking squire huddled by the embers of the common room fire, his pale face lit by the remnants of the fire.

'Sir John requests your immediate attendance,' the young man said.

I may have uttered further blasphemies, at least until I realised that this *had* to mean that I had a *sauvegarde*.

I dressed in the warmth, or relative warmth, of the hearth, and put on a heavy cote and walked up to the castle. Sir John was in the gatehouse, issuing orders.

'Sir William,' he said.

I bowed.

'The Duke of Lancaster and the Earl of Warwick are hard pressed by the French,' he said, conversationally. 'Anything that could go wrong, has gone wrong. Plague, dysentery, treason ...' He glanced over his shoulder. 'I need to get a convoy to the duke, and no fucking about. Will you take it?'

'No *sauvegarde*?' I asked.

'No fucking *sauvegarde*!' he spat. 'Damn it, Sir William!'

I shrugged. 'I supposed I should ask the wages,' I said. 'But instead I'll ask the distance and what force?'

'If I strip Guisnes and my own garrison, I can give you twenty hobilars and as many archers,' he said.

Well, I had been bored.

'To Harfleur?' I asked.

'To wherever young Lancaster has retreated.' Sir John shook his head. 'All my news is five days old.'

I blinked. 'You want me to cross war-torn France in late autumn, with a virtually undefended convoy, to an unknown destination?' I asked.

'That sums it up nicely,' he said.

'Sweet Christ,' I muttered, or some such.

And then, of course, I volunteered.

Because I was bored.

'I'm not coming,' Fra Peter said. He said it with flat finality, and the heavy disapproval of a maiden aunt.

I loved him, but we had different interests. So I handed him all my letters from the prioress for Avignon, keeping only those for Rome. We embraced.

I could tell that he had things to say to me.

But we were both wise enough not to say everything that came to mind.

CHAPTER THREE

NORMANDY

September 1369

By the time my convoy left the gates, I'd been pared down to just ten archers and ten hobilars, which made me angry. I might have saved my excess of spirit. The hobilars were the most useless soldiers I'd ever been cursed to command, and twenty of them might have broken my spirit altogether.

Ah, Jean, you wish to know what a hobilar might be when he's at home? It's an English term – but some say Welsh and some say Irish. It's a term for an armoured cavalryman who is not a knight, nor yet a man-at-arms – usually just a man with a helmet and aventail, and perhaps a good maille shirt or even just a coat of plates, on a bad horse, with a spear. In my father's day they'd dismount to fight – spearmen on nags, intended to keep up with the archers and knights on a raid.

Mine were vicious social climbers and garrison clerks playing at knights. My troubles with them started before we were at the gate, when the 'Vintner', or corporal commanding them, started giving orders to the wagoners.

I rode over.

'I'll give the orders,' I said.

'Who are you?' he asked, with no attempt at civility.

'The man in command of the convoy,' I said.

'Get fucked,' he said.

Considering he was in a besmottered haubergeon and a rusty aventail, and I was in spotless, if rain-swept, plate, he might have backed down. But he didn't. And I had to assume, based on his stiff neck and his swearing, that he was at least a veteran, in which case, alienating him would have been foolish.

I used Percival to out-manoeuvre his horse, cutting him off from his troops. It was a non-violent demonstration of my superior horsemanship – and my superior horse.

'Commanded quite a few convoys, have you?' I asked, my voice relentlessly cheerful.

'One or two,' he said.

'I was at Poitiers and Brignais, and I have spent the rest of my time fighting the Turks,' I said. 'So let's not be fucking around, eh?'

It didn't work. 'Fuck off,' he said. 'I don't know you. You ain't garrison, so you ain't shit to me.'

I nodded. 'I don't suppose having Sir John tell you I'm in command will change your mind?' I asked. 'Because based on the state of your horse and your armour, you're utterly incompetent, and I don't plan to die because you don't know how to conduct a convoy.'

That got his attention. 'What the fuck are you talking about?' he asked.

'Your kit is a disgrace,' I said. 'And your hobilars are no better.'

'Men-at-arms,' he said.

'I've seen brigands with better kit,' I said. 'Look at that slovenly arse.'

The man was having trouble managing his horse, and his gambeson was not buckled. Nor would it ever be, as he was overweight and it looked as if it had been made for a much smaller man.

The Vintner didn't even turn his head.

'I don't know who the fuck you think you are, but—'

I dumped him. It didn't take Fiore. I just reached down, took his foot, and unhorsed him.

'Shut up,' I said. He was in some very cold dung and mud. 'You are relieved. Good day.'

He got up.

I turned my charger so that I loomed over him.

'Don't make further trouble,' I said. 'Or I'll just drop you again. Right?'

Nine hobilars.

I hated all of them by the time the crenellations of Guisnes were vanishing on the endless flat of the Pale, and we were riding into the forest which I had hoped would cover our movements. The nine of them combined surliness with ineffectiveness to a level I had never before witnessed in soldiers. Three of them pretended to be knights, or at least nobly born men-at-arms, and styled themselves squires. I discovered this when I ordered them to scout ahead.

'That's pricker work,' said a small fellow with a bold moustache as red as my own. 'I'm a gentleman squire.'

Prickers are Northern horses, used to run down Scots raiders.

Well, here's the rub. I was used to being obeyed. I was used to being Sir William Gold, a 'great knight', a donat of the Order of Saint John, a captain, or at the very least, a corporal, in the well-arrayed armies of Savoy or Siena or Verona or Milan.

I wasn't used to a parcel of rogues who viewed me as an enemy. They saw themselves as veteran soldiers. They had plenty of spine, but it was all directed at me, and in five long miles with some very slow bullock carts, I learnt that they knew *fuck all* about the conduct of a convoy in enemy country.

I was angry. But I'd had words with myself, and God, for that matter, about anger, so I swallowed it and tried to think of how to handle these useless idiots.

I wasn't in the mood to argue, and I wasn't yet ready to kill them all, so I gathered my own pair of archers and rode off into the forest of Guisnes, looking for the French and buying myself time to think. I found nothing to make me shy, but Christopher found a shod hoof-print well off the road, and that put the fear of God into me. I rode back to find the convoy halted about a hundred paces from where I'd left it, and the 'rearguard' that I'd assigned closed up to the main body.

'Why are we stopped?' I asked.

Everyone looked sullen.

'You wasn't here, like,' someone said.

'So you stopped? In France?' I asked. 'And who, I wonder, is watching the road behind us right now?'

Red Moustache was the boldest hobilar.

'Who the hell could get behind us?' he asked. 'We're only two miles from Calais.'

Red Moustache had never met Timurtash. Or John the Turk, or Ewan the Scot.

But I had.

I rode up to Red Moustache. He was on a pretty good palfrey, and he himself looked capable. I kept my temper entirely in check. I had thought this out, for once.

'What's your name, sir?' I asked.

'Geoffrey Hales, squire-at-arms,' he said.

'I am Sir William Gold,' I said. 'Geoffrey, I'd like you to take command of the rearguard. I'd like you to pick two of our "men-at-arms" and three archers, and stay three hundred paces behind us. If we are attacked, I'd like you to respond. Do you know how a rearguard responds to an attack on a convoy?' I asked.

Pleasantly.

He had green eyes. There was some humour in them – he was a preening cock, but not a fool. He thought about it for as long as it takes to say a paternoster.

'No,' he said.

Thank God. A straight answer.

'I'll come and explain in an hour,' I said. 'Hopefully the French will leave us that long.'

I smiled, he smiled, and I had one man who I might trust with a little authority.

Mother of Mercy, they were useless. The other two argued, even about going on the rearguard.

It was a grey day, and the October rain was falling – not in sheets, but just a sort of damp wind that from time to time increased to being a little stronger. By the time we'd gone another mile, a horse was lame.

Christopher, without a word, dismounted, got the man off his horse, and examined the lame horse's foot. He took a stone out and then another, and then shook his head.

'Badly shod,' he said. 'I would need tools.'

'Sweet Christ,' I said. 'You're a farrier?'

The black man shrugged. 'My Lord, I have done many tasks.'

'How about scouting?' I asked.

He smiled.

The wagoners were capable men. I had eight wagons, all full to bursting, all pulled by teams of bullocks – big, big cattle with huge heads. They were slower than honey in January and stronger than a charging knight.

They were, in truth, a little slower than a walking man. And while that seemed a curse in the first few miles, as we went on through what

273

was, at least technically, still England, I realised that I needed them to stay slow because I needed to train my hobilars.

The archers were another thing entirely. All ten archers were old men of thirty-five or even older. All had decent horses and good haubergeons or gambesons, most both. They were bored and none of them seemed to want to give orders or help in any way, but they all knew the game and they obeyed.

The closest among them to an officer was an old pirate named Dick Thorald from Saint Bees in Cumbria. He wasn't a master archer because he was too lazy, but he knew how a convoy worked.

'How would you like to go out and scout ahead?' I asked.

'No, thankee,' he said.

'Good, then. Pick two archers to go with Christopher there, and you take charge of the carts.'

He smiled a snaggle-toothed smile, as if admitting that I'd put one over on him.

'Blackie knows his way around a horse, eh?' he asked.

This is how you know a typical, lazy, competent veteran. Dick hadn't even been in earshot when Christopher examined the lame horse, but the Cumbrian already knew that the black man knew horses.

I was glad that he was feeling chatty.

'Yes,' I said. 'His name is Christopher.'

'The Moor,' Dick said. He showed me his snaggle teeth again. 'I were at Poitiers,' he said.

I smiled. 'Then you remember when I was a cook,' I said.

'Cook's boy,' Dick said. Another man might have made the correction with malice, but Dick was too lazy to be malicious. 'Aye. When'd you get knighted?'

I nodded. I didn't think he was challenging me, and I might have just this one chance to communicate my ... *experience* to my 'men'.

'At the Siege of Florence in '65,' I said. 'Hans Baumgarten knighted me on the field.'

The Cumbrian nodded. 'Good fer thee, lad,' he said, his accent thick and buttery. 'Raaight. Thee ga'an hevt'a craic. Aas stoppin' ere wi' the fuuckin' carts. Eh?' He smiled.

It took me time to interpret his dialect.

'Thanks, Dick,' I said. 'Or should I say, Master Thorald?'

'Sweet Chraist,' he said. 'Maaster who?'

And so we rode on through the rain. Some harness broke and was repaired. A heavy wagon put a wheel over the edge of a tiny bridge, and I dismounted with three archers and put my shoulder to it until we had it back into the gravel-lined ruts of the muddy ditch that passed for a road.

I trotted my riding horse back to the rearguard, which was at least at the right distance.

They were inattentive, had no flankers, and weren't watching the road behind us. I shrugged to myself. Instead, I complimented Master Hales on his distance, and then began asking him questions about the terrain around us.

You catch more flies with honey than with mustard.

In fact, we were well along our day's track, perhaps twelve miles from Calais. The day was still wet, and the farms we passed had mostly been burnt long enough ago that the charred timbers shone with water. To the east, a deep ravine broke a line of low hills, the first real terrain since we'd left Calais. To the west, towards the coast, it was mostly flat. All of this land had been in tillage recently, and then deserted. Thirty years of war and the plague had cleared it of peasants, and covered what should have been arable land with a stubble of young trees, thickets and fens. But a discerning eye could make out the ruins of old houses, the litter of a hovel done in wattle and daub, the line of a broken fence done in hurdles, the hedge at the centre of a field of weeds.

I saw it as a series of vignettes. I could run my eyes over it and pick out all the places I'd put an ambush, a counter-ambush, a roadblock, a single archer meant to be an annoyance ...

I turned to the other hobilars, subtly including them in the questions I asked Master Hales. None of them was Sir John Chandos in disguise, nor yet John Hawkwood. But Hales had a head on his shoulders. The rest looked like brigands, or just fools. One was a slim boy so young that I wondered that anyone paid him at muster. Another was fat.

'So if that old farmstead was full of brigands ...' I said. I smiled.

Hales chewed the end of his moustache. His companions looked bored. When I'd almost despaired of an answer, Hales cocked his head to one side.

'Do they block the road?' he asked.

Listen, I'm not saying it was a brilliant question. Merely that Master Hales was … engaged.

'Say they do,' I said. 'Listen, my friends. It would only take a single log across this track to stop our wagons for as long as it takes a good priest to say Mass.'

'Sweet Saviour,' the youngest said, crossing himself. Well, at least he had the imagination to see it in his head.

The other man, dark-headed and much given to lice, was looking out over the field of brambles to our right. Behind him, the three archers tried to look invisible. I had time to note that almost all the archers had better horses than most of the hobilars. Probably they were paid better.

Aha.

Hales shook his head. 'They block the road and start killing the wagoners,' he said.

'Yes,' I said.

'I guess I'd go across the field here,' he said, peering into the rain. 'Blessed Virgin. I suppose I'd ride all the way out, to stay in the cover of that line of hedge – come in the back of the old farmyard. Assuming there's a way in.'

We rode along a way.

'Is that the right answer?' he asked.

We were now passing the abandoned farmyard. The young hobilar flinched when he saw the man who'd been hanged with a cooking chain from the old oak tree in the farmyard. Birds had been after him, and what was left of his flesh was black, as if he'd been burnt. I knew that smell.

Jesus Lord Christ. I knew that smell. The smell of France in 1358. The smell of death. For a moment, it took me back.

I shook it off. Although I promise you that a grey rainy day in autumn is not the best time to find a rotting body dangling from a tree.

I looked into the yard, and saw that the old farm fence behind the rubble of the barn walls was down. I pointed this out to Hales.

'So was I right?' he asked.

He was actually eager for my approval, and he'd thought it through well enough. I hated them all less, and I decided to give him some actual military advice.

'There is no right,' I said.

He looked disappointed.

I shrugged. 'If you do *something*, it's far better than doing nothing. If you do *something* with spirit and a little art, you increase the odds that your enemy makes a mistake.' I smiled. 'Yes. Your flanking might do it. Might arrive too late to save us, or just in time, or might panic the whole ambush into running. Or there might be a second ambush right there by that stream, and you take the first crossbow bolt and the plan is wrecked. See?'

'So what's the right plan?' Master Hales asked, trying to hide the whine in his voice.

'Whatever works,' I said. Probably too much honesty.

Mid-afternoon found us a couple of miles from Fiennes, where, based on what Sir John Burley had told me in Calais, I could expect a forti-fied town with an English garrison, and a good night's sleep before I went off across Normandy into hostile territory. Because I knew war in France, I was treating the English Pale as enemy territory. It only needed a few dozen of the Duc de Bourgogne's men to decide to make a little raid, and we'd be knee-deep in Frenchmen.

I called a halt, set a trio of watchers, and let them eat a little sausage and cheese while I rode ahead to Christopher. I found Gregory Fox first. Gregory was already acting like a veteran. He'd put an old grey hood over his steel cap and he was behind a tree, just below the ridge line of the next big rise of ground, watching the ground towards Fiennes.

He gestured south. 'Chris is out there,' he said. 'He has two archers with him.'

'And he left you here?'

'Yes, My Lord.'

'He saw something he didn't like?' I asked.

Gregory wasn't a man of many words. So he nodded.

As I started forward, he said, 'Tracks.'

I reined in again. Looked south towards Fiennes and north to my convoy, with the same indecision that the old Roman centurions probably had in similar situations.

I no doubt swore, and rode back to my convoy.

I had the convoy moving again in a quarter of an hour. It was mid-afternoon, we were all wet and cold, and the hobilars, who had no cloaks, were miserable. I told Dick to keep everyone moving, listened to his incomprehensible Cumbrian reply, and then I changed to Percival, took a lance from the wagons, and rode back over the ridge. Gregory Fox was still at his post, and I motioned for him to join me.

'No Christopher?' I asked.

'Nothing moving down there,' Fox said.

Nothing to be done but look for myself. I was reduced to being my own scout.

We went forward down the ridge. To the right, broken ground covered in scrubby trees. To the left, farm fields given over to small trees and tall grass.

If there was an enemy force out there ...

If they'd snapped Christopher up, or killed him ...

I'd missed this? I wondered at myself.

We trotted along the trail for a mile, moving fast, and then I paused to look at the tracks in the mud where a very small rivulet crossed the road. Shod hooves – impossible for me to count how many. Broken grass to my right and to my left.

'Wait here,' I said, and took my warhorse downstream. Percival turned slowly and stepped along the narrow stream bed like a great lady crossing a farmyard, feet lifting high.

My heart sank. Actually, it felt more like it swelled to fill my chest entirely. I felt as if my new breastplate was too small.

More tracks crossed the stream twenty paces to the west. I rode back and found the same. An experienced raider, hiding his tracks by spreading his people out in a stream crossing. Wary, but not careful enough.

I took a deep breath. I thought I was looking at twenty to thirty men. Easily enough to take ... or to destroy my convoy.

I rode back to Fox, who was at the crest of the low rise that had probably once been the bank of the stream.

'I want you ...' I said, when there was a high-pitched whistle to the south.

I looked that way and saw Christopher, his dark skin distinctive even two hundred paces away, riding down on the neck of his horse. The two archers were right with him, like a horse race coming down the road. Then they vanished into a dip of ground.

Behind them were half a dozen men-at-arms. They were not unlike our hobilars, although better mounted – coats of maille, lances, helmets. They were riding at a good clip, if not a full gallop.

I stood in my stirrups, looking left and right. Not an ambush, then. No one was coming through the brush, unless they were masters of the art.

Pilgrim barked, coming out of the thicket west of the road.

I swore. We were about to be in a fight. I didn't need a dog, and I sure as hell did not need my nice dog getting killed. On the other hand, his presence told me that my flank was secure. Dogs know when men are hiding.

He barked again. He was a smart lad, and he was reading my body language and assuming that things were wrong and that he, like any good dog, could fix them.

Percival liked Pilgrim, and he settled under me, convinced by animal logic that if Pilgrim was with us, everything was going to be fine.

'Go home!' I shouted.

Pilgrim looked puzzled.

Of all the foolish problems.

'Gregory, I'm about to charge those men,' I said. 'I want you to dismount and shoot into them as soon as I'm through them.'

'Through?' he asked. He was *smiling*.

'I'll go through them if they don't put me down,' I said.

'Got it,' he said.

I kept my visor up long enough to see him slip from the saddle and string his bow.

'Pilgrim, stay,' I spat, and slammed my visor down with my right hand. I walked Percival across the little stream and reined in. 'Fox, grab him by the collar.'

An untried horse, untrustworthy troops, a dog, rain . . .

Just another day in France.

I had time to pray, and I did. That was *not* like France in 1358. I checked my new sword and my new dagger and shook my head.

Christopher crested the low rise that was really the old bank of the stream. His mouth opened as he saw me and then . . .

He was passing . . .

I touched my spurs to Percival's sides . . .

The two archers burst over the rise . . .

I passed between them, and their pursuers were *right there*, and my lance found a breastplate as if it had a mind of its own and I unhorsed the man. In fact, he *and* his horse went down, and Percival jumped the rolling horse, almost unseating me. I swear to my maker it was the longest, highest jump that horse had ever made, and I was slammed back against my saddle, lost my perfectly good lance ...

I was through. I'd dropped one and I was through them. I turned Percival, who didn't turn like my glorious Gawain or my lost Gabriel, but had to slow and slow. I lost precious moments bringing him in, but I got my long sword off my belt, which, if you have never had to do such while mounted, is quite exciting.

I got Percival's head all the way around, and managed to get a fleeting eye-slit view of the road to the south. I had to know if they were a raiding party or a vanguard.

The road appeared empty.

Percival burst forward – or rather, back the way we'd come.

The Frenchmen were almost as inexperienced as my hobilars. Two were stooped over the broken body of the man I'd unhorsed, and the other three had crossed the little stream, where Master Fox had shot one dead with a single arrow. Instead of riding Fox down in the thicket and killing him, the other two were reined in on the road.

It was more like murder than fighting. They were young, and foolish, and in shock.

I blew back through them like a winter wind. I don't particularly remember what I did, but it was all Fiore – a pommel locked around a neck, a throw from an armlock. I killed none of them, praise God, but left two more face down on the road, thrown from their mounts. One man had managed to evade my reaching sword blade, and another was dismounting to get his crossbow. The two of them, as if by prior arrangement, turned to flee in perfect unison, but Christopher and one of the archers had already turned *their* horses and were crashing through the tall grass, outflanking them and cutting them off. Christopher and his mount leapt the stream like a centaur and gave a whoop.

Pilgrim emerged from the brush, spooking the crossbowman's horse, and he was thrown.

The other man, caught by Greg Fox stepping out from the brush with an arrow on his bow, raised his hands.

'Jesu,' Christopher laughed, as he bound their hands.

One man was dead – the first I'd unhorsed. His falling horse had rolled over him on the gravel surface, crushing his ribcage. The rest were virtually unhurt.

'Bury him,' I said to the prisoners, in French.

They obeyed. Faster than the hobilars.

About ten minutes later, the convoy caught up and passed over the creek, the hobilars wide-eyed at the little huddle of damp Frenchmen.

Dick Thorald grinned at me.

'Awreet, then!' he greeted me. 'Ar we gaana share't ransoms, then?' the old rogue asked.

'I don't know,' I said. 'Did you take anyone?'

He grinned. 'Shares!' he said.

And that made some sense.

Then, as my precious convoy rolled into Fiennes, I rode back to collect the rearguard. I was extremely pleased to find that Hales had two archers out in the flat country to the west, as flankers. My hands were shaking.

Even through the descending darkness, we could see the gatehouse of Fiennes in the distance.

'My Lord,' he said suddenly. 'You took all six yourself?'

I was still watching the darkening countryside.

'No, I had help,' I said.

''It's still ... quite a feat of arms,' Hales said.

I couldn't stop myself.

'Not really,' I said. 'They were as useless as you lot.'

He winced.

But I was feeling ... happy. I let the rearguard clip-clop past me, so that I was alone with the falling darkness. I dismounted, knelt at a roadside cross, and prayed for the man I'd killed. Here's his little cross in the book.

But then, I had the oddest thought. I thought of fighting a very angry Boucicault, not far from where I was kneeling – and the ease with which he'd unhorsed me. I thought of being a routier.

The pale moon was just rising in a glow of cloud, and I turned to Percival, muttered some endearments, and got a foot in a tall stirrup.

I'd been such a desperate young man in mismatched armour. I had come a long way from that boy, I think. I got myself back in the saddle, turned Percival, and trotted to the gate of Fiennes.

*

The garrison of Fiennes was in a bit of a panic. The 'Captain', who was not much of an improvement on my hobilars, was an older squire from the Crécy generation who managed to simultaneously hold the French in contempt and be afraid for the Duke of Lancaster.

'I don't know you, sir,' he said.

I dismounted and Christopher, God bless him, took Percival, took my helmet off my head, and put a cup of hot cider in my hand. Fox took the helmet, and then, in the inn yard, started stripping off my harness.

'William Gold,' I said, pointing at the device on my shield.

The black spur rondels showed against the scarlet in the darkness, as did the order's eight-pointed cross.

'Oh, aye,' he said. 'What are you doin' with all those prisoners?'

'I assumed I'd send them back to Calais,' I said.

He shook his head. 'I don't have the men to guard them,' he said.

'I can't take them with me,' I said.

'Kill 'em off, then,' he said.

I took in a long breath and released it slowly. Had I missed this, really?

'No,' I said. But I was too tired to argue with him. I could make my own plans. 'What's it like south of here?'

'There's at least two raiding parties out there,' he said. 'We saw their smoke today, and yesterday, too. Burning villages to the west.'

War in France. I kill your peasants, you kill mine.

'There's a rumour that the duke and the earl have been badly defeated,' he said very quietly. 'Somewhere south of the Somme.'

I nodded. 'I find it hard to believe that the French could beat us in a straight fight,' I said.

'Your words to God's ear,' he said. 'But Bourgogne is a decent captain, and du Guesclin ...'

'Whatever is happening,' I said, 'I have to take this convoy through. Know anything about the terrain?'

'If the duke ain't been beat,' he said, 'he'll have to get across the Somme. We did, back in Crécy year.'

'I was six years old,' I said.

He finally smiled. 'Blessed Virgin, young sir. I was five-and-twenty. But we crossed at the ford at Blanchetaque. It's terrible, chancy, dependent on tide and the will o' God ...'

'But all the Crécy veterans will know it,' I said.

He nodded. 'An' the duke won't want to turn thirty miles inland.

There's not another good crossing until Abbeville. And Abbeville's bridge is a castle.'

Well. That made my work all the easier. I went and found Dick Thorald and Hales, and I told them to get the men together.

There was a great deal of grumbling. But, thanks be to God, no absolute disobedience.

I gathered them in the mostly empty stable wing of the inn – twenty-nine men, including Christopher and Gregory and the wagoners.

'I've spoken to the castellan of this town,' I said. 'We have about three days' travel to the sea-ford at Blanchetaque. We'll find the duke's army there, or close enough.'

Silence. Not even muttering.

'We had an easy day today,' I said. 'Tomorrow we'll be in France—'

'That was an easy day?' Hales asked. I think he was used to being a wit, and used to being allowed to speak.

'Anyone die?' I asked.

Hales looked away.

'If no one died, it was an easy day,' I said. 'Listen up, lads. The *reason* it was easy is that the Frenchmen out there are as bad as we are. But once we go south, there will be more and more of them, in worse terrain, and we'll have to be as wary as a fox in a farmyard and as slick as a greased pig to get through.'

Heavy silence.

'So, a few things. First – I took five Frenchmen today. Two are knights, one is a squire. The ransoms will be shared. Everyone shares – wagoners included. That goes for any other ransoms we take.'

Now I had everyone's attention.

'Second – in one hour I will inspect your horses and tack. I expect all the horses to be rubbed down, bedded on good straw, watered and fed. I expect the tack to be dry and oiled. I want to see your swords and scabbards, and your maille, and the archers' spare bowstrings and their quivers. For tonight, I'll spare you an inspection of your clothes.' I smiled. 'Because today is an easy day.'

I smiled around, as if I expected to be obeyed.

'Finally, we will leave Fiennes at Lauds tomorrow. I'll have Fox wake you.'

God, I wished I had l'Angars, or de la Motte, or Lapot, or Richard Grice. Or Bibbo, or Ewan ...

But I didn't.

'Dismissed,' I said.

I turned and walked back to the common room and began cleaning my own kit.

It was an hour after Lauds when our last wagon rolled out the gate of Fiennes, but I was not ill-satisfied. The horses were in semi-acceptable shape, and most men had a dry cloak over some hastily polished maille. Most of the armour had been oiled or tallowed straight over old rust, but it was all serviceable. I hated them less – indeed, a combination of my little feat of arms and my offer to share the ransoms had worked a bit of a miracle. No one was very fond of me, either, but we were moving.

I had to move without Christopher and Fox, whom I was sending back to Calais with a report and with our prisoners.

'Pick up fresh horses and come straight back,' I said.

'Yes, My Lord,' Christopher said.

The castellan had a change of heart and added four mounted men, so that I didn't have to worry quite so much, but I spent a precious minute explaining, in good French, to my prisoners exactly how lucky they were to be escorted back to Calais, instead of being hanged in chains by the roadside. Then I distributed all their armour and weapons among my hobilars. The breastplate fitted Hales nicely, and made him look more like a true man-at-arms. I gave the biggest man the only good iron gauntlets, and appointed him to lead my scouts.

I spent most of the morning with my rearguard, on Frank. I got him to canter up the column all the way to the vanguard before Sext, and we rolled south. The road ran through the woods. We passed a pair of streams with intact bridges, and then wasted two hours building a structure to support the carts at a third stream, which was full of water and about six paces wide. Downstream, I found a ford. Shod hooves.

I was trying different men in different roles. Today's vanguard commander was the pudgy man in the ill-fitting gambeson, who now had good iron gauntlets. His name was Robin Wall, and he was someone's bastard son, and not anyone very important. He was from Lincoln – mild as a clerk. Except that he had a touch of madness in his eye. He kept looking at his iron-clad hands.

'Young Robin,' I said, conversationally. I called him 'young' because he seemed like a boy to me, despite being at most perhaps ten years my junior. 'The men who we took yesterday will have twenty friends, and they're likely looking for us today. Stop looking at your pretty iron hands.'

'Yes, sir,' he muttered.

The mad eyes roved over me and they went to the wood line of the next ridge.

We were, quite literally, beyond the pale – the Pale of Calais. We were in France, and every hand would be against us. Luckily, at least in the short run, the frontier we were riding through had been burnt, raped and murdered for forty years. No one lived there except some feral pigs and some very dangerous-looking wild dogs.

Pilgrim was unconcerned with wild dogs, but the feral pigs drove him into fits of noisy barking.

It wasn't raining. I thought that it was just possible that we'd get through to the Somme without a contest. But I wasn't betting on it.

'Ever been in a battle?' I asked Robin.

'No,' he said sullenly, like a younger man.

'If you were going to hit us, how would you do it?' I asked.

'Wait until we make camp, surround us, and demand we surrender,' he said. 'Maximise the captures and the profit.'

I smiled. 'You've been a routier!' I said.

He flushed. He had pimples, and he was overweight, but his mind was thin and wiry.

'Nah,' he said. 'I just think about it, like.'

I nodded. 'And if you see a road block?' I asked.

He gave me a nasty smile. 'I turn this old plug and ride off west across country and let them have you,' he said. 'No one will chase a useless fuck like me if they can have the convoy.'

'Excellent thinking,' I said.

'Why'd you give me the gauntlets?' he asked suspiciously.

I shrugged. 'Do they fit?' I asked.

'Yes,' he said.

'Good,' I said, and rode back to the main body, where, for an hour, Thorald entertained me with his Cumbrian. It was a little like listening to Greek or Turkish, except that I understood both of those languages pretty well. But there was a cadence to it, and after a bit, with a few memories of John Hughes, I had something of the meaning.

Mid-afternoon, I took a young archer, Gosford, and rode well ahead. It was risky, but my choices were limited. We crossed another stream with no bridge, and then turned back half a mile and chose a campsite with room to turn all the wagons. Gosford was young enough to see it all as an adventure, so I left him alone to start a fire and collect wood, and rode a very tired Frank back to the column, where I changed horses and told the wagoners that they only had two miles to go.

It wasn't a long day, but it was uneventful. By dark, we had the wagons circled, the cattle in an abandoned field. It had two good walls, and we closed the other two sides with an abatis of felled trees.

'See to your horses,' I said. 'We're going to have trouble out in the open. Better that you're cold than your horse is cold.'

Saint Michael was smiling on me, though. We had a mild night, and my guards stayed awake.

So did I, mostly, with Pilgrim pressed against me, wrapped in my riding cloak. The only part of me that was warm was where the dog was, and I had plenty of time to be worried about Christopher and Fox and every other decision I'd made. I rose four times to check my posts. I wished I had another knight. A trustworthy officer.

I had been *bored?*

We had no trouble getting underway in the early morning darkness. We were almost out of firewood and no one had slept particularly well on the damp ground under the big wagons. I made sure everyone had some hot cider, and then we were rolling. They warmed themselves bridging the next stream, while I put half the archers across to watch over us, and before Sext we'd already made ten miles. Off to my left, Wailly – that is, I hoped it was Wailly – sat amid ploughed fields, smoke rising from hearths in the pleasant morning air. Wailly was a walled town, loyal to the king of France.

I rode up to Robin.

'An ambush could come from any direction,' I said, 'but watch Wailly. Watch for riders, watch for movement.'

Robin looked a trifle less sullen. 'Aye, sir,' he said.

I rode with him for an hour, and then rode all the way back to my rearguard. With eight wagons who at least knew to stay together, a rearguard behind an advance guard in front, and two archers well out ahead, my whole column covered half a mile. Frank went up and down, up and down, as we passed Wailly. I breathed better when I could no longer see the place.

South and south.

We made about three miles an hour. That was if we didn't have to rebuild a bridge. The road was a track, mostly just two wagon-wheel ruts rolling between old stone walls or hedges, from time to time, a turnaround or a little side path where two big wagons could pass each other. The ground to the east was getting rougher and steeper. Off to the west, towards the coast, I was convinced that there was a parallel road, and that my adversaries, if they existed, were on that road, possibly sleeping well at Wailly and then shadowing us.

Or maybe not. Maybe I was making the whole thing up.

I didn't think so.

The big wagons rolled on. I rode up and down, up and down.

I managed to worry a great deal, and I forgot to eat. Once again, I rode forward with Gosford, and we chose a campsite. It reminded me of being the cook's boy in Poitiers year. I'd learnt to choose a campsite from the head cook. I wondered where he was now. Fifteen years.

About Gosford's age, I reckoned.

He was a quick study, though, and we found a nice site, with water and an old sheepfold with an unburnt shack. I went in, had a look, and nodded.

'Good eye, lad,' I said.

He blushed.

We made camp in time to start fires and cut wood. There were some trees down in what had once been the farm's woodlot, and we had axes in the wagons and a saw, a fine thing that someone in London or Ghent had made. I kept the archers at the firewood while the hobilars tended the horses – all the horses, including the archers' horses. We had some salt pork and some Venetian rice. I got two men on cooking. Odd to have rice in France.

'Have a bit o' sausage,' Fox said.

I wanted to hug him. He'd brought four spare horses and he had wine, which we shared very carefully so every man got a brimming cup and drank it off on the spot. I'd been around, and I wasn't going to let one man bully four or five rations out of his mates.

Christopher told me what he'd seen, which wasn't much.

'Scared spitless the last three miles,' he admitted. 'Something or someone shadowing us, and I could feel it but couldn't see naught.'

I drank off my wine with everyone else, and then told off four men, all archers, for an evening patrol, which I took out myself, riding a mile each way along the road as the last light vanished from the sky.

And then, I slept well.

The next day we rolled south through a steady rain. Rain is uncomfortable and makes a camp almost unlivable, at least in October, but it has this virtue – lazy, under-trained French knights and peasants don't make raids or patrols in the rain. I squandered the last of whatever coin I'd won by sharing the ransoms on the French knights, and pushed them forward as rapidly as animal flesh and human flesh could stand, and got some surly replies, which I ignored.

Towards nightfall, the steady rain began to increase. It was perhaps two hours past Sext, but already we only had perhaps three hours until dark because days are short in October. I needed to camp, but we were now out of the 'border ground' around the English Pale. We were in France. The towns were fortified. Even the villages, those that had survived being burnt by both sides, were fortified. Most of the fields were in tillage, and I could see animals in paddocks, although it was clear that someone knew we were coming and was moving everything into the castles – us, or Lancaster coming the other way. I confess that I'd spent the whole day hoping that the duke's prickers would ride up to me and I'd be off the hook for the whole thing, but as I say, two hours after Sext and it was clear I needed to camp.

I galloped ahead with Christopher and Gosford. We were moving fast because I had an ominous sense of apprehension – that 'nameless dread' that can come upon you because you forgot your visor pins, or because you can feel an enemy ambush.

We were moving along a road, a better road, lined in tall hedges and studded with trees. It came around a sharp bend, and there was a farm cart with four peasants quarrelling.

We snapped them up, which is to say that, like a good routier, I charged them, took their wagon, and in a moment had all four men as prisoners. The wagon proved to contain two entire families – men, women and children.

I separated the men and demanded information. I learnt this from

Hawkwood – have spies, recruit guides, pay them well and keep them separate.

The nearest town was Nouvion, already cleared and abandoned by the Duc de Bourgogne. Beyond Nouvion was Sailly-Flibeaucourt and Le Titre, which my new guides assured me were prosperous hamlets.

Remember that I speak French as well as any French peasant, and in the same Norman French patois – 'waaiy' for 'oui', and everything spoken in the nose. In a few minutes, Jean, the prudhomme I took first, was complaining about Jacques, his useless neighbour who'd made them late and whose malfeasance had landed them all in this scrape. Jean seemed to have forgotten that I was his captor.

Jacques, when I questioned him, was nearly useless in his terror, but his wife, Marie, was a very religious woman who'd made all the local pilgrimages. I got the feeling she may have been a bit of a busybody, but that was no business of mine, and from her I heard about the church of Le Titre and the abbey south of Sailly-Flibeaucourt.

'That's where Monseigneur le Duc is forming the *Milice*, and where all the chevaliers are to go with their vassals,' she said artlessly. 'The herald said that the English were only a day or two away, and we had to flee.'

'And is the ford open at Blanchetaque?' I asked.

'Oh, *oui, monsieur*, for was it not just yesterday that my sister and her fool of a husband crossed the ford with their silver and left it with us ...' Marie's hand went to her mouth.

I was still mounted, leaning into the back of the wagon. Marie's glance went to a barrel by her daughter.

They all paled.

Luckily for them, I've been a bad man, and killing a family of rich peasants and taking their silver, which I was perfectly capable of doing, was not on the day's plan.

I smiled slowly, so they knew that I knew they had a barrel full of silver.

'As long as your directions prove out,' I said in good Norman French, ' I won't search your wagon.'

My little convoy made a cold camp in the church of Nouvion. It was dry, and we didn't burn it or anything else – truth to tell, in the rain, it might not have caught. We ate sausage and drank wine. I put

Greg Fox on the two families with Gosford. Men-at-arms can find any excuse for a little warmth on a cold night, and I wasn't tolerating any of it. After a cold supper, I questioned the men and women again, and made a little map – see it here, in my book of hours?

In the morning, there was a bright sun. I went out with six men – Hales and Gosford and the best mounted hobilars. As I expected, we saw a mounted patrol off to the east, towards Sailly-Flibeaucourt.

'Back,' I said.

I got them under cover, threw my cloak over my armour, and walked along the hedge, my sabatons catching on everything. But I had it in my head that if we were seen, we were done. I assumed that the Duc de Bourgogne was on my side of the Somme, getting ready to dispute the passage of the river with Lancaster.

Let me note that I was dead wrong, as you'll hear, and yet, in my error I was right to be afraid. There were French troops forming on the north bank of the Somme, but they were local men under local captains.

I watched the French patrol silhouette themselves against the skyline twice, and generally show the brightness of their harness all along a slightly divergent track to the east.

'Back,' I ordered.

The seven of us picked our way carefully until a ridge hid us, and then rode like the wind for Nouvion.

I sent the wagons west, because Marie the goodwife said that the 'old wagon road' ran that way and made a wide swing on slightly higher ground before turning back east to the ford – a longer distance, but the first two miles almost directly away from where I assumed the French army to be. I had Robin Wall take his advance guard in front of the wagons, but I held the rest of my people in Nouvion. I loopholed two peasant houses on the south-east side of the town and waited.

I didn't have to wait long.

The French patrol came along the road led by a knight in excellent modern armour. He had two crossbowmen with him on good horses, and the rest of his people were spread out behind him in no particular order.

We took him immediately. I simply let him ride between my two little fortified hovels, and then tossed him off his horse and Christopher put a dagger under his chin. He never knew what had hit him. His crossbowmen surrendered to Gosford and Fox and their drawn bows. Then the archers in the hovels loosed at the men on nags coming behind, and they killed some ponies.

The rest of them ran.

The smaller crossbowman swore like an Italian.

'You're a long way from home,' I said, in that language.

He rolled his eyes. 'Hell, damnation and plague,' he said. 'Fucking idiots.'

My young knight looked as if he planned to burst into tears.

The Italian just shook his head. 'I told him. And told him. Too fucking stupid to make war.'

I watched my archers move out to where they'd dropped men on the road, and loot the bodies. There were two francs-archers taken – really, just wealthy peasants dressed like soldiers. The king of France thought that by putting men in gambesons and aventails, he could make them into English archers.

'They're worthless,' Hales said. 'Let's just kill them.'

I remember raising an eyebrow. 'Are you worth a ransom?' I asked.

He gulped visibly.

'Then don't go around killing such,' I said. 'Strip them and release them.' I looked around. 'But not until we pull out.'

They had good basinets with aventails of maille, which I used to improve the kit of two of the poorer hobilars. The young knight armoured another hobilar, the youngest – a man so young and thin-faced as to be somewhere between a ferret and a slip of a girl. His name was Thomas Fenton, and he blushed constantly and had a stammer. But he fitted the armour, and instantly became, after me, the best armoured man. He got the young knight's charger, too.

'How old are you, Fenton?' I asked.

He blushed. And hung his head.

'Fenton,' I said, as patiently as I could. 'It's not a complicated question.'

'No, My Lord,' he mumbled.

Beyond him, two archers were looking through one of the abandoned houses. One gave a shout and emerged with a ham.

I waved at Dick Thorald.

'Get them mounted and get out of here,' I said.

'Awreet,' he agreed. Well, I assumed he was agreeing.

I motioned to Hales.

'Take everyone but young Tom here, and Gosford, Fox and Christopher. Find the wagons and stay with them. If you come to the Somme, halt and wait for me.'

Hales looked solemn. 'Yes, My Lord.'

I was never really comfortable with being 'My Lord', but I was a baron, three times over. I never used the titles except in letters, but I suppose word had spread.

Now wasn't the time for humility.

'Right, then,' I said.

He put his hand to his visor and rode away.

We watched the roads from the church tower, or rather, I did. I watched for more than an hour, until I saw, first, dust, because mud dries fast, and then the glint of metal.

Christopher had produced a dozen apples he'd 'found' and I was eating one, trying not to look down. I'm not really much better than Fiore at heights. I watched the French force move up from the south and east. This time, there were more than two hundred of them, and they came on two roads. But they moved up to the hedges that lined the distant Sailly-Flibeaucourt road – Gosford called it 'Sally-Flubber'. Then they halted.

I'd already thrown my apple core away. I was ready to ride, and ride fast.

But the French commander hesitated. The rapid annihilation of his patrol hadn't provided him with any actual information beyond that there was an enemy force in Nouvion. Fleeing men and stripped prisoners count every man twice, or perhaps fifty times.

The French commander began to deploy into the patchwork of fields east of the town. He had more than two hundred men. And he was very cautious.

'Garn!' Gosford said. 'They's all cowards.'

Christopher glanced at me. 'Look,' he said.

A few horses were coming forward – someone with a pennon.

I was playing with my beard. Below me, Fox had all the horses. He was looking up at me, his face a question.

I climbed down from the church tower. Gosford followed, and Christopher stayed to warn us of any change.

'Gosford, you and Fox get back to the houses we fortified. There's a small retinue coming down the track. Put some arrows in them at very long range and then slip back. Do *not* be seen. Understood?'

Fox, who had been making war for precisely one week, nodded as if he understood. Gosford nodded as well.

'Go,' I said.

I mounted Percival and told Tom to wait.

'Here they come,' Christopher said from above me. And then, a chuckle. 'And there they go.'

Minutes went by – too long. And then Gosford appeared with Fox.

'Don' think we hit nuffin',' Gosford admitted.

'Let's get gone,' I said. 'Christopher?' I called.

He dropped off the last of the wall and vaulted into his saddle.

'Still running,' he said.

'Sorry?' Fox said.

'I still don't understand,' young Tom said.

I led the way out of Nouvion, on the same road I'd sent the wagons. We rode slowly, careful not to raise dust, but out of some superstition I didn't talk until we were a mile or more clear of the little town and its now-distant church tower.

'The French commander thinks we're the Duke of Lancaster,' I said.

'What?' Gosford asked.

'Why?' young Tom asked.

'Of course,' Christopher said. He grinned.

'And now he's going to waste another half an hour planning his attack,' I said. 'Or he'll just wait for someone with a bigger title to come and take responsibility.'

The sun was bright, and high in the sky. We passed through a big oak wood as the road turned south and more south. As we emerged from the woods, I could see the Somme estuary off to the west. The sea was a remarkable deep blue.

I was alternating between an excess of spirits and a black fatigue. I was fairly certain I'd fooled the French into leaving me a route to the ford, but until I was across, I had to fear it would be held against me, and until I saw the state of the tide, I knew I might just be locked at the edge of the ford for hours. If I found the ford. And then I had to find the duke. And I was out of forage for my horses, and food for my people.

It was just before Sext that I caught my convoy. Over towards Sailly-Flibeaucourt we could hear church bells. I knew it was Sailly-Flibeaucourt – I knew the road was turning back east, away from the sea, just as Goodwife Marie had said. I rode up my column, greeted Hales and Thorald.

'Seen young Robin?' I asked.

'Nah,' Thorald said. He shrugged.

I passed him. The bells stopped ringing. I trotted Percival up to my riding horse and changed, swinging a very tired leg over my saddle and heading out to find my advance guard.

'With me,' I said to Fenton and Gosford. 'Christopher, see to the horses. Fox, help him.'

I might need my warhorse at any moment.

Off to my right, the river got closer and closer. It was enormous, at least by military standards – fifty paces wide, and flowing strongly with the October rains and some mud.

'Jesu Christ,' I muttered, or some such blasphemy.

But as I rode east and south along the bank, I saw signs that the river was running lower, and I could see sand on the edge of the mud, and mudbanks in mid-stream. Low tide was coming. Tide in the Mediterranean is usually measured in hand spans, whereas in the Atlantic it's measured in fathoms. A low tide might be ten or fifteen *feet* lower, and the ford at Blanchetaque was probably only practical at low tide.

I needn't have worried about Robin Wall. The pudgy man was resting his horse at the edge of the ford. He had two archers dismounted in cover, and had sent another man across to test the depth.

I wanted to embrace him.

'Well done,' I said.

He flushed, and I realised he wasn't really much older than Tom Fenton. The age I'd been when I was a cook's boy at Poitiers.

But he was resting his horse like a professional, and his archers looked as if they were ready for anything.

'It's going to be rough getting the wagons across,' he said. Then he flushed again because he assumed he was wrong.

I rode out into the river, my riding horse communicating her unease at the current, but it was very shallow over hard sand and gravel. Shallow, but a rapid current.

'Master Wall, stay here and hold Master Hales and the convoy until I return. Who's the archer crossing the river?'

'Bill Morse. We call him Buck.'

I nodded. 'I'm going to scout south,' I said. 'On me!' I shouted to my comrades and we were away, splashing through the ford.

I'd expected to find something at the ford. The French? The Duke of Lancaster's prickers? Finding it empty unnerved me. Now I was alone in a darkened room, so to speak, and I needed to know what was happening, no matter how bad the news was.

Remember, it was possible that the duke was already taken, or had fought a battle and won it, or was still all the way south by Harfleur. And yet, when I'd reckoned the distances and the marches he'd be making, and I'd be making, I'd hoped to run into him at the Somme. And of course, I thought the French army was at Sailly-Flibeaucourt. I thought I'd got around the French and there should have been an English army . . .

Why am I telling this to you, Master Froissart? Because most men have no idea how battles happen. I wanted you to see how wrong I was about the location of the French host, and to try to understand how blind we were, moving around the countryside of France.

At any rate, we dashed down the road, heading almost due south. There were tracks on the road – tracks of carts, and unshod horses, mules, donkeys, an ox. But no peasants at all.

Oh, I was rattled.

I generally attack things that frighten me, so we rode hard, and fast, straight south, or as straight as the road to the ford would let us. We went up a shallow valley to the hamlet of Cahon. I knew it was called that because that's where Marie's sister who was married to a fool lived.

Through Cahon. I admit I could have been taken on the narrow track between the first two houses, exactly as my young prisoner had been taken that morning. Except that I was moving faster, and slapped my visor down as I went between the buildings, but I might have saved my effort. The little hamlet was empty, and we pushed through and rode south for another mile, and then another.

Nothing.

I reined in at the top of the first low ridge since the ford, where the road turns west towards Quesnoy-le-Montant. I could see up three narrow valleys whose streams ran down into the Somme, and I could see for a couple of miles.

'Damn it to hell,' I said.

Was I on the wrong road altogether? Had I missed some basic instruction? Instead of a war, I was in an empty country, as if the plague had taken the living. I best remember closing my eyes and opening them, as if this would change the reality.

Only the absence of peasants suggested that there were armies close by, and the absence of something is always a bad proof.

'Master Fenton,' I said. 'Please ride back to the convoy ...'

I wasn't sure what I was going to order. Once the heavy wagons tried to cross the ford ...

The ford, which was going to be full as soon as the tide came in. I had limited time to make my decision.

Far off to the south, perhaps a mile and a half, something moved. At first it was like watching a spider spin a web out of the corner of your eye. Then the tiny movement repeated a few times and there was a sparkle, and then a little flash of light as the sun caught something.

My heart beat faster.

Here's a tiny stone against which to brace your foot when you are desperate. English columns tend to sparkle more than French columns. The French had some bright armour, but generally they cover it in cloth – thick outer gambesons to absorb the shock of our arrows and keep them from shattering. Just the splinters from a volley of arrows can blind men.

French archers, with the exception of the Picards, aren't worth much. Our people tended to wear their armour bare – white, as some call it. And that means our people sparkled more at a distance.

Or so I hoped, because what I was seeing was shining like Saint Michael and a host of angels.

Of course, closer up there was rust and grease, and the white armour had a brown tinge. But closer up, there were the red crosses of Saint George scattered through the troop. They were Welsh cavalry on ponies, and they were moving fast.

When I released my breath, I felt as if I hadn't breathed in days.

'Master Fenton,' I said.

'Sir?'

'Go and tell the column we've made contact with Lancaster's army and we'll have further instructions,' I said.

Then I thought of the tide, the time of day, and the position of the duke's army. I couldn't wait for someone else to make my decision for me.

'Bring the wagons across,' I said.

There it was. Done. I'd committed, right or wrong.

The Welsh passed me back to the Earl of Warwick, who was commanding the van. He was a big man, as I have said, with a week's stubble on his cheeks and a perpetual scowl. I'd seen him at Poitiers, where he fought brilliantly, but it was clear he didn't remember me.

He handed his basinet to a page. He was, after all, an earl.

'Never heard of you,' he said.

'My Lord Earl, the Captain of Calais sent me with a convoy,' I said.

'Sweet Christ – across Normandy?' he asked. 'Where the hell is it?'

'Just coming across the ford at Blanchetaque,' I said.

His eyes met mine. 'You crossed the ford?' he asked.

'Yes, My Lord,' I said patiently.

'Today?' he asked.

'An hour ago,' I said.

He waved to his knights.

'Go!' he said.

I didn't see any way they could fail to find the ford, but the knights looked both exhausted and haunted. Every man of them had a thick stubble of beard and deep black marks under their eyes.

'My Lord, Master Gosford here can be your guide ...'

Warwick turned his head like a falcon. 'Gosford?'

'Yes, My Lord. I know the way. Dead simple, 'tis.'

'I do not know the tide,' I offered hesitantly.

'Yes?'

'But I fear that the ford will be closed before the army can come up. That's why I ordered my wagons across.'

'What's in your wagons?' Warwick asked.

'Arrows and salt pork,' I said. 'Some beef. Some wine.'

Warwick glanced back at the second convoy of knights and men-at-arms coming up the road. Their horses were in terrible shape, and at the base of the ridge I could see a mob of men on foot.

'Well, Master Gold—' he began.

'Sir William,' I said.

He glanced at me. 'Sir William,' he said, mildly enough. He was clearly not used to being corrected, nor yet so much a tyrant that he couldn't accept such.

'My Lord ...' I met his eyes.

'We're hard pressed,' he said. 'The Duc du Bourgogne and his captain, Hugh de Châtillon, are right on our heels with four times the men we have. We lost men in our rearguard yesterday to men-at-arms out of Abbeville. We have some plague and some other pestilence, and they don't, damn them.'

I looked back towards Sailly-Flibeaucourt.

'But ...'

Luckily, I didn't shout my incorrect theory on the French deployment to the rooftops. I had to assume that Warwick knew what he was talking about, which meant that the force at Sailly-Flibeaucourt was a local force. But a deadly one, capable of blocking the ford.

'My Lord, there's a French force of perhaps five hundred men just across the river,' I said. 'I deceived them this morning.'

He raised an eyebrow. 'You saw five hundred with your own eyes?' he asked.

'Yes,' I said.

'Sir John!' he called to an older knight in a fine German armour with a boxy breastplate. 'Keep moving!'

You need a camp, I thought.

But I wasn't in command.

The Duke of Lancaster looked like a Plantagenet, from his long straight nose to his bright blond hair. He had a small circlet of gilded brass on his basinet. He was the king's fourth son, the Prince of Wales's younger brother. Prince Lionel's younger brother, too.

And there you were, Chaucer – not a dozen horsemen away from me. One of our many meetings.

I dismounted and made a reverence.

'Sir William Gold,' Warwick said. 'With a convoy from Calais.'

Lancaster looked south, and then back at me.

'Sir William says that the French have a local force of five hundred on the other side of the Somme.'

The good duke swore. Now, to be fair, I met him at a terrible time – in a campaign in which he'd accomplished little, had been dogged by pestilence, had failed to take Harfleur or to deceive Bourgogne, in the year the Plantagenet Empire began to crumble and his wonderful wife died. No blame to him. But he sat on his horse like a stunned bull.

Then he looked at me.

'What does Sir William know of war?' he asked.

He wasn't looking at me. I was a person of no account. He was looking at Warwick.

Chaucer, you were then still a squire in the court of the duke. You spoke up on my behalf and said some very formidable things. Lancaster actually looked at me for the first time.

'Not your first campaign, then?' he said, and suddenly he was a different man – a man capable of humour. And correction.

'No, Your Grace,' I said. 'I was at Poitiers,' I added.

Heads turned.

The Plantagenet eyes met mine, and the image of a falcon was even clearer.

'Speak to me, Sir William. Speak freely.'

Remember, I was kneeling on the road in my harness. On one knee, anyway.

'Your Grace, the French have five hundred men in the towns just beyond the river,' I said. 'If you can get a force across immediately, they'll be easy to deal with – they're militia. But the tide will come up and close the ford.'

'When?' the duke asked.

Do you guess? Or tell the truth?

'I do not know, Your Grace,' I said.

Warwick shook his head, but another man in good armour put a hand on Warwick's bridle. He was older – in his fifties or sixties.

'We fought here in Crécy year,' he said. 'The ford is open for about four hours, then closed for four to six.'

An hour after Sext. Darkness three hours away, the tide already coming in – perhaps open for another two hours. The French crawling up your backside, and another force just across the river.

It's popular these days to blame a great deal on Lancaster – nay, Chaucer, you are hopelessly biased. But in that hour, he was a great captain. He woke like a bird of prey, gave a squawk, and then settled to making good decisions.

'My lord of Warwick,' he said. 'Get thee across the ford if you can, and destroy whatever force you find there. I will hold the ford if it is in my power to do so, and cross in the morning.'

'Yes, Your Grace,' Warwick said.

Then he began coughing.

As it proved, Warwick had the sense to take a third of my wagons as he passed. He got his Welsh cavalry across the ford and made fires before dark, and I sent Gosford and Tom Fenton with the earl, and gave him the young knight I'd taken prisoner. I kept the Italian. And I released all the peasants, and begged Warwick to see their wagon clear of our army. He coughed and agreed. He was a chivalrous man, even worried and sick, and is that not the very definition of greatness?

It was in my mind that Warwick might slip back into Nouvion before the French seized it, but he was more cautious, and merely sent out some of his light horse and made a small camp.

The rest of my wagons came across to the south side. My wagoners watched as the barrels were taken away by exhausted men. Some ate the meat uncooked.

The archers looked terrible. These were retinue archers, England's best, raised by great lords for hard currency from the veterans of Crécy and Poitiers and Auray and fifty other fights. In a good retinue, every archer had as much armour as most French men-at-arms, and rode a good horse with another for emergencies.

These men were as thin as Greek saints, or fence rails, and their horses were no better, where they had horses at all. It wasn't quite a mob, but the main body lost cohesion as soon as the cargoes of the wagons were released, and had the French caught us eating, they might have had us all to ransom. As it was, the best-disciplined retinues, like Warwick's and Hereford's and the like, got their fires lit and their cook kettles going, and their archers got a full meal and then some.

Anywhere I went, men looked at my horses. My riding horse looked bigger than Lancaster's charger – the army's warhorses were in as bad shape as the archers' ronceys.

Well. It's odd to relate what Chaucer said and what I said, when the man is sitting right here. Correct me, if you like. And a little more of that cider.

Where was I?

Ah. I found Chaucer, here, sitting on a salt-beef barrel, already empty and upturned. Somewhere, a cooper was going to scream bloody murder. Barrels were supposed to be cleaned, knocked down to staves and returned, but the army was burning them or using them as seats.

'William,' Chaucer said. 'You cannot have any of my beef.'

There's a greeting for you.

I told him I'd missed him in London, and he shook his head.

'I wish we were all in London,' he said. 'Comfortable at the Savoy Palace, listening to the good duke tell us about his campaign in France.'

'Bad?'

'Hell,' he said. 'And I've been here before. I know the smell and the sound.'

Chaucer hadn't been present the whole campaign. He was far too senior an officer to be used as a messenger, and he'd been in England until shortly before I landed, when he'd been sent with money and letters from the king.

'Châtillon could have had us any day of the last five,' he said. 'But they fear us. They still fear the goddamned English from Crécy and Poitiers.' He shrugged. 'And they are as short of money as the English crown. It is a wonder to me that they keep fighting when neither of them can afford to pay.'

I looked around. 'This is worse than I expected,' I said.

'The duke is all that's keeping us together,' he said. Then his eyes met mine. 'Christ, food helps.'

I decided to play the game the way I'd played it as a penniless squire, or perhaps rather better, so as darkness fell, I took a small tun of wine from the last wagon to the Duke of Lancaster's fire, and handed it over to his military steward, a man that Chaucer knew well. That got me an introduction to the duke's fire.

The duke with a belly full of beef and a cup of red wine was a much more politic, and even chivalrous man. He motioned for me to approach and drew me up when I made to make a reverence.

'I've never been so happy to see a food convoy,' he said. 'My army is in tatters.'

'Your Grace,' I said, 'I wonder if you'd let me take my hobilars out at dawn, or even now. As we are better mounted than most of your people.'

It was impolitic to say, and given how badly my hobilars were mounted, it spoke to just how terrible the campaign had been for the English horses.

The duke looked at me for a moment.

'Yesterday, Châtillon snapped at my rearguard,' he said.

One is not allowed to interrogate a prince of the blood. I glanced at Sir Nigel Loring, an older knight and one of Lancaster's most trusted men. I knew Loring well enough, from the years after Poitiers.

'Where is Châtillon now?' I asked.

Loring looked down his nose at me.

'Somewhere hereabouts,' he said.

Now, I'm as English as the next man, and I can shout for Saint George as loud as any, but in that moment, I had a very real temptation to ride off and leave them to it. Except that Sir Nigel and the young duke and many of the rest of them had made war in Spain and France. Perhaps they just hadn't faced Albornoz or the Turks.

'I could go and find them,' I said. 'Right now.'

'You plan to do a deed of arms?' a younger knight asked.

No, you fool. I plan to find out how long we have until we're attacked.

But the field of war is the stage of chivalry, so I drawled, 'Perhaps.'

Well. No one actually told me that I couldn't. There were retinues acting like soldiers, and morale had increased with food. When I gathered my patrol, my men surly for being required to tack up in the dark instead of lying down to sleep, I saw pickets being posted. I found an emaciated master-archer from Hereford's's retinue, another Thomas, posting them.

'What's the password?' I asked.

He glanced back at the fires. 'Didn't get one,' he said.

'Salt Beef,' I said. 'Counter-sign Salt Pork.'

He laughed when his stomach rumbled. 'And you are the duke of ...?' he asked, the sarcasm clear.

'I'm the Duke of Making War like an Army,' I said. 'I'm taking a patrol out into the dark and I don't want to get a shaft in my belly button when I come back in.'

He nodded. 'Right you are, sir,' he said.

I took ten men out into the darkness. Hales was relatively eager, and so was Wall, to my surprise. As I said, they were all loud in their surliness, but it was a different surliness from the first day's.

Riding in the darkness is not easy. Even on a road, on a moonlit night, you can miss things. Horses fall, like people. It's dangerous.

Off the road, you have to move very slowly. You can be surprised by anything – a bull in a field, a wasps' nest your horse didn't see, canes or brush full of snags or prickers, low-hanging branches that bop you in the head or sweep you from your saddle.

In a hundred horse-strides, I knew that Christopher and I were the only men who'd ever done this before. So I divided us into two teams – one going south and west up one little valley, and one going south and east up another.

Hales looked at me. 'Why's the Moor in command?' he asked.

'He's done this at night,' I said. 'Haven't you, Christopher?'

'I've stolen a great many horses,' he said. 'But only from Moslems, I promise.'

We split up and I went south and east, got lost at a fork in the road I'd missed, went back, and finally got us over the second ridge.

And there were the French. Thanks to God, they had no more discipline than the tired English. They had four ragged lines of fires, and a field of picketed horses just waiting to be stolen, and a handful of pavilions. I could smell their campfires as soon as I could see them.

I spent a third of the night riding all the way around their camp. I couldn't count tents, but I could count horses and fires, and they didn't have much in the way of guards – a few men, close in by the fires.

I was tempted to go for their horse herd. But I had no other veteran horse thieves with me. If I'd had John the Turk ...

I missed him. I missed all my friends and comrades, and Hales was not an adequate substitute, although he was learning quickly.

It took me an hour to pick my way back, but I did it unobserved, and we found Christopher closer in, with a prisoner, a local squire who'd wandered too far from their camp.

We took him to the Duke of Lancaster, and got some sleep.

The morning dawned pink, and the army's baggage started across the ford as the tide went out. But by the time the sky was fully light, it was clear that the army wasn't getting across in a single tide. Time was running out, and before the duke knelt to say his morning prayers, a line of armoured men became visible at the top of the valley to the left front, or south-east.

Lancaster got us formed quickly enough. He put the most dependable retinues in the centre by his banner, and sent most of the broken men away with the wagons. There were a dozen wagons of sick men – some had plague, and some just couldn't walk any more.

All in all, we had about five hundred knights and men-at-arms who could wear harness and bear arms, and perhaps a thousand archers, or fewer. Some of them complained that they couldn't fully draw their bows – cramps, or exhaustion, or sickness. So our actual force to cover the ford was less than one sixth of our opponent's, and as we watched the French come down the valleys, the mismatch in force began to seem absurd.

I could see Châtillon's personal banner to my left front, and his war banner as Master of Archers to the king of France. I counted more than eighty pennons and bannerettes. Altogether, I thought he had perhaps two thousand men in decent armour – not so very much more than we had.

On the other hand, withdrawing across a ford in the face of the enemy is very difficult. Every man who crosses the ford is not fighting in the rearguard. Your pool of available men is diminishing as you retreat, meaning that in the end, your rearguard is almost inevitably overwhelmed.

I stood with Chaucer here, and Hales, and Fenton, and a handful of English men-at-arms. We were in our harness, watching the enemy. Fenton was young enough to ask questions, and soon we had a lively debate going about how best to get across.

Sir Nigel Loring was passing our position and he dismounted.

'What have you gentlemen decided?' he asked. He could be both debonair and humorous, especially with food in him.

They'd all been arguing a moment before, but now they were all silent.

I met Sir Nigel's eyes and said nothing.

He nodded, as if we were old companions. And the Earl of Warwick joined us, although he didn't dismount.

'It's a bit of a puzzle,' Warwick admitted, and coughed.

He'd been back and forth over the ford since dawn, swimming his horse until the tide fell.

'Sir William?' Sir Nigel asked. 'Chaucer speaks well of you. Give us your counsel.'

I didn't want to. I knew exactly what I'd do, but I didn't know if they had it in them – exhausted, diseased men on tired horses.

'How do you cross a ford in the face of the enemy, Chaucer?' Warwick asked. He smiled. 'According to all your dead Romans?'

Chaucer, I'd always assumed you were the perfect courtier – that all your bitter statements were saved for your drinking companions. I was wrong.

'My old Romans would say that you should avoid getting into this situation in the first place,' Chaucer snapped, and then added, 'Your Grace,' in an unrepentant tone.

Yes, Geoffrey, that *is* what you said.

Sir Nigel frowned, but old Warwick laughed, as did most of the younger men-at-arms. Their laughter emboldened me. They were in better shape than perhaps I'd guessed, or mayhap I'd forgotten how hardy the English can be, when the dagger is at their throats.

I looked at Chaucer, who was flushed, and then at Warwick.

'We should attack,' I said.

Fifteen minutes later, I was standing in full harness with Warwick and Loring and the Duke of Lancaster.

'Lay it out for me?' Lancaster said. 'I'm not dead set against it, Sir William, but perhaps you are used to Italians and your ideas may not ...' He didn't finish his sentence. He often did not.

I was looking at Châtillon's banner.

'Your Grace, the French fear us. If they did not, they'd have been on us in the dawn. Half his force is militia from the towns. Your Grace, I'll be bold and say that I *have* faced men like them in Italy. They are resolute if well fed and well led. I doubt either is true here.'

Lancaster was looking up at Châtillon's army.

'We send your banner across with your retinue,' I said to the duke. 'Either that will draw them, like a provocation in a sword bout, or it will not. If they come down off the heights, we attack, and you, My Lord, come back and finish the job. If they stay on the heights, they don't mean to come down, and we keep marching until everyone is across.'

Lancaster looked at Warwick, who bent over, coughing, and there was blood on his hand. But then he smiled at me.

'Best plan I've heard this morning,' he said.

Loring nodded. 'Your Grace, if we defeat them, we buy all the time we need. And were not the king your father's orders to bring the French to an open battle? Here we have one.'

That clinched it with Lancaster, and he nodded.

'Very well. My retinue crosses and becomes the reserve, eh? They'll believe that. It's what that damn lawyer Charles of France would do – retreat first and leave his men to fight.' He nodded at me. 'Thanks, Sir William. We hear great things of John Hawkwood. Clearly he is leading a fine school for chivalry.'

I almost spoke out – something like you would, Chaucer.

Are you mad? John Hawkwood's never met chivalry. He likes to be paid.

But I decided it wasn't the moment.

I had no real command. The English formed in fairly tight ranks to cover the ford. The lack of Lancaster's men, the best armoured and the best trained, was obvious – my hobilars were as well armoured as many. Listen, in a long campaign, especially one where you ride fast over broken ground, many men – aye, most men – will start abandoning things they don't need every day. Like lances, and heavy helmets, and gorgets, and ...

Right. All discipline had not broken. But we only had perhaps a hundred men in cap-à-pie, of whom I was one and Fenton another, God save us. I put Hales behind me, and put Fenton in the front rank because full armour is better than skill in a close fight. I moved around a little, making sure that at least in my small band, the archers had lanes down which they could shoot. I showed them how we did this in Italy, in the old days of the White Company, and I was pleased to hear old veterans on either side of my little group start to order their own men in the same way. Listen, in great battles like Poitiers, we'd put all the archers in clumps with men-at-arms between them. But on a frontage of perhaps five hundred paces, blocks of archers would just have offered the French places to break our line. It was already a different war. I've already mentioned, I think, that the French had taken to wearing heavy cloth gambesons *over* their armour, to soak up arrows and prevent the shattering of the shafts. And when du Guesclin took the field ...

It didn't bear thinking about. I was next to Loring's retinue, and we locked up with their formation and then 'invited' the men of the next small band to close up to us and not leave a gap.

The young aristocrat next to me was from the Welsh Marches. He wore a lot of brass edging on his armour, and he had money.

'Sirrah, if you would take the care to have *all* of your men-at-arms stand against the French, I'd have no need to close over to you. Or are your *hobilars* afraid?' he asked in his aristocratic Norman French accent.

I smiled. 'Ever been in a fight?' I asked.

'I am Sir Richard—'

'Don't care who you are. Ever been in a stour? With more than a hundred men?' I waved my hand at Loring's men and mine. 'The deeper you are, the harder you are to break.' I smiled, reached out a hand, and smacked his left pauldron in a friendly way. 'Just tuck in. Put those lads in the second rank, shorten your front, and leave room for your archers to loose.'

He had a nice helmet, but his visor wouldn't stay up – they usually don't. He was holding it with his hand.

'I've done this a dozen times,' I said. 'I promise you it will work.'

Sir Richard, whoever he was, showed more sense than I expected.

'Very well,' he said.

He began to re-form his retinue.

As it proved, he and I were standing together in a friendlier mood when you walked up, Chaucer.

'The duke is retiring his banner right now,' he said. 'May I make my stand with you, William?'

I introduced you to young Sir Richard. But my eyes were already on Châtillon's banner.

I wasn't disappointed. Châtillon didn't even wait for the duke's leopards and lilies to reach mid-stream. He dipped his personal banner. Moments later, the royal banner of France and the 'Master of Archers' banner dipped. And then, with a long, untrained ripple, the whole French army started down off the low ridge.

307

Here's the thing, friends. In war, once you give an order like 'attack the English', you are no longer in command. That's not always a bad thing. If you have a dozen eager, competent young captains, and they know their business, and you choose the right moment to attack ... well, they should get the job done.

But if you have a large, unwieldy and unpaid mass of men who don't know or trust their officers, and think the enemy may be unbeatable ...

'Look at them come on,' you said, Chaucer. 'Christ, I didn't know there were so many Frenchmen in all the world.'

Now, Geoffrey, I love you like a brother, but when I looked up the ridge, that's not what I saw. What I saw was how much faster the men-at-arms moved off than the militia, whose brilliantly painted heavy shields caught the sun in a particular way and whose ranks just weren't so eager to get to grips with the English. And some brilliant planner had interspersed the militias with the men-at-arms, so that their hesitancy left broad gaps in the French lines.

I also saw that many of the French knights had left their shields with their horses. They had short spears, or long swords. And they'd abandoned as much armour as our people had.

But we had war bows, and they didn't. They had some good crossbowmen – but they were slow, and they didn't move and fire with any alacrity.

They came on. Their line was a third again as long as ours and they were deeper, at least in places. On the other hand, whoever had formed their line had virtually ignored the terrain below the low ridge, so that the paths of two big blocks of men-at-arms or knights were blocked by farms and farmyard walls. They each deviated ...

I was looking to the centre. Watching Sir Nigel, who was just fifty paces from me.

We were going to win or lose in the seconds after Sir Nigel gave the order to attack. If the English were sufficiently motivated and all moved off together, I was confident we'd triumph. If any of our people hesitated ...

Sir Nigel stood in his stirrups. He was an older man, in his fifties – one of the last of King Edward's captains still in the field. He was calm, and tall, and old – a good combination.

'Englishmen!' he roared. He didn't clear his throat, or anything

– an excellent performance. 'Keep your ranks, listen for orders, and we'll all be a little richer in an hour!'

There was a satisfying growl from the ranks.

'We're going to attack!' Sir Nigel roared. 'When I say halt, six shafts from every archer. And then we'll charge. Listen for my trumpet. Now, are you ready?'

They didn't roar. They growled like lions. It was a terrifying sound, and I remembered why everyone feared the English. I saw men who looked like scarecrows suddenly lick their lips and make a joke, or give the French a two-finger salute.

His banner dipped.

The French line was perhaps one hundred paces away. The French were almost at the base of their ridge, and their line was now more of a mob. A hundred paces seems so close it's almost intimate, but Sir Nigel had his own ideas of how to fight the French.

We started forward, and the closing speed of the two armies doubled.

The French stumbled to a stop. Not all of them, mind. Just most of them. It was all spirit – the English went forward all together, a five-hundred pace line unbroken end to end. The French line was much longer now because they were spreading out as they moved – but it was chaos in the centre, and now they simply stopped.

They were afraid of us, and rightly so.

'What'a ferk's 'ee at, 'en?' spat Dick Thorald behind me. I couldn't understand him, but his tone of doubt carried.

Gosford felt the same. 'I could feather any three Frenchies here,' he said.

But Loring understood spirit. He was taking us *close*.

'Halt!' rang the order.

The French were mostly immobile, perhaps fifty paces away.

'Six shafts!' Sir Nigel roared.

All down the line, master archers called the words.

'Nock!' 'Draw!' 'Loose!'

They were a polyphony of orders. Our thousand archers had perhaps fifty different master archers, so that someone always seemed to be saying 'Draw'.

The arrows began to fall like a wicked, dark sleet. They struck with a sound like a boy rattling a stick on an iron fence, but repeated a thousand times, and the arrows overhead were continuous, as each little contingent loosed at its own pace. The best-trained men had shot their six, closed their quivers and exchanged bow for sword and buckler before the least-trained archers loosed their last shafts, but the whole exercise took about a minute. A minute to launch six thousand shafts. Two hundred and fifty pounds of hardened steel and ash dropped on the French in a minute.

Right in front of me, the royal banner of France went down. So many men were hit that it looked as if a giant hand had been waved over them. At fifty paces, with good lines of fire, hardly a shaft missed. Most of the archers were shooting flat, instead of lofting.

The last archers were tossing their bows backwards over their heads and drawing their bucklers off their hilts. And behind us, I could see the Duke of Lancaster coming back over the ford with his whole retinue mounted. They were moving rapidly to my right.

The centre of the French army began to waver and shake like summer wheat in variable winds. The militia had actually taken fewer casualties than the men-at-arms because of their shields, but men had been hit, and most of them had never seen a man die within a few feet.

Sir Nigel was watching the duke move out of the ford.

He knew, as I knew, that we'd already won. Now it was just a matter of the scale of the victory. So he was holding us back, waiting for Lancaster to ride around their flank. He gave him almost a minute – a long time to stand there with your archers grumbling that they could have killed more Frenchmen.

By then, the Abbeville militia who had been so bold the day before against Lancaster were coming apart like a ship's sail ripped by the wind. The well-armoured front rank of the militia stood its ground, but most of the ill-armed men behind were running.

The French commander, Châtillon, stepped out from under his personal banner and shouted something in French, and waved his sword. He turned towards us, clearly intending to charge. A group of well-armoured Frenchmen followed him, and they began to trudge towards us. But no one else joined him.

Loring's trumpet sounded.

Our entire line went forward, men-at-arms and archers, starvelings and scarecrows. Most of the French didn't wait for our onset. They started to run when we were ten paces out, but the centre men-at-arms, the best armoured, stood their ground. Hugh de Châtillon ran at us, his sabatons kicking up clods of earth like a destrier, and he ran right at me. He was a big man, my own size, and he had a big sword in his hand, and a dozen gentlemen of France at his heels.

He and I met sword to sword. We'd both slowed from a dead run for the moment of impact, but he expected me to block him. Instead, I crossed his sword with mine in both hands, half-swording, and then I rotated and threw him into Hales, tripping him as he passed. He fell face first, and Hales took him prisoner by sitting on him.

For perhaps the time it takes to say a paternoster, I was in a thick fight. I took three wounds, none of them deep but all of them danger-ous – a stab under my left arm that, thanks to God, only went in a finger's width, a cut across the back of my left thigh, and I have no idea from where it came, and a sword that went into my visor and stuck, the sword's point perhaps the width of a piece of parchment from my right eye. I'd already dropped Châtillon and another man, but the swordsman who got his weapon into my eye-slot then used it to throw me, levering my body with his sword on my helmet, trying to force the point another inch or two into me. It took long enough that I knew that if he fell straight atop me, his weight would prob-ably drive the point in. Even as it was, I was only alive because my armourer was brilliant at hardening steel.

I went backwards. As it proved, I tripped over Châtillon behind me, and I went down hard, my helmeted head slamming into Hales's breastplate so that I saw stars and smelt copper.

But Tom Fenton put his shoulder into my opponent, and he lost his grip on the sword … The man fell off to my right, and there was a pain in my eye and the sword was gone, wrenched *out* of my visor by the fall.

By the time I got to my feet again, we were collecting ransoms.

We took virtually their whole army. They were on foot, far from their horses. The duke took Châtillon from me – or rather, from Hales – but he compensated us both handsomely. That's another tale. Lancaster's charge was more like a crowd of servants clearing the boards after a feast than like a decisive cavalry action. By the time he turned their flank, most of their knights were throwing down their swords.

Here's how close I came to death – my eyelid was cut.

CHAPTER FOUR

FRANCE

Late 1369 – 1370

Blanchetaque should have been a great victory. But we had to retreat – we had no food, and no cavalry to pursue our beaten foes. We withdrew north, and the French went into winter quarters. Our little victory had no effect on the war beyond enriching those of us who'd taken a good prisoner. And unlike the desperate victories at Poitiers and Crécy, we retreated afterwards.

And our army kept dying. Men who'd stood their ground at Blanchetaque died over the next four days. Some simply fell on the road. The army had the plague, and while I can't pretend to understand the deadly, ugly killer, I can tell you that my own eyes saw that it kills the ill-fed and exhausted faster than the strong and well rested. By the time we reached Fiennes, we'd lost another three hundred, and when we reached Calais, the great Earl of Warwick died, as if, having seen his army to safety, he could relinquish command to a higher power.

And despite our losses, the Duke of Lancaster and the Captain of Calais were desperate to keep us out of the port. Despite terrible weather, we were ordered to camp outside the walls. Ships came, almost immediately. It's a black time in my memory and I may have lost a week, because by then I was as tired as the rest. I'd kept my handful of men at work – there were too few shoulders capable of levering a wagon out of the mud, or rebuilding a bridge. And after Blanchetaque they were mine. Even an old devil like Dick Thorald was willing to do whatever I asked, I think.

Regardless, by the third week in November we were at sea, and well before Christmas I was back in London, living out of a knight's cell at Clerkenwell. I found my people lodgings around London. The speed with which the Crown abandoned the men of the army was incredible to me, and the difficulties thrown in the way of common archers and lowly hobilars in claiming back wages had the look of intentional obfuscation.

Thorald came back to me after we'd been in London a week. He told me that the exchequer had told him and Master Hales that they could have their wages as garrison soldiers in Calais, and not in London. In the end, after appealing to Sir Robert Hales, the Master of the Order in England and sometimes an officer in the king's government, I simply loaned all of my men their wages, and put in a claim in my own name. Nan's father found me a barrister, and he had me write a letter to the Captain of Calais ... and to make a shorter tale of it, two years later I received all their back wages. I had money, because Lancaster purchased Châtillon's ransom from me in gold.

This is how you squander armies, my friends: by not paying the real cost of war – that is, the subsistence and maintenance of the men, aye, and the women, who put their bodies into the storm for their king, or merely do the laundry or fix the wagons. As I keep telling you, Master Froissart: war is a team sport.

After I handed out money to all and sundry, my sister invited me to Buckland for Christmas. I went, taking only Christopher, heedless of the distance and the snow – a calculated risk, as the southern part of England is usually temperate, and was in the winter of 1369.

I returned from Buckland to hear that Sir John Chandos had died in France, the best English knight of my generation, and the best captain. The reign of horrors had no end, and the war had taken on a dark cast for all Englishmen.

Back in London, healthier in body and mind despite the news, I was determined to travel south when the Channel was open. But fate, or the Lord, had other plans for me, as you will hear. At Clerkenwell I found a summons to Kenilworth, the country seat of the Duke of Lancaster, but before I could arrange to travel, I found that the duke was at the Savoy Palace in London. I attended him without delay, in my best clothes, a suit of blood-red scarlet cloth and dark fur, with my spur rondels worked around the edge of the hood in gold thread. God, I loved that hood ...

You don't want to hear about hoods. You want to hear about war.

Very well. The fight at Blanchetaque had not won the war or gained England anything, as I say, but it had served to raise my name to the notice of the duke, and I was welcome at his court. My irregular status only increased my fame. I, a modestly well-known mercenary, had fought for free.

In truth, my three captures and their ransoms were worth two years' wages in Italy. I kept my Italian crossbowman for a while. His name was Giovanni, and he was from Capua, and had led a chequered life involving most of the armies of the world. I left him with the order, where he became a brother sergeant, and led a very different life. He's still at Clerkenwell, and he has such a fund of stories, Messire Froissart, as would make your pen shatter with amazement.

I attended the duke, and was welcomed, in a distant way. I cooled my heels in various antechambers, admired the superb architecture and the plasterwork, more like Italy than England, and the windows, which were enormous, and the food, which was mostly cold. But the Savoy was close to the Temple, where I tended to go to pray, and my man of law worked close by, from an inn. I'd hired him for professional assistance on understanding English military contracts, but now we were exploring the purchase of various lands, as you may hear.

I received and sent letters constantly. I was in the same place for the first time for years, and I had time to read, to spar with strangers in the yards, to write and to read more. I wrote to Fra Peter Mortimer in Avignon – naturally, Fra Peter had got a *sauvegarde* the moment the French army went into quarters, so he was gone when I returned to Calais. I answered letters. Sir John Hawkwood didn't seem in any particular hurry to have me back, but he did mention that he was eager to have more Englishmen, and suggested that I assemble a reinforcement for him.

I thought about that. I saw an opportunity to serve Hawkwood, and to restore my reputation in England and perhaps take permanent service with the Duke of Lancaster. I really didn't know what I wanted, yet.

That's not true. What I wanted was Emile. I took no leman and loved no woman, although I did see Nan a few times, and had a fine dinner with her family. I thought of my children, and told myself they didn't need me.

In late winter, the plans for the coming campaign took shape, and the duke summoned me in person and invited me to raise a retinue for his new campaign. I took my men from the hobilars and archers I'd taken on my convoy. I offered retinue wages and I spread my net wide. I wrote letters to men I knew all through England, even to my sister, looking for archers.

I had an entire company, at least a small one, in Italy, but they were too far away. And from what I gleaned from you, Chaucer, and the titbits dropped by Loring and the duke, we would have an early campaign in the spring, perhaps a *chevauchée* south into Provence. A country I knew, and the best part of my route to Italy. Profit and honour in one package. I had a letter from Pierre de Murs in the name of the Green Count, giving me my liege's permission to serve the Duke of Lancaster on the condition that I did not serve against the count himself, but with a coda that stated that the count was doing his all to avoid direct service to King Charles of France.

Janet wrote to me from Milan, saying that Hawkwood was annoyed at his contract with the Visconti, who were 'tight-fisted misers'. He had a contract for two hundred lances, and he had my fifty. I had my own contract, although Janet hinted that the Green Count was not as happy with his brother-in-law as he had been.

I had a letter from Richard Musard, who professed himself delighted that I was alive, and told me that he, too, would be serving the duke in the spring. He'd purchased an estate in England. He recommended I do the same.

And I had a long letter from Fiore. He'd heard from Nerio, who, he said, was bored. Fiore mostly discussed the fighting at Cascina, in which he'd no doubt played a glorious part, but I gleaned that Nerio might be wanting us back in Romania. And I still had children at Chambéry, and I wondered if the Green Count had sent Bernard to fetch young Edouard back from Lesvos.

I wondered if there was still a lemon tree, and I cried a little.

Looked at now, from here, I realise that I just wasn't ready to go back. The time between Emile's death and Camus's death was like a trip to Purgatory – the madhouse, the assassins and the poisons, the plague. Even now, tonight, I think this is the most detail I've allowed myself to think about all of it in many years, except once, as you'll hear.

I wasn't ready to go back. And no one seemed to be calling me back.

I wrote to Nerio, asking for clarification. I wrote to Miles Stapleton, asking if he wanted to fight in France. I wrote to John Hughes, asking if he'd like to return to the life of arms. I combed the Southwark stews with Christopher, looking for men.

Eventually I decided to make a full campaign with the Duke of Lancaster, and then to take any of the men I'd raised to Italy as a reinforcement to Hawkwood's Englishmen. I put that proposition quite frankly to every man I approached. I sat in the Swan, a beautiful inn and brothel right on the river, with as much glass as the Savoy and a great deal more laughter. I had a regular table where I recruited, with Dick Thorald sitting on one side and Christopher on the other, and one of my man of law's clerks writing everything down. My indenture from the king, which was not very different from an Italian *condotta* or contract, specified twenty men-at-arms and forty archers, all mounted.

Listen, the details of the indenture won't interest you, but let me say that in some ways the king of England and his son paid better than the Italians – and you were paid most of it in advance, to pay for wages and equipment. But the government was notorious for paying the back end very slowly, or not at all. Men like Sir Robert Knolles had dozens of lawsuits pending against the very crown they fought to defend. And already, with the careful eye for finance I'd begun to develop as Emile's husband and as a commander of a company, I was seeing the fraying end of the English war finance. There was not enough money. There were not enough horses, or ships to move them to the Continent, and my young banker in London told me quite bluntly that the Italian money people were placing their bets on France.

I was rich enough to make more money – that is, I could pay my costs up front, in hard specie, which actually saved money – and because I knew Sir Robert Hales, the Grand Prior of the Order and the acting treasurer of England, I was reasonably sure I could get my bills paid.

Nor did I recruit only veterans. I wanted some likely young men, tough and eager. There are times when the passion of a man with no experience of war is preferable to the blank stare and stubborn resistance of a veteran.

I saw to it that they all had lodgings, a decent roncey, a shirt of maille and a good bow. I wanted every man to have a buckler and a good stout sword. I ran some sword and buckler drills in the Swan's spacious yard, with the girls watching from the balconies all around as if we were a troupe of mummers come to do a Passion Play.

My men-at-arms were a different story. After some remarkable shows of aristocratic privilege, I decided that I lacked the pedigree to recruit the sons of noblemen. I was snubbed a dozen times, and I found the attitudes remarkable. In effect, I was told repeatedly by snobbish young dandies that fighting in France was for 'them' – in this case, the half-gentlemen and self-styled squires and sons of professional knights, the growing population of men who made their living by war. The sons of the aristocracy didn't see war in France as their duty or their inclination.

I sat with Richard Hales and young Thomas Fenton in an expensive inn north of the Temple. Unlike Southwark, here I had an empty table and no takers.

'We could just make our own, like,' Hales said.

'My thoughts exactly,' I said.

Of course, the world believed that it took a life devoted to arms to make a knight. Italy had taught me that all it took to make a good man-at-arms was good armour and a summer or two of training.

My little retinue picked up an excellent contract from the Knights of Saint John. The Grand Prior wanted all the old armour at Clerkenwell and elsewhere to be cleaned and remounted, if immediately useful, or sold off as scrap, if too old or damaged. I gathered all my new archers, put them under Hales, and had them catalogue and clean the armour. Then we picked the pieces we wanted and sold them to ourselves at scrap prices, with the prior's full approval and thanks.

Late winter. London was a muddy, icy hell. A young girl trying to bathe on the Thames steps fell in and was swept away to an icy death. There was a nasty riot in Southwark over enforcement of the bishop's court and the treatment of the whores. The royalist side was badly beaten, and some buildings were burnt, and a few of my newly recruited archers looked sheepish and nursed burns and broken knuckles.

I'd chosen eight young apprentices or runaway yeomen's sons as future men-at-arms and started training them. Easter was coming, and I'd already become tired of my Lenten fasts, and there was a girl in Southwark who looked increasingly toothsome to me, despite my Lenten vows and my memories of Emile.

Chaucer here sent a boy to Clerkenwell, and I was summoned to meet the Duke of Lancaster.

Well fed, in his own Savoy palace, the duke was a very different man, and, begging your pardon, Geoffrey, one impossible to like. Even back in the spring of 1370, Lancaster was hated in London for his high-handedness, his snobbery, and his iron-clad belief that he was above the law and above London.

He was a complicated man – no simple snob, he. While his court and the king's competed for the most remarkable and ostentatious display in buildings, in clothes, in dogs and horses, he was also the patron of the most ascetic of the anti-clerical priests – men like Wycliffe and his friends. I say nothing against Master Wycliffe, except that I have always suspected that his anger against the Pope and papal powers had more to do with the constant preferment of the Pope's favourites over Master Wycliffe than any real theological difference. And I have very much enjoyed, over the years, hearing parts of his Gospel read out in English, although as my own Latin improves I have come to understand even what a bad priest sings.

Regardless, in the spring of '70, Lancaster still wore all black for the double bereavements of his duchess and his mother, and Master Wycliffe was an infrequent visitor, and Lancaster's servants were the enemies of every right-thinking London apprentice. The man himself was back and forth between the wars in France and his own court in England. Nan's pater said Lancaster intended to abolish the Lord Mayor of London and replace him with a royally appointed captain. If that plan was ever made, it was a terrible idea, but I suspect it was merely the sort of thing men said about Lancaster.

Any road, I made my bow and waited my turn, until the churchmen ahead of me had had their say. On that occasion, as I say, Wycliffe read out a section from Luke, and we all applauded him, and despite his taciturn nature, he left beaming.

'How may I serve you?' the duke asked me.

He was seated on a low throne. I could smell the warm hippocras in his cup.

'Your Grace summoned me,' I said.

One of his courtiers whispered in his ear.

'Ah. Sir William, it has come to my attention that you are raising your indenture here in London.'

'Yes, Your Grace.'

'I have immediate need of a goodly body of men. This is a situation where ... appearances ... matter.' He took a sip of wine and looked at me.

'Appearances, Your Grace?'

'Clothing. Armour. Horses.'

I understood. 'Yes, Your Grace. I think my men can make an excellent show.'

Lancaster looked around. 'Good.'

He was thinking about something else, and I was not important enough to be offered wine. I saw him consider it and decide *not* to offer the wine. It was the manner in which he made enemies.

Fortunately, I'd learnt my manners under the Count of Savoy, who could be every whit as difficult.

'The Lord of Coucy, our good cousin, is coming to London, and then to my father's court, with his wife, my sister,' the duke said. 'All of my own men-at-arms are already in France. Would you be so kind as to meet the good Lord of Coucy, and escort him to my father? And, Sir William, this is a more important commission than it might appear. Look the part, if you please.'

I made my reverence, and before I could leave the chamber, Chaucer here was at my elbow. You remember?

He said, 'William, Coucy is only here to spy. We want to look prosperous, and as if we have an endless tide of good archers and fit young men-at-arms.'

'While in fact we're scraping the barrel and my men-at-arms are mostly urchins and runaways,' I said.

You gave me your twisted smile – ha! That very one, eh?

I thought then that you were holding something back, and you were, were you not?

Then I blessed my stars that I knew Nan and her father. Nan's second husband was a fripperer – that is, a man who sold used clothing. Nan's father was a mercer who sold cloth, and through Gregory Fox I recruited a small phalanx of out-of-work tailors.

In two long days, I turned my hobilars and yeomen's sons into gentlemen, wearing tight-fitting cotes-hardie in the Italian style, with high collars and deep-cut sleeves on the over-gowns. They got long gowns for feast days, and boots for riding and good sword belts and a dozen other things. It cost me a fortune.

So what? How often does a man get to escort Enguerrand de Coucy? He was, at the time, married to the king of England's daughter – a love match, everyone said. His mother was a cousin of the Green Count, but then, he was related to virutally every aristocrat in Europe. He was, with the Duke of Lancaster, reputed to be the richest knight in the world. He'd lived in England half his life, as a prisoner and then as a bridegroom, and he was related to most of the crowned heads of Europe. I'd seen his banner at Blanchetaque, but not the man himself – he was scrupulous in serving both of his kings.

Coucy was landing at Rye, and we collected our new clothes, polished our harness, mounted our horses, and rode out of Southwark to the applause of the clergy and the girls of the Swan and a dozen other inns, and made our way across Kent.

Coucy came off an English ship, as unruffled as a cat that always lands on its feet, magnificent in red, white and blue, with hose in all three colours and an over-doublet of quilted silk with embroidered garters on it, as he was a knight of the Royal Order. His wife, the Princess Isabella, was as pretty as a picture in a book of hours, all pink and dark blue and gold, in the latest fashion, with a heavy houppelande of midnight blue lined in squirrel, falling away from a magnificent belt of enamelwork and silk. I made my reverences in my own best clothes, wearing a breastplate over my embroidered scarlet for the first and last time.

'You are very daring, to put that scarlet so close to that hair,' the princess said as a greeting.

She had one of those faces – heart-shaped, with carefully frizzed hair in one of the French styles and an elaborate linen cap that was very English. She was trying too hard to be young, and her face wore a perpetually silly expression of feigned surprise that was accentuated by powder and rouge.

'Perhaps it's a warning to his enemies,' Coucy said. He smiled – a courtier's smile. 'But we have friends in common, do we not, Sir William? Pierre de Murs? Jean le Maingre of glorious memory?'

I bowed again. 'I am lucky to count Pierre de Murs among my

friends, and the good Marshal was always more of a mentor than merely a friend.'

I had a sudden picture of being unhorsed violently in a field south of Paris.

'And my cousin, the Count of Savoy, is wont to sing your praises ceaselessly,' he said. He smiled, and this time the smile went to his eyes. 'I welcome the opportunity to spend a few days with so notable a soldier.'

'I'd like to know why my brother isn't here to meet me,' the princess said.

I flushed at his praise – the more so as no one else in England seemed to know who I was or what I'd done. I turned to her, a courteous reply ready to meet her vacuous expression, but there was a look in her eyes that gainsaid her make-up. Wry intelligence pierced the veil and then was hidden again.

'My lady, the duke your brother commanded my attention ...' I began.

I'd planned a courtly reply to this very question, as I had no idea why Lancaster wasn't here in person.

'Blessed Virgin,' the princess said with an affected yawn, cutting off my speech. 'Am I to spend the next few days being bored, as well as damp and cold?' She looked at me. 'Are you dull, Sir William?'

'Yes, my lady,' I said. I bowed. 'But a dull blade may be sharpened, and a dull silver polished.' I gave her a smile and nodded. 'Perhaps a few days of my lady's company ...'

'Damme, you are bold,' she said. 'My father must be waxing desperate for escort captains if he sends one as chatty as this one.'

Her words carried a sting, but her smile was frank and considering. She had a reputation as wilful, unbridled and difficult.

'Dear heart,' Coucy said, 'he's fought almost everyone in the world. I misdoubt that he's afraid of us.'

I laughed. 'My Lord, I'm afraid all the time. My first fear is that I'll be late in taking you to my lord the king, and my second fear is that you'll catch cold here on the wharf. I have horses, and your escort awaits.'

I led them down to the stone wharf, and the princess surprised me by mounting like a man, splitting her heavy skirts and riding astride. She looked at me, gauging my reaction, and smiled.

'Women can ride quite well, if they please to, Captain,' she said, as if I'd never known another woman who could ride. I thought on my sister and remained silent.

I left them with Master Hales after a brief introduction, and made sure of the Lord of Coucy's train of goods, which went into three heavy military wagons, and his train of servants – three women and five men. I had horses. They weren't much, and I had a pang for my beautiful Arabs and all the horses we'd brought from the Holy Land. It seemed like another world.

'You're the man who fought all alone on the bridge at Meaux?' he asked me. 'Under the eyes of all the ladies of France?'

'I wasn't alone,' I said.

The princess was hawking as we rode, and we weren't making very good time. On the other hand, the weather was magnificent – English spring at its most glorious. It was as if Princess Isabella had brought the spring with her.

She was thirty-seven or thirty-eight – not a blushing maiden. She'd married late, and was said to be a wanton. I didn't see a sign of it. I saw a woman who pretended to such things, the better to deceive men into underestimating her. Her inner woman was like Sister Marie, or my Emile – she was her own mistress. And Coucy treated her accordingly. They were allies, and I ... *liked them.* Coucy was much better at being a great noble than either Amadeus of Savoy or the Duke of Lancaster. Perhaps he was more intelligent, or simply had better manners, but he never showed reserve, and he at least appeared interested in what was said to him. He already knew Hales's name, and he treated Hales as a peer, despite the fact that he had to have known, the moment the man opened his mouth, that he was not really of the knightly class.

'Were you not?' the princess asked, allowing her small falcon to settle on her hand.

'Madame, there were at least four of us, including Tom Folville and some French knights. And an archer, Sam Bibbo, who saved us all, in the end.'

She handed her falcon to one of her ladies.

'I know who you are,' she said accusingly.

I must have looked puzzled.

'You married Emile d'Herblay. Murdered her husband, too.'

'Now that, my love, is a slander ...' Coucy said.

She grinned at me. 'Emile was there. At La Marche. Wasn't she?'

Damn, that woman was quick.

'Yes, Madame,' I said.

She gave me a glance full of meaning.

'D'Herblay—'

'Pulled the wings off flies,' Coucy said.

The princess glanced at me. 'You love her?'

Just for a moment, I could not speak. My eyes filled with tears, and my face blotched, I could feel the heat rising.

'*Mon Dieu*, what have I said?' the princess asked.

I wiped my eyes on my new chamois gloves.

'My lady died. Last year. Of plague.'

I'm not altogether sure I'd had to say those words out loud up until that moment, and they stuck in my throat.

She reached out a small, gloved hand and took mine.

'My mother died in August, Sir William.'

Just for a moment, she was yet another woman – caring, pious, even motherly.

At our third manor house in as many days, we were met by a royal messenger who directed us to Rotherhithe, on the Thames. King Edward was hawking there.

I was glad of the messenger because I didn't know the way to the manor, or what to expect. He was a very young man, one of the endless Scrope clan.

'Just keep me out of their way,' he said. 'I haven't any fine clothes to wear, and I need a nap.'

He looked at me, as if inviting some question.

I couldn't think of any.

'Chaucer told me to look after you,' he said kindly. That is, for a slip of a seventeen-year-old to be kind to a veteran captain of twenty-nine or so. 'Do you know anything about what's going on?'

'No,' I said.

'Queen Philippa died last year—'

I was not in the best of moods. 'I know,' I snapped.

'Don't bite my head off, there's a good fellow. Only trying to help out. The king has a leman ...'

I may have rolled my eyes.

'Is this any business of mine?' I asked.

'Named Alice Perrers,' Scrope said. 'A very fine piece, all in all. His ... time ... with her ...' He chuckled. He thought that he was very witty. 'It isn't public yet. They are at the falconry lodge together.'

I cannot now remember why I was so impatient. Horse tack needing repair? A sick horse? An angry man-at-arms? Who knows? I merely remember slapping my gloves on my leg armour.

'Out with it, lad. The king's affairs are none of mine.'

'We don't think Isabella knows about Alice Perrers,' he said at last, in a bit of a squeak. 'And Lancaster has had a flaming row with his father. So he's not there. Or here. He was supposed to greet his sister here. Instead, he's at Kenilworth.'

You see, friends, all of this had a certain ring of familiarity. I'm not really a bluff soldier. I'd been a cook's boy, I'd run a brothel, and I had, in fact, spent two whole years as a sort of military courtier to the Prince of Wales, and that much again with the Count of Savoy. I knew how the game of court was played.

And I suspected that I was not privy to everything. From titbits that Coucy had let drop, I thought he was there to test the waters for a new truce with the king of England. He didn't look like a spy to me. In fact, I gathered from him that as he had estates in both England and France, he *wanted* peace. He seemed very interested in crusade. I was accustomed to duplicity in the Holy Land and Italy. Coucy was not a bluff, open fellow, but I thought he was an honourable man.

But what I did know was that, as captain of Coucy's escort, this was all far above me.

'I'll take my lord and the princess to this falconry lodge,' I said. 'And then I'm done with the whole business, and the king's likes and loves are none of mine. Nor yours.'

Scrope shook his head. 'If you could just ... delay them. A day or two. Until Lancaster sees reason and returns to court.'

Just then I thought, gracious God, this is what Chaucer does every day. What Musard puts up with for the count.

'Two days,' I said, hoping I was doing the right thing.

'Chaucer asks it,' my sprig said.

I went straight to Coucy.

'My Lord,' I said on bended knee. 'I wonder if you'd condescend to spend another day here. There is some trouble ahead that I'd like to avoid.'

Coucy smiled. 'I am always in favour of avoiding trouble. Tell me about Alexandria.'

That night, at dinner, the princess smiled up at me. I was serving her because none of my 'men-at-arms' were good enough to carve at table. Sweet Christ, I was busy in the kitchens, running a school for squires. The cook was in a panic because he'd only planned one dinner for the great ones, and here we were with no jugged hare. And so on.

'Why were we delayed today?' she asked sweetly.

As I say, I'd come to quite like both of them.

'I was asked to delay you, My Lady,' I said.

Coucy almost spat food. He took a drink of wine, and then laughed so hard I was afraid for the trestles holding the table boards.

She smiled at me and gave me her cup to drink – exactly the sort of petty compliment that Lancaster didn't understand. That told me that I had gauged the test correctly. She already knew.

'Are they hiding my father's mistress from me?' she asked.

I shrugged. 'My Lady, I really am a soldier. My understanding is that we're waiting for your brother to return to court.'

'Did you know Lionel?' she asked suddenly.

'I met the Duke of Clarence on a number of occasions,' I said.

'Tell me of his wife?' she asked. 'I'm told that she is the most beautiful of all the women in the world.'

The food was getting cold. I waved to Tom Fenton, who came in with a good soup and a steaming bowl of herbs and greens in butter that I'd all but cooked myself. Tom was desperately nervous, and he tried to bow and balance an enormous pewter platter, and the end result was that he tipped about a third of my greens onto the floor.

'Fucking hell!' the boy spat. And then froze.

Coucy and his lady began to laugh aloud.

Later, after they'd dined, Coucy waved to me, handed me his napkin to fold, and said, 'When you've had your own food, come and sit with me, Sir William.'

So I did. I wolfed down my greens and some roast swan, and the cook's masterpiece, roast boar, which I confess was as good as I ever tasted. I swallowed a cup of wine, gave Tom Fenton my professional captain's 'just wait till your father comes home' glare, and went up the steps to the solar.

'My apologies, My Lord, My Lady ...' I began.

'I've certainly heard the words said before,' the princess said.

She was lying on a long couch, with a book in her hand. Her lady-in-waiting was by her. She had five women by her, but only one was a real 'lady'. She was Anne-Marie de something, and had large brown eyes and seemed tolerably friendly.

'Now tell me about Violante Visconti,' she insisted.

I probably looked uneasy.

'Sir knight, I've listened patiently as you and my husband have killed half the men in Europe with your tales of Alexandria and Italy and France. *Please* sing me a love story.'

So I told the Italian Wedding, in as pleasant a light as I could manage.

Somewhere in there, I realised just how intelligent the princess was. So I was almost prepared when she held up a hand for me to stop my tale.

'Who killed my brother?' she asked suddenly.

I looked at Coucy. He was standing by the room's deep and very modern fireplace.

I had a sudden realisation that these two were master players in the game of courts and power, and that none of this was about the king's leman or Lancaster's anger.

Coucy smiled without mirth.

'Sir William,' he said patiently, 'you are leading an escort composed of peasants' sons masquerading as knights because the English army is already in France.'

'My father has been sleeping with Alice Perrers for three years,' Isabella said calmly. 'And you served an entire campaign beside my brother, and I'll wager a glove against my best horse that he never asked you about Lionel.'

My answer, no doubt, showed in my face.

'I'll never rule England,' the princess said. 'But by Our Lord, Sir William, I won't see our name trampled. Bohun told me that Milan's deranged son ...'

There's an expression: 'out of the frying pan, and into the fire'. How had I imagined that I'd simply been chosen at random to escort the most powerful lord in northern France and a princess of England?

In that moment, Chaucer, I blamed you. I assume now you didn't know any better than I, and that Lancaster must never have questioned you, either.

The princess watched me steadily.

I'd been set up.

'Did you *ask* for me to command your escort, My Lady?' I asked, and I suspect there was a squeak in my voice.

'Of course,' she said, with a smile.

'I think we should allow Sir William to sit,' Coucy said.

Anne-Marie brought me a stool and smiled in what I had to think was sympathy.

I glanced at the princess.

'Anne-Marie is my shadow,' she said. 'She can hear anything you have to say.'

I was handed a cup of wine.

'Tell me,' the princess said.

So I told her. I had sworn no oaths, and nothing that I said was hurtful to the Count of Savoy. I laid it all out from beginning to end, and it took hours. I had to go back to my own days as a routier to explain Camus, and even then, I could see that she doubted my statements about a certain house in Vigone.

Coucy did not. He was still by the fireplace, his face slightly averted – you might have said he was staring into the fire.

'I think I understand,' he said. 'It's the Bishop of Cambrai, is it not?'

I shook my head. 'I loathe Cambrai,' I said. 'But in this case, I fear that Camus acted on the orders of Prince Fillipo, who was himself deluded.'

'But the Prince of Achaea is dead,' the princess said. 'And so is Camus. So ... do you think that the Duke of Milan is responsible? In any way?'

I thought of Gian Galeazzo asking me what he could do to rid himself of Prince Lionel, a year and more earlier in Milan.

It is her fault. She is so beautiful, he said with the absolute self-centredness of a madman.

It was a little like carrying the deadly new explosive powder in barrels. You know that if you do the wrong thing, they can burn or even explode.

Did I really think that Gian Galeazzo ordered Clarence's death? If I said so, that die was cast.

I looked at the king's daughter, and thought, *if you say everything you think, you could start a war.*

Did Milan kill Prince Lionel?

Hawkwood is serving Milan.

The Green Count is serving Milan.

The papacy is fighting Milan.

The papacy is backing the king of France against the king of England.

Would the Duke of Milan allow his royal son-in-law to be murdered for his son's ...?

'I don't know,' I said at last.

Coucy smiled at me. 'You have been very careful not to mention your friend Richard Musard,' he said.

I sagged. Not since Juan di Heredia had I met people like them. Both of them.

'We will have a discussion with Sir Richard,' the princess said.

'Lucky Richard,' I said, a little too loudly.

Isabella laughed. 'You didn't think much of my brother, did you, Sir William?' she asked.

I looked away. 'In fact, I liked him very much,' I said.

'Ahh,' she said. And then she said, 'He was one of us, and he represented England.'

'My Lady, I did what I could for him,' I said. 'Richard and I both insisted that all his food be tasted, all his visitors screened. But he—'

'He didn't take you seriously.'

I shrugged. 'He didn't fully ... make use of Richard. The Count of Savoy sent Sir Richard to protect your brother.'

Coucy smiled. Isabella frowned.

'Tell me, Sir William,' she said. 'Are you going back to Italy?'

'After this campaign,' I said.

She nodded. 'I can be a useful friend,' she said. 'I would greatly appreciate your letters, the more especially if you would continue to look into this ... matter.'

'Milan and Prince Lionel?' I asked.

She smiled. 'Precisely.' She waved a hand. 'For me.'

*

The next day, we stayed in because of the rain, and Tom Fenton redeemed himself by finding us a trio of very damp musicians who played while we danced. Princess Isabella knew a hundred dances, and she was a good and patient teacher, and my 'men-at-arms' had a crash course in both dancing and serving at table from two of the greatest aristocrats in Europe. The princess insisted on pressing every woman in the house, from the slattern to the cook, into the dancing. Coucy, who was no fop but a hardened soldier, found a stock of hard cider and broached it. As day made its way to evening, we served a meal that I'd cooked part of in my arming clothes to a hall filled with servants and masters dancing together. It was as if the Lord of Misrule had come among us. Coucy, in his accented Norman-French-English, was drinking with Dick Thorald in his accented Cumbrian English, and while I found both of them hard to understand, they seemed to understand each other very well.

I danced repeatedly with Anne-Marie. Her very inscrutability made her charming. The occasional smiles I won from her seemed well won.

I went to bed alone, and very drunk, and realised that it was the best time I'd had since Emile died.

The next day, silent and surly, we rode north and delivered our precious cargo to the manor of Rotherhithe. Just before Isabella rode through the gate, she turned to me and seized my hand.

'May I count on you?' she asked.

Behind her, Anne-Marie met my eyes. She smiled slightly.

'Yes, My Lady,' I said.

'Good,' she said. 'You see? You were not dull at all.'

She pasted the mask of giddy amusement on her face, tittered, and rode in under the arch.

Coucy nodded, a smile in the corner of his mouth.

'I saw the king of France bow to you,' he said.

He rode in.

I sat, a little sad to see them go.

In June, we sailed for Aquitaine. I had met my full indenture and been mustered and approved – if not paid. We arrived after the prince had mustered his vassals and marched. I had every opportunity after we landed to measure our strength against the army the prince had led to Poitiers – an army that was thought, in the summer of 1355, to be

329

too small to overawe the king of France, or even the Gascons. Yes, in that summer, the prince had had almost six thousand men, and now we had perhaps a thousand men-at-arms and a thousand archers.

The years had not been kind to England. I'd gone to Italy and missed a decade, but as far as I could see it, King and Commons had won a war with France and then dismissed it as completed business. France had used the last decade to rearm. The king's inveterate jealousy of his son's success at Poitiers caused him to behave badly to the prince in matters concerning Aquitaine, and this was the upshot – the prince was trying to hold a third of 'La Belle France' with an army of fractious, treasonous vassals and a handful of Englishmen. In the summer of 1370, even reliable vassals were watching the dissolution of the Duchy of Aquitaine and looking over their shoulders at the king of France.

It was all coming apart. Most of the king's good captains had died; Chandos just that winter, tripping on his own long gown and getting an axe in the back. I stood on the wooden wharf in Bordeaux, watching my horses come ashore, and I had a feeling that was rare for me – an expectation of defeat. We were marching to face the Duc du Berry, the Duc d'Angoulême, and my old friend du Guesclin was on his way from Spain with two thousand men. We were supposed to stop them with a handful of retinues led by professionals. It seemed insane.

We landed at Bordeaux on the third day of June. I remember it well because the next day, the fourth, is my name day, and I paid for a feast in one of the taverns I remembered from '56 – the Three Foxes, where I had run a string of girls with Richard Musard, and played at being knights while actually being pimps. I also found the armourer and his wife who'd sheltered me in the spring of '56 and fed them, too. I had the pleasure of watching Tom Fenton teaching a French girl the dances he'd just learnt from the princess of England. It was a different inn – no obvious prostitutes and better food. Bordeaux had prospered under English rule.

My little retinue had already been mustered, and although I'd expected to be in Lancaster's service, I found that I was under the orders of Sir Walter Manny, a Hainaulter who had served the king of England for almost fifty years. The man appeared older than a cathedral and as strong as a castle, and just as grey. In fact, I believe he was just sixty as I turned thirty.

I knew a great deal *about* Sir Walter, and I knew many men who'd served under him, but I was still worried when he came down from the castle to inspect my retinue two days after my name-day party. My unease communicated itself to Hales and Christopher and then to my men, who were as polished as a day's work could make them.

Manny spoke with a distinct Flemish accent, and wore the very latest in Bohemian plate armour. He had no fat on him, and his horse was the best I'd seen in Aquitaine.

He reminded me of John Hawkwood, right down to the large hat. Manny's was of scarlet cloth embroidered with his arms in black and gold like a wasp, with a charge of Garters.

He smiled. 'Sir Villam Goldt, I beliefe?' he said, and took my hand.

We were both on horseback. I was in my full harness, and I led him along the ranks of my retinue.

As I say, we'd already been mustered and I brought my muster-roll in case I was challenged, but Manny was no clerk. He looked at bows and counted bowstrings and asked Gosford to hand over his sword, which he examined.

I'd formed my people in the Italian manner, which is to say my men-at-arms were in front, each with an archer and a mounted page. Beyond this, I had ten 'extra' archers under Christopher. They formed to the left of the men-at-arms in two neat ranks.

Manny nodded to Hales. 'Your men-at-arms look like fops,' he said, his words clipped.

Hales flushed.

I bowed. 'We were used as an escort for the Princess Royal,' I said.

Manny nodded. 'So I understant,' he said in choppy Flemish-English. He smiled at Christopher. 'He ees a Moor?' he asked.

'Aethiopian,' I said.

Manny looked interested. 'You vere at Alexandria?' he asked. 'Dine vit me, and ve'll tell each other tales. Your retinue ees in excellent order, but you know this, *hein?*' He pulled on his reins but then glanced back. 'Who pays the pages?'

'I do,' I said. 'This is how we do it in Italy.'

He nodded. '*Eh bien*,' he said, and rode away.

And that evening, after a good dinner and some tall tales, Manny

331

nodded, as if his gaze could penetrate the wall and see my men.

'I like your men very much,' he said. 'I haf asked for you – you and Belmont and Musard. Ve are very short on professional soldiers, thees year.'

I was delighted to find that Andrew Belmont had an indenture, as did Richard.

'May I ask our plans?' I said.

Manny made a face. 'Ve must vait for the Duke of Lancaster and all our knights,' he said. 'The prince ees in ze north, watching Berry's army that ees around Perigord.' The Hainaulter shrugged. 'I vill tell you ze truth, Sir Villam. I do not think ve vill zee any fightink. Berry is a cowart, and the prince is very sick.'

June gave way to July, and Andy Belmont arrived. The two of us had virtually identical retinues, and Manny placed us together. He had us to dinner, and after we'd eaten, he turned to me.

'Sir Villam, will you be villink to serve under Master Belmont?'

I nodded. 'Of course, Sir Walter. I've served under Andy before this.'

Manny turned to Belmont. 'And you? Vill you serf under Sir Villam?'

Andy bowed. 'Of course. I've served under him before, too.'

Manny nodded. 'This is gut.'

I had used my first days to fatten my horses, but as it became clear that we were not marching into Limousin immediately, I started training my retinue the way I'd always wanted to train. I took them out on day-long trips over the broken country south of the port. The second week in July, with Manny's permission, Andy and I went out together, headed east into the mountains, and literally showed our flags to the lords of Libourne and Coutras. We had several 'encounters' with local men-at-arms, none of them violent, but my people looked better every trip out, and our horses were getting harder.

We heard that du Guesclin had arrived at Toulouse and was leading a great army into Limousin. In a professional way, I was rather looking forward to meeting du Guesclin. I suspected our contingents were a match for his Spanish veterans, but time passed, and du Guesclin turned north.

Andy and I didn't need to be told which of us was in command. We scarcely ever disagreed, and he was the calmest, most easy-going professional soldier I've ever known. He almost never took offence at anything, and we usually laughed instead of sparring.

Richard Musard arrived while we were in the east country. His retinue was every bit as good as ours, and the same size again.

'Did you meet the Princess Isabella?' I asked him.

He rolled his eyes. 'Oh, yes,' he said. Then he grinned. 'This is going to be like old times!'

'No brothel,' I said.

His grin vanished, but only for a moment.

'No brothel,' he said. 'We could make that our war cry.'

Andy was almost as happy to see Richard as was I, and we had several drunken evenings at the Sign of the Three Foxes before Sir Walter sent us south, along the border between Aquitaine proper and Armagnac. With sixty men-at-arms and almost two hundred archers altogether, we had enough force to command respect, and in fact, we were unchallenged all the way down to Agen. At Agen, the Comte d'Armagnac had a fortified bridge over the Garonne, and we took it. It wasn't in our orders, but the three of us, old comrades and veteran routiers, wanted to make names for ourselves, and I owed Armagnac a blow or two.

There's no fight to describe. Our whole force was mounted. We hired guides, moved fast, and paid good silver to have scaling ladders built, the English way, of oak, with sections that bolted together. We stormed the *bastide* at Agen from both ends, taking both towers at the same time, just before daybreak. We took no losses and seized, by happy chance, almost a thousand silver deniers in local taxes that the garrison had just collected.

Manny was delighted with us. We gave him his share of the money and dispersed the rest among our people, and then rode out again. This time we went almost to the walls of Condom. I made damned sure my villains didn't burn my *bonne amie* from her little castle south of the city, nor did we harm anything belonging to my former landlady, but we did destroy the count's summer hunting lodge after taking all the wall-hangings and some silver.

I had forgotten war, in France. But now I remembered – burn the enemy, take his goods, ride away. Very much like banditry, anywhere else. I did it well – my archers and my former hobilars saw me as a good captain. I was, in fact, a very expert routier.

In Limousin, the Duc du Berry and du Guesclin seemed to be everywhere, taking town after town and castle after castle, and our little successes in the south were not a good balance. Manny and the prince, who came down while we were absent to greet his brother the Duke of Lancaster, wanted us to strike a blow into Armagnac that would distract the French attackers, but the truth that I'd begun to recognise was that this was a war about money, and we, the English, were already running out. Most of the districts of the Duchy of Aquitaine could not, or would not, pay their taxes. The king of England had attempted to finance the war out of his own private funds, and was now out of money. In Normandy, Sir Robert Knolles, the veteran routier more of Camus's stamp than I could like, was trying to fight a war as a business, as if he were in Italy. A war of burnt houses and forced 'taxes' collected from peasants who could never defend themselves.

But by the Lord, it was not what I wanted. Sitting on my warhorse, looking down at two older women and a man watch their hovel burn ...

One of the women turned to me. She started by begging me, but after a few words, she suddenly filled with rage.

'I don't care if you kill us all, you prick! You son of Satan! You have burnt my farm and destroyed my food, you fuck! All my work! My linens! Every fucking thing I've made since I was a girl!'

By then she was hammering her fists against my horse, and my leg armour. Her husband, terrified, dragged her off me, and fell on his knees in the road.

Hales, at my elbow, all but spat.

'Stupid woman! Tell it to Armagnac, your so-called lord! He betrayed the king of England.'

'I don't give a fuck!' she screamed. 'I have done nothing but work, do you hear! I have worked my whole life, you fucking criminals!'

'Shush, my dear, my heart,' her husband said. 'They will rape you and kill me.'

I took a gold noble from my purse. I always had one – I gave them as rewards for the best, bravest actions from my people. A year's wages for an archer.

'I'm sorry,' I mumbled, ashamed.

I dropped the gold coin on the road.

Christ, I was not a routier any more. Even as Hales suggested that

334

we kill them all and make an example, something made a *ting* against my breastplate.

The woman had thrown my gold coin at me. And hit me.

I shook my head. 'Don't touch her!' I spat.

Still flushed with shame, I turned my horse and rode away.

'We should have hanged her,' Hales said.

'I need to go back to Italy,' I said. 'We have rules there.'

However, our raids, tiny pinpricks that they were, had an effect on the entire war. Armagnac feared enough for his lands that he left the Duc du Berry's army at Limousin and marched south with all his vassals. Sir Walter Manny, who remained the master planner of the war in Aquitaine because of his wide service and reputation, thought that we might have reached the end of the campaign.

But early August saw the arrival, or rather, the return of the Earl of Pembroke, Sir John Hastings. The earl was twenty-three years old, one of the great peers of England, and knew considerably less about war than my horse. Pembroke was said to have quarrelled violently with Sir John Chandos. There were men in Manny's retinue who muttered that Pembroke's incompetence had killed Chandos, whom we all regarded as England's best knight.

Regardless, Pembroke refused to allow Manny to continue in command from Bordeaux. He demanded that all of us march up country to join the Prince of Wales at Cognac.

I was present when their disagreement almost came to blows. We were in the castle, awaiting the dispersal of a shipload of supplies. Manny had invited the captains of the retinues for a cup of wine while we waited to make our marks on the tally sheets.

Pembroke came accompanied by his captain, who was as young as he was himself. He was in armour. Manny smiled, and bowed.

'You honour us, My Lord,' he said.

'When will we march for Cognac?' Pembroke demanded. 'With these supplies, you have no excuse to remain here.'

Manny smiled. Unfortunately, it was exactly the smile that fathers use on errant children, and it ignited Pembroke's wrath – which was, I promise you, not that difficult a task.

'I will not be gainsaid!' the earl shouted.

'As a matter of policy—' Sir Walter began.

'Be damned to your policy! You routiers are all the same, cowering here where it's safe and nipping at the French like brigands robbing a corpse.'

The earl's roving eye made sure to find me – and Andy Belmont, too.

Manny was patient. 'My Lord, I am obeyink zee orders of my sovereign prince. He entrusted into my 'ands—'

Pembroke spat. 'I am a peer of England,' he said. 'I'll give the orders here.'

'Uh-oh,' Andy said softly in my ear.

'My Lord,' Manny said crisply, 'I haf less than a thousand men, and I am holdink the Comte d'Armagnac in my hand. This is the policy of the king of Englant.'

Pembroke got red in the face. I thought at the time that he was playing a role – that he knew we all thought him a fool, and he revelled in it, somehow.

'When I want advice from a foreign adventurer, I'll ask for it. I am marching for Cognac.'

'I am not,' Manny said. 'I await the Duke of Lancaster.'

'I order you!' Pembroke spat.

'I do not recognise you as havink the authority to order me.' Manny bowed. 'I mean no disrespect.'

'You are a knight-banneret, a foreigner, a damned hedge-knight ...' Pembroke spoke too loudly. 'You surround yourself with these routiers.'

He glanced at me.

Well, he wasn't making any friends.

Manny shrugged. 'I am sorry that you tink all these things,' he said. 'But King Edward has ordered me—'

'King Edward is in bed with his mistress and I am here!' Pembroke shouted.

Andy blinked. 'Italy's lookin' better and better,' he muttered.

Pembroke marched north two days later, with about a hundred lances. Manny held the rest of us back for a few days – mostly to show his irritation, I suspect. Then, when he heard firm news that Lancaster was at sea, our force, about a hundred men-at-arms and two hundred archers, started north for Cognac. Manny led us as far east as he dared, so that we might be seen by du Berry's patrols, and on the fifth day of August we had a skirmish near Pillac. I wasn't in it, as I was further north, but Richard unhorsed a Gascon knight and took him prisoner. Armaganac, who rivalled Pembroke for his military acumen, read our movement as an attack, and began concentrating his forces to face our non-existent attack, while we raced north and joined the prince at Cognac.

Jean de Grailly, the Captal de Buch, was there waiting to receive us, a big man on a truly magnificent horse. The Captal had often been our leader in the 'old days'. He'd tried to stand up for us, and he and John Chandos had tried very hard at Calais to win the prince's forgiveness for me and for Richard.

And now he welcomed us warmly. Richard and I dismounted and made our bows, and the Gascon lord took us by the hand and raised us.

'Ah,' he said, 'my good gentlemen. Now I think we will raise some hell. It's been dull here.'

Cognac was not big enough to contain even a small English army, and we had to camp. I didn't own a pavilion, and so I paid some local peasants to run me up a hovel of wattle and daub. I was charmed by how different it was from a similar hut in Sussex – different hurdles, and less straw. But it was sturdy enough and I shared it with Christopher, so that's where the Captal's squire found me.

'My Lord,' he said. 'The prince is summoning all of his officers.'

I collected Richard and Andy, and we followed Sir Walter Manny through the river gate into the city proper, and then up to the castle. The hall was full of men – the Captal's knights and most of the prince's men, as well as all the officers. For an army of fewer than three thousand men, we managed to have a hundred officers, and it took too much time to get us to be silent.

I hadn't been close to the Prince of Wales since the day in Calais when he'd told me that I was not welcome to serve on his tournament team. My feelings about him were deeply divided. I understood his actions in the autumn of 1360, but I didn't love him for them.

The prince was not in armour. In fact, he was lying on a litter, and his skin was grey. He looked like a much older man. An older, bitter, angry man. The years had not been kind, and despite my feelings, it hurt me to see him like this. I remembered his noble calm at Poitiers, and the moment at which he ordered the Captal and his reserve to charge.

The Earl of Pembroke hovered by him, like a mourner at a bier. Just by him was Edmund of Langley, the Earl of Cambridge, the prince's younger brother. He was perhaps a year younger than I, and had a large retinue, almost four hundred men-at-arms and archers. He was tall, like the other Plantagenets, and sandy-haired, and looked more cheerful than Lancaster or the Prince of Wales. In fact, he looked the most like Princess Isabella.

And by them were two men I knew all too well – Sir Percival de Coulanges, whom I'd last seen as Peter of Cyprus's chamberlain, and Florimont De Lesparre.

I saw Lesparre with real shock. A year before, we'd fought in Milan. He had been part, wittingly or not, of a plot to kill Prince Lionel. Now he was within an arm's length of two more English princes. I thought of Isabella's charge to me.

Balanced against that, I knew Lesparre to be too proud to be an assassin. The man was no friend of mine, but I didn't see him as a witting pawn. Unwitting, perhaps.

I was still recovering from my shock when the prince spoke from his litter, his voice low and quiet, but such was the respect we all felt for him that we were perfectly silent. No one even coughed.

'The Chevalier du Guesclin has brought his men-at-arms from Spain and joined the Duc d'Anjou at Périgeaux.' He coughed. 'The Duc du Berry is at Limoges. Laying siege.'

'Limoges is one of our most important towns,' the Earl of Pembroke said with unnecessary authority.

In fact, I don't think that there was a man in that room who needed to be told anything about Limoges. It was one of the richest towns in Aquitaine, and well fortified, with a *cité*, a walled town around the cathedral, and a *château*, both fortified, and a citadel.

'We should march on Du Berry immediately,' Pembroke said.

The Captal looked at Pembroke as if he had worms crawling on his surcoat.

The prince cleared his throat. 'Du Berry outnumbers us more than two to one,' he said.

And Sir Walter Manny spoke forcefully. 'Ze moment ve move, du Guesclin is behind us. *Hein?*'

338

'With more men than we can hope to raise,' the prince said. He coughed again. 'Perhaps when my brother of Lancaster joins us?'

'We can defeat any force the French throw at us,' Pembroke insisted. 'Remember Crécy and Poitiers, my prince.'

I couldn't see the prince well – he was flat on a litter that rested on four heavy chairs. But I saw his head turn.

'I never forget Poitiers,' he said into the silence.

The Captal turned away – disgusted, I think.

Andy Belmont glanced at me, and Richard looked pointedly away.

As we emerged into the smoky air of the upper town of Cognac, Richard spoke our thoughts.

'Too many royals and not enough soldiers,' he said.

Andy was fiddling with his gloves. 'It's as if we've *become* the French,' he muttered.

Later that afternoon, we understood that Sir Walter and Pembroke had debated strategies in front of the prince. Manny was insisting that we should use the same tactics as du Guesclin. We should send our best retinues deep into the enemy's lands, raiding and burning, to force the break-up of the French armies and to keep our forces fed at the expense of the enemy.

Pembroke wanted a battle. And he freely used words like 'traitor' and 'coward'. In effect, he argued that Limoges, the centre of banking in the province and the location of the most expert enamellers in the world, had to be protected. Manny argued that Limoges was virtually impregnable, and that we could be more Fabian in our response. Thanks to reading some of the ancients in Latin, I even knew what 'Fabian' meant.

The debate was still raging when Lancaster came up the road two days later, with another four hundred men in excellent array.

The presence of three sons of King Edward in one small army had all sorts of effects. One was that the Earl of Pembroke, despite being a peer of England, was not really in the first rank of aristocrats any more than Walter Manny or I. Lancaster and Cambridge and the prince himself were going to have all the commands.

And despite our worries, the presence of no fewer than three royal sons of King Edward was having an effect all by itself. Suddenly we had some Gascon lords coming into Cognac, shame-faced at earlier defections, or apologising for their late arrival. The Captal gathered them into a force.

I noted that there were no d'Albrets. Bertucat, the family black sheep, was serving us ... rather, serving himself. He was leading a routier company, raiding everyone. Otherwise, they were all out for the king of France.

There were also more scions of great houses than there had been in the fifties. All three of the Plantagenets had a dozen or more sons of the great in their retinues, and this served to drive former routiers like me and Walter Manny to the margins. Despite the relative competence of the king's sons, and I'd wager any one of them might have made his living making war, the men in their trains were high-ranking amateurs who thought that scouting, foraging and patrolling were beneath them.

But Manny still had the prince's ear. He was famous as a planner and the king had always relied on him, and he continued to argue that the veterans be released in all directions to raid the heartland of Berry and Armagnac. The prince, who'd led some of the greatest *chevauchées* ever waged by Englishmen, was inclined to adopt his point of view.

And then the city of Limoges fell.

Limoges should never have fallen. Not only was it magnificently fortified and well garrisoned, but the citizens were loyal to the king. They had received a wide variety of privileges from the king, and from the prince as ruler of Aquitaine. Their wares were respected worldwide – indeed, Princess Isabella wore a 'Limoges girdle', and so did almost every fashionable, rich man or woman in Europe.

The Duc du Berry suborned Limoges with money. He was a collector – the richest collector of jewels and fabrics in Europe – and his approach to war was to buy things. I confess that this witticism came to me from Richard. He paid the bishop of the city to get him to open the gates to the lower town, and then sent a cartel to our prince, imagining that the victor of Poitiers was too sick to respond. In fact, like some giddy boy, he sent five challenges in a single afternoon. It was the twenty-second day of August, and as each arrived, the prince's anger became more obvious.

The last of the Duc du Berry's messengers found the Prince of Wales at dinner. According to Tom Fenton, who was serving at the dinner, when the challenge was read out, the Duke of Lancaster told his elder brother that the city had been betrayed by the bishop, Jean le

Cros, and that the bishop had told his cathedral chapter that he, the prince, was dead in order to get them to sign the capitulation.

The prince rose unsteadily to his feet.

'By my father's soul!' he snarled. 'I will snatch Limoges back from this renegade priest.' He glared around. 'Who will avenge me on this churl?'

His hands shook on the stick he used to support himself. But friends, the insult went through all of us. Our beloved prince was sick, and this French 'collector' thought that he could insult us.

We arrived before Limoges on the tenth day of September. Manny's contingents were the vanguard, and we arrived ahead of the others and put a cordon around the city. Of course, we lacked the soldiers to start a siege, but we threw up hasty barricades on the roads and laid out a camp.

The Duc du Berry, despite all his boasting, was gone. He'd withdrawn as soon as he heard that the dreaded English prince was moving, and he abandoned enough of his camp as to save me from having to purchase a pavilion. And as we swept through and picked up his sick and wounded, I learnt that while he had a two-day head start, he was moving very slowly because of his baggage, and was only at Ràzes.

I changed horses, rode back to Manny, and he opened his visor.

'Sir Walter,' I said, 'I'd like to pursue du Berry. I have fresh horses for all my people, and I can at least sting the bastard.'

'One hundret against six thousant?' Manny asked. But then he nodded. 'Don't take foolish chances, *eh bien*?'

None of the three of us – that is, Richard and Andy and I – needed to be told. We went after him, a hundred men after six thousand, as Manny said. At dawn on the twelfth day of September, we caught his rearguard in the hills north of Ràzes – a dozen knights and several hundred men-at-arms, most of them not in armour, and quite a few baggage wagons. They seemed to think that it was a beautiful day for hawking. They had no pickets. The first the rearguard knew that we were close was when I unhorsed the commander.

I swept up the road with all our men-at-arms and Andy Belmont, while Richard took all the mounted archers and beat up their quarters, taking hundreds of prisoners.

North of Ràzes, some of du Berry's household knights made a

stand. They were good knights – well trained and well horsed and, to be honest, they cut a swathe through my former hobilars and my new-minted men-at-arms, unhorsing a dozen of them. Fortunately for us, they had no support, and their initial success made them too bold. Andy and I had hot work for several minutes, holding them until the sheer weight of numbers took them down. But down they went – we took three, killed one, and the rest ran.

To my infinite satisfaction, we ended the skirmish with the Duc du Berry's pennon that his knights carried as their flag. We also took the captain of his guard.

Sadly, we didn't get much of the duc's own baggage, which was accounted as incredibly rich. Instead, we had to content ourselves with twenty good ransoms and a remarkable amount of clothing, some food, and a fine haul of horses. But we did take one memorable mule. I can only assume that someone in the duc's household rose late and threw important items onto the mule. Dick Thorald, an old campaigner, spotted it after the fight on the road and took it.

By Our Lady! A year's wages for my entire company, taken in a moment. On that mule were a servant's clothes, a *malle* of the duc's household items – his ivory reliquary, his gold and ivory comb, a silver and onyx mirror, six beautiful silk shirts, all dirty, an embroidery kit with needles, a pair of pointed shoes with gilt-silver chains that needed repair – and a gold statue of the Virgin. And an enamelled knight's belt. Probably Limoges work – twenty-six panels, solid gold, enamelled over with images of the Blessed Virgin, each slightly different. One of the most beautiful things I'd ever seen.

'Dick, we have to share,' I said.

I thanked God I'd been sharing all my own captures.

Thorald smiled. 'Awreet,' he said. 'Just giv'est mirr an' al caw it fair.'

I took me a moment, as usual, to get through the sounds.

Mirror.

I smiled and handed over the beautiful thing.

'Fer ta missus,' he grinned.

By the rood; somewhere in Cumbria is a woman with a mirror worth a baron's ransom. I hope she liked it.

By the time our little column returned to Limoges, the prince had arrived in person, travelling on a litter between two horses, and his army was properly investing the town. I met Florimont Lesparre in the streets of the camp. He was the more surprised, and he reined in his charger.

'I remember you,' he said. 'I suppose you are one of the routiers that the prince employs to do the dirty work.'

I smiled. 'I know who you are, too. Much easier when you wear your own coat of arms.'

This last quip was a reference to his fight with me at the Italian Wedding, when he'd worn Camus's arms.

He flushed.

I smiled more.

But our good work against du Berry's rearguard did win us the notice of the prince. Despite Lesparre's efforts – or perhaps I wrong him and he did nothing – we were summoned, still unshaven and covered in dust, to his presence. I was in arming clothes, and I walked out of my pavilion immediately, so that as I walked I realised that I was still wearing my greaves on my lower legs. I did have the presence of mind to have Christopher grab the little embroidered pennon we'd taken from du Berry's knights.

Walter Manny met us at the entrance to the prince's hall. He was staying at the Benedictine abbey south of the city. His court occupied most of the buildings, and he was using the monks' refectory as his receiving hall.

'Fuckink brilliant,' Manny whispered.

In the hall, the prince sat on a low-backed chair of carved and inlaid oak that had, by its decorations, been intended for visiting bishops. The Captal stood by him, and the Duke of Lancaster stood at the windows, looking out over the city.

'Sir Walter Manny,' said a door ward. 'Sir William Gold.'

The prince looked up.

He looked better. There was more life in his posture than there had been at Cognac, and his eyes had the flash they'd had in the fifties. His shoulders were stooped, and he had a shawl over them, but he was girded with a knight's belt and a sword.

I fell on my knees. I hadn't really intended to do so, but there it was – he was, in every way, my prince. Despite everything. Richard did the same, and Andy Belmont stood behind us.

The prince looked at the two of us for so long I was afraid. My heart beat fast, and I thought, perhaps because of Lesparre, of Peter of Cyprus keeping me on my knees for an hour.

'I know you both, of course,' he said warmly.

He waved to the Captal, a little pettishly. His wave told me that he was frustrated by his own physical disability. The Captal stepped forward, held out his hands, and raised us both to our feet.

'Are you two inseparable?' the prince asked. 'You were in the old days, were you not?'

Richard glanced at me, and smiled.

'He's difficult to be rid of, Your Grace,' he quipped.

The prince smiled, and gave a wheezing laugh. 'You have served the Count of Savoy,' he said. 'Both of you.'

'Yes, Your Grace,' we said together.

'And John Hawkwood,' Belmont said, unbidden.

The prince smiled. 'I wanted to praise the three of you for your pursuit of du Berry,' he said. 'You have proven him craven, and redeemed my honour, for which you have my thanks.'

We all bowed. Christopher bowed low and presented the duc's little pennon. The prince waved, and a servant gave Christopher a purse of gold nobles. He waved to the Captal.

'The citizens of the *château* have held out loyally, and they have just handed over the keys of the upper town to my brother,' he said. 'But my former friend the bishop seems determined to hold the cathedral, and he has a garrison.'

He looked at me. 'I don't have a tournament team on which to place you, Sir William. But I'd be honoured if you would lead an assault with your friends.'

I bowed to the floor. Listen, most of you know what this meant, but I'll say anyway. To lead an assault under the eyes of the prince would be one of the greatest honours of a life of arms. You know whereof I speak, eh, Froissart?

'At your command, Your Grace,' I said.

It was almost an apology. And I still treasure it.

Limoges should have been nothing, after du Berry fled. The French had left only about two hundred men-at-arms as a garrison. They had almost no archers – and the citizens were violently pro-English. The commander, Jean de Villemur, did what he could. He took hostages from the pro-English citizens, armed those who appeared loyal to the king of France, and when we started to mine under the walls, he started a counter-mine.

On the evening of the seventeenth day of September, the Duke of Lancaster sent me a message to be ready to lead my men-at-arms early the next morning. I passed the word to Richard and Andy, and then I wrote some letters and slept well, and in the morning, Christopher had me armed cap-à-pie before the sun was in the sky. I led my dozen newly minted 'gentlemen' along the edge of our camp and met with Richard and Belmont and their men-at-arms. I expected ladders.

In the ruddy, salmon-pink light, the duke looked cheerful.

'Good morning, Sir William,' he said. 'It's a curious form of reward, the one my brother has given you.'

This time, he waved to a squire and I was given hot spiced wine. See? My status had changed.

'How so, Your Grace?' I asked.

'We're going down to fight in the mine,' the duke said. He glanced at Richard. 'I fear there's not room for all of us. Will you lead the assault on the breach?'

Richard looked at the unbroken curtain wall.

'Breach, Your Grace?'

'We'll have to win the fight in the mine, and then fire the supports,' Lancaster said.

Richard nodded. 'As you will, Your Grace.'

Lancaster turned to me. 'Have you ever fought in a mine?'

'I can't say that I have,' I allowed.

The duke looked over his own knights.

'Nor I,' he said.

Here's the manner of it.

The miners dig under a wall, their intention being to open a hole big enough to collapse a wall section from underneath. In the old days, we'd dig out under a section, prop it with big trees, and then set fire to the supports. If this worked, the fire would weaken the supports and the wall would crash down.

The invention of gunpowder had made mines even more deadly. Nowadays, the engineers will pack the hole they dig with powder and ignite it, blowing the wall above into the heavens. I've seen it done well, and I've seen it done badly, and I've heard the muffled thump as some poor bastard sets off his own powder and dies like a soul in Hell.

In the case of Limoges, our mine had gone in under the wall very quickly, but the garrison had counter-mined, or dug an answering tunnel across ours. Our people had propped about forty paces of wall, and there was 'some' powder. These tunnels, by the way, were about the width of a man's shoulders, about four feet high, and dark as pitch. Don't imagine torches or cressets. Imagine darkness like the tomb. Imagine it hot. Imagine that the ceiling is held up by some props made of branches, and dirt falls on you every time your helmet brushes the ceiling, which is constantly, and you must walk with knees bent and head bowed.

In armour.

Men can only go down those tunnels one at a time. So the combat is very personal. Most men fight only with daggers. Indeed, behind us, Lancaster's knights – and they were all belted knights, young, rich men in very good armour – had mostly stripped their leg armour and had rondel daggers or baselards in their gauntleted fists.

They all looked terrified.

I looked up at the curtain wall. My desire for a 'good deed of arms' was at odds with my knowledge of the art of war.

'Your Grace?' I asked.

'Sir William?'

'Am I ... correct in assuming that the French captain has to surrender soon?' I asked. 'He has little food. And no hope of relief.'

Lancaster raised an eyebrow. 'Sir William, you are welcome to decline the honour.'

I sighed. I took off my sword belt, unbuckled my scabbard and put it back on, the sword naked in my steel-clad fists. I had my dagger close, and I had Christopher tie the end of the scabbard to my maille so it couldn't slip away.

'I'd like to go first,' I said.

Lancaster nodded. 'My brother would insist that you be allowed,' he said. He bowed. 'But if you'd rather ...'

I smiled. 'Your Grace, I am not afraid to fight. I merely hate waste.'

I glanced back at the young men behind him. If the mine collapsed, we could lose a lot of well-born men.

I went to the head of the mine, where two heavy pilings defined the opening of a tunnel.

'What did my brother do to you?' Lancaster asked quietly. 'He believes that he has made too many errors in his life, and he seeks to make restitution for them all. I find it difficult that he imagines that he has failed.'

I tried to avoid his eyes. I was looking for the space inside myself to pray. Suddenly, it was all real – I was going to fight. It wasn't a game. I was going to fight underground, in the dark.

But Lancaster worshipped his brother, or so I'll guess – and he wanted to understand.

'Please, Sir William?' he asked. 'Something about a tournament—'

'It's a long story,' I said. 'If we both survive the next hour, Your Grace, I'll be happy to share it.'

Then I knelt, and slowly, in Latin, I prayed the Lord's Prayer. Until I was calm.

I went down into the mine. I had to climb down a ladder, in sabatons. Perhaps you think I'm foolish to wear sabatons, but I have always worn them – feet are very vulnerable. Horses step on them, and so do men – and in the dark ...

I got to the bottom. The passage went off to the right, and there were three miners watching their tunnel with a crossbow.

'It's the duke,' someone said, and they were all bowing to me.

'His Grace is behind me,' I said.

'Mother Mary, I wouldn't go down that tunnel for love nor money,' said the man with the crossbow.

This is the stage of chivalry – a tunnel five feet high and three feet wide, half a dozen miners as the crowd, your own prince as your judge. Otherwise alone, in the darkness.

I thought of Emile. I thought of Christ.

I thought of Camus, and all the people I had killed, and I stopped, put my hands on my sword hilt, and prayed again. I wished I'd had time to confess. I thought of my sister, of my daughters and my son, who I hadn't seen for a year.

And I thought of the Duke of Lancaster, feeling his way along behind me in the darkness, and to be honest, I wished it was Richard Musard or Andy Belmont.

I dropped my visor. In total darkness, a little less vision wasn't going to do any harm.

I started forward. I made it about ten feet, dislodging bits of earth from the ceiling with the point of my basinet and from the floor with the toes of my sabatons, and then there was a snap.

The crossbow bolt hit me right in the middle of the breastplate. It left a small dent in the metal and the bolt shattered, throwing shards of splintered ash everywhere.

I sat down, hard.

Try and get to your feet in a tunnel five feet wide and four feet high, wearing head-to-toe plate armour over a shirt of maille. I promise you this will not prove as easy as you think. If there was light, you might amuse your friends. As it was, I had to turn *away* from the dark tunnel and get to my knees, and then stand, and then turn around. It seemed to take an hour, and all that while I expected a spear or a dagger in the back.

'What happened?' the duke asked suddenly out of the darkness behind me.

'Crossbow,' I said.

I didn't like the sound of my voice. Scared and winded.

I went forward again. It was harder to make myself go forward the second time.

I went about forty feet along the tunnel this time, my sword gripped at the hilt and half sword, probing ahead with its point. After the first ten feet there was no light at all, and my helmet cut me off from most of the sound. I had my visor down because it made no sense to have my face unprotected in these absurd conditions, but I was breathing hard, my back ached already, and I was soaked in sweat.

I hadn't fought anyone yet.

I went forward with my left foot, sliding the back foot up as the front foot advanced.

This time, by luck, I caught the moment when the crossbowman opened his lantern. The light shone – he had a partner.

The tiller moved, as if by magic, and the bolt flew. This time it skipped off a wall and then brought earth out of the ceiling, changed course, struck my armoured foot and vanished into the loose dirt on the floor.

I took three or four gliding steps forward, my breath coming in gasps.

The crossbowman and his mate ran for it. As they turned, the crossbowman's mate dropped the lantern, and the candle guttered, and in its light I saw a fully armoured knight and a man-at-arms with a shiny breastplate. The man had a lit slow match, and he had a long, iron club on his shoulder like a Flemish *goedendag*.

I wasn't waiting to talk. I got my point up to waist height in the light of the dying candle, and I flicked a thrust forward with one hand, and my opponent made a wild parry. Wild, but successful.

He came forward with his parry – a trained man.

I went forward to meet him, rotating my blade off his parry, catching it back in my left hand. Suddenly we were so close that I could feel his warmth, and his steel forearms slammed into mine. He had a dagger.

I had a long sword. I tried to push the point down past his hands into his gut below his breastplate, but the point caught on something. Anyway, he had a coat of plates with a fauld, as I learnt by pressure – I couldn't see *anything*. But I had his hands – somehow I was pinning one or both to the side of the tunnel. I slammed my pommel forward, caught it on the low tunnel roof, ripped it free, and some of the roof collapsed, dry earth falling on us both. He flinched, and I got my sword free and clipped him with the pommel. I couldn't see a thing, and had no idea what I hit. But I had him. I pushed forward, using my size and strength and whatever advantage I'd just gained with my pommel, and he was pushed back, his shoulders behind his feet ...

I got a sabatoned foot over his feet and I ground the steel edge of my shoe down into his bare instep. Behind him was the man with the *goedendag*, except that it wasn't – it was a handgonne, and it was pointing at me. My knightly opponent was going down, and I had no choice. I left him behind me and struck forward, almost falling, arms flailing.

The gonner's match-hand was shaking so violently that he couldn't get the match down on his powder. I cut the match hand by the guttering light of the candle, almost severing it from his arm, and the man fell back, a scream just forming in his throat, and there was another armoured man.

And then the candle went out.

I knew I was in the chamber where the two mines met – it was wider here, a long low chamber under the very walls. I pushed forward at the next knight, and got a sabaton tangled in the dying gonner. I fell. My helmet hit something.

It was completely dark except for a single pinpoint of dull orange – the gonner's match. The gonner was screaming, and something struck me on the breastplate as I tried to get to my feet. At least one of my opponents had found me in the dark, by luck or skill.

Thank God for good armour.

I slashed with the sword that, thanks to God, was still in my hand. I was on one knee ...

There was a flash of light – not white light, but angry and red. A *whooosh*.

And then another.

The dull sound of dirt falling. The scream of a soul damned to Hell for all eternity.

Something hit me very hard in the head and right shoulder. And my mouth was suddenly full of dirt, my eyes full of smoke.

Understand, I could see nothing. There was pressure against my back and my legs – something had hit me hard ...

By luck, or God's will, I passed forward to get at my opponent. Finding no resistance, I went forward again.

The floor moved. I was on my knees without intending to be, and it finally came to me that the mine was collapsing. Or had collapsed.

Sweet Christ. To be buried alive has to be one of my many fears, and among the worst. I tried to push forward, but I was cautious. I couldn't face falling to the floor, face down as the dirt fell ...

I managed half a step. There was a beam down ahead of me – one of the big supports that was supposed to prop the whole ancient wall above my head until we were ready to bring it down.

I stopped moving.

Everything seemed to have stopped. I had to cough, and cough again, and somewhere in the dirt and smoke, there was other coughing.

No light, no breeze, and I wasn't entirely sure which way I was facing. Behind me, a low crackle, and a dull orange that told me how thick the smoke was. Fire.

How much powder was down here?

Panic.

Coughing, to my front – maybe to the left. The intense smell of sulphur and of frying pork. Someone was burning.

Under the fallen prop, or over it? That stopped me for many heartbeats.

In the end, like many life decisions, it was easy. There was a clear space above it, and no space below it. I went over it in no time at all, after my long hesitation. I went towards the coughing, my sword tapping like a blind man's stick.

The coughing stopped.

I have seldom been so terrified. The darkness was *absolute*. I kept closing my eyes and opening them, hoping to get some hint, some hope of light. Strange patterns played inside my head, and the smoke had the taste of sulphur.

Hell is dark. Hell has no light, because light is the grace of God.

My sword's point scraped dirt. How far had I come?

I turned my shoulders, finding my right shoulder to be very painful. I went left, and there was a clear space. My sword point found wood. And under the wood, a man. Over the wood, dirt.

I knelt. The man wasn't pinned. A beam had fallen on his unhelmeted head. His breathing was odd, but he wasn't dead.

I wasn't in the mood, there in Hell, to kill anyone.

I took a few breaths, got my arms locked under his, and dragged him into the little clear area I'd just vacated. Then I tried going the other way. The smoke was better ...

There was a breeze, and I could hear voices. Shouts, even.

Above me, something shifted, and there was a loud *crack*.

Dirt fell. And the orange glow behind me leapt up for a moment.

Fire and smoke, sulphur and darkness, oppressive heat.

Hell.

I wagered everything on the sound of voices. I got my sword blade under the unconscious man, the flat against his back, one hand on the hilt and the other at the point, and I pulled as fast as I could. He was out. I got him up high enough that I was just dragging his heels, and I stumbled backwards into the Stygian darkness ...

CRACK!

Behind me, there was a roar, and then there was a swirl of motion, a taste of dirt and something rotten, and I fell backwards, dragging my unconscious burden with me. I suppose that I panicked again. I knew it was the wall above us cracking and settling, and that we were dead men.

I pulled him, moving backwards like a crab. Falling back, sitting up, dragging him ...

It took me time to realise that there was a little light. And a ladder, going up.

I had passed under the wall. I was inside the city.

I got my wounded companion to the head of the ladder after three attempts, drank off the pitcher of water that the workers had thoughtfully left in their workings, retrieved my sword, and crept to the edge of the hole. It was cut into a stable wall where the building was against the foundations of the town. I climbed the ladder. No opponents. I went down, stripped my rescuer of his armour and helmet to lighten the load, and carried him to the mine-head.

Then I sat, my legs dangling in the mine-hole, and rested. There were a pair of muffled thumps, down in the tunnel, and another rush of sulphur smoke came past me.

A crash outside.

The opposite wall of the stable was long boards pegged to the cross-timbers, and the gaps between let in the slanting sunlight. It was still morning. I felt as if a year had passed, and yet it had been less than an hour.

I made my unconscious man as comfortable as I could and went out of the stable into the town. I looked back at the wall beyond the stable – it had more than half collapsed. And there were men fighting in the rubble piles of the breach – a dozen or more English knights fighting as many French. I was behind, and to the side, of the French.

It was almost a relief, after the hell of being under it. I stepped down off the remains of a catwalk, slid down a collapsed wall section, threw my sword around the neck of a French knight and demanded his surrender.

It took us two assaults to take the town, and even then it only fell when loyal citizens opened one of the gates. The fight in the mines had gone all wrong, and the Duke of Lancaster had taken the knight I was fighting after a quick fight. He proved to be the garrison commander. But the same collapse that prevented me from getting back, cut him off on our side.

I had a cruelly wrenched shoulder, a turned ankle – acquired later in the day, stepping badly on the loose stone of the breach – and two more prisoners to ransom.

And then we got into the town.

Listen, this is the hard part. The bad part.

When we were forming up to go into the breach the second time, word came from the prince that we were to offer no quarter. Hales was there, and Fenton. Young Robin Wall was already down, a bash in his thigh, and Gosford was dead. We had taken heavy losses in the first assault, and there was a growl from the men as the herald told us not to offer mercy to the defenders.

But before the assault went forward, the Captal appeared on the dead ground below the breach.

'The prince has cancelled his orders!' he roared. 'Quarter is to be given! The townspeople are to be spared!'

Men grumbled. I heard them, and I knew it would be bad.

And it was.

When the gates opened, the garrison continued fighting at the breach for another amount of time. I was sword to sword – I can't count time then – but I was fighting with every part of me, and I had not yet noticed the turned ankle because I was in the maw of the beast. At one point, Musard and Belmont and I cleared almost five yards of the breach, just the three of us. Up and up – my sword broke somewhere on the slope. Then I was fighting with someone else's spear, and then with my dagger and the butt of my broken spear, and then the French men-at-arms were kneeling, begging for quarter.

I smacked Tom Fenton in the head with the butt of my broken spear when he went for a kneeling man. He turned on me like a mad thing, and I stepped through him and dropped him over my thigh.

Andy Belmont grabbed three Frenchmen and shoved them down the breach.

'Move!' he roared.

There's a real professional. A massacre costs money. He was saving the ransoms.

But off to my left, an archer in the duke's livery raised a maul and slammed it down on a French knight's head from behind, crumpling his helmet and drenching the man's shoulders and aventail in his pulped head.

The archer whooped with satisfaction, and the butchery of the garrison began.

Now, I've heard a lot of foolish talk about Limoges. It was bad. But it wasn't Alexandria. First, the so-called *cité* was taken by assault. By the laws of war, no quarter need be offered to soldiers in an assault.

But more importantly, we didn't kill the people. The citizens. Most of them were on our side – they opened the gate for us.

The French had murdered their hostages when the gates opened. We found the bodies.

Oh, it was all a chivalric tournament, in the autumn of 1370. Limoges wasn't the hell that Alexandria had been, or other towns I've seen taken by storm.

But by the saints, it was terrible enough. A third of the town burnt, and over two hundred citizens died, and more than half the garrison was massacred.

But the idea that the prince demanded the murder of the town is foolishness. It was his town, for the love of God.

PART IV

ITALY

1371–1373

CHAPTER ONE

AQUITAINE AND ITALY

October 1370 – August 1371

Limoges was the prince's last campaign, as you all know. It was a small victory in a year of defeat, and it did, for a while, shore up the collapsing wall that was the Duchy of Aquitaine.

Sir Walter Manny took the three of us and our retinues on a thrust into Limousin, and we discomfited Armagnac again in early October, but by then the prince was getting ready to sail for England. The Earl of Pembroke was to be made a Knight of the Garter. That should tell you all you need to know.

Sir Walter was also returning to England. Andy Belmont had a place in the duke's retinue.

And Richard Musard was returning to the service of the Count of Savoy.

'I had a letter,' was all he said.

But I knew he was disappointed, or worse than disappointed, in England.

'I'm for Italy,' I told Sir Walter, as the leaves turned in the highlands north of Perigord. We were a day's march east of Limoges, near Pontarion. As far east and south as Manny's raid was going.

Sir Walter glanced over my command. I had seventeen men-at-arms left, and about thirty archers, and almost a hundred horses, as well as a handful of *bonnes amies* and sutlers and hangers-on. I had sixteen good wagons and the loot of a fairly successful autumn, and, most of all, I had a stunning amount of gold from the sale of the gold statue of the Virgin.

'A week's travel, if I'm not stopped,' I said.

I looked at Richard. He nodded. He had as many men-at-arms as I, and almost as many archers.

Manny nodded. 'I vill miss you, Musard. And you, Goldt,' he said. 'You and your frients reminded me of the old days.'

We touched gauntlets and parted. I embraced Andy – he was going back to England.

'I'll be in Lancaster's retinue next year,' he said. 'You'll see.'

'I believe you,' I said.

And Belmont shook his head. 'Damn,' he said. 'I almost want to go back to Italy.'

But instead, he threw his arms around me, and we parted.

Richard formed his men and came with me. He was going back to the Green Count.

As my wagons began to roll over the top of the pass that led east, I turned back. So did Andy. Richard waved.

'Send my regards to Janet!' Andy called.

A week later, we were rolling into Chambéry. We'd got some wry looks and had one day of out-racing a French patrol to the bridge at Pont-Neuf, and I'm almost certain that I misled the Duc du Berry into assuming that there was a grand *chevauchée* rolling into Provence, but we fought no battles and burnt no farms. I paid hard silver for our food, and when we crossed the Rhone at Givors I paid the toll for all my wagons to a terrified toll-collector, and we had a little feast on the far bank because I could see the mountains of Savoy, and we were, to all intents and purposes, *home*. The morning after we passed through Chambéry, I encamped on my own estate and decreed three days' rest.

I had been gone more than a year.

I am a lucky man. Lucky in my lord, and lucky in my friends.

The count sent Sam Bibbo to me with a message, and we talked the night away, and I joined the count for a day's hunting. I handed over letters from the Prince of Wales and the Duke of Lancaster, and was received like the prodigal son. And that evening, after dinner in one of the count's lodges, I was presented with the Emperor's sword.

'You left it somewhere,' Count Amadeus said. 'Your friends went and fetched it back for you.'

Attached to the belt was de Charny's dagger. And my old purse.

And this little book of hours, without which I wouldn't be able to recite this story.

Sam Bibbo told me all about the ransom – the chagrin of the Comte d'Armagnac, and the difficulties he made.

I'm leaving out Richard's reception. If I was the prodigal son, Richard was the apple of his eye, and he was embraced, cosseted ... He deserved it. And he'd brought the count some excellent men.

The next day I spent with my daughters and sons. Edouard, who had grown enormously in a year, was distant at first, and then bursting with stories of life on Lesvos that made me weep. I had been so happy in Outremer. *We* had been so happy ...

I had brought them balls made of hemp covered in leather, and we rolled them at candles, to everyone's delight. I had a sword for Edouard, a good one, if small, and a dagger for my son Richard. I had a toy knight that Gregory Fox had made, complete with cloth 'maille' that could come off, and a dagger and a doll for Magdalene. And from Limoges – paid for, by God, and not taken in a sack – was a set of buttons done in Emile's arms in Limoges-work for Magdalene's first proper gown. I was a very popular father for a while.

But everything in Chambéry was new. My children had new tutors and a new seneschal, who didn't much like the look of me. Bernard and Jean-François were cautious in their comments. Edouard was the lord, now, and his seneschal was above criticism. Apparently.

It's what I had wanted. I wanted them to continue their lives without me, so I wouldn't have to bear the day-to-day knowledge of my loss of Emile. But a year later, it seemed like an incredibly foolish decision. Perhaps it was Limoges, or perhaps just Camino and a few months as no one important in England, but I wondered why I didn't want to be the lord of some estates in Savoy and play with my children.

Then I went to the chapel of her castle on Sunday with Bernard and Jean-François, and I remembered why I'd made this choice. It was the longest service of my life. I expected Emile to come in late, as she often did, and when Bernard brushed my sleeve, just for a moment I thought it was her. I left the little church weeping like a babe. It was all around me – her smell, her furnishings, wall hangings, a chair we'd once ... Well. It was too much.

A year had passed. Nothing was really different, and that night, rather than sleep in her castle, I gathered my things and went back to my own little manor, where my troops were billeted.

The Green Count had troubles of his own. The fall of the Prince of Achaea and the death of Prince Lionel had loosened the foundations of trans-alpine politics in a way that shook Savoy itself. The Visconti immediately demanded the return of all the towns they'd given to the Duke of Clarence as dowry for Violante. I had brought letters from the Prince of Wales for Lord Edward le Despenser, who was supposedly acting as steward of all of Lionel's surviving holdings, but the English chancellery in London was far behind in time. Le Despenser had sold Clarence's holdings to the Marquis of Montferrat for sixteen thousand florins about the time I was landing at Bordeaux and celebrating my thirtieth birthday.

Oddly, everything that followed was due to le Despenser's decision, which was a surprisingly venal one. When I think on the Italian Wedding, I often wonder how many men – and women – died as a result of the web of conflicting policies that resulted in that unlucky day.

As soon as Galeazzo Visconti heard that le Despenser had sold the 'English' holdings to the Marquis of Montferrat, he declared war. And the Visconti insistence on reclaiming the towns 'given' to the Duke of Clarence and 'reclaimed' with Violante ended up threatening the Green Count and his Piedmontese state and overturning the diplomacy of Europe.

Again.

On Christmas Day of 1370, I would guess that there weren't two hundred men and women in all of Europe who understood how intricately interlinked the war between France and England was with the conflicts in Northern Italy. The linchpin of the two theatres was the Pope. Pope Urban, the fifth of that name, known to many of us as Guillaume de Grimoard, died in Avignon on the nineteenth day of December. His death was known in Chambéry by Christmas Eve, and all the calculations hung in the air pending the election of a new Pope.

Urban had been the enemy of Milan, and the king of England had married his son to Milan's daughter. Urban had been a gifted man and a patron of my beloved Father Pierre Thomas – a crusader in his heart, and a man who kept the Benedictine Rule even as Pope. But in his heart, he was French. He had many faithful English servants, but he remained a Frenchman in his heart and in his diplomacy, so his hatred of Milan translated into an English alliance with Milan.

The Green Count was the ally of Milan, and thus could be trusted to keep his forces out of the war with England, despite his alliance with France. The Holy Roman Emperor was the ally of the Pope against Milan, but the ally of the king of England against France. It was all beautifully balanced, like a troupe of acrobats, each standing on another's shoulders.

But it couldn't last. And now Urban was dead.

And my own thoughts were almost as complicated as the diplomacy of Europe. I suppose that I had imagined ... It's difficult to rebuild my thoughts now, but I supposed that, despite my reservations, or perhaps without any real thought, I imagined that I'd return to service with the Green Count. I was, by then, a fairly polished military courtier. I was acceptable even in the Prince of Wales's court, and I was valued in Chambéry.

Listen, my friends. I have known men, brave men, who have done nearly impossible things, and yet are terrified of heights – you know I mean Fiore. Yet Fiore is continually finding himself in high places, because he forgets. That's perhaps how it was with me. I thought that I could stand on the heights of my memories of Emile. I was wrong. I needed to flee. I could not endure daily contact with her ghosts, and they were many – the ghost of her dancing, the ghost of her walking down a corridor, playing with Maggie or Isabelle, tossing Richard in the air, opening a present, mounting a horse, kissing me in an alcove ...

She was everywhere.

But fortune was with me in a number of ways. First, there were letters for me in Chambéry, and I had the time to digest them. I had a letter from Hawkwood, a very civil one, addressing me by all my titles – I could see that it had been written out by Janet. He suggested that he would appreciate my return in the spring, if that could be arranged, and he asked me to send his respectful greetings to 'that most eminent lord, the Count of Savoy'.

Hawkwood used one line that I hoped he composed himself. 'Without you, William Gold, I feel as if I'd left home with an empty scabbard, and no sword.'

Janet, who sometimes dealt with his correspondence, added a scrap of papyrus with a note that suggested that Bernabò Visconti was very slow in paying, and that Hawkwood might be looking for a contract in the northern war, by which she meant the coming conflict between Saluzzo and Savoy.

I had another letter from Fiore. This one was from Greece, and I laughed aloud to find that Fiore, who affected to despise Nerio, was with him.

'I found that I could no longer stomach the service of Mammon, in this case, the Visconti. Bernabò is actually a beast, and his constant performance of a man above both law and morality sickens me. Hawkwood's tolerance of Visconti's behaviour led me to this step, and whenever Nerio takes my gloves or behaves like a pompous arse, I remind myself that I could still be watching Bernabò act like a tomcat on a public stage.'

Fiore was serving Nerio. I found, on reading further, that he'd raised a dozen lances of his own in Udine and taken none of mine, except his squire.

There was a long and somewhat bombastic letter from Nerio, the gist of which was that Corinth was expanding as a port – that he'd established trade relations with Constantinople and Venice and he was starting to trade in currants and wine. And that he had his eyes on Athens. He reminded me that I had a *condotta in aspetto* or a 'contract in waiting', and he suggested that in a year or two he'd want me to bring my companions to Romania for a campaign.

I had a report from l'Angars, detailing the gains and losses and profits of the year in which I'd been gone. I looked at the handwriting and realised that Janet had written this, as well. And I noted that l'Angars' figures didn't add up.

I fire-hardened and sharpened a couple of quills, intending to write my own replies, but instead I sat in a cold solar with four neatly prepared pens and stared at the parchment I had in front of me, neat and ready for my thoughts. At some point I rooted in my old purse for a sharper quill knife, and found of all things, my little collection of scraps of parchment with the long, twisting S.

Of course, I'd had them in my purse. My old purse, that the Armagnacs had taken from me, and Bibbo had restored.

I had no further thoughts. I missed Fiore. When he was about, I could always beat my thoughts into submission with a little swordplay.

I didn't *know* what I wanted to do. I felt disconnected – from my friends, from my family, such as it was ... from my life. I imagined going back to Buckland, signing over all my worldly possessions to the order and becoming ... a retired knight? At thirty?

But as I say, Fortuna smiled on me, or God. The next day, I rode hunting with the count, and received an invitation to return to his palace for wine. We were discussing a deed of arms for his Christmas court. It's not part of my story, but the count was clearly worried for his chivalric reputation. He had discovered the harsh reality that participation in the world of politics is bad for one's ideals.

Or perhaps I'd discovered that.

Regardless, I rode back to his palace in snow – a beautiful late afternoon. From the ridge above the town, we could see smoke curling from every village for miles. The snow on the trees was a magnificent contrast of light and dark, tinged red by the afternoon's last glow. I found it all beautiful, and yet in some other way it didn't move me as it might have.

We rode down to Chambéry, and I handed my riding horse over to Christopher and went inside with Richard Musard and Ogier and a crowd of other men I knew, and liked. Despite that, I felt alone, insulated from their Yuletide cheer by my own absence of purpose, my own empty thoughts. Or confronted in corners by some memory of Emile – ambush after ambush.

I settled in a chair to nurse my cup of hippocras, and found myself looking up at a priest and a tall nun in a long black habit. Just for a moment, I thought she was my sister – I was in an odd place inside my head.

Not my sister, but Sister Marie. My second piece of *fortuna*. Standing with Father Angelo.

'You came back?' I asked.

Father Angelo had left the Holy Land with my company, and had functioned as our chaplain for several thousand long miles.

'The count, may God bless him and his house, found me a nice church and congregation to be my very own,' he said.

'Verona?' I asked. Angelo was Veronese, a De la Scala.

He shook his head. 'No. I have fallen in love with the Piedmont.'

I turned to Sister Marie. 'Seeing the two of you together is like old times. Has the count found you an abbey?'

She made a face. 'Not exactly,' she said. 'My abbess wanted someone to go to Avignon and I made sure she chose me.' She smiled. 'Actually, I suspect she meant me from the first. We don't... get along.'

She changed the subject and asked about Edouard and Magdalene. I offered to take her to see them. Father Angelo promised to visit us, and took his leave.

Sister Marie looked at me for a long time. By then, we'd eaten with the count and we were sitting by one of the palace's enormous fireplaces, watching a big log burn.

She put a hand on mine. 'You are not doing well,' she said.

I frowned. 'I'm fine,' I said.

She raised an eyebrow. 'Really?' she asked.

She turned and watched the fire for a while. I remember asking her about her own family, about her convent.

She told me some things. I knew that Marie was well-born – her convent was somewhere up the Rhine – she knew the Count of Savoy, for example, and Emile d'Herblay. She had enough familial connections that she generally got her way with her convent and the Pope. And she told me that, in effect, she'd returned to her convent and found that she couldn't manage the combination of obedience and boredom.

'I'm not against work,' she said. 'I don't even mind doing the scut work – I've washed a few floors.' She smiled bitterly. 'Father Pierre Thomas ruined me as a nun,' she said. 'He let me think for myself. Now I think about God and Jesus and theology in a whole different way. I've read most of the scholastics, and I find it very difficult to return to the daily image of Jesus as my Holy Bridegroom and other pabulum for novices.' She met my eyes. 'Was it bad, with the prince?' she asked suddenly.

I shrugged. 'We burnt some peasants,' I said. 'The usual.'

She looked away. And back at me.

'We are two of a kind,' she said.

I nodded.

'You are a professional soldier, a *milites*, and you find war to be—'

'Tiresome,' I said. 'And you are a nun, and you find being a nun to be ...'

She laughed. 'Tiresome. A fine word. Listen, William. I have thought a great deal about you – indeed, Michael and I talked about you all the way back to Paris ...'

I smiled at the image.

'We made a great pilgrimage, and you turned it into a military campaign. Perhaps it was a brilliant campaign – in the end, you killed Camus.' She raised her hand. 'I won't even argue that Camus needed killing. I'm not pious enough to tell you that. Merely that instead of looking for God, you found a sword. And you used it. And Emile—'

'I don't really want to talk about Emile,' I said.

She shrugged. 'Too bad, William. Emile wanted to take you away from Hawkwood. You know that? She wanted you to stop risking your life for other men's petty wars.'

I was immediately hot with anger or fear. My eyes filled with tears and my face flushed. I hated what she said about our pilgrimage, and I knew it was true.

'I am a knight,' I said. I can't say whether I said it bitterly, or angrily, or perhaps fatalistically. 'I fight.'

'May I tell you something about yourself that I think you already know?' she asked.

'No,' I said.

I was full of anger, and yet, at the same time, aware that she was not the legitimate target. I loved Sister Marie too much, thank God, to unleash my anger at her. So I rose and walked out into the snow. I remember only that Pilgrim followed me. And I stood in the stable, weeping angry tears while I tried, almost blind, to saddle my horse. I rode home in a rage of moral cowardice.

The next day, I awoke to find that Sister Marie and two other sisters were ensconced in my small buttery, chatting with my cooking staff in good Savoyard French.

'I want to see your children,' Marie said. 'And I'm not easily put off.'

'I'm sorry,' I said.

And I truly was. This woman had been through *everything* with us – Alexandria and Lesvos, and all that came after. She had been closest, I think, to Father Pierre Thomas.

As we rode out into the cold, clear air, I found myself telling her about all of it since I'd left her – about my sister and London, about the campaign in Limousin, about Limoges ...

Pilgrim seemed to love snow, and he bounded through it, a reckless display of his spirit, while Marie asked a dozen questions about Isabella, the princess of England, and then about Lionel ... and his death. When I spoke about these things, I began to see what mattered to me and what did not.

We came to Emile's castle, and stayed a few hours. The children loved Marie and my very wet dog, and perhaps even me, and Marie was welcomed with an effusiveness that made me a little sorry.

We were on the ride back when she turned to me.

'William,' she said, 'you have been like a brother to me. I cannot stop myself from telling you this. You do better when you fight for something in which you believe. There, 'tis said.'

I probably smiled. 'That is no news to me,' I said.

She looked at me. 'You cannot decide what to do,' she said.

I may have shrugged.

'I know what I want,' I said suddenly. 'I want to live on Lesvos with Emile. Can you give me that?'

'No,' Marie said. 'Nor can God give you that. But you must find something. Or you die in someone else's war, doing something on the edge of evil for a cause in which you do not believe.'

That night, I realised that everything I had done for more than a year had been stop-gaps and fillers for life – even the Camino. I'd simply gone from one short-term goal to the next without much in the way of volition. Without ambition.

I thought of my conversation with Fiore, so long ago, when he asked me about the morality of fighting for the Visconti, whom we despised, against the Pope, whom we, for the most part, liked.

I have, ere this, and at this very table, admonished those of you for whom war is a profession that the butcher should not hate the cow – that we should follow the profession of arms without hating our opponents. But I will confess the failing of such a dispassionate way of war. Hate is strong, and full of justification. If the French are evil, then fighting them is justified, and no more need be said, or considered. And without such simple justifications, the knight can find himself like a priest with questions about his faith.

At the edge of despair.

Is this all there is?

*

Sister Marie announced her intention of staying at Chambéry until Twelfth Night was past and perhaps the snow cleared out of the passes a little, and as she was welcome at the count's court, she lingered. In fact, the count offered her a convent in Savoy, and I think she was sorely tempted. And I also think that she stayed to save me, and I honour her for it. It was a dark winter. I might have lost myself in a woman, or in some fighting – perhaps both. In fact, Marie snapped at me that perhaps if I had a leman or paramour, my simple sin might make me less difficult.

I was shocked. 'You, a nun, counsel sin?' I asked.

She shrugged. 'Perhaps I'm a poor theologian, William. But I note that while none of that interests me much, some of you seem to value it very much.' She smiled. 'As Father Pierre Thomas used to say, I'm a Christian, not a fool.'

Still, I couldn't take her advice. If it was advice.

When I wrote my first letter, I found that it was to Princess Isabella. In it, I outlined what I knew about the Duke of Clarence's death, and what I'd learnt at Chambéry. It appeared that he'd died at Alba, not Pavia, as I had been led to believe. Although, to be fair, he died immediately after Emile, and I had probably not paid as much attention as I might have. I spent some evenings with Richard as we went over what he knew, but he had, for the most part, been in the field dealing with the consequences of Achaea's death. He hadn't been with Lionel at his death, either. We both lamented that Doctor Albin and his Caterina had lost their places – they'd have known everything.

'The staff broke up very quickly after the duke died,' Richard admitted. 'Everything was hasty. I had no one to whom I could report except Hereford, and he didn't know anything about Italian politics or what we'd been doing with the count.' He shook his head. 'And you lost your wits—'

'Emile died, Richard,' I said. 'And I've known you to lose your wits over a woman.'

He started to take offence. Instead, he sipped wine, looked at me, and nodded.

'I apologise, brother,' he said. 'You are correct.'

Alba was a rich, ancient city, and it was property of the dukes of Milan. It had been part of Violante's dowry.

I wondered if she knew who had murdered her husband. I wondered if she cared. I wondered if Emile, had she lived, would have been able to get her to speak.

I confess that I even wondered if there was anything to be gained from working out how he died, and who had killed him.

At some point, I remembered that in the fight in the madhouse, we'd taken Black-Beard. That is to say, I knew that it had happened. At some point, penning my letter to the princess, I realised that I might know a man who held the answer. It was all too likely that Black-Beard was dead – Fiore might just have strung him up.

But I suggested in my letter to the princess that I'd keep looking into it. I realised that I had a reason to go to Alba, and that I wanted to return to Hawkwood. It's odd, because serving Hawkwood didn't offer me a cause – not a cause I believed in. And perhaps the only part that Sister Marie had wrong is that men like me don't really believe in causes. We really believe in people, and I preferred Hawkwood to the other leaders available to me. Except maybe Savoy, and he was living in a castle full of Emile's ghosts.

Maybe. Or maybe I just preferred Hawkwood.

But as the passes began to clear over the Alps, I made arrangements to take my little band of Englishmen over the passes as Sister Marie's escort, at least as far as Alba. I sent Hawkwood a letter informing him that I would be returning.

I had a last audience with the Green Count. Really, it was nothing so formal. I was with his chancellor, getting a set of *sauvegardes* and passes signed for all my people when he came in, almost as informal as we had been in Venice. He handed a notary his comments on some legal matters, written in wax. He looked over my shoulder.

'I think I need to speak to you, Ser Guglielmo,' he said.

So I followed him along the hall to his private solar, and was invited to sit. He was in a golden-green brocaded silk doublet with a high tulip collar in the best Milanese style. Fox admired the count's clothes, for good reason, and as usual he made me feel dowdy and underdressed.

When we entered his solar, the first thing I saw was a chessboard of ivory and ebony.

He waved at it. 'The board is empty, being set for a new game,' he said. 'I am reliably informed that Pierre Roger de Beaufort has been elected Pope. Another French Pope – this one even more "French" than the last.' Savoy nodded to me. 'In this, at least, I am more Italian than French. He will be called Gregory the Eleventh, and he's going to try to make peace between England and France.' He looked at the chessboard.

'So nothing will change,' I said.

'Urban was a great Pope,' the count said. 'He had intelligence, humility and energy.' He shrugged. 'If England fails to defend Aquitaine, I will come under heavy pressure from the king of France. I'm fighting this summer with my own vassals against Saluzzo,' he said carefully. 'So ... I will continue to pay for your lances to serve with my brother-in-law ...' He looked at the door. As if he was afraid of being overheard. 'But only, I suspect, until autumn. This season – perhaps one more after.'

I felt a shock go through me, the way you do when lightning strikes close by.

There was a soft knock. A servant entered, set up a side table, and served us both wine. And then took himself out.

'You are a man of excellent discretion, Ser Guglielmo,' he said. 'I have very little love for your John Hawkwood, but I know he did us good service last year in Milan. I want you to ... suggest ... that the board is changing.'

I thought this through.

'And that you may choose not to provide the Visconti with a company of lances?'

He gave me a small nod. 'You know I find it very ... difficult ... to be at war with the Pope,' the count said. 'And everything is connected.'

I thought of my conversation with Fiore. And then I thought of Albornoz, the Pope's general.

'Hmm,' I said, or something equally non-committal.

'When we marched to save Bernabò from the Emperor,' the count said, 'I saw the possibility of Milan being drowned by the rising tide of the Holy Roman Emperor and the Pope, two great rivers joining together.'

He steepled his fingers.

I could only wait. I had my own appreciation of the situation, but to hear it from the Green Count's own lips was far better. It was exciting.

'Now, I find it possible that the Visconti will take all of Tuscany and add it to Lombardy. And then I will be a vassal. And the Pope will stay in France. And Florence will fall to Milan. A great many things will happen, and none of them good. Sometimes, Ser Guglielmo, I feel like the only adult in a room full of children. Why can't they be satisfied with what they have?'

Of course, I might have muttered something about his treatment of the Prince of Achaea. And yet, despite taking Achaea's lands, I knew that the count had more honour than most of his peers. He was, for the most part, satisfied with his domains.

'Sometimes,' he said, 'I think that I am neither the black pieces nor the white pieces.' He glanced at me. 'Sometimes I wonder if I'm the board. Why can't the Visconti behave like gentlemen?' He looked away. 'Why couldn't Pope Urban stomach a few insults and work for the Union of Churches?'

I was not my place to answer, so I didn't.

'I begin to think . . .' he said, and hesitated. 'That the Visconti need . . . limits.'

Well, well.

He talked to me about the expenses of my company for a bit. He asked after all the new recruits I'd brought out from England. I admitted that I was paying for them myself.

'Good,' he said. 'Because if my cousin the king of France were to find that I had on my payroll a company of lances who'd just raided his vassals in Armagnac, I might have to do a great deal of explaining.'

'My Lord,' I said, when it was clear he was done with me, 'you are saying, in fine, that I should suggest to Sir John Hawkwood that the game of princes in Italy is about to change?'

He nodded. 'Something like that,' he said.

'And for myself,' I said, 'you anticipate that at the end of this year, you will not renew my contract?'

'Bah. Perhaps never – perhaps another year,' he said. 'Ser Guglielmo, you, personally, are always welcome at my court and in my councils. But next year, I do not envision hiring . . . *professional* soldiers.'

Or maintaining them for your Visconti relatives.

Ah. Italy. Why had I missed it?

Because the wine was better, that's why.

*

Spring wasn't even a rumour when we crossed the passes and came down into Turin. The passes were full of snow, but it was hard-packed and dirty, and relatively easy to travel if you had a good horse and it wasn't your own thin-soled shoes on the ice. I had letters from the count and we had excellent lodgings, and then we rode on. Sister Marie had no hesitation in going with me to Alba, where we were too many men, too well armed, and too many Englishmen. Gregory Fox tried to ask some questions for us and was rebuffed. Lionel of Clarence's men had been rapacious and violent after he died, and Alba had no good memories of his lordship, and his court was completely dispersed. Already, every aspect of the town was back in the hands of the Visconti.

Marie took her sisters to a Benedictine convent and asked what questions she could. I had a different approach. I dressed down and asked around our tavern until I found out who might be hiring cooks and cooking staff. Everyone in the cooking business remembered when the English duke had died, and that his household had been broken up, almost immediately.

I was careful, but apparently not careful enough, and I wished I had men like Witkin to cover me – I knew I was followed whenever I left our tavern. My Italian was good, but not good enough, and the trail was a year old. I gathered that, with time and money, I might come to know what had happened to Clarence's cook, but I couldn't find her. I did learn her name – Caterina Labriza. It was rare, but not impossible, for a woman to be head cook in a great household.

My little company received daily and irritating attentions from the Visconti podestà, who wanted us gone and threatened to sequester our weapons, despite my letters indicating that I was in the service of the Visconti as a knight in Hawkwood's *condotta*.

The podestà simply *wanted us gone*. He was automatically suspicious of any Englishman, especially armed, and in effect, he *was* correct – I was looking into Prince Lionel's murderer.

After four difficult days, we rode on. Sister Marie, who was as interested, by then, in the tale of the death of the English duke as I, declined to sail from Genoa, which might have been the easier route. Instead, we escorted her to Pavia on the Via Francigena, one of the twin capitals of the Visconti empire. I had memories of Pavia, and none of them particularly good.

I had assumed that as hireling soldiers of the Visconti, we'd be lodged and dismissed. I had forgotten my own notoriety, and after seeing Marie to the Hospitaller priory for the night, I was summoned by no less a personage than Count Galeazzo.

The count greeted me in a marble-lined chamber I'd never seen before – fancy veined marble in pinks and greens and blacks and purples that, for my taste, made a chaotic profusion of colours that weren't in the best of taste. They did show off the family riches, and the confusion of patterns in the stone were, I thought, allegorical of the endless Visconti plots. Or perhaps the way they saw the world.

He was sitting on a gilt chair that would have been a throne for most men. He had a small gilt side table by him, with wine and white cakes, as if the table might make him look less like an enthroned emperor.

'Ah,' he said. 'Sir Guglielmo. The swordsman. We are most pleased to have you return to our armies.'

I bowed. What other response could I make?

'I have before me a number of …' He smiled. 'Eh, what shall I call them, messire? Complaints? Cautions? Comments? Reports?' He smiled at me. 'I gather that when you visited our town of Alba, you and a nun made certain …' He met my eyes. His were like those of a bird. Shiny, and expressionless. 'Certain enquiries.'

Well. I'd had an hour to prepare my responses. And I had learnt a great deal in my years as a courtier.

'Enquiries, Your Grace?' I asked.

He leant forward. 'Don't play stupid with me,' he snapped.

I met his eyes. 'Enquiries?' I asked again.

'You were looking for the Duke of Clarence's former cook and household staff,' he said.

I shook my head. 'I'm sorry, Your Grace, but you are mistaken. I was providing an escort for a nun of the Benedictine Order who has been the papal legate's Latinist. I only visited Alba looking for any English soldiers who might remain, as Sir John Hawkwood ordered me to recruit Englishmen.'

'You enquired after his cook,' the count said. 'At the orders of the Duke of Lancaster.'

I began to understand the scale of his suspicions, and the level of trouble in which I found myself. On the other hand, he didn't know who was making the enquiries.

I allowed myself the appearance of a retreat.

'I may have asked after the cook,' I said. 'If your sources are so well versed, Your Grace already knows of a certain house in Vigone ...?'

He was fretting. Perhaps I was supposed to have folded immediately, or perhaps he was just bored. His eyes were elsewhere.

'Yes, yes,' he said. 'Camus and his madhouse. A pestilence that you and your friends cleared away.'

I had a thought. I suddenly thought of Black-Beard, and the message he'd forgotten in his grate – the signature like a long *S*. Or a snake. Or a viper.

I almost swore aloud. It must have shown on my face. We took him in that fight, and then I rode off in pursuit of Camus. Perhaps the man had died. Perhaps ...

'We took prisoners,' I said. 'I was just following up an ... accusation.'

Now I had Count Galeazzo's full attention.

'You took prisoners? In the madhouse?' He was dismissive. He waved his hand. 'None of their testimonies could be reliable.'

I nodded. 'Exactly. So I thought that I would look further into their madness.'

I was making this up, but I had him. And the more I thought about the various attempts on the Green Count and his wife and the Duke of Clarence, especially the one right here in Pavia ...

'Do you now serve the Duke of Lancaster?' he asked.

'No, Your Grace,' I said.

I smiled. My smile was meant to rob my statement of veracity, because I knew, with a drip of cold sweat on my spine, that I needed a great name to keep me from being dumped into an oubliette.

He nodded, picked up a cut quill and chewed on it, showing his nerves as clearly as if he'd mentioned them aloud.

'There will be no more questions about these people,' he said. 'Is that clear?'

I made a face.

'Gold, you are a nobody, and I can have you killed and your body destroyed without a trace,' he said softly.

The change in him was so sudden that it was as if I was talking to someone else. The great lord was gone, replaced by ...

The viper of Milan.

'Quite clear, Your Grace.'

'Your friend the nun, your sword-teaching friend, your squire, your horse. I can make them all simply go away. Understand?'

I looked at him. I was stunned, and terrified – but also angry. And also ...

This was the real man. A man for whom threats like this were a natural weapon, to be deployed against any threat.

He raised an eyebrow. 'It's all a simple misunderstanding,' he said, switching suddenly back to the great lord. 'My poor son-in-law died of overeating. He wasn't used to rich Italian food. I understand that English food is poor and thin.' He waved a hand. 'There is no more to know. Do you understand me?'

'I understand very well, Your Grace,' I said.

I rode south with Sister Marie and her sisters, just to be sure. And I told her in no uncertain terms of the threats that had been offered.

Marie said what I had been thinking. We were a day north of Reggio Emilia, more than halfway between Milan and Bologna. We were sitting outdoors, in a grape arbour covered in new leaves with well-carved benches and a long table that still had some dried grapes from the previous year's harvest stuck to the surface. The inn had seen better days. The arbour was built into the back of the big fortified inn, with a view of the Enza river. Marie's sisters were playing chess at another table. My ruffians were in the common room, making as little trouble as Dick Thorald could manage in them. Sam Bibbo was scouting the road. We were, for the moment, safe.

'The Visconti either killed Prince Lionel, or are so worried at the possibility of accusations that they act as if they're guilty.'

I nodded.

Marie made a face. 'You thought Camus did it for ...?'

'For the Prince of Achaea,' I said. 'And I agree, it didn't make sense, even then.' I looked at her. 'None of it makes sense, to be honest. And I have to assume that this Caterina Labriza woman, the cook, is long dead. Whether innocent or guilty, the Visconti will have rid themselves of her.'

'Hmm,' Marie said. 'Labriza is not a common name,' she commented. 'And the Church has a long arm. And hates the Visconti.'

'Hmm,' I said. 'I will find out what happened to the prisoners we took in Vigone – probably tomorrow. My company is a day's ride away.'

'Any notion how to get three nuns through a war?' she asked.

I returned to my company like a well-loved son to the bosom of his adoring family, and if Lapot had been my John the Baptist, I was luckier for it.

Witkin was on road guard with Ewan and Gospel Mark and Claudio Birigucci and Beppo. Even Beppo embraced me, and then tried to kiss a nun, who screamed, and there I was, back in the midst of my people. Before an hour passed, I had Marc-Antonio's arms around me, while de la Motte tried to tell me about every action the company had fought and Sam Bibbo went to find l'Angars.

L'Angars came into my pavilion, which was, of course, *his* pavilion, and threw his arms around me in turn, and behind him was Sir John Hawkwood, whose habitual foxy expression had been replaced with a slight smile that, on him, indicated real pleasure.

'Gold!' he said. 'You didn't hurry, I see.'

'I brought fifty new men,' I said. 'Englishmen. Some Scots and Welsh.'

Hawkwood virtually beamed – by which, as it was John Hawkwood, I mean he smiled a little more.

'I hope the Count of Savoy is paying them,' he said.

Very little had changed, I could see.

My other reunion was with Gabriel – perhaps the finest warhorse I've ever known. He was fat, and a little out of shape – but Marc-Antonio had him. I curried him myself while Marc-Antonio and I laughed about my impersonation of him.

'My father was somewhat perplexed,' he admitted. 'And I'm touched to say that he paid the ransom before I understood what was happening.'

I made sure he was repaid from my Venetian banker. But that for later.

I was home.

The only man who was missing was Gatelussi, who had taken the Greeks and gone back to Lesvos. I couldn't blame him – he was a prince, and had a life ruling his domains ahead of him. I promised myself I'd write him a letter, and then I dedicated several days to

375

riding around Reggio Emilia and making contact through enemy lines with the Prior of the Knights Hospitaller in Bologna, by whose good offices I passed Sister Marie on towards Rome. I also got a good look at the defences of Reggio Emilia, which were formidable.

A week later, and it was as if I had never left, and I confess that the death of the Duke of Clarence was no longer anywhere on my list of military duties. Hawkwood had several excellent officers – William Boson and Richard Romsey come to mind – but as the English seemed to be doing both the operational planning and the logistics for our army, we were under strain. Our army was composed of some Milanese professionals under Ambrogio Visconti and his half-brother, my sometime friend and comrade Antonio Visconti, and a heavy German contingent under Johann Flach von Reischach, who had defeated Hawkwood himself a few years before.

I'm wandering off my road, but the point is that the moment I rejoined Hawkwood I was put to work, and my duties were far beyond my own company, which suddenly consisted of almost seventy lances. But instead of training them or holding a muster, or any of that, I spent two days reviewing l'Angars' paperwork for the Count of Savoy, sending in reports, and then I was scouting the works at Reggio Emilia where Hawkwood intended us to lay a siege. No sooner had I ridden the whole circuit of the walls than I was tasked with bringing in a convoy of food and camp supplies from Milan, which, thanks to God, I met halfway up the Via Francigena and didn't have to escort from Milan proper. By then, I was both afraid of the Visconti and increasingly unwilling to put myself in their power.

You are welcome to imagine me in some sort of moral quandary as I helped Hawkwood set the siege of Reggio Emilia in motion on behalf of Bernabò, while simultaneously loathing the whole family. But it seemed a piece with the politics of Italy in the year of Our Lord 1371, as our army, composed of English, Germans and Milanese, all pretended to be a 'free' company with no masters, and while the Lord Bernabò sent 'warnings' to his neighbours like the Lord of Mantua, Gonzaga – himself a newly created tyrant – suggesting that we were bandits and thieves and he himself was powerless to stop us.

'The last time you and Ambrogio pretended to be "free companions" not in service to Milan,' I said to Sir John, one beautiful afternoon in late May, 'Albornoz defeated you and a lot of men died.'

Sir John didn't even glance at me. For a man who'd been beaten a dozen times in the last ten years, he was very touchy about his defeats.

'I share your hesitation,' Sir John said. 'Let's take Reggio Emilia. Then we'll discuss the rest.'

If you want to know the key to Sir John's greatness, it was in that statement. He was a fine soldier, a solid tactician, to use an old Latin word – a fairly good man-at-arms, although I've known better. He was very subtle, especially in negotiations, and he could lie – and his ability to lie was unmatched. Also, he was almost never afraid, at least of men. Or God.

But his real power was his ability to focus on one task even when he had another task in hand. Sir John had increasingly complex relations with the Visconti, as I was soon to discover, and there was a lot going on in the summer of 1371. And despite all of that, we were going to take Reggio Emilia, because that would increase his reputation and give him a more secure bargaining base, which would allow him to affect all the various cogs and gears that were whirling around him. He never lost sight of ... anything.

So we probed Reggio Emilia and the papal army probed us. But the Pope hadn't paid his people that winter, and no one was responding to our aggressive patrols. By Our Lady, even my trip towards Bologna with Sister Marie had been virtually unnoticed and unopposed.

Did I mention that our war in Italy was complicated? We were fighting the Pope and his coalition, and we'd been specifically tasked by Bernabò to keep the Gonzaga lords of Mantua neutral. But Ludovico Gonzaga, the ruler of Mantua, had a son, Feltrino, and he had made himself Lord of Reggio Emilia a few years before and seemed ill-disposed to give it up to Lord Bernabò.

In other words, Mantua was neutral, but Mantua's son was the Lord of Reggio Emilia and was fighting for the Pope. And he was an easy petty warlord to hate. The day we opened our siege, an English archer, John Lake, was wounded and taken prisoner, and the Reggians shot him, still alive, off a trebuchet. He was dead as soon as it fired, of course, but the deliberate horror of the killing had the opposite of the local tyrant's intended effect. He meant us to be terrified. Instead, we were all angry.

Ambrogio thought it was just a piece of theatre, and said so. Antonio actually smiled, and as I was there, all I could think was that the Gonzaga and the Visconti were birds of a feather.

Sir John merely smiled his very slight smile.

The next day he summoned me. He was armed and armoured, sitting on an excellent warhorse at the head of our camp, which was itself fortified. Nights were cold, and all our people were in little hovels built of wattle and daub – solid shelters with their own hearths. Down by the river, a line of women did laundry, and the sound of their young voices rose to us on the breeze. I rode up, and he waved me over.

'William, we have a problem,' he said.

I nodded. We had a host of problems. I was thinking of hiring a notary just to keep track of all the things I had to do.

'Money,' Hawkwood said.

I must have nodded vigorously. Listen, I'd brought my company's payroll from Savoy – just three months in gold. For my full company, three months' pay represented almost four thousand gold florins, a terrifying amount of money to guard. Let me put this another way. I had money from my wife, and three good estates that paid an income. If I had to pay my company of seventy lances for three months, I'd be a pauper.

And that's for seventy lances – roughly two hundred and fifty men. Seventy fully armoured men-at-arms, seventy armed squires, and seventy archers. A variable number of pages, usually armed, but mostly there as horse-holders and grooms.

So – money.

Hawkwood looked at me from under his eyebrows.

'You paid your men,' he said.

'Yes,' I agreed.

'I wished you'd spoken to me first,' he said. 'Milan hasn't paid the summer wages yet, and I have people who haven't been paid for almost a year. Now they're even louder in demanding money.'

I saw his problem, but I wasn't going to withhold my men's pay because the Visconti couldn't cover their debts, and I said so.

Hawkwood shook his head. 'I would only have asked you to go somewhere else to pay them. Anyway, it's done.'

'What's wrong with the Visconti?' I asked.

Hawkwood glanced at me. 'They're out of money,' he said. 'Everyone is. The Pope can't pay, and now the Visconti can't pay. But like children, they continue to squabble, and to expect us to dance to their tunes. Bernabò keeps offering me estates and bribes to keep fighting, as if, by enlisting me, I'll keep the war going.' He shrugged.

'Do you refuse them?' I asked.

Hawkwood grinned mirthlessly and I saw that he was really ageing.

'Of course not!' he said. 'I take them, and send another letter demanding the wages.'

'And the Pope's no better?'

Hawkwood was watching the walls of Reggio Emilia.

'The Pope has some very important advantages,' he said. 'Better banks, and a widespread system for collecting funds.' He waved a hand as if slapping away an insect. 'That's for another day. But after we take Reggio Emilia, we will ... slow down.' He smiled wickedly. 'And perhaps start taking our wages in direct contributions, like the old days in France.'

I had nothing to add.

'William,' Hawkwood said, 'tell me about the Duke of Clarence.'

I looked around.

Hawkwood smiled his fox's smile. 'No one to overhear us.'

So I told him. In detail.

He nodded thoughtfully. And his eyes met mine.

'I have a letter from Bernabò,' he said, 'demanding that you cease asking questions. I have had a conversation with Ambrogio that was ... difficult.'

He watched me like a hawk. I nodded.

'Bernabò and Galeazzo do not agree themselves as to our strategy,' he said. 'And as I say, they aren't paying. And your count's little war in the Piedmont is heating up. I want you to keep an eye on all of that. And, William, I really do want to know what happened to Clarence.'

I nodded.

'But I want you to be very careful,' he said.

'You don't need to tell me,' I said.

I rode straight from that meeting to my pavilion, where I grabbed Marc-Antonio.

'Black-Beard,' I said.

I had to remind him of the whole episode. And then he called to

Ewan, who came in and said he'd been wounded, which I remembered.

They didn't know. *They didn't know.*

I began to fear that Black-Beard had escaped. I knew I'd put him down, but if no one had bound him as a prisoner ...

I wrote to Fiore, but that letter could take months to deliver and more months for a reply to reach me.

It was mid-June before I was able to think about Clarence's death again. I escorted convoys and skirmished with some very unmotivated papal mercenaries east of Reggio Emilia, a skirmish whose most memorable feature was that one of their men-at-arms, unhorsed in the initial mêlée, surrendered to Pilgrim. As knights do not usually surrender to dogs, it was perhaps the high point of the summer. Pilgrim sat on the man, unable to penetrate his armour, but he stayed down, very much afraid.

Anyway, the knight clearly wanted out of the war. It was becoming increasingly clear that the Pope wasn't going to rescue Reggio Emilia.

It was also clear that the Lord of Mantua, Ludovico Gonzaga, was not actually neutral. He was sending food to his son Feltrino, and we didn't have the manpower to fully encircle the town.

I had other problems – the small but very real problems of command. Bibbo's return moved men around in my company, and the fact was that I had two different bodies of men – the veterans of the Holy Land, under l'Angars, and the 'New English', as almost everyone called them, under Hales and Fenton, with Thorald as their master-archer. The problem was that men like Grice and de la Motte and Lapot had far more experience of war and command than Hales or Fenton. And my veterans were resentful of serving under Hales, who was acerbic when he should have been funny, and aloof when he should have tried a little friendship.

So, in late June, I nearly lost half my people in a botched raid on one of the city's outskirts. We were only saved from being ambushed by Dick Thorald's sharp eyes and suspicious nature, and we had to run all the way back to our camp with our tails between our legs.

Sir John had a few choice words for me, which culminated with, 'You're too kindly with your children. Shake them up, or I'll do it for you.'

That hurt, and I was probably red with fury, but a day later I knew he was right. I placed Lapot in command of my left division as corporal, with de la Motte as his standard-bearer and lieutenant. Hales collected his pay and left me, and I had a miserable week, as I had liked Hales. But he went off to serve Hereford, and Fenton stayed, as did Thorald.

We had other problems. Sir John's Company was edging towards mutiny. The lack of money was crippling, and our own patrols became as lacklustre as the papal mercenaries we faced. Nor was our situation improved when we all learnt that the Count of Savoy had engaged Anichino Baumgarten, a well-known scion of the Baumgarten mercenary family, for a very high rate of pay. I confess I felt a trifle betrayed myself. The count was paying Germans to do his fighting. The news was softened by the knowledge that the Germans were going to be garrisoned in the Prince of Achaea's former domains. Listen, I loved serving with Hawkwood – I enjoyed that he called me his sword. But I'd have left him in an hour to be in direct service to the count, especially in a war that had some causes and consequences I understood.

Closer to home, Lady Janet returned. She had gone home to settle matters of her own estates – the crown of France was powerful enough that the rule of law was re-established in southern France. Hawkwood had clearly thought she'd never come back. I won't say that he disliked her, merely that her desire to serve as a knight was no longer 'convenient'. He didn't need women in armour. His company had changed a great deal – he had fewer archers, more Italians. It was still the best military organisation in Italy. But it wasn't the grim assemblage of veteran routiers it had been in '64.

Take that as you will, Janet brought with her a great deal of gossip from the French and Savoyard courts. Indeed, it was she who brought us all the news of Baumgarten being hired by the Green Count. And the terrible tale of the rout of all the English armies in France, which she told with the relish of a Frenchwoman for the defeat of her personal enemies. Knolles' forces scattered and defeated, hundreds of Englishmen killed or captured.

I was appalled, and yet not surprised. I'd seen the confusion in the commands, and the pettiness of some of the officers, at first hand.

She sat in my pavilion. It was early evening, high summer in Lombardy. Fields of wheat glowed in the last of the sun, and

Christopher was whistling a *Sanctus*, and the smell of our cook fires mostly covered the smell of our privies. I had red hangings inside my tent, all tied back to cool it and catch a little breeze. Janet sat on one of my chests, and I sat on the other, like figures in a romance or a painted manuscript I'd seen at Pavia, except that the manuscript didn't include a large boar-hound perched on the bed. Pilgrim would sit *between* any two people, as if to be the focus of all attention.

Marc-Antonio served us wine, and then I motioned to him to sit. I had Christopher as a squire, and it was high time Marc-Antonio was knighted. I had sent to his father, asking his advice about the young man's future. He'd been with me enough years to deserve his own lance, at least. Alternatively, his father might want a professional soldier for Venice. In the meantime, I was accustomed to treating him as a younger peer, and Janet had always liked him.

She was wearing a kirtle with a knight's belt over it, a heavy, practical baselard hanging from the belt. Janet was a remarkably attractive woman, despite a broken and badly set nose and a little too much brightness in her eyes. She had muscles on her muscles, and she was tall and deep-breasted. It was odd – I've said this before – but I seldom thought of her as an attractive woman. When we'd taken her from the town where she'd been assaulted and her father killed, we'd all stayed clear of her a bit. Later, she was Richard Musard's lover, and then Andy Belmont's, and all through that she was a 'man-at-arms'. She was a comrade, and that was that. Except that occasionally I'd see beneath the armour, so to speak.

I mentioned that Andy sent his regards, and she smiled.

'I always liked him,' she said, as if she hadn't always liked all her lovers, which may be the truth of it.

'He was a damn good companion in France,' I said, and told her a few of my adventures in France. She nodded.

'The count sent you a letter,' she said with a smile.

She produced it from within her kirtle, and I read it carefully, enjoying the man's flattery. It was remarkably empty of anything *but* flattery.

'He might have saved the parchment,' I said.

She smiled her slightly twisted smile. A sword cut, many years ago, had made her lips very slightly uneven.

'He values you,' she said. She was playing with her dagger hilt.

'You know that he's eventually going to break with the Visconti, don't you?'

There it was. I tensed.

She raised an eyebrow. 'Come on, William,' she said.

I glanced at Marc-Antonio. He nodded.

'I agree, milady,' he said. 'All the players are about to change.'

I probably cursed, or blasphemed, because I had really liked my life – as a military courtier, as an elite messenger. As Emile's husband, rather than as a routier. And when the game changed like this, when all the chessmen changed sides, men like me were often the ones who lost most.

Janet smiled. 'I want to go back to wearing armour,' she said, changing the subject. 'Will you please plead my cause with Sir John, before I break his head with my sword hilt?'

I smiled. 'Why ask Sir John?' I said. 'I'll take you and your people right now.'

She had three lances of her own, excellent people, Flemish archers.

She smiled, and that smile was so big that it seemed you could fall into it. Janet was not given to many smiles. It was nice to see.

'I accept,' she said. 'Damn it, William! I won't make trouble.'

'I have most of the old lances anyway,' I said. 'I'll put you with de la Motte.'

I didn't know it, but taking Janet, who was an expert lance *and* a very literate noblewoman who could act as my notary, served to drive another small wedge between me and Sir John. Like the money, it wasn't a major issue, but it annoyed him, and he made a few pointed remarks, which I was old enough, at the age of thirty, to ignore. It still seems odd to me – I'd solved a problem for him.

Janet changed my professional life. She was a detailed planner – she thought well ahead. I thought that I was expert in these matters, but once I gave her the authority to requisition or purchase food and wagons, she began to plot to feed us weeks in advance. She put money into the grain market, buying wheat that had not yet been harvested. She knew bankers and pawnbrokers, and she laid out a scheme by which we'd become our own bank to lend money to our soldiers in the winters, saving usury fees and making a small profit.

She also kept a calendar, so that we remembered all of our various appointments and assignments. Each morning, she instituted a meeting at which she would run through the day's activities and missions. Some men resented her, but de la Motte and l'Angars and Lapot were all her old friends, and none of them felt threatened by her. In two weeks, we were the best fed, best looking of the contingents around Reggio Emilia. Janet made the time for us that I used on training them.

I began to remember what I liked about war. The practice. The comradery. The feeling of purpose. Because my troops were still being paid, I had more latitude with my discipline than Sir John, and I could keep my men patrolling. Consequently, Sir John kept us busy.

In summer, I had a letter from Sister Marie in Rome, delivered by a friend of Father Angelo's, a priest from the Vatican who showed me a ring with a donat's cross carved in it.

'I was to deliver this directly into your hands,' he said.

I put the ring on with delight, having lost mine in France. Father Angelo, who had been home in Verona and only recently returned to us, his mercenary flock, put a hand on the man's shoulder.

'I am to tell you that this really is Father Cosimo,' he said, 'and I have known him all my life.'

All the security was revealed when I saw the contents of the letter.

'I have found the Labrizas,' she said. 'There are two families, who seem to be interrelated. But there is a lay sister in a convent near Mantua with that name, and a monk here in Rome remembers that she has a sister who is a famous cook.'

This is what I meant when I said I forgot about Clarence's murder until June. To be honest, I'd almost forgotten the whole matter. Again. This time, in the routine, day-to-day running of my company.

On a positive note, I suspect my lack of action had lulled Ambrogio and Antonio into assuming that I had reacted as might be expected to the Visconti threats.

I summoned Beppo.

'I have a difficult matter for you,' I said.

'Beppo was born to undertake difficult matters,' Beppo said. 'Imagine, if you will, *illustrio*, how difficult it is for Beppo to attract a woman, and yet how very often Beppo is successful, and there you have a measure of how fit he is for the most difficult activities.'

Sweet Christ, how I loved Beppo. Next to Janet and Bibbo, the most useful member of my compagnia, or perhaps neck and neck with Christopher.

I gave him the name of the convent. It was south and west of Mantua itself.

'I need you to visit this convent—'

'Oh, the good sisters will love beautiful Beppo ...' he muttered.

'Tell them you are a demonic apparition,' I said.

He shook his head. 'Always ends badly for the demon,' he said. 'What, then?'

'I need to know if there is a sister formerly known as Labriza,' I said.

Beppo looked at me for a long time.

'This is the Clarence matter,' he said.

Well ... Beppo. The man knew things. I shouldn't have been surprised.

'Yes,' I allowed.

Beppo looked at me like a man buying an old horse. I waited him out. Finally he spoke.

'*Boso*,' he said cautiously. 'Do you remember sending Beppo to watch Alba?'

I did not.

'The week ...' He looked away. 'After your wife died,' he said.

In his hesitation, I saw suddenly how careful they were all being around me. Grief is an odd thing – a high wall against reality, in many ways.

'No,' I admitted.

He nodded. 'Ahh,' he said. 'Beppo apologises, *illustrio*. Beppo had assumed that you stopped asking questions ... for reasons. Beppo knows a few things about threats, eh?'

'I don't understand,' I said.

Beppo pulled at his demonically forked beard. The man had a terrible face, as I've said, and then he proceeded to wear a forked beard. It was almost gallant, how he played to his own deformities.

'You have never asked Beppo what he learnt at Alba,' he said, and shrugged. 'Beppo assumed that the good knight had been threatened by the Visconti and wanted everything forgotten.'

I might have laughed. Grief is indeed like a high wall. I had no memory of sending him on a mission – that was lost in so many other things – but when he recalled it to me, I could just see it, so to speak, as if through a tangle of thorns.

'Beppo didn't find the vial of poison or the dagger,' he said with a self-exculpatory shrug. 'But everyone Beppo spoke to thought that the Visconti did it – most especially the young one, Gian Galeazzo.'

I sat back, feeling as if I'd been blind.

'But—'

'Beppo has no hard evidence,' Beppo said. 'But Beppo knows a few things. One is that the Milanese doctor ran the night the duke died. And was found a few villages away, with his rings cut off and a broad smile under his chin.' He made a throat-cutting gesture. 'Another is this Labriza woman. Beppo heard of her. Beppo never heard that she was Mantuan.' He smiled evilly. 'Perhaps Beppo is not the only smart one.'

I got up, walked out of my pavilion, and walked all the way around it. And then went back and sat with Beppo. I just had to be sure we were not overheard.

'You think the Visconti ...?'

Beppo played with his beard. 'Beppo is very careful about what he says about great men. Beppo is especially careful when the great men routinely kill men like Beppo for stealing a chicken or a rabbit, much less fucking serious shit like this.'

I nodded.

'But,' Beppo said, 'you treat Beppo like a man. Beppo is loyal – when he's well paid, eh, *illustrio*? So here's what Beppo thinks, in his private heart.' He lowered his voice so that it was little more than a coarse, garlic-coated breath. 'Gian Galeazzo always wanted the English princeling dead, and in the end, he found people who would do it for him. And then his father, who wanted his pretty towns back, sent in his assassins to clean up. It was never Galeazzo's plot, until his son did the deed. But once it was done ...'

I could see it. 'Gian Galeazzo used Camus's people?'

Beppo shrugged. 'In this, I am ignorant.'

I thought of the slips of parchment. Of the statement that 'we could be paid twice'.

'Find me this nun?' I asked.

'Beppo is loyal, and Beppo is usually brave,' the ugly man said. 'But *illustrio*, you are sending Beppo with a lit torch into a room full

386

of black powder. Antonio's men watch everything you do, *Illustrio*. Beppo assumes you know this.'

I looked at him, considering.

'And to this, let Beppo add ...' He looked away, outside and then back. 'If if Beppo leads the Visconti to this nun, she is dead.'

'Fuck,' I suspect I said. I remember thinking *how on earth did I get into this?*

Beppo nodded.

'I need to think,' I said.

Sometimes, God moves in mysterious ways. Perhaps I say that too often, but then, God just keeps on moving.

Hawkwood summoned me. I went, already worried that I was somehow found out – that he was going to warn me that the Visconti were coming for me.

Instead ...

'I need you to make a slight navigational error,' he said.

I knew that tone – the fox had a plan. I was perfectly willing to engage in some mischief on his behalf.

'Where to, My Lord?' I asked sweetly.

'I want you to burn the Gonzaga palace at Guastalla,' he said. 'It's really just a glorified hunting lodge. Sack it thoroughly. Take anything of value. Kill anyone you fancy needs killing.'

The two of us pulled out our various itineraries and looked at distances and practicalities.

'Why Guastalla?' I asked.

Hawkwood smiled the fox's smile. 'You know that our opponent here is Gonzaga of Mantua's son, eh?' he asked.

'Of course,' I answered.

'Bernabò offered him money for Reggio Emilia,' Hawkwood said. 'Felestrino Gonzaga turned him down, and said, "My father will keep me supplied until Hell is full." It's Mantuan food that is flowing into Reggio Emilia, and we lack the manpower to stop it.'

Just to be sure, we didn't lack the manpower. We lacked the gold. If our troops had been paid, we'd never have let a single convoy through. Even as it was, my people were making a good profit hitting their convoys, and Pilgrim was getting fat on Mantuan sausage, but that's another story.

I nodded. 'So we're going to deliver a message,' I said.

'Exactly,' Sir John said. 'We'll "mistakenly" burn a Gonzaga palace, and perhaps the father will stop sending the son food. All a terrible misunderstanding.'

I drew a little picture to show myself the relative positions of the Gonzaga palace-town at Guastalla – about halfway between Reggio Emilia and Mantua, off to our east.

'I assume this town is where the convoys are built up?' I asked.

Hawkwood nodded.

'Shouldn't you send the troops who need to be paid?' I asked.

Hawkwood laughed. 'Damn,' he said. 'You're more of a routier than I gave you credit for. No, I want a message sent, not the whole-sale rape of a duchy. Send your lads. They'll do a professional job.'

'Give me a day to prepare,' I said.

I gave l'Angars very exact orders. I duplicated them to de la Motte, and then I sent Janet, in armour, with l'Angars, because she has decided 'views' on the discipline of soldiers and I knew she'd make sure we were, for the most part, gentle as lambs.

When we rode out of Hawkwood's camp before dawn, we went north, as if we were meeting the latest of our own food convoys from Milan – in fact, I sent six lances under Tom Fenton to do just that – and then I turned east. My pilgrim itineraries said it was twenty miles.

Just east of the hamlet of Sesio, I found two farmers with a cart, watching two women cutting wheat in a nearby field. I scooped them up.

'Gentlemen,' I said, 'I need guides to Guastalla. I can make this the best day of your lives, or the worst.'

Both of them agreed that they would prefer to have the best day of their lives, so I separated them, giving one to Beppo to watch, and the other to Marc-Antonio.

We moved quickly after that. East of Cadelbosco di Sopra, we crossed the boundary stones of the old Demesne of Mantua, but you mustn't imagine that we did so with any fanfare. Northern Italy is a patchwork of polities, and it's like a quilt that's been repaired too many times, so that the edges fray and the patches on top of the patches lose their colour. Were we in Mantua yet? Hard to tell.

But Mantua wasn't at war with the Visconti, and regardless of all my precautions, there was no force of lances waiting for us at the border and no ambush deep in the countryside. Fighting Turks had probably overprepared me for Italy. Timurtash Bey would never have allowed my force, unobserved, so close to his master's capital.

We were moving in broad daylight, at a trot. We had spare horses, and we didn't need to stop at crossroads because our peasant guides were both terrified and greedy. My prickers, who were mostly older pages led by Christopher, had the sheep and cattle cleared off the roads before we got bottlenecked.

A little after the bells for Sext, we rode into Guastalla. My archers already had the town gates – l'Angars had secured the Mantua road and northern side half an hour before, against no opposition. The town didn't even have a communal guard on duty.

I rode into the square opposite the small Gonzaga palace. Next to the church, it was the best building in the town, a mid-sized brick and stone structure that aped the manners of the Visconti without in any way rivalling their sheer magnitude.

The podestà and the head of the town council were waiting for me. They didn't have halters around their necks, but that was the idea – de la Motte had spared no effort in terrifying them.

'Gentlemen,' I said, with what I hoped was a terrible smile, 'do you know why I have come to visit you?'

The town councillor had no idea. I looked at the poor man. A prosperous merchant, he was probably wondering in that moment why he had spent time and money winning an office that was bidding fair to get him killed.

The podestà was a Mantuan lord, and he had both bluster *and* an understanding of why we were there. All read in the stiffness of his back and the set of his lips.

'Your routiers will pay for this insult,' he said.

I nodded at the small palace. 'You serve the Gonzaga, yes?' I asked.

'I have that honour,' he said. 'And if you take any action—'

'Spare me,' I said. 'I have a sword and you do not. Let me be clear. This town is the location at which the Lord Ludovico Gonzaga assembles the relief convoys for his son, the Lord Feletrino, at Reggio Emilia. You don't have to shake your heads, gentlemen. I not only know it to be true from men I've captured –' and I smiled again – 'but I have taken the trouble to seize the tax lists held here, and my notary assures me that you are taking taxes in kind and shipping them to Reggio Emilia.'

The town councillor's face spasmed. His mouth opened and closed like a fish out of water.

'Yes,' he said.

The podestà glowered. 'Fucking peasant,' he said.

'By the laws of war, this town and all in it are now mine, forfeit,' I said.

'The town is unprotected!' the councillor cried out.

'The more fool you,' I said. 'Your town was participating in a war. Perhaps you should have arranged to guard yourselves.'

'He told me!' the man suddenly shrieked.

The podestà shrugged in a way that said he thought he and I were 'men of the world' together, and I should understand.

I nodded. '*Illustrio*,' I said, addressing the merchant, 'I suspect that the podestà has very little to lose in this matter, while you and your people have a very great deal to lose. So I will be brief. I will destroy the palace to its foundations, as a message to my lord. If you want your town intact, you can ransom it. Otherwise, the town and the church will be included in my lesson to your lord.'

'You are making a very grave error,' the podestà said. 'The Visconti have promised that my lord would be neutral.'

I nodded. 'Yes,' I said. 'I'm sure we all believe whatever the Visconti promise.'

He flushed red.

In less than half an hour, the merchant was back, with four fellows. By then, the palace was looted even of wall hangings. We packed everything into the carts that we found in the palace courtyard – carts rounded up to be used in the next convoy to Reggio Emilia.

I had two men who understood the new black powder, and they were placing their barrels in the basement – aye, and stirring the contents. If you ship powder already mixed, the charcoal can separate out from the saltpetre and sulphur, or so I'm told.

'We can pay you a thousand gold florins,' the merchant said.

'Two thousand,' I said.

He gulped.

'Spare me your insults,' I said, before he could speak.

'We will be fucking beggars,' he said.

'No,' I said. 'But if you don't find two thousand florins, I'll cheer-fully make you beggars. Forever. Stop fucking around.'

It's easy to overawe a man when you are atop sixteen hands of magnificent warhorse, in full armour, and the man is on foot below you without even a dagger. In fact, I rather liked the merchant – he wasn't oily or evasive. His anger was perfectly sensible, and he was afraid like an intelligent man, not like a coward.

And I suppose you might expect that I'd feel guilty, extorting money from the merchants of Guastalla. But I didn't. They'd made a serious mistake, as had their lord. Now they were going to pay.

I wasn't even going to burn their houses.

It was all a great deal more civilised than in France.

Before we fired the charges on the palazzo, I sent Beppo with Marc-Antonio and two Italian pages off into the countryside to find the convent. Have you forgotten it? I hadn't. This is what I mean by 'God's will'. The raid on Guastalla was the perfect cover for Beppo to go to the convent, and I was pretty certain that I'd deceived the Visconti spies as to my intentions at least twice over. Even if they had an agent concealed among my own people, which I doubted, that agent would have to look through the chaos of the sack of a palazzo to see Beppo slip away.

We stayed in Guastalla through the night, in full possession of all of their gates and public buildings. Whereas an army of mercenaries can vanish in a town of a hundred thousand people, like Florence, my two hundred and fifty were effortlessly in charge of Guastalla, a town of five thousand.

Beppo returned before first light. I was sleeping under a cart in the palazzo courtyard – I didn't want to be available to an assassin.

I poured water over my head.

'What?' I asked.

'Your Marc-Antonio did the business better than Beppo,' he said. 'We found the nun.'

'Let's get her,' I said.

'She no longer matters,' Beppo said.

I was too sleepy for this.

'She's dead?'

'No,' Beppo said. He liked drama. 'While Marc-Antonio speaks to

391

the sister through the grille, Beppo is visiting the kitchen. The cook is there, *illustrio*. She is in the abbey kitchen, cooking. The Labriza. Remember, I have seen her.'

'So,' I asked.

'Beppo has her,' he said. 'She knows her life is over. She spoke to Beppo.'

'Christ,' I said. 'Where is she?'

'Outside,' Beppo said. 'We need to be rid of her.'

'What?' I asked. I was still asleep.

'She *knows*, My Lord.' Beppo's voice was again a garlic-laced whisper. 'And she knows that the Visconti killed her parents. Just a month ago.'

'Christ,' I said.

'Beppo thinks it unfair that Beppo was granted this face when his sins are so very venal, and Gian Galeazzo Visconti is beautiful like an angel and yet he kills people's parents to cover his other murders.'

'Christ,' I said. Again. The Visconti have that effect on me.

'Listen to Beppo,' the twisted man said. 'We cannot ever be seen with her. Or we are all dead. We need to be rid of her. Beppo was tempted to do it himself – as mercy, the way you kill a badly wounded friend.'

His voice was quiet and terrible. Beppo had lived a harder life than I had, and sometimes he reminded me.

'Listen,' I said. 'Take her to Venice. To Carlo Zeno.'

Beppo considered me for a moment.

'Yes,' he agreed. 'Good. Beppo hates killing women.'

Venice. The most powerful state in Italy, except perhaps Genoa. One of the few states that the Visconti could not, under any circumstances, offend. A place where I had powerful friends. And where Albin and his wife Caterina were.

'No one will look for you, moving east while we withdraw west,' I said. 'Take Marc-Antonio.'

'Yes,' Beppo said. 'You are a good man. Beppo needs money.'

I had two thousand florins in gold. I gave him a hundred, and another hundred for Marc-Antonio.

'I need to speak to her myself,' I said. Perhaps I was just stubborn.

So there, in the ruddy light of an August dawn, I met the cook, Labriza. She was a big woman, and she didn't look like a cook. She was strong, attractive as only an experienced older woman can be, with a hard set to her mouth and surprisingly beautiful hands.

'*Ma donna*,' I said.

She looked at me and looked away.

'Tell him what you told Beppo,' Beppo said.

So she did. She said it all, in detail – more detail than I'll tell you. She wasn't sure who had killed Clarence, but it scarcely mattered, because she knew, as the head cook, who had tried to bribe her to kill him in the weeks before.

When she was done, she shrugged.

'When I was offered the position,' she said, 'I thought that I was made, you know? My life was settled.' She smiled bitterly. 'Instead, I was a dead woman.'

'I'm sending you to Venice,' I said. 'I have friends there. You will be safe. With a little luck, we will find you a great house in which to cook.'

She looked at me. 'I have a daughter,' she said. 'Save her, and I will pray for you all my life.'

'Fuck,' Beppo said. 'Fuck.'

It took hours to secure the daughter, and we burnt some barns to cover our movements. I suppose that makes me a bad man, because those peasants had done nothing to warrant the burning of their barns, but war is war, and investigating the death of a member of the Plantagenet family had become a kind of war.

After a silent Sext, I sent my advance guard down the road towards Sesio, and an hour later, with no ill reports, I sent my convoy of gold and loot in their wake. Under an oak tree outside town, I shook hands with Beppo and Marc-Antonio and gave Marc-Antonio my little store of twisted parchments with the letter *S*. They rode off north, towards Mantua, dressed like travellers.

I'd done what I could. I prayed, then and there, to God to protect them.

As I rode through a brilliant August day, I considered what I knew, and what there was to know. And I wondered ... Honestly, I wondered if it mattered. The Visconti were vain, greedy, arrogant bastards who wanted absolute dominion – but then, so were most of the lords of Italy. So, in fact, was the king of France. The morality of it all was sticky.

On the other hand, I had made a promise to Princess Isabella.

I didn't need anyone to tell me the consequences of the letter I was contemplating.

In the end, it was the knowledge that the Visconti had killed the cook's parents in their attempts to find and kill her that decided me.

I was angry. Perhaps I was angry with God, for taking Emile. Perhaps I was angry with Count Amadeus, for hiring a German. But in some way, I was angry with princes, for the way they treated people. And that focused on the Visconti. I could write a secret letter to Princess Isabella, and there would be consequences – most of all, a change in the English alliances.

But damn it, I wanted justice. I wanted more than just a letter to a woman who might or might not have the power to take action.

No one got in our way as we retreated across southern Lombardy.

Which was lucky for them.

We rode back into the army camp north of Reggio Emilia on the first day of September. I turned all the money and loot over to Hawkwood, and he used the money and loot to pay his two hundred lances. He was scrupulous in handing me back almost a third of it, which I put in the bank against a darker day.

'You put the town to ransom?' he laughed. 'William, you have always been a lion on the battlefield, but this is the first time I've seen you as a master of the monetary element of this profession. Two thousand florins? You're not my sword. You're my banker!'

I was happy with his praise, although some of it was two-edged. I told him the story of the raid, and detailed to him what I'd told the podestà.

'Beautiful,' he said.

'I have another matter to discuss,' I said.

Hawkwood sat back. He had a good iron folding stool with a tapestry seat, and he often placed it against the central pole of his pavilion so that he had a backrest. The more time you spend in harness, the more you want to rest your back.

'Money?' he asked.

'The Duke of Clarence,' I said.

Hawkwood nodded. 'I see,' he said.

He called his squire, a young Englishman whom some men claimed was Hawkwood's brother, and told him to clear the pavilion for fifty paces around and stay away. We heard the commotion outside, but the men had just been paid at least part of their wages, and discipline was good.

'Speak,' he said.

'Gian Galeazzo had Lionel killed,' I said. 'Galeazzo sent his killers to clean up afterwards.'

'You are certain?' he asked.

I shrugged. 'I wasn't there,' I said. 'Short of that, yes.'

Hawkwood drank off his wine. He was staring out of the door.

'You know, William,' he said, 'in many ways, I wish you hadn't told me this. And then, on the other hand, I knew it all along, and I had to expect that you'd stay on it.' He looked at me over the rim of his wine cup – a silver chalice from a church, by the way. 'Once you get on something, you never let go. You're like a dog with a bone.'

He glanced at Pilgrim, who reacted to the word 'bone' in English with an enthusiastic tail-wag and a strongly indicated desire to bark, but he was a good boy and stayed silent.

'Dogs bury bones,' I said.

'William,' he said in admonishment.

We sat in silence for a moment.

'Do you have evidence?' he asked.

'Yes,' I said.

That surprised him. 'Where?'

'Safe places,' I said.

He stared out of the door again.

'How safe?' he asked.

I frowned. 'As safe as I can make them,' I said. 'I very much doubt that the people who are responsible could find them – or even, having found them, act.'

Hawkwood pursed his lips. 'Don't be hasty,' he said. 'Let's take Reggio Emilia.'

I agreed.

CHAPTER TWO

REGGIO EMILIA

September 1371 – June 1372

I t was less than ten days later that the Lord of Reggio Emilia handed over the keys of his city to Hawkwood, and led his soldiers and baggage wagons north and east on the road to Mantua. Young Feltrino was full of bluster, and Hawkwood was bored, hearing him out.

'My father will make you pay for the destruction of our town!' Feltrino spat.

'Your town was unharmed,' Sir John said. 'Your palace was destroyed.'

'You have no idea what we can do to you …' Feltrino said.

Hawkwood smiled. 'Well, on the other hand, you have an *excellent* idea of what we can do to you. Please send your esteemed father my regrets that he allowed himself to become embroiled in a war for which he was unprepared.'

As I say, in the end, Feltrino rode away.

Almost immediately, we became the garrison of Reggio Emilia. No papal army threatened us because they were covering Bologna to the south. There were a thousand rumours, all the usual – that the Holy Roman Emperor was returning to the field, that the Pope was going to attack Milan directly, that Venice and Genoa were close to war. We heard rumours from the Piedmont, which was not so very far away. The Green Count appeared to be throwing in his lot with the Marquis of Saluzzo, against whom he had initially appeared to be at war. Savoy was edging closer to war with Milan.

Meanwhile, Bernabò negotiated with Hawkwood for a new *condotta* while not having paid for the previous year and further, demanded that we restore the money we'd taken from the Mantuans and pay reparations. Sir John responded in his subtle way, not by telling Bernabò that we'd done it to get Gonzaga to stop sending his son supplies, but in a much more evasive manner. He reminded Bernabò that he had not paid the company, and pointed out that as we were apparently a 'free company', we owed no allegiance to anyone – a thinly veiled threat to keep the very rich city of Reggio Emilia for ourselves.

In late October, Bernabò came in person.

He came with a company of good lances, and a pair of beautiful sisters who were both his lemans, and he was the same boorish, violent man I'd known two years before. Yet now, seeing him fondle his mistresses or drink to drunkenness, I thought him to be the best of the Visconti, not the worst. He wore his sins openly, and he, at least, had a sense of humour. He settled with Sir John in one evening, and produced hard specie to pay the back wages – or rather, to pay about half of them, claiming that the loot we'd taken from Mantua would pay the other half.

'You told me to return it,' Hawkwood said.

'That's between you and Mantua,' Bernabò said.

'That's not the tune you played this morning,' Hawkwood said.

Bernabò shrugged. 'The truth is whatever I tell you it is,' he said. 'I'm paying the gold.'

Hawkwood nodded. 'You have paid half the gold,' he said.

'I'm telling you that you've been paid,' Bernabò said, as if, by saying it, he could make it true.

Hawkwood shook his head. 'That's not how it works,' he said.

I had a letter from Fiore, disclaiming all knowledge of Black-Beard. The rest of the news was better – Fiore was coming back to Italy, with Nerio. I got that news in October, and within a week we had a truce between the Pope and the Visconti. I took some leave and met them in Florence in December, and we celebrated Christmas together. Nerio was collecting money from relatives, and Fiore looked more prosperous than I'd ever seen him.

Marc-Antonio and Beppo also met me in Florence.

That was a good Christmas – the Christmas of 1371. We heard Mass at one of the smaller churches, and we bought each other presents in the market and then we went and listened to Landini at the Servite friars. He played on their organ for a while and then sang with the choir, and we were all transported.

That night, Nerio spoke of his frustrations and I of mine. Nerio was depressed and angry at how difficult it was to move the Catalans out of Thebes, and I spoke of my problems with Hawkwood and with war.

Nerio waved his wine cup. It was late. We were the only guests in a public inn, and even the servants were in bed, though they'd left a good store of wine out for us.

'Fiore tells me that your Prince Lionel was murdered,' he said.

I hushed him. 'We don't say these things out loud.'

Nerio laughed. 'Fuck that,' he said. 'The Visconti are just another family of criminals risen to power.'

Fiore laughed.

I shook my head. 'I had forgotten you, Nerio,' I said. 'I forgot that I had a friend who was so powerful that he could mock the Visconti.'

'Not powerful enough to take fucking Thebes,' he said. 'I need two thousand men and I don't have the funds. I don't suppose you'd come and fight for me for a year for free?'

I shook my head. 'I can't afford it,' I said.

'Nor can I,' Fiore said.

'Tell me about your murdered prince,' Nerio said.

So I did. I told him the whole thing. I cried when I came to Emile's death, and Fiore and Nerio put their hands on my back.

'You loved her so much, and yet you went off to bed with that Miriam woman,' Fiore said, sounding a little like an elderly aunt.

'Fiore,' Nerio snapped. 'Don't be an arse.'

'I don't understand!' Fiore said. 'I told him he was behaving badly and he tried to hit me.'

Nerio gave me a look of commiseration, but he put an arm around Fiore.

'Fiore, the rest of us often do the wrong thing,' he said.

'I have noticed this—' Fiore put in, and Nerio drove over him.

'But having done the wrong thing, we continue to live and breathe and have tempers and opinions,' he said.

Fiore nodded. 'But I told him ...'

Nerio smiled slightly. 'My dear Fiore,' he said. 'What have I taught you in Corinth?'

'Not always to say what I think – indeed, my mother often said the same, but in this case ...'

I'd never seen it before. Fiore was silenced by Nerio's look.

Nerio glanced at me. 'So Gian Galeazzo killed Clarence to arrange the return of his sister,' he said. 'Why'd he ever allow her to marry him, if he's such a little cock?'

'That's what I see,' I said.

Now Fiore was nodding with me. 'Unnatural,' he said. 'Despicable. I saw it with my own eyes.'

Nerio pursed his lips. 'And then Galeazzo sends killers to silence anyone who could talk.'

I nodded.

Nerio nodded again. 'But ...?'

I smiled. 'But I have some evidence and some witnesses put away.'

Nerio nodded again. 'Of course you do,' he said. 'William, I love you beyond all other men. In this you are unique. What do you plan to do about it?'

'I don't know yet,' I said. 'What are you doing about taking Thebes?'

He smiled. 'Shipping cargoes of currants,' he said. 'And saving my money.'

Christmas healed me. Perhaps not absolutely, but if I learnt one thing from my year of darkness, it is that friends are important, and two weeks in Florence with Fiore and Nerio were more restorative than victory or money.

Neither of them had any better idea than I had of what to do with the information I'd gathered. And to write it all out in a letter was to sign my own death warrant, and the warrant of the messenger, if we were discovered. And I suspected I was followed all the time – Nerio commented on it.

The last night, Fiore was playing with the four new pairs of gloves he'd purchased. Pilgrim was watching the gloves with far too much interest. Nerio was lying on the bed, the way he often did in the old days, before Alexandria, when we all lived together in Venice.

'Tell your friend the English princess,' he said. 'Let her deal with it. She's rich, powerful, and your duke's sister.'

Pilgrim leant towards Fiore, and I put a cautionary hand on his head.

'Come to Greece with me,' Nerio said. 'Sit in Corinth and blackmail the Visconti for a great deal of money.'

I probably gave a start. Nerio shrugged.

'I'm tempted to do it myself,' he said. 'It's a good secret. With it, you could bind an alliance or write a death sentence.'

'Mine,' I said.

'Not if you are in Greece,' Nerio said. 'They're not *that* powerful. This is the great secret that the bastards of this world don't want you to know. They're just not that powerful. From Greece you could shout this to the rooftops. Who'd stop you? The Turks?'

That wasn't my idea at all. I wanted to tell Galeazzo what I thought in person.

And I wasn't sure when, or how.

I went back to Reggio Emilia, and duty.

I'd bought Janet a pair of jewelled gloves in Florence, and she loved them, and it was while she embraced me that I thought to ask her.

'Do you know Enguerrand de Coucy?' I asked.

'Not well,' she said. 'But I have met him a few times.' She smiled her slightly twisted smile. 'He's a good man, in a very determined manner.' She glanced at me, almost shy, which was rare for her. 'He's one of the few men I've ever known who wanted to hear my fighting stories.'

Well. That bore some thought.

By late February, when all the roads were rivers, it was clear to us in Reggio Emilia that both the papacy and the Milanese were using the truce to raise money. Indeed, my letter from Nerio at Venice said that the money supply was limited because the Pope and the Visconti had borrowed everything they could, and no one had any hard currency to lend him.

He mentioned in passing that he'd seen Albin. I took that to mean that he had checked my arrangements and found them to be sufficient. He also sent me a new helmet, a remarkably beautiful one by my favourite Brescian armourer. It locked under the chin and had a beautiful tall plume-holder that would allow my people to see me on the battlefield, and Janet gave me a magnificent red *panache* to wear in it.

I already missed Nerio and Fiore both, but Fiore said Nerio wouldn't come back.

In March, when a watery sunshine betokened the arrival of a false spring, the papal captains began to move all along the Via Francigena. My little company's pay arrived from Savoy, indicating to me that the count was not yet breaking with the Visconti and relieving me of my greatest short-term anxiety. If the count had not paid, I would have had to take service directly with the Visconti, or find another contract. Hawkwood was right about me – I wasn't really good at the financial aspect of war. The pay convoy also brought me word of the death of John of Montferrat, who was holding a great deal of the land that the Visconti wanted, some of which had been the Duke of Clarence's – and who was, incidentally, a member of the same Palaeologoi family as the Emperor in Constantinople.

There was a great deal going on, and I wasn't as well informed as I would have liked.

But Janet was.

When we paid our troops, we'd made an astounding profit, mostly because Janet had been lending them my money at interest all winter, and now we collected. It seemed a little harsh to make a profit off my own soldiers, and I put the money we made aside to use on the company – better armour, fresh horses.

I won't bore you with the intimate details of running a company of mercenaries, but I will add that better discipline and trust in command saves money and makes everyone richer. Regular payments build trust and discipline, too. My people tended to look after their horses, and we still had the largest stock of Arabs in northern Italy – indeed, de la Motte had taken to breeding them in camp. But because our discipline was better, our horses lived better and longer, and we had more remounts.

The soft year – and it had been soft, before Reggio Emilia – had been good for us, and the winter in a city had given everyone a good rest.

Which was good, because suddenly the Pope had money, and the war that had been cold went hot in a matter of weeks.

In April, the man whom Messire Villani described as the '*Maestro di Guerra*', my old friend and enemy Galeotto Malatesta, the Lord of Rimini and one of Italy's most famous captains, finally achieved his lifelong ambition and was appointed by the Pope to command the papal armies at Bologna. Malatesta reminded me in many ways of Sir Robert Knolles – he was an able captain, and he was capable of financing his own war and running it like a company, for a profit.

That's where the similarities ended. Knolles had been badly defeated by the French because he lacked the social status to keep his captains together. Malatesta was one of Italy's great lords, and in addition to his all-around competence, he had a great name. He had also been playing the game for a long time. According to Villani, he was born in the year of Our Lord 1305, which made him older than Hawkwood – a solid sixty-seven years of age.

Almost immediately, the pressure on our front at Reggio Emilia increased, and all thoughts of the murdered Duke of Clarence vanished into the morass of daily patrolling, foraging, raids on the enemy and covering our own. Every day I wished for Giannis's stradiotes and John the Turk – but even without them, we had enough veterans of the Holy Land to hold the edge in cattle-raiding and horse-stealing. Hawkwood's men were paid at least part of their arrears, and they took an active part, and Ambrogio's Italians were almost as adept as we. Only the Germans, who preferred the day of battle, took little part in the patrolling.

Tom Fenton began to shine as a junior corporal, despite never having been to the Holy Sepulchre, and when he lifted a German captain's entire horse herd, he was the hero of the hour. The Birigucci brothers gave daily demonstrations of how much like life in the Scottish borders it was to be raised in central Italy, and Ewan and Mark and Beppo and Christopher raised hell wherever we rode. Janet took a long ride all the way around Modena, deep in the enemy's lands, and reaved an entire herd of beef destined to feed the papal armies.

All things told, May was a marvellous month for the 'English' and our Aethiopian, Hungarian, French, German and Italian friends and allies. By the end of the month, we'd lost only four men and gained in both repute and gold.

Hawkwood began to smile more. And late in the month, he ordered us forward.

'We've pinned his ears back,' Sir John said pleasantly, as our little army trotted down the road from Reggio Emilia, heading south-east towards Modena. We had about a thousand men, all mounted – about half English, and thus about one eighth archers. The Germans were the most heavily armoured, the Italians were usually the best hand-to-hand fighters, but we were the best organised, and we had the best horses. In fact, my people had *so many* horses that we left half our horse herd safe at Reggio Emilia.

Hawkwood was right. We'd won the patrol war out in the fields and at the crossroads and in the night. It had been hard work at first, but like a few flakes of snow in the Piedmont becoming an avalanche, each little raid and crossroads duel had magnified our superiority until the enemy abandoned the night altogether, and feared to ride abroad in troops smaller than a hundred men by day. They were taking their forage from the farms *behind* their positions.

And Hawkwood had bought the peasants. He did this mostly by buying provisions and preying on the papal logistics instead of the local people. It was a very successful system which I have striven ever since to emulate.

Malatesta retreated for two days, and then we discovered that he, too, was a canny old fox. He'd built himself a fortified camp with a wetland and a river in front of him while we were concentrating on his supplies. Now he marched into it and called for the militias of Bologna and Modena, and in a day we were outnumbered, camped in a bad position without enough clean water, staring across a swamp at Malatesta, who was no doubt laughing.

But it was fox versus fox, and Hawkwood was up to the strategic challenge. He sent Romney north, looking for a bridge or a ford, and me south, downstream. Greg Fox, who was still in Italy watching the fashions, found a stone bridge about four English miles south of our camp, and no guard, and I sent every man I could lay my hands on to hold the end of the bridge.

We decamped before the midges came out of the swamp at Matins, before the sun was up. With good guides, we retreated into the out-skirts of Rubiera and then turned south, leaving our campfires burning and our tents up behind us.

We rode fast, on open ground by the banks of the Secchia river, and we crossed the bridge in good order without meeting any opposi-tion. This sort of manoeuvre can only be attempted when you have the peasants on your side to ensure secrecy and to guide you in the darkness. When you hear of an exploit like this, you ask 'Why doesn't everyone perform a night flank march?' but in this case, and every case

I've known, it is the preconditions of the flanking move that ensure its success. It is not foolhardy bravery. It's careful planning and good guides.

And a little luck, like Greg Fox finding the bridge.

Malatesta awoke to find us on his side of the river and marching north, turning his flank and marching for Modena. He had no choice but to abandon his camp and come to face us. Our mounted army was faster than his footmen. He had a shorter distance to march.

In the end, we faced him across a patchwork of hedged fields and small irrigation ditches as the sun rose in the east. There was a ground fog, as there often is in Italy, and it was slow to burn off. We could see Malatesta's army moving – flashes of steel and coloured pennons above the low fog.

I was with Romney and Antonio Visconti, Ambrogio, his half-brother, and Hawkwood. We were all mounted. I was already on Percival, with Marc-Antonio right behind me. Pilgrim was chasing rabbits and generally annoying his master.

Hawkwood was as he always was – calm, precise. We were discussing how we'd form, when Tom Fenton, who'd been out with our light horse, cantered up and pointed at the fog.

'My lords, I believe that Messire Malatesta is coming straight for us. Now, if you please, messires.' Fenton, bless him, already had good Italian.

Hawkwood stood in his stirrups and I was reminded of Sir Nigel Loring.

'Well, well,' he said. He sat, and sawed at his reins. 'Never mind details. Get them formed, Richard. Sir William, attend me.'

Together we cantered down the long column of archers and men-at-arms, Pilgrim bounding along beside me, and some men cheered the dog. He was very popular. Hawkwood used the same words over and over, one of his little tricks for being obeyed precisely.

'When you arrive at the front, go in the direction that Richard Romney directs and form front immediately. Stand your ground until I order you forward. Now go!'

He must have said those words twenty times, in English, in French, in Italian and in German.

Antonio rode by me, as his Italians were near the rear of our force with my small *condotta*. He didn't smile at me – our friendship had, at some point, died. It seemed unfair to me, as he owed me his life several times over and several hundred ducats as well, but then I've noticed throughout my life that if the balance of a friendship tilts too far to one or the other, resentment forms.

Now, I had perhaps seventy lances then, and Antonio perhaps fifty in his own name. Together, we were perhaps one tenth of our army. Hawkwood rode with us all the way to the head of Antonio's knights, who were formed across the road like a wall of steel, in the best Milanese plate.

'Gentlemen, I want you to sweep out, on horseback, and embrace Lord Malatesta as if you love him,' Hawkwood said. He mimed his orders, sweeping his armoured arms in a wide bear hug. 'William will go north, and go around the left, and Antonio will go south, and go around our right.'

Antonio Visconti flashed me a smile. It was the first smile I'd had from him in the whole campaign.

'We come in from the flanks, eh? Perhaps we shake hands in the middle?'

I took his hand then.

'Split our ransoms?' I asked, like the old days.

'Never!' he said.

He regretted it, later.

Of course, he was still a Visconti. But it's better to go into a big fight trusting your allies like brothers, than to go in worried they'll leave you to die. And anyway, just in that moment, I didn't care that he was Bernabò's bastard son. I loved him.

That's what it's like, when you trust your captain and your comrades. And Hawkwood radiated confidence and ease.

'You two lovebirds be careful or people will talk,' he said lightly, and Antonio laughed.

And then we were away, on diverging courses like arrows shot from a bow.

After the battle, as you'll no doubt hear, I came to understand what Malatesta had decided and how he'd made the decisions. In the early light of morning, he mistook our forming up and dismounting for complete disorder in our ranks. And he acted decisively.

He ordered an attack. And his blocks of infantry rolled forward so fast, for footmen, that he had victory in his grasp before we were dismounting.

Hawkwood read him instantly and responded. It was like watching two expert swordsmen fence with thousands of men.

I went north, as I had been told, passing along behind the Germans and Italians who were the left division of our little army. All along the ranks, they were dismounting, horse-holders stepping forward to take the warhorses and hackneys and ronceys – a mob in total chaos. Our 'line' looked like a sheep pen on shearing day, with men going in all directions.

Just beyond the helmets of the German men-at-arms, we could see Malatesta's infantry deploying, and the Romagnol knights, resplendent in silks and pennons, matching us as we moved north. They were riding behind their line as we rode behind ours – Malatesta's parry to Hawkwood's *riposta*.

I pointed them out to Tom Fenton and my men-at-arms.

'We're going to have to beat them,' I said.

Janet barked a laugh. 'We've been beating them for five years,' she said.

I was already on Percival, as I have said, and all my men-at-arms were on their best, and I had to compromise between a need to get into position as quickly as possible and a desire to save our horseflesh for a decisive charge. We rolled left behind our line, Malatesta's household knights rode parallel behind their own line, and far behind me, Hawkwood sat calmly on his big charger and waited patiently for Malatesta to make a mistake.

We came to the end of our line – a hundred mounted crossbowmen under a Visconti captain. They were dismounting, too, sending their horses to the rear. We had to make a long, slow detour around an olive grove to avoid their chaos, and for five very long minutes I lost sight of the battlefield.

We emerged from the olive grove to find a drainage ditch, wider than Percival wanted to cross, blocking our path, and I cursed. My prickers swept up and went off to the right and left, riding along the ditch.

'Damn, damn,' I muttered, standing in my stirrups.

I was close to the river, which would put an absolute limit on my ability to ride around Malatesta's flank. The drainage ditch probably ran right into the river. I wished I had Turks, or Stradiotes – some light cavalry who'd already have been out and found me a path. And it was my own fault. I should have sent Christopher earlier.

So all I could do was mutter 'damn'.

Sam Bibbo sat on his charger, silent, waiting orders. Sam was, by the by, as well armoured as any man-at-arms – full leg armour, good maille and a brand-new breastplate. Most of my veteran archers were men-at-arms with bows. They were too valuable to leave light-armed, and yet it meant that I was very short of men who could crawl through undergrowth and find a path.

Damn. Damn. Damn.

Time was passing, and the full-throated roar of the god of War came on the morning breeze as Malatesta's attack went home against the centre of our army.

'Farm bridge, farm bridge!' came a call like a war cry.

It was coming from my left, further to the north. I turned Percival, pushed him recklessly through a thorn brake with Pilgrim at my heels and burst into another set of fields. There was a sort of cart track, and in the distance, perhaps four hundred paces away, the river.

A flash of armour – a man waving.

Caution said that I should ride to this supposed bridge and have a look. Hawkwood's need said I should trust my scouts and go into action immediately.

'On me!' I roared.

Marc-Antonio and de la Motte came crashing through the brush, followed by Grice and then more men-at-arms. L'Angars caught up with me. We were a mob, but I didn't think I had time to re-form. I led the way down the farm track, assuming that it was the road to the farm bridge.

It was. But when I saw the 'bridge', my heart went cold.

It was perhaps six thick boards, supported by a single pair of pillars.

'Blessed Virgin,' I muttered.

Greg Fox and a dozen other archers were already across, and there was a sparkle of sun-dapple on armour beyond them.

Now or never.

'Cross in pairs. No more than two at a time, no pushing, no crowding.' I turned to l'Angars. 'You stay here and make sure my orders are obeyed. If that collapses, we're fucked. Understand me, sir knight?'

407

He tapped his visor. 'Got it, M'sieur le Cap'n,' he said.

'*En avant!*' I called.

I led the men-at-arms immediately to hand. I crossed with Marc-Antonio and Pilgrim. De la Motte came with Lapot and looked back at mid-bridge, as Percival's hooves hit the end boards with a terrible hollow sound. The bridge looked as if it hadn't been badly maintained since a slovenly farmer had pegged it together in Roman times.

I will never trust someone else's scouting report again, I thought, as fervently as I prayed, 'Blessed Virgin, let me get my knights across.'

Italian knights were emerging from the line of poplars at the edge of the next field. I waved to Ewan.

'Engage them!' I called.

All the archers, the scouts, dismounted. There were nine of them. But there was Mark and there was Ewan, Greg Fox, Christopher, Witkin.

Italian knights are very good. They have tremendous spirit, and they are magnificently well trained in all the chivalric arts. But they are old-fashioned with regards to armour. Many of them just don't have the silver to buy the latest stuff.

Witkin's first arrow, loosed at about two hundred and fifty paces, at so high a loft that the concept of 'aiming' was ridiculous, plummeted from the heavens like a thunderbolt of Jupiter and, by sheer luck, went up to the fletchings in one of the Malatesta knight's warhorses, just behind the saddle.

The horse sank to its knees, and the Italian formation, such as it was, suddenly resembled a wasps' nest that's been kicked.

Sam Bibbo, who'd just crossed the bridge, cuffed Witkin in a friendly manner and rolled off his horse, his bow coming into his hand. Dick Thorald was with Bibbo, and he pushed his reins into the hands of a terrified boy, no more than ten or eleven, and ran forward with more energy than I'd ever seen from the old Cumbrian.

'On me, gentlemen!' I called.

I meant it exactly. I was forming every man-at-arms as they crossed, the dribble slowly becoming a company – ten, then twenty. My whole force was intermixed, so when archers crossed they dismounted by the other archers, who were not in anything as formal as a line. In fact, what it resembled was a shooting contest. Men bickered, and the sound of wagers floated on the air.

'Red and yellow nob – see 'im?'

'*Ah, vraiment, mon amis! Eh bien, le petit homme avec les moulins rouges.*'

'I see 'im, the bastard.'

'*Ah! Eh bien!*'

'That must o' hurt, mate. Should a' bought isself a better 'elmet, eh?'

Bibbo bellowed, 'Less talk and more arrows!'

The Malatesta men-at-arms were taking hits and they didn't like it, but they were all veterans and they had an idea of how mad it would be to try even forty archers in an open field.

They melted away. These weren't untried Frenchmen at Poitiers – these were men who'd seen as much war as my men. They were gone as fast as a cloud crosses the sun on a windy day.

'Get them mounted!' I called to Bibbo.

He waved an arrow at me.

I turned to de la Motte and Janet. 'I'm going after them.'

'We should wait for our archers,' de la Motte said.

Janet said nothing.

'Let's go,' I said. I remember waving for my page to bring Gabriel up, so that I could change after a charge.

I turned Percival across the field and waited for a volley of crossbow bolts to show me the error of my ways. But as Percival's big hooves raised dust from the wheat field, nothing rose from the far wood line except a hum which I would later find to be wasps, disturbed by the Italian knights, as you will hear.

Pilgrim barked, an unexpected sound from such a well-trained dog. Percival was excited – ears up, well gathered, nostrils wide. I looked back and my corporals had the men-at-arms well formed and closed up – forty or so men and one woman, crossing the field in a cloud of dust. My heart rose.

I'd forgotten how much fun this could be.

We hit the thickets at the edge of the next olive grove at a trot. I crashed in, my armour and my powerful horse making me confident that I could get through the edge, and there were paths carved by the Italians, and a dead horse right at my feet. Percival gave a sort of skip as he cleared the dead horse, and we were in the midst of the trees.

And the wasps.

His eyes rolled, and then he gave a skip like a much smaller horse, and almost had me off. He was backing, and I had sharp lances behind me, so I touched him with my spurs and he was off. He was a fine horse, but after five or six stings, he'd had enough, and we were moving through an olive grove at a gallop.

I was saved by my new helmet and my excellent harness. Percival went along a sort of lane between the trees like an equine thunderbolt and only small branches played on my body. By the grace of God, my visor snapped down with my first attempt to close it, and then I was hunkered down in the saddle as if I was jousting, but my lance was gone, torn away by a tree, and it was all I could do to stay on my maddened horse's back.

We were flying – that's how it felt. I realised as a fist caught me in the gut that my wasp-stung horse had leapt another ditch and we'd landed heavily. Warhorses aren't great leapers, but Percival had *just* managed it.

I was clear of the trees and I could think. Something flashed in the corner of my eye. I was hit on my reinforced left pauldron – a sharp blow that was somehow different from a branch scraping away at me – and Percival was turning under me ...

Colour. All around me. Silk and steel ...

Sweet Christ, I was in the middle of Malatesta's men-at-arms. Blows fell on me like rain, but I was moving fast, and they were all facing the wrong way, as I'd exploded into them from behind.

I had no weapon to hand.

I took a thrust in the back. Someone was fast and well trained, and it *hurt* – the point went through my maille and through my gambeson, too. In those days I never wore a backplate.

And then I was clear. We were racing along, a full gallop, and I'd gone through the Malatesta column and now we were riding across another wheat field, the young shoots of green flashing by the very limited vision of my barred visor. I used my knees and Percival responded, turning to my left, and again, and more – a wide circle.

When I was sure that I had him under control, I reached down for my sword. It pleased me enormously when I found the Emperor's sword still belted to my side. The hilt had caught on a dozen branches and not ripped free, which is why it's always worth the silver to get good leather-work. Your sword will never be any use to you if it's not there.

No sign of Pilgrim. No sign of the rest of my men-at-arms, either.

I drew the Emperor's sword, and turned my horse to face the Malatesta men-at-arms.

There were about a hundred of them. Go ahead, Chaucer – make a face. I was there and you weren't.

I waved my sword. I assumed someone would come and face me in single combat, and I wasn't wrong. Italian men-at-arms can be accused of many things, including poor horse care and bad discipline, but they cannot be accused of cowardice. Four different men came at me from different parts of the column, and being Italian, none of them would give way to the others.

Four to one is bad odds.

Better than one hundred to one, however.

I didn't have a lance, either, so I did my best to become Fiore. I put my sword in a low *garde* on my left side and rode off *to* my left. Listen, when you face a left-hander, always press his left side. Push against the weapon and you negate his advantage. Against multiple opponents, treat the situation as if they are all left-handed. Rotate them left.

My first opponent had a fast horse and a white surcoat with lions and roses. He came at my left side, and I lined up with him as if we were jousting. My sword found his lance point and I performed Fiore's parry, lifting the spear point up and over my horse's head in a long glissade, and then using my bridle hand around his unprotected neck to sweep him from the saddle.

I ended up with his lance. I had it backwards, but as I swept around to the left, I rotated it in the air and put the Emperor's sword under my left thigh, pinning it to the saddle with my leg as we turned. Simultaneously I thought two thoughts – that I wished Fiore had seen me do that, and that I'd come a long way since I couldn't face Boucicault in the lists.

I ended my turn quite close to the Italian men-at-arms watching. Every eye was on me – some men raised their visors or slipped their great helms off their cerveleurs.

Bless him, Percival was not flagging. I didn't use my spurs. We lined up with two of the men chasing us, and I aimed for the left-hand one, who was slightly in the lead.

He was a good jouster. Fifty paces out, he raised his lance and saluted, a pretty play, and got his lance back in its rest with a flourish.

I didn't unhorse him, and he didn't unhorse me. Our lances exploded, and in the confusion of the moment of the hit I thought he'd killed me, as something was bad and then it wasn't – pain, twisting, Percival stumbling and then turning under me.

He'd only ripped away my left pauldron, which vanished into the wheat. A very good score in a tournament, but here ...

The third man was blue and red, and his lance caught my right arm, tagged the vambrace like the blow of a fist in a tavern fight, and he was gone, and I was twisting away, still up, still capable.

I took the sword from under my leg. The last man, the fourth, was in black and yellow, and he'd ridden wide, intending, I think, something modestly unchivalrous, like coming up behind me. But now he was alone, and he did something noble – he dropped his lance and drew his sword.

I slowed Percival with my knees, and we went in close, horse to horse, and Percival reared. I managed to stay on, but I had the feeling that we were rearing a great deal more than the other horse. I covered his first cut, a heavy, overhand cut from a high *garde*, and then he was falling away and I'd done nothing. Percival had overwhelmed his horse. Percival was an excellent fighter – one hoof or the other had landed *hard* and the other horse was rolling on the ground, probably killing his rider.

I turned us, guessing that the other two would be right behind us. My right arm hurt – I wondered if it was broken, the pain was so sharp.

We were almost at a stand and Blue and Red had his horse at a canter, and I got Percival's head around, my hand high and the sword on my left side. I cut into the other man's lance without thought, on reflex, and my counter-cut slammed into his helmet – mostly a wasted blow against an armoured man but not entirely. He didn't come off, worse luck, but he kept straight on, stunned and out of the fight for a few heartbeats, and I went sword to sword with the man who'd been a good jouster.

He made a cut from out of distance as his horse shied at the dying horse on the ground. I snapped a one-handed cut from my right side, very flat, at eye height – in truth, unless the Blessed Virgin pulled his helmet off his head, a wasted blow. But he covered it with a desperate swing, both hands on the hilt of his sword.

I went for Fiore's *punta falsa*. I rotated my own sword like an hour-glass, taking the momentum of his parry and using it to turn my blade to the inside of his, leaning out over Percival with my shield hand to take my own sword at mid-blade, trapping his sword above my shield.

It sort-of worked. Which is to say that the movement of the horses and his desperate counter-parry caused me to miss putting my point into his eye-slot by a finger's width. My point scraped down his helmet, a harmless blow, except that it went down the *left* side of his helmet so that my hand went across his throat. I used it as a lever to throw him from the saddle. His own horse's forward motion did the rest, while Percival rotated under me like a dancer.

The last man of the four was Blue and Red, and he was having trouble turning his horse. One of his reins had come off, or broken, or maybe I'd cut it – I had no memory of any such.

The Italians on the farm track were cheering him.

He was still trying to get his horse to turn. I stood my ground, Percival between my legs blowing like a dragon. His whole giant frame was shaking with fatigue.

I saluted with my sword. My arm hurt.

The Italians didn't exactly cheer me, and some of them began to shout very rude suggestions in Italian, but they were chivalrous men and they waited for their last champion to control his horse and finish me.

They were still shouting at him when l'Angars came out of the trees at their back with fifty men-at-arms and crushed them. It happened so fast that I had a moment of disbelief – it was like the moment when a sandcastle goes down under a wave. Gone.

In another moment, a dozen Italians were bursting past me, riding for their lives. My opponent came over and surrendered himself to me.

Now that the fight was over, my arm stopped working. I'd apparently performed a creditable version of the *punta falsa* with a broken right arm, but having done it, the arm now hung at my side. My arm and shoulder burnt with a malevolence that caused me to look at it several times for blood.

Armour will protect you from cuts, but not from sheer impact. The lance hit to my arm had broken it right through the steel. My

413

new helmet had held against everything thrown at it, but I still felt stunned. I wasn't quite sure where l'Angars had come from.

'You were going to fight them all yourself?' Marc-Antonio called.

'Forgot it was a fight and thought it was a horse race, more like,' Janet said. 'Guillaume, are you still capable?'

Her French was heavily accented, but men laughed anyway.

Percival was done, poor fellow.

'Horse,' I mumbled.

No one likes to give up their charger on a stricken field, but Sam Bibbo gave me his, one of our half-Arabs.

'Boys'll be along soon,' he said with a slow smile. 'An' I never mind being late for a battle.'

So I got my leg over the tall saddle with a powerful boost from the master-archer, and then tried to get my bearings.

There was the river.

So Malatesta had to be the other way.

We rode far enough that I began to fear that somehow, in my addled state, I'd gone wrong. But Ewan waved. He was trotting across a field with yet another line of poplars beyond it, and the sounds of combat floated to me.

I assumed that the battlefield lay beyond the poplars. I turned to Christopher, who was at my elbow. I remember he was cursing our page, who'd vanished with Gabriel.

'Take my pennon and get Ewan. Go to the point where the enemy line is anchored and wave the pennon. L'Angars – form here.' I waved.

Janet laughed. 'Someone's back inside his head.'

'Form up!' l'Angars bellowed.

De la Motte wheeled his people into line by my standard, as my little personal pennon seemed to leap across the field in Christopher's hands.

I counted quickly. I still had most of my people, almost seventy men-at-arms and another seventy armed squires in the second rank. In a battle of two thousand against four thousand ...

Perhaps the margin of victory. Or perhaps too late to do anything but scare the looters. I had to be practical – I was late.

'Dick!' I called to Thorald. 'Take six men you like. Get back to the last woods and mark them. If we come that way, we'll be in a hurry.'

'Awreet,' he sighed.

That had to do for covering my retreat.

I missed Percival, as my new mount was stubborn and kept putting his head down to eat the young wheat sprouts. I didn't blame him – I was hungry, too.

'Forward on the standard at my order,' I said.

'I rather like being cavalry,' de la Motte said, and men laughed, because we usually fought on foot.

'I like it when William does all the fighting,' Janet said, and more men laughed. 'Let's see if he wants to go and fight Malatesta by himself.'

'I love you all!' I spat. More laughter.

My pennon was waving, far down the field near the western corner of the field. Our people must have been hard-pressed.

But maybe not yet broken.

'Let's go,' I said.

Then Christopher moved, and he and Ewan began to wave. I had no idea what they were saying. I opened my visor again and looked right and left. My line was well formed, but how exactly was I planning to go through the poplars? Was there a stone wall in that patch of woods? A ditch?

Listen, friends, when you read one of the chroniclers describing a battle, it's all cavalry charges and infantry stands, but from my saddle, battles are won and lost by feeding your horses and knowing where there's a bridge over the drainage ditch or a path through the trees.

I could see daylight past Ewan's head – then I could see that it broadened. They were marking one of those farm paths that punch through the hedges and tree lines of northern Italy. I assume they're for farm wagons and workers.

And there ... and there ... the sun flashed on stone. The poplars were many trees deep, like a thick line of pikes, and there *was* an ancient wall between their roots.

'We're going to form a column of fours without halting!' I roared.

I roared it four times because sometimes you just cannot hurry, and having everyone understand is more important than anything else. If we lost our order here, we'd never get it back.

I pulled out of my line.

'We're forming from the centre!' I roared. 'Ready!'

Most men had their visors up again. If we took a crossbow volley, a great many men would die, but then, if there were crossbows concealed in the poplars, Ewan and Christopher would be dead. And they weren't.

Unless it was an ambush.

'Go!' I ordered.

And as crisply as we did it on the training fields behind Reggio Emilia, my lead four went forward at a trot, and then a pair of riders joined them from each side, the wings shrinking in at a diagonal as the line became a column.

The column went forward into the gap, and the sound changed.

We were entering the main battlefield from the north, turning the enemy's western flank. As it proved, we came in well behind them, perhaps a hundred and fifty paces from where the Visconti men-at-arms, on foot, were giving ground slowly to a huge press of Romagnol and papal infantry. The dismounted crossbowmen had already taken cover in the olive groves, but were still peppering the papal troops with bolts from the trees.

As soon as my standard came in past the trees, the crossbowmen began to cheer. It was a thin sound, but the Visconti men picked it up. I could see Ambrogio's standard and a crowd of dismounted papal knights around it with their own banners. Our line was broken in places, and yet somehow still holding – or rather, the tendency of Italians to fight for rich ransoms was keeping them from finishing Hawkwood off.

I've been known to take a few ransoms myself, to be fair.

Again, in a storybook, when you arrive in the enemy rear, you win the battle. But I had a hundred and fifty horsemen, in a battle of seven thousand men.

'Let's go!' Janet shouted. She was excited. Battle always excited her.

Perhaps it was my broken arm, or my unlovable horse, but I was not in a hurry to throw my cavalry at the enemy rear. I had a suspicion that my little command was far more dangerous as a threat than as a reality.

'*Do not charge!*' I managed to roar. 'Stay on me. Form line! Slowly! No rush, gentlemen! Make it tight!'

There was a little grumbling. But our horses were not fresh – everyone had fought once already. And the English are not as wild as the

French. No one ran off, and we managed to keep it together. The crisp column of fours emerging from the trees performed a quarter-wheel to the right, and we began to deploy the way we'd formed column, from the centre to the wings, which is the fastest way if you've read your Vegetius.

It seemed to take forever.

And yet, while we were unfolding like a pavilion being set up, the papal militia to our right front began to give ground. Suddenly they were throwing down their pavises and their crossbows, crashing through the poplars to our right, headed north towards the camp they'd abandoned that morning.

I let them go. They were a big block of men and I hadn't had to fight them, and as they ran they exposed the flank of the papal men-at-arms fighting Ambrogio. And *they* were already looking over their shoulders at my standard.

Bless them, the Visconti men-at-arms who'd been slowly pushed back by the militia were now free. They took a breath or two, looked at their beleaguered comrades to their own right, and began to fall on the rear of the papal men-at-arms.

The enemy flank was beginning to unravel, and I hadn't done a thing except appear.

It was Borgoforte all over again, except that this time we had enough men to *actually* make a difference, if deployed correctly. I pointed with my left arm at the papal standard, which was set high on a great wagon in the middle of the field.

'Gentlemen!' I shouted. 'Let us emulate Saint Michael and cut the head off the dragon!'

'My best battlefield speech,' I muttered to Janet.

I got a loud cheer, and my heart rose to see most of our archers come out of the gap at a trot, all mounted, led by Sam Bibbo. I turned my borrowed horse and rode over to him.

'Follow me, pick up our prisoners, and look as mean as hell,' I said.

Our archers were mostly so well armoured that they looked like knights, if you didn't look too close.

Bibbo began to form the mounted archers two deep – a smaller second squadron behind us.

'Pages have the ransoms,' he said.

I'd forgotten the ransoms, the Italian knights we'd taken in the first skirmish. If this went badly, we'd be very happy to have some important people to trade for ... us.

In the centre of the field, the men by the big wagon, the *carroccio*, were looking around. Most Italian commanders kept a reserve by the *carroccio*, the very best men of the militia and the knights. Malatesta was an older man and a traditionalist, which, worse luck, meant that his best knights were waiting by the papal banner.

And I couldn't wield a sword or a lance. In fact, l'Angars, who often wore a big red sash around his waist instead of a sword belt, used his sash to tie up my arm in a sling. He was fast and economical.

'Not the first time it's been used this way,' he said gruffly.

He hurt me cruelly, but I kept my head moving back and forth, watching my people form, and when he was done I pushed my visor down until it clicked against its cunning little catch.

'Forward at the walk,' I said into my visor, and l'Angars repeated it, and we started forward.

The *carroccio* began to move. It was a giant wagon drawn by eight warhorses, with wheels nine feet high and a gigantic papal banner flying from a pole thirty feet above the bed. There were guild crossbowmen in the bed of the wagon, and they were very good. My new helmet took a blow so hard that I was almost unhorsed – at two hundred paces, no less. My neck hurt. My arm hurt, my shoulder hurt, and then all that fell away and my battlefield clarity took over.

To my right, I could see John Hawkwood's scallop shells moving forward. To my front, there was movement. The *carroccio* guards were looking, first at me, then the other way.

A group of knights went forward from the *carroccio*, lances levelled – maybe fifty. They were charging at Hawkwood's banner.

Their movement revealed Malatesta himself. He was in full armour, with his great helm slung on his back and his fierce grey moustache emerging from his aventail, his destrier magnificent in a silk caparison woven with his red and yellow chequy barred argent. He had a white wand in his hand, and he was pointing at something to his own left, which was virtually straight ahead of me. I couldn't see it through the limited vision of my visor.

As I watched, his horse moved forward, towards Hawkwood.

We were still moving at a walk, and my horse was not bad at knee signals, so I let go of my reins and opened my visor.

418

'L'Angars,' I said, 'let's get Malatesta.'

L'Angars grinned, and beyond him, de la Motte and Lapot also grinned.

'Your best speech ever,' Janet said behind me, and everyone laughed.

'Visors down!' l'Angars called.

Suddenly men and horses went down. De la Motte was gone, as if swatted by a giant hand. The damned crossbowmen with their heavy arbalests.

I reined in, turned back to Bibbo.

'New plan!' I yelled. 'Get the *carroccio*!'

He waved, and the archers began to turn to their left, increasing speed. I slapped my visor down again and pushed back into the front rank.

'Trot!' I said, raising my left hand as a signal.

Malatesta saw us. We weren't that far away. Later I knew why all his attention had been on Hawkwood, but now, he saw me and rage filled his face. Rage at interrupted victory. He had Hawkwood. He was about to win ...

Now he was about to lose.

'Lances!' l'Angars bellowed, and seventy lance points came down.

Janet punched past me into the front rank without a comment. I'd have hit her, except that I realised that she had a lance and I didn't, so I rode the charge in the second rank.

Malatesta's bodyguard was about fifty knights, all his own people. They didn't really have enough time to change front and charge, but they were damned good, and we came together like ten thousand cooks beating all the pots in the world. Janet unhorsed some poor bastard, her weight slightly forward, graceful as a steel lily. I had time to wonder if she could have taken Boucicault, as I'd seen her beat Belmont and do well against Fiore, and then we were through, riding in an empty field.

Empty, except that to my right, Hawkwood's household knights were breaking the papal centre with their axes. Empty, except that Antonio Visconti was coming the other way, his knights gradually collapsing the Romagnol left.

In a hundred heartbeats, the papal army went from the edge of victory to utter defeat. I've never seen it happen so fast. Their apparently beaten foe turned on them and their flanks collapsed, and their hopes ran out like blood from a heart-shot stag.

Janet's horse was better than mine, and she was probably still a better rider. She turned, her unbroken lance already erect, looking for a new foe like a bird of prey hunting rabbits.

Her helmet wasn't as good as mine, though. I could see things she couldn't, and while she looked, the prey I saw was Malatesta. He'd never got his great helm back on, and his lance was broken, and he was trying to draw his sword.

I rode at him. I was five horse lengths away before I remembered that I had no weapon and no useful right arm. But I remembered a story that I'd heard in France from a famous tournament fighter, and I trusted my helmet and my armour.

I came at him from the side. He was trying to turn his charger and draw his long sword at the same time. He had a magnificent, gold-decorated sword, probably a gift from the Pope, and I don't think he'd practised getting it out. His arm wasn't long enough. The straps were caught on the back of his saddle, and his horse just kept turning to the right, away from me.

It was like a game – like playing the tournament mêlée game at Krakow. I'd played it with Fiore. I'd even played it left-handed.

I lay low, the cantle of my high-backed saddle in my gut, reached out with my shield hand, and got the bridle of his horse. And Sam's horse turned at my command and went off to the right, towards Hawkwood.

Malatesta cursed.

But I had him. I had his bridle and I was literally pulling him out of the battle.

Rage, fury and fear are great drivers. Malatesta ripped his sword off his belt without getting it free of the scabbard and he thrust at me, a stout thrust. He was over sixty, and his thrust was as strong as one of mine. But it struck the back of my helmet and skidded.

I didn't let go of his bridle.

He swung, a great two-handed blow, but it wasn't at my left arm, where I had his horse. That might have done some good.

Instead, he hit me across the back. But my gambeson, my maille, and the *scabbard still on his sword* kept me alive.

I was still far from Hawkwood's men, and they were on foot. Behind us was a gigantic dust cloud rising from the mêlée as if the knights were on fire. Out of it rode Lapot, as if he'd had enough of the dust, except that he pointed the head of his horse at Malatesta and he flew.

Malatesta hit me again, a ringing blow to my left rerebrace above the shield, but the hardened steel held. My shoulder hurt. But I had him.

'God damn, Gold!' he roared. 'God damn!'

He took a moment and pulled the scabbard off his sword, but we were still moving towards the English lines.

'God damn!' he called again.

I pulled savagely at his bridle, and Sam's horse swerved left and I almost unhorsed him.

He snapped a cut at me, one-handed. It hit my helmet and my ears rang, but the steel held and I swerved again, trying to shake his seat.

He got both hands on his hilt, cocked all the way back so the sword shone behind his head. Lapot caught his hands as he passed behind and threw him from the saddle. The old knight went down like a hanged man cut down from a gibbet, and I reined in immediately.

Now my head hurt in addition to my shoulder, my arm and my back. Despite which ...

I knelt by Malatesta, who, I was delighted to see, was alive and alert.

'Fuck it,' he said. 'I'm not getting up.'

When Bibbo came, we gave him some water.

I had the biggest capture of my career.

And the papal army was destroyed. It came apart around us, as I knelt by my prisoner, and most of the papal infantry, who were guild militia from Bologna, surrendered to Hawkwood's people, or Antonio Visconti's, or mine. And we didn't want them, but it being Italy and not France or Spain, we just took their weapons and let them go, instead of massacring them or turning them into mine slaves.

That's one of the reasons Italy was better.

The knights, we ransomed. And the great battle cart of Bologna and the papal banners. We ransomed those, too.

I was in a strange place. I hurt, and had a broken arm, but I wasn't really wounded and I could still give orders. Malatesta hadn't really made many mistakes. The one-sided result of the battle wasn't because he was a fool, but rather that he'd trusted his men to win before we could come at his flanks.

He told me, in detail, while we watched the end of the battle.

People rode up to me, asked questions, asked for orders, and Pilgrim, shame-faced and covered in wasp stings, came and had to be cossetted. Eventually Sir John came and joined us, and then Richard Romney, and by the end of the afternoon, we had most of the knights gathered, drinking wine. The casualties were relatively light because so many men had surrendered.

De la Motte was alive, although he had a broken arm and two broken wrists from his fall from a dying horse – bad luck, but hardly lethal. Lapot had a bad cut on his left wrist that showed bone. A blade had gone in between the cuff of his gauntlet and his vambrace.

Best of all, I managed to remember Marc-Antonio. He'd fought well, and taken two good ransoms, and he was completely untouched. I led him to Sir John Hawkwood.

'I can't raise my arm,' I said. 'Do me this favour.'

Hawkwood smiled with genuine pleasure. But to me, he said, 'You'll just have to pay him more.'

He knighted Marc-Antonio with the Pope's sword, and old Malatesta gave him the buffet.

I'd forgotten the thrust to my back until Janet saw blood running down the back of my left leg, a darker red against the red of my hose, and she snapped a dozen orders while I wobbled. I think it's curious how much worse I felt when I saw the blood than I'd felt a moment before. I think I went out, because my next memory is of lying on a pallet of straw. One of the Italian doctors was looking at me, and he and Janet had an argument, and then he went out of the tent.

'Fucking idiot,' she said. 'Listen, William. This is going to hurt.'

She wasn't joking. Whatever she did went through me like a lance. In fact, she poured wine on the wound, and they put some vinegar on a sponge and ...

'*Christ* almighty lordofheavenandearth!' I said, or something similar.

'Sleep,' Janet said.

Her squire, Markus, a German lad of fifteen or so, pushed a pillow under my head.

CHAPTER THREE

MODENA, ASTI

June 1372

As was all too often true in Italy, the day after the Battle of Rubiera, we thought we'd crushed the papacy and won the war for Milan. We'd taken their most famous commander. We'd captured more than half their knights.

Nothing could have been further from the truth. In fact, all the victory did was to show the depth of the papacy's resolve and their financial resources. It also began to show how many of the 'neutrals' hated the Milanese. Niccolò d'Este, the second lord of Ferrara of that name, had long been an ally of the Veronese against Milan, but now he stepped forward to be the Captain-General of the papal forces. We were still tending our wounded and trying to bargain with our captives when d'Este moved six hundred infantry into Modena and began bringing up his chivalry – hundreds of knights – until his military camp under the walls looked like an army.

Hawkwood watched all this with something approaching satisfaction.

'I want you to sell me Malatesta,' he said.

'You get half anyway,' I pointed out.

He smiled. 'I need Malatesta to be back in the saddle,' he said. 'I'd rather face a cautious old soul like Malatesta than d'Este, who has very little to lose. In addition, Bernabò hasn't actually paid us yet, and I'm not really interested in fighting two battles in one year.'

'You're not disappointed that we didn't grab Modena?' I asked.

'I'd have been disappointed if all the useless sods patched together a peace and left us without work,' he said with a vicious smile. 'A big, fat victory with lots of ransoms and cash for every man? Perfect. Even better if it has no effect on the war.'

It was difficult to discern whether he was being sarcastic or literal.

We were looking across a dozen fields at the gabions marking the earthworks that d'Este had thrown up to cover his camp. Behind us were some of our Hungarians, covering our reconnaissance.

'What happened to our Turks?' I asked.

'Gone back to fight in Greece,' he said. 'They went with your Greeks, which probably tells you something.'

'Listen,' I said, 'I have Bretons and Normans and Picards, Englishmen, Scots, Irish ... I have a whole war serving together in my company.'

'As do I,' Hawkwood agreed. 'Men can live in harmony, as long as they have a common enemy.'

I laughed at such accurate cynicism.

'Anyway, I miss the Turks and the Greeks,' I said. 'Sir John, can we win this war?'

He looked at me as if I was a fool. 'Win? Against the Pope?'

I was still thinking about Sister Marie's contention that I needed to fight for something in which I believed. The victory at Rubiera had been so crushing ...

'William, do you remember our "siege" of Florence? Back in '65?' He held up a hand. 'Stupid question! It's where you were knighted, eh?'

I grinned, remembering the fight at the barriers. And Baumgarten. 'I remember,' I said.

Sir John was watching Modena. 'I'm getting old, William. I forget, and I assume you young people do, too.'

It was one of the most human things I'd ever heard him say.

'We had perhaps six thousand men,' he said. 'We couldn't even seal the gates of Florence, much less make a meaningful scratch on the city walls.'

I nodded. I've spoken to you gentlemen before about the difficulties of 'winning' a campaign with very few men.

Sir John pointed his white staff of command at Modena.

'If I wanted to prosecute this war to the fullest of our abilities ...' he said, and he smiled at me to indicate that nothing was further from his mind. '*If*, mind you ... I lack the men and resources to push the papal forces out of Modena. As long as d'Este, who's no prize, has two good captains and a thousand men, he'll hold that city forever. And then? Let's just say I could take Modena?'

He looked at me. I saw it all now. I'd been locked in my tiny world of command, worrying about fodder, and pay rates, and promoting senior lances, and burying dead men and arranging for their favourite *bonne amie* to have a portion of their earnings, all of which could have used the judgement of Solomon and all the lawyers in London.

And here was the stark reality.

Sir John drove on. 'I take Modena and I face Bologna,' he said. 'One of the richest cities in Italy, with a big, healthy garrison and an international treasury from the Pope. I could no more take Bologna than storm Heaven, and I'm not inclined to pretend to try.'

'What are we doing, then?' I asked.

He looked at me. 'We are professional soldiers,' he said. 'We do what we're told, within certain limits. Speaking of which ...' He nodded. 'Remind me about the Duke of Clarence.'

Six months since I'd assembled my proof – perhaps a little less. I'd told him everything ... But we'd had a siege, a war ...

So I told him again. And I repeated my assumptions. That young Gian Galeazzo had done it, and his father had killed people to cover for it and make sure he got his towns in Piedmont back.

Hawkwood nodded and then he laughed. It wasn't even bitter.

'So that arse Despenser had the right of it all along,' he said. 'But I wanted proof. You said you had proof?'

I shrugged, which hurt. Everything hurt, and I had piercing headaches and days of incredible fatigue – too many blows to the head. And some very dark days ...

'I suspect,' I said, and then I paused to choose words, thinking of Chaucer here, and other clerks I've known. 'I suspect that if we had a King's Justiciar, and a jury, we'd hang him. That much proof.'

Hawkwood didn't look at me. He was looking at Modena and d'Este's camp.

'Damn me to Hell,' he said. 'You have *proof*?'

'Yes,' I said.

He nodded. 'That's bad.'

I knew what he meant. If all we had was suspicions, well, we'd be just more angry Englishmen. But the Visconti couldn't afford proof. Enough people already hated them.

The irony was that neither Galeazzo, the monster, nor Bernabò, the other monster, had done it.

'Damn me to Hell,' Hawkwood said again. 'You told me all this before.'

'I did, at that,' I agreed.

At the time, I worried he was getting old. In retrospect, I think that he needed to have the information reviewed when it was convenient. He was, after all, the fox.

We passed the summer at chivalric games. They weren't really chivalric – they were merely games. We had the occasional skirmish, but for the most part, we offered various terms to arrange a duel – Hawkwood and three knights against d'Este and three knights, that sort of thing. Hawkwood played d'Este's chivalrous nature like a gittern, claiming that one site was too wet, another too close to the enemy camp. In July, I was appointed to the team, and I arranged that it would be a contest of six knights against another six. I met the Marquis d'Este and was favourably impressed. He was a good knight, and a thinker, if not much younger than Malatesta.

After four meetings and some very good wine, I realised that d'Este had no more intention of fighting than Hawkwood. He was delaying while he built his army. Hawkwood was delaying because mercenaries make as much money waiting as they do fighting.

I had other interests, by then. Because one day, while my right arm and my back were healing, I went with a group of my knights and senior men-at-arms into Reggio Emilia for an evening of entertainment. I'm not sure exactly what I expected, but we'd been invited by a local lord and Hawkwood had arranged for the great hall of the castle to be decorated. We had mummers present a sort of 'triumph' for Sir John and Ambrogio, whose vanity had grown as vast as a summer thundercloud, and as loud.

'Ignore him,' Hawkwood said to me.

'He's claiming that he won the battle,' I pointed out.

Hawkwood shrugged. 'As long as he pays the money,' he said, 'he can make any claim he likes.'

After the play, and some dull Latin poetry that only half a dozen of us understood, there were a dozen local maidens, heavily escorted, and music for dancing, and food. We'd been in the city for Christmas, and no maidens had been produced, and I wondered, idly, what it was like to be sixteen and asked – forced? – by your father and mother to go and flirt and dance with dangerous barbarians.

It didn't hold any charm for me. I was about to decline to dance when my eye fell on Janet, who was dressed, for the most part, like a noblewoman, in a beautiful rose-pink kirtle of silk and an equally magnificent overdress of dark blue brocade trimmed in pearls and squirrel fur. It was a little heavy for summer, and a few years out of fashion – but at the same time, it was the best garment in the room. And she was wearing a small fortune in jewellery, as she did when she chose to wear women's clothes.

She glanced at me. It occurred to me that she probably wanted to dance. So, knowing that no force on earth could make her do anything she didn't want to do, I made my best reverence, all the way down on one knee, and asked if she'd do me the honour.

She laughed. 'You'll do, Guillaume!' she said.

She spent the next hour and more showing me how to be a better dancer. If you've been listening, you'll know that Janet taught me to dance, when she was teaching me to look and act like a gentleman, back in '63. And she was a divine dancer, which is probably why she was such a devastating fighter – in top physical shape, with near-perfect tempo, she floated while other girls bobbed up and down.

Ambrogio had been the centre of attention for the local maidens, with Antonio Visconti as a close second. As Bernabò's sons, they were demigods. Or demi-satyrs.

But after an hour, Ambrogio came over and put a familiar hand on Janet's arm.

'Do me the honour of dancing with me, and I'll show you how a man should dance.'

Janet was a terrible failure as a woman – she never flirted and almost never simpered. Nor did she lower her eyes, or pretend interest in men, or any of those things. So she flicked her eyes towards Ambrogio.

'No thanks, My Lord,' she said.

He was already reaching for her hand. He snapped back as if she'd struck him.

'What?' he asked clumsily, before his vanity caused him to draw himself up. And then he bowed. 'If you'd rather hobble around with this clod –' he favoured me with a smile – 'I won't interfere.'

'My thanks for your understanding,' Janet said. 'And please get your hand off my arm.'

Ambrogio withdrew, his face as red as blood.

'You are so very good at making friends,' I said.

She was flushed. 'I hate being touched,' she said. 'And it's disgustingly hard to kick a man in the groin in two layers of skirts.'

I had a hand on her shoulder and I took it off.

'I don't mean you,' she said. 'Dance. I love to dance, and you are already better.'

'My back hurts.'

'Stop whining and dance. Why are men so resistant to dancing?'

Janet glanced over at the Italians around Ambrogio. They were laughing.

We did a simple circle dance, and then a more complex dance for three couples called 'Jealousy', that I had danced in Verona and already knew, to Janet's delight, and we mimed our parts, tormented by love and jealousy, and made people laugh.

Antonio Visconti crossed the room. Some of the good feeling from the battle remained – he smiled at me.

'My brother is very angry,' he said. 'What did your woman say?'

Janet made a face. 'I'm not anyone's woman,' she said.

Antonio had ridden with us long enough to understand his error.

'Ah,' he said. 'My apologies. Ambrogio believes that all women belong to him, like our father.'

Janet nodded. 'It's not an uncommon error,' she said. 'Among men.'

Her hand was on the long dagger in her belt.

Antonio turned to me, virtually ignoring her.

'What have you done?' he asked suddenly. 'I hear things.'

No need to pretend ignorance – I had no idea what he was talking about, and said so. Antonio glanced back at his brother.

'Galeazzo is out for your head,' he said. 'You've saved mine a few times. So I'm trying to return the favour.' He leant in. 'What the fuck did you do? Sleep with Violante?'

He was serious.

'No,' I said.

'They want you dead,' Antonio said. 'So offending my brother right now is not a good move.'

428

I swore.

He put his hand on my arm. 'I mean it, Guglielmo. Go somewhere else. Galeazzo has a long arm and he's a hater. Far worse than my father, who could forget you between one slut and the next. Whatever you did, please go where I'm not asked to kill you.'

Well, there I had been, thinking him ungrateful.

'Thanks for the warning, Antonio,' I said.

He smiled. 'Eh, you've saved my worthless carcass at least twice,' he said. 'I could have been hanged on a rotten tree in Naples. A bad death.' He shuddered. 'I don't forget.'

And here I thought you had.

I turned to take a cup of wine from a page and Janet knocked it from my hand.

'I heard all that,' she said. 'You're not drinking anything else we haven't seen poured.'

The page apologised as if he'd dropped the cup – probably a good move with Italian lords, who can be quite touchy.

'Come,' Janet said imperiously. 'I know a place we can dance without interruption, in perfect safety.'

In another woman, it might have been an invitation, but Janet generally meant exactly what she said. We collected our cloaks, hats and horses and rode down into Reggio Emilia, and then out of the northern gate for almost a mile in the warm air. I was silent, trying to imagine how I could evade Galeazzo's assassins. Trying to decide, still, what I should do. I needed to tell Isabella of England.

'We're here,' Janet said.

'Here' was a whitewashed inn with heavy old timbers that might not have been utterly out of place north of the Alps. It had Italian arbours and a healthy smell of wine and garlic and olive oil laid over the scent of cat piss and horse manure.

Inside, we found wine and musicians, and everyone seemed to know Janet. They treated her like a great lady. Two different servants waited on her at all times, and another on me, and she paid lavishly. Musicians were produced – two were travellers, one an old drunk who had to be jerked awake and softened up with wine before he'd play. But when he played, it was like listening to a stubble-cheeked, blurry angel.

'Now we can dance in peace,' Janet said. To the stubble-faced drunken angel, she said, 'Play me some Landini.'

We danced. And Janet invited some of the others – some workmen, a scholar, a prostitute and a young girl travelling with her father. We danced in circles and as couples. We leapt like Saracens and hopped like the Milanese and swept about like the French, and I was drunk, and drunk on the music.

And very late, I was stretched on a good feather bed with Pilgrim on the floor beside me, already snoring like big dogs the world over. Janet was looking at my wound, her sword-hard hands on my back.

'I think you'll live,' she admitted. She was fairly drunk herself. 'It's bleeding more than I'd like,' she allowed, and gave a violent hiccup.

I tried to remain immobile while she re-bandaged me, but the room was spinning and I was trying very hard not to throw up. She finished and sat heavily on the bed.

'I need to go to my own room,' she said.

'People will talk,' I said, with a laugh. My head was spinning less.

'Not my people,' she said in her usual severe tone. 'I don't keep people who talk.'

I thought of Christopher, who was sitting downstairs making eyes at one of the inn's maidens.

'Neither do I,' I said.

'What are you going to do?' she asked, pressing my hand slightly.

'Try not to throw up,' I said. 'Talk to Hawkwood.'

She leant over. 'I'm not sure we're in the same conversation,' she said.

'You mean Ambrogio?'

'You are so very intelligent, on the battlefield,' Janet said. Her eyes were bright.

And I finally understood. I understood a hundred things – a thousand. Looks, actions, meanings.

I reached up and very cautiously, in case I had this wrong, I put a hand behind her neck and pulled.

Lust hit me like a wave, and something more – something more powerful than lust.

We kissed a long time, fully clothed. Janet was so ... different. Hard. Soft. Tall.

Not Emile. There's no other way to put that.

She rolled me on my back and sat on my hips.

'Now that we're here,' she said, and smiled, 'I'm not sure I'm ... ready.'

'Ready?' I asked, stupidly.

'Oh, Guillaume,' she said.

She rolled off the bed and left the room, leaving me in a drunken, lust-filled, confused state. A knock at the door raised my hopes, but it was Christopher with a jug of water.

'Drink it,' he said. 'The lady says so.'

I was still confused the next day when I rode into camp – confused and cautious, aware of how easily a man could be killed, riding the roads of Italy. Janet was by me, dressed as a woman but with her sword at her side, and she was as pleasant and as acerbic as ever.

'Can we …?' I began.

'Later,' she said. 'I think that I have played you a dirty trick. Later.'

Well. It wasn't as if I didn't have other things to think about, but I found my glance lingering on her, and realised that for the second time since Emile's death, I was finding a woman attractive. Not the small attractions of a fine ankle or a low-cut dress – I am a lovesome man, and I note such things almost without thinking. But I saw other signs. I saw her broad, capable hands with long, swordswoman's fingers and I liked them. I saw the slight curl of her lip where the sword cut had marred it, and I liked it …

You get the idea. I was flirting with being smitten. Smitten with an old friend.

And I enjoyed it.

I also had no hangover, probably because I'd drunk the water Christopher brought. I arrived back in camp alive and sober, determined to make my decisions and move on. I needed to tell Isabella of England. I needed to stop hiding from the problem, before the problem changed me.

And I knew that Hawkwood was changing. Hawkwood was not the kind of man who lived and died by his ideals – indeed, he was a very practical man. But I could tell that the Visconti murder of the Duke of Clarence didn't sit well, even with his flexible morality, and that it was sitting there like a bad dinner being slowly digested.

It didn't help that Bernabò declined to pay the month's double pay that was traditional for a major victory. Considering that Rubiera was hailed – indeed, still is – as one of the masterpieces of war of the last forty years, it was a stunning oversight, and Hawkwood had reason to feel slighted.

I doubt that it helped that Ambrogio claimed the victory for his own, either, no matter how Sir John pretended it did not.

No assassins came after me. I set Sir Marc-Antonio to watching me with Witkin and Ewan and Sam Bibbo, and I began to consider who could be my messenger north to Enguerrand de Coucy and Isabella. I knew we were being watched.

In mid-July, Ewan and Witkin caught a spy, one of the Visconti grooms. Witkin killed him without my permission, and Ewan told me in no uncertain terms that this was the way these things played out.

So I was only a little surprised when, towards the middle of August of 1372, after a visit from Visconti officers and a long council in Hawkwood's pavilion with Ambrogio present and me excluded, I was summoned to join Hawkwood. I passed Antonio on the way in.

'Run,' he said in a whisper. 'Please.'

That chilled me. And then I was in the tent with Sir John, alone except for his squire and Richard Romney.

'William,' he said.

'I gather this isn't good,' I said.

He motioned to his squire, and the young man handed me a cup of good wine.

'My Lord,' he murmured in English.

'Withdraw,' Hawkwood snapped at the young man. 'Romney, stay.'

When the squire was gone, Hawkwood stood.

'Amadeus of Savoy has thrown his feudal army into Asti, up north,' he said. 'He's at war with Bernabò.' He glanced at me. 'Ambrogio just suggested I massacre your lances, or at least kill you and take your lances.'

'Good Christ,' I said, or words to that effect.

Romney nodded. 'Sorry, Sir William,' he said. 'Antonio stuck up for you.'

'How do they know ...?' I began.

I was about to blurt out my fears – that the Visconti knew that I knew their secret about Clarence. I forgot for the moment that Romney wasn't in on the secret.

Hawkwood all but put his hand over my mouth.

'Don't make this worse than it is,' he snapped. 'Ambrogio thought I should kill you because of your loyalty to the Count of Savoy.'

I let out a breath. 'Oh,' I said.

'Or at least that's what he said,' Hawkwood went on, with a meaningful glance.

'Your contract is with the count,' Hawkwood went on. 'Not with me. And you've been paid for the year ... More than that I cannot say. So I assume that you will not be coming with me. Because Ambrogio and I are going to the siege of Asti, to fight for Gian Galeazzo.'

I looked at Hawkwood. 'You are ... letting me go?'

Hawkwood shook his head. 'Good lord, lad. You are my sword. I'm not *letting you go*. I'm getting you clear before the explosion happens. You have some nice estates in Savoy. Don't lose them. Take your lads and go to Savoy. Don't go near Pavia or Milan. That's my advice. When your contract's up, we'll have you back. And happy.'

Romney nodded.

'Richard, give me a moment with our William,' Hawkwood said, and Romney shook my hand and left.

When he was gone, Hawkwood looked at me. 'I believe in contracts,' he said. 'It's a very limited form of morality, but it suits me. I have a contract with Bernabò, and while he hasn't paid, I'm also married to one of his daughters and I'm beholden to him.'

I nodded. 'I understand.'

Suddenly I understood a great deal.

'No, young William, I'm sure you don't,' Hawkwood said. 'If your Count of Savoy has a brain in his head, he'll employ you immediately. And you'll be fighting us at Asti.' He frowned. He was angry, and sad – two things John Hawkwood seldom allowed himself to experience. 'I went to a great deal of effort to build a future for us in Milan,' he said. 'Galeazzo has tossed it all away. Now it's all going to fall. Yes. Go to Asti and fight us.'

'Never!' I said.

'Immediately,' Hawkwood said with his fox-like smile. 'Listen, lad. I'm about done with the Visconti, despite my wife and my lands. But I'll see my contract out. And you'll do the same. That's the game, eh?'

He was a very cautious man, off the battlefield.

I had to think about what he'd said for a moment.

As if to reinforce my guess, he said, 'And you know something that ... perhaps I could use as a shield. If it comes to that.'

'A shield?' I said, stupidly.

But I knew, almost in the same instant, what he meant.

He was preparing to change sides.

I was his message to Savoy. And the Pope. And my knowledge of the Clarence murder was going to be the lever he used to get his wife and fortune out of Milan.

I blinked. Why, exactly, had I wanted to go back to Italy? But I owed John Hawkwood, just as Antonio owed me. Life and fortune.

Hawkwood was looking at me with the flat, level gaze I associated with him on battlefields.

'You understand me, William?' he asked. 'Because my wife is currently being watched by Visconti bravos. And Ambrogio seldom lets me out of his sight. *Do you understand?*' he hissed.

'Yes,' I said. 'I'm your pricker and your herald.' I said it very quietly, and his eyes lit up.

'That's my William Gold,' he said. 'Get out of here before Ambrogio has a go at you himself.'

'No goodbyes?'

'None,' Hawkwood said.

Four hours later, and my convoy was rolling. It was, perhaps, the best demonstration of the level of organisation that Janet and I had achieved – the level of training that l'Angars and de la Motte had helped me reach.

De la Motte was on his new horse, with his right arm in a sling – both arms broken, and both wrists, by the fall at the Battle of Rubiera – and we hadn't fully healed, any of us. But he wasn't too injured to ride. One wagon sufficed for our wounded. When I told Janet we'd leave no one behind, she accepted without a question.

'What are we doing?' l'Angars asked.

'Rejoining the Count of Savoy, who is now on the other side,' I said. 'As of right now, we are a free company for all practical purposes. I'm paying wages, until Savoy accepts us or rejects us. The Milanese may want us dead.'

'Ah,' he said. He grinned. 'This must be the price of fame about which I've heard so much.'

He reached down to pat Pilgrim, who was riding on the tailgate of the baggage wagon. Janet looked down the column. It was raining.

'How do we avoid Milanese troops?' she asked.

'Bernabò is moving a new army down to Reggio Emilia on the Via Francigena,' I said. 'Galeazzo has an army at Asti. They *can't* have any other troops. So we take the Genoa road for sixty leagues and slip around Piacenza from the south and west and see if we can get into Asti before Gian Galeazzo and Hawkwood close it up. It'll be two weeks before they can surround it.'

'I don't want to fight Hawkwood,' Janet said. 'He has no love for women, but he's always been fair to me.'

'If I give you my word that we won't fight Hawkwood?' I said. 'That, in fact, he's ordered this, will you keep it to yourselves?'

Janet smiled her little smile. She has two – a broad smile with a hearty laugh for when she hears a good joke, and a little smile that she gives when she thinks she's smarter than other people.

'Perfect,' l'Angars said.

Our convoy discipline was excellent, nor was there any reason that it shouldn't have been. We had almost two hundred men who knew that they had large sums of money due to them from ransoms and battle bonuses. As the pay had been regular, it never occurred to them that Savoy might decline to provide double pay for the decade's greatest victory over his ally, the Pope. I wasn't sure of my own welcome.

Italy.

Why did I want to go back to Italy?

Just north of Reggio Emilia, in the teeth of the driving rain, we passed the inn where Janet and I had *not* made love, and I turned us west, into the hills. I paid outrageous sums to some very happy peasants for guides, and kept us moving. We were two hundred and fifty men and women, fifteen wagons, five hundred horses. We crossed the river at San Polo d'Enza and the next at Langhirano, moving like lightning, at least by the standards of convoys with wagons. We made camp in the hills and ate four wagons' worth of food, and our horses consumed all the forage we'd brought and more that we bought ... or stole.

We stayed that night on the banks of the Taro. We slept for six hours, rose and marched north and west again, parallel to the Via Francigena but ten miles west of it all the way. I had Marc-Antonio take scouts over to the main road, and they saw Bernabò's column moving south. Again, the advantages of having made war in the Holy Land told, as we evaded Bernabò's pickets effortlessly.

We crossed the Taro at Fornovo, and two archers fell in and had to be rescued. Pilgrim swam across and then looked both thin and miserable, and Janet told him he was a very wet dog, which he was. I took pity on him and wrapped him in my dry cloak, which was foolish of me.

But the wagons made it across without further event, and then we were on a better road network. I sent out twenty scouts and then followed them north, back to the Via Francigena, and we cut in behind Bernabò, heading north as he headed south, and we marched away on the best road in Italy, making three Italian miles an hour. The second night, we negotiated beds and forage in the great monastery of San Donnino, and we paid in gold for our food.

I got everyone under cover. It was still raining, and even the monastery's dozens of outbuildings couldn't contain our entire horse herd. I needed broad plains and abundant grass and money, and I was already terrified about what I was doing.

On the other hand, I'd got around Bernabò's army and I was well ahead of Hawkwood. I stood on the brick *demi-corte* behind the monastery's main building, watching the drizzle and trying to imagine how the roads ran for the next two days. The monastery was a very lucky find and we wouldn't sleep as soft again until Asti. Indeed, we were about to enter the Visconti's inner domains.

Inside, in the refectory, Janet was sitting with Marc-Antonio and Christopher. Marc-Antonio was writing to Janet's dictation. She was changing the loads in the wagons. Lapot was standing behind her chair, taking notes on a wax tablet.

I sat down, ate an excellent bowl of something with beef in it, over pasta, drank a cup of wine, and felt much better.

As if she could read my mind, Janet reached over and put her ink-stained hand on mine.

'We can do this,' she said. 'We can do it like no one else.'

I nodded. Lapot winked.

Marc-Antonio raised his head, looked at me, and blinked.

'If you'd told me, when I was weeping in my father's spare room,' he said, 'that being a knight would mean getting soaked to the skin and sitting in wet clothes writing out "buy" orders for grain . . .'

'Yes?' I asked.

He grinned. 'I'd have come anyway. Good point.'

'Exactly, Sir Marc-Antonio.'

'Ah,' he said, glancing unintentionally down at his knight's belt. 'Sir Marc-Antonio. I love the sound of those words.'

'Keep writing,' Janet growled.

'You are buying grain?'

'The abbot thinks we serve Bernabò,' she said quietly. 'Possibly, being Italian, he merely pretends to believe we serve Bernabò, so that he can take my silver.' She flashed me a smile. 'And I'm paying him in *good* silver.' She smiled. 'It occurred to me that if we arrive at the siege of Asti with our wagons full of grain, we'll be even more popular.'

'You are a great woman,' I said.

'I know,' she said.

'I wanted to pay the abbot in notes on the Visconti,' Marc-Antonio said.

Janet looked at me. I understood Marc-Antonio, but I agreed with Janet.

'We're not going to steal grain from the monks,' I said.

Janet turned to Marc-Antonio, and I looked at her profile, and thought, *I'm falling for Janet. Not a good idea.*

He handed over his carefully written-out bills, drank off his wine, and looked at me.

'Do I get to raise my own lance?' he asked.

'Ask me after we reach Asti. If Savoy is paying, then yes.'

Marc-Antonio grinned. 'I will be a famous *condotierro!*' he said, pumping his fist in the air. Lapot put an arm through his and took him away, leaving me with Janet and her ink-horn and her accounts.

'Don't you think it's odd that while we march up and down Italy, fighting for the Pope, and then Milan, and now possibly the Pope again ... we can pay for our grain with money from our ransomed "enemies" who used to be our allies, from the same banks we used before?' She looked up at me. 'This is a bankers' war, fought on credit, by rich idiots who tax their peasants to play the game, and it's about as effective as playing *Calcio* to decide who holds a city. Or maybe we could have wrestling matches, or fight in the lists. Cheaper, and easier on the peasants.'

I sat down and poured more wine. The refectory was a beautiful space – beautifully made, spare wooden benches of a light-coloured wood, heavy pine board floor, and whitewashed stone all around us.

There was a podium where a monk would read during meals, and behind it was a magnificent Saint Michael done in stone – very old.

I opened my mouth to speak, and she shrugged.

'I'm tired and ill-humoured,' she said.

'Everyone is,' I agreed. 'One more day – two at the outside.'

At some point in the moment, we were holding hands.

She looked at me – no flirtation, no come-hither.

'William, do you know what I like best about you?'

I grinned. 'Nothing comes to mind.'

She nodded. 'I like that you let me be whatever I like, and that includes being a lance.'

She was wearing an arming doublet that had seen much better days, and a pair of hose that might have been embarrassing if they hadn't been covered with a pair of ruined high boots. Her hands were strong on the wine cup, and her hair was tied back the way a man's would be.

She glanced at me. 'I have ... feelings for you. But they're not as important to me as my place in the company.'

I nodded.

'I won't become a *bonne amie*. I'm not a courtesan or a wife, either. I have a suspicion that you'll turn out to be Richard Musard all over again.' She shrugged and drank wine. 'I'm not doing this well. I meant to tell you how much I wanted ... you.' She shrugged. 'Fuck it. William, we go back too far to be lovers. I'm sorry I started down that road.'

That was a punch in the gut.

But I'm good at various forms of combat. I pasted a smile on my face, and drank some wine. Then I raised my cup.

'Too bad,' I said, toasting her. 'But I think I see.'

She nodded. 'Listen, William. I'm a year older than you. I'm smaller than most men, and my bones hurt all the time.' She made a face. 'I have maybe three more campaigns in me, if no one puts me down.' She met my eyes. 'I love it. Being a knight. Even in a bad cause.'

'As do I,' I agreed.

She leant over suddenly and just barely touched her lips to mine. It went on far too long, and then I was sitting back. She was bright red.

'I'm an idiot,' she said.

'Me too,' I said. 'I need to sleep.'

I got up, finished my wine, and went to my bale of straw. Alone.

We were rolling before the sun came up in the morning, and by the grace of God, the sun *did* rise and the rain was over, and we kept rolling through a late August day with a cool breeze and dustless roads. I had officers out ahead so that horses were watered by rotation. We had halts every two hours. We were making *better* than four miles an hour. At Piacenza we were terrifyingly close to Pavia and Galeazzo. I could all but feel his malign presence beating on me from the east.

But we turned west again, and now we were marching *out* of the Visconti lands. My scouts were working hard, and they were well in front. I had Beppo and the Birigucci brothers half a day ahead.

It was too dangerous to stop so close to Pavia, so we kept marching into the dark. The horses complained and the oxen on the wagons showed the whites of their eyes, but I had good wagoners and I offered them double pay to keep on through the night.

And on we rolled. Five miles, and another five – past sleeping villages and inns locked tightly. By Matins, we were our own harbingers. No one had heard of our coming, and we rolled on – Oviglio, Masio ...

At Castello di Annone, the sun was rising and we still hadn't lost a man or a woman. I crossed the little Roman bridge and was cheered by a dozen of our *bonnes amies* who were sitting on their mules by the roadside, eating a grilled fish they'd just bought from a boy. I bought one, too, and ate it with them. I gave the tail to Pilgrim, and bought another for Christopher and Janet, who came up with the wagons.

Ewan rode in before we were all across.

'There are Visconti troops on the road,' he said rapidly. 'They aren't even armed – their weapons are in their wagons.'

My guide of the day was a young, very intelligent-looking peasant named Roberto. He had the thin, ascetic face of a Greek saint, and he spoke more thoughtfully than most young men. He looked at me and fingered his short beard.

'Eh,' he said.

'Yes?'

'Heh,' he said. 'There's a road through the mountains.'

'What road?' I asked.

He looked fearful. 'Other side of the river,' he said.

'You mean, if we recross the river, we can go through the mountains?'

439

'Yes, lord,' he said.

I looked at Janet.

All the *bonnes amies* groaned, and one swore by Mary Magdalene, and then we recrossed the bridge. We climbed and climbed up into the mountains, and if the Milanese saw us, we had no hint. Everyone was very tired – no one is good with the loss of a full night's sleep, and Thorald looked like he might die.

But we plodded on, up and down. Azzano d'Asti and Montemarzo and fifty switchbacks in three hours.

But then we saw the castle at Asti. The Visconti were across the river, and didn't hold the bridge, and then it was all easy.

'Sir Guillaume d'Oro,' Pierre de Murs said. He wore a slight smile. 'My lord the count is very ... interested ... to see you.'

'I am eager to see the count,' I said.

I gestured at our baggage wagons. All my people were in full armour and carrying their weapons.

'The wagons are mostly full of grain,' I said.

De Murs laughed. 'You are full of surprises, Sir Guillaume.'

An hour later I was standing in the hall of the Castello. The count was dressed in half-armour, with an emerald-green cote-hardie cut to fit over his breastplate, and a gold knight's belt at his hips.

'Sir Guglielmo,' he said, looking up. 'Have you really brought your entire company?'

'My Lord, Sir John Hawkwood ordered me to come,' I said.

I'd had four days to plan how I delivered Sir John's message. Now I had his full attention.

'Sir John Hawkwood *ordered* you to leave Bernabò's army and join me?' he asked.

'Yes, My Lord.'

The count waved to young Roger, who really needed to be placed with a knight. He was too pretty and too old to be a page, and had been for two years. Roger brought me wine with a flash of a smile.

'My Lord,' I said, 'Roger needs to be a squire.'

Roger beamed at me.

The count frowned, and then looked at Roger.

'How old are you, messire?' he asked.

'Sixteen, My Lord,' Roger said.

The count glanced at me. 'Sir Guglielmo, is it really your intention to serve me here at Asti?' he asked.

'Yes, My Lord,' I said.

The count smiled. 'Then, Roger, you can do no better than to find yourself arms and take service with Sir Guglielmo. You will not find a better knight.'

I thought Roger might put his arms around my neck. I gave him a smile.

'Run along,' I said. 'You have armour?'

He paused.

'Find Marc-Antonio,' I said. 'Sir Marc-Antonio, my former squire.'

When the boy was gone, I faced the count.

'So it has happened,' I said.

When the count went to war with the Visconti, it wasn't just a sea change, it was a symptom of changes throughout the world of diplomacy.

The count tapped his fingers on his side table.

'Yes,' he said.

'I have brought seventy lances,' I said. 'I can serve you for feudal duty, but I will need money for my people.'

He nodded. 'I can only afford to pay you as feudal troops,' he said. But then he smiled. 'At least, officially. Thank you, Guglielmo. I have several vassals whose service is ... not what I expected. I will send them home and retain you. You will want to send your horse herd west, with mine and Montferrat's.'

He clasped his hands, a ring winking like fire on his right hand.

He waited.

'Is this the chessboard you imagined?' I asked.

He smiled. The black and white board was there, on his side table.

'Yes and no,' he said. 'The English are in a state of collapse that I had not anticipated, and the Visconti are more successful than I expected. The victory at Rubiera ...' He smiled. 'I'm sure that you played a great role, but I might have been happier if you hadn't been so effective.'

'Now that we're servants of the Pope again?' I asked.

'Is this what passes for a sense of humour in England?' Savoy asked. But his mouth curled. 'I think I prefer the Pope, even this Pope, to the Visconti.'

And anyway, you will end up holding Asti, a very rich city.

'And the other matters?' he said carefully.

'Sir John's contract expires in September,' I said.

Savoy raised an eyebrow. 'I am not in a position to employ him,' he said.

I nodded. 'The Pope is,' I said.

Savoy looked at me, steepled his hands, and then rang a little silver bell.

A servant appeared.

'Sir Richard, if you please,' Savoy said.

We chatted about horses and how best to move them before the formal siege began.

Musard came in, embraced me, and poured himself a cup of wine.

'Your friend Sir Guglielmo here wishes me to be the go-between for Sir John Hawkwood and the Pope,' he said.

Richard glanced at me. 'Yes,' he said. 'An excellent notion, as long as Sir John can be trusted.'

Savoy flushed. He drank off his wine. Then he smiled.

'What a world,' he said. 'Very well. I suppose he's not much different from Coucy, except in breeding.'

'We're employing Coucy for the Pope,' Richard said to me over his wine cup. 'You know, because you defeated Malatesta and d'Este isn't up to the job.'

I nodded. 'Do you send messengers to Coucy?' I asked Richard.

'Never more than six a week,' he said.

'Can I send a letter?'

'Absolutely,' Richard said. 'Welcome back to the side of right and good.'

I grinned. 'The whole time I was with Hawkwood, I was serving the count,' I said.

'He has you there,' Savoy said. 'We're the ones who changed sides.'

He said it with enough bitterness for a cup of aloes, but he managed a slight smile.

When I had my letter for Princess Isabella ready, I had Janet copy it out fair, and Marc-Antonio made a second copy and then a third. The letter outlined my allegations and the proofs, where I had them, in detail – the testimony of the cook, the scraps of parchment, what I knew of Black-Beard. I put it all down.

442

One copy went to the princess. As it turned out, I had reservations about lone messengers crossing Lombardy, and I sent Marc-Antonio with Beppo and the Biriguccis. I gave the second copy to the count, and watched him read it.

'Yes,' he said at the end. 'You know, before Achaea, I wouldn't have believed it. I didn't think people worked that way.'

I had nothing to say to that.

The third copy I sent to my bankers in Venice, with a convoy of merchants, disguised as a copy of my company's accounts. As insurance. It would sit in a vault, and hopefully no one would ever read it.

And while I did these things, Gian Galeazzo, twenty-year-old son of Galeazzo Visconti and murderer of the Duke of Clarence, came up with 'his' army. He had three thousand lances and another two thousand Milanese infantry, and a small horde of pioneers and peasant workers.

I felt an enormous relief as I watched them open their siege lines. I was happy to face the Vipers of Milan across the fields and walls. I looked down at the banners as the enemy camp was set. I could see Hawkwood's banner close to Gian Galeazzo's. I could see Ambrogio Visconti's banner, and Antonio, his half-brother and my sometime friend. Richard pointed out the new men – Italian captains that I didn't know, Ruggero Cane and Jacopo dal Verme. And Father Angelo, whom I hadn't seen since Christmas at Chambéry the year before, pointed out a distant relation, Cavallino di Cavalli.

'You must be a long way from your parish, Father,' I said. 'I'm fairly certain that none of my people has been to confession since we lost you.'

'I am working my way from the top to the bottom,' Father Angelo said. He laughed. 'Life as a parish priest may be too dull for me.'

I grinned. 'You know you're always welcome with us,' I said.

He looked out over the walls. 'Now that you are fighting for the Pope ...' he said, and let that hang.

It was a formidable host of professionals – the best money could buy. Against them, Otto of Brunswick, who was the lord in command of Asti as regent for the very young Marquis of Montferrat ...

You are following along, yes? The Paleologoi of Montferrat were the owners, although both Savoy and Visconti also claimed Asti under various pretexts, and Savoy had thrown in his lot with Montferrat to protect his own claim and back the Pope against the Visconti ...

Eh bien. I feel I have to remind you, because I was there, and I had to remind myself from time to time how the sides aligned.

The 'enemy' had built a big *bastide*, as large as the siege mound at Borgoforte. We were cut off from the outside eventually, and we ran out of some luxuries. The siege rolled on through August, but the truth was that the issue was never in doubt. We had two thousand men, excellent captains, and enough food for a year. Gian Galeazzo had bickering captains, some problems with disease, and very little stomach for a fight. We heard that Sir John proposed an all-out assault on the outworks, and Gian Galeazzo's councillors declined to allow the army to make such a risky attempt. There were raids and counter-raids. My people continued to show a real flair for stealing horses on dark nights, and Ewan and Christopher together proved an irresistible and truly international force in night-raiding; a man born south of Aegypt in Africa and a man from beyond the Wall in Scotland united to make war in Italy.

Spies told us that Hawkwood proposed an assault a second time. For my part, I don't think Hawkwood ever intended to make such an escalade. I think he was needling Gian Galeazzo, who paraded his men every day like a boy playing with his toy soldiers.

Perhaps stung by such taunts, Gian Galeazzo surprised us in late August by sending a challenge to mortal combat. The challenge specified the Lord Gian Galeazzo and four knights against the Count of Savoy, and four other knights.

Otto of Brunswick was a big man, even for a German – old enough to have grey in his hair, and strong enough not to care.

'This is a child's idea,' he said sharply.

The count looked at Richard. We were having our daily meeting before we went to our posts. All the officers had sections of the wall and pie-slices of the town to defend.

Richard nodded. 'My Lord,' he said, 'given that you are the most famous knight in Europe and he is a stripling of twenty, you can only lose if you fight. If you kill or wound him, you are a bully. If he kills you, he's a hero.'

'And he's my sister's son,' the count said.

He shrugged, glancing at me, and I wondered if he was thinking of the Prince of Achaea. Or of Lionel of Clarence.

'We have to at least pay lip service to the idea of this duel,' Otto of Brunswick said.

The count smiled mirthlessly. 'I have the perfect men for the work. We can prevaricate with the best of them,' he said bitterly. Because really, for all his faults, my count was a true knight, and when challenged, he wanted to fight. 'Sir Guglielmo? Sir Richard?'

He meant me, and he added Pierre de Murs.

'You don't have to come,' I said to Richard.

'I wouldn't miss this,' Richard said. 'Anyway, I'm a knight of his order – I can't say no. Are you going to loose your bolt?'

We were walking down into the lower town from the castle, leading our warhorses by their bridles.

'What bolt?' Pierre de Murs asked.

I smiled. 'Gian Galeazzo hired assassins to kill the English Duke of Clarence,' I said.

De Murs stopped walking. 'Christ,' he said, the only blasphemy I ever remember hearing from him.

Richard smiled. 'You see?' he asked de Murs. 'Never a dull moment with Sir Guillaume.'

De Murs glanced at me. 'Should we be in armour?' he asked.

'Absolutely, ' Richard and I said together. 'I'll get the count.'

Two hours later, and I was somewhat surprised to be sitting on Gabriel facing John Hawkwood. He was with Ambrogio and Antonio, a man I didn't know, and Gian Galeazzo himself. We were at the south end of the fortified bridge over the Tanaro river – heralds had agreed this was neutral ground for a parley. It was a beautiful August day. The mountains were magnificent to the north and west, and the river sparkled in the sun, and the grey stone was warm.

They brought a dozen men-at-arms, all Milanese bravos in full armour. We had the Count of Savoy, on a green caparisoned charger, and Pierre de Murs, and Richard, and Ogier and me. Behind us were no men-at-arms, because that's what the truce had specified.

'And *that's* why we wear armour,' Richard said, looking at the numbers gathered by the river. 'He wouldn't try a straight-up assassination, would he?'

The Visconti camp rose on a hill in the background, capped by their massive earthwork.

Hawkwood smiled at me, five horse lengths away.

'William,' he called out. 'This is Ruggero Cane.' He pointed out the man I didn't know.

'I don't believe he would,' I said to Richard.

I rode forward, assuming that it was better to be hanged for a lion than a lamb. I stripped off my right gauntlet and shook Cane's hand.

The Italian smiled. 'I gather we aren't fighting just yet,' he said.

Gian Galeazzo was fidgeting. 'What are we doing?' he called out sharply.

He was trying to keep his voice low – trying to be the great man. His horse was betraying his nerves. Horses are like that.

I looked at him, and something rose in my throat, like a lump. Anger? Fear? It wasn't easy to diagnose, but the closest I can come is *disgust*. Here was a young man, one of the wealthiest and most power-ful in the world, and he was already a monster. *And he was pretending to be a knight.*

Pierre de Murs had been chosen as our spokesman, and he rode forward.

'My Lord, the Count of Savoy declines your challenge, as he is your uncle and you are not of an age to ...'

Visconti flushed. The flush made him look still younger. He had pimples, and he still had the lean build that comes before the bulk of muscle forms, and his beard and moustache were very thin. His horse turned as he communicated his anger through his knees and thighs.

'Not of an age!' he spat. 'Come and fight me, you treacherous coward.'

Antonio was looking away. Even Ambrogio had the good grace to look sorry.

Pierre de Murs had probably never heard his master, the Count of Savoy, referred to as a treacherous coward. He was silent a beat too long, and then he shook his head as if shaking off a blow.

'My lord suggests that you choose a champion to represent you—'

'Fuck this, you pompous arse,' Gian Galeazzo said. 'I'm not talking to your women any more, Uncle! Come and fight me! I'm not afraid you'll murder me the way you murdered Filippo!'

Now Sir John was looking deeply uneasy, and Ambrogio had a hand on his cousin's bridle. Ruggero Cane had a look of disgust on his face that raised him in my estimation.

Count Amadeus, the Athlete of Christ, the man who'd saved

Constantinople and tried to save the Church, was speechless with rage. He looked as if he'd taken an arrow in the gut, and his eyes all but threw thunderbolts.

I walked Gabriel forward. I felt fear, and anger – that odd weakness in your biceps that means you are in the grip of something else.

'Gian Galeazzo Visconti,' I said.

'Don't …' Hawkwood said. But he didn't say it with much effort.

Gian Galeazzo looked at me. In his arrogance and his anger, he didn't recognise me. Another servant – another cog in someone else's machine.

'Another fucking English barbarian,' he spat.

I smiled. 'Be more moderate, My Lord. Your uncle would kill you in a single pass, which these gentlemen must have advised you. And unlike them,' I said into a near-perfect silence, 'I have seen you fight.'

Then he knew me. 'Ah, the sword master,' he said. 'I thought you were in my service? When did you change sides?'

'I was never in your service,' I said.

'I don't pay much attention to when the servants come and go,' he said.

He was trying to ignore me, but I had moved my horse right in by his horse, and Gabriel was not afraid of his stallion, so that the two began to snort and skirmish. Ambrogio reached for my bridle.

'This is the man,' he hissed.

I backed Gabriel one step, so that Ambrogio grasped empty air.

Ambrogio drew. He had a short sword, or a huge dagger, the length of a big man's forearm and very broad at the hilt, and as soon as it cleared the scabbard, a number of things happened.

Antonio rammed his horse into Ambrogio's horse.

My horse, tired of tangling with Gian Galeazzo's horse, began to rear.

Richard cut in front of the Count of Savoy and roared, 'Ware!'

The Visconti men-at-arms put their visors down.

And John Hawkwood turned his horse. He had a beautiful, huge beast of a horse, and he blocked the Milanese from their lord.

'Hold!' he roared like a lion at bay.

I noted that Ruggero Cane followed Hawkwood, turning his horse side-on to us, offering us no threat and preventing the Milanese men-at-arms from crowding forward.

Ambrogio was a true Visconti, and he didn't believe in half measures. He cut at me with his short sword. As we were at a parley, I didn't have a helmet on, and he cut at my head. But he tried to feint – we were very close, almost breastplate to breastplate – and his hand went back behind his shoulder and the blade rotated as he went from *fendente* to *reverso*.

Fiore had had an answer for that, too, even on horseback. Ambrogio hesitated too long, ceding the initiative, and I was above him as my horse half reared. I tapped my spurs and got my right hand between his hilt and his head and caught a piece of his cross guard and a finger – not much, but enough. My horse fell forward and weight and momentum ripped Ambrogio backwards, wrenching his shoulder. Gabriel went perhaps three strides forward, and I ripped Ambrogio from his saddle, right over his cantle, and dropped him on the ground. I ended up with the sword, backwards, in my hand.

Behind me, Richard had also pushed forward, protecting the count and further spooking Gian Galeazzo's horse, which tried to rear in limited space, collided with Ambrogio's horse, and threw him. It was a long, slow fall, and Gian Galeazzo hit hard, just as I got Gabriel around.

Richard was already backing his horse.

'I didn't touch him!' he shouted.

Gian Galeazzo was roaring with pain and humiliation. His men-at-arms were trying to press past Hawkwood and Cane. I got my horse back between de Murs and Musard.

'Kill them!' Gian Galeazzo shouted.

Ambrogio was stunned, his shoulder wrenched, and he was still trying to get to his feet. He might have been a bad man and a bad knight, but he was one tough bastard.

'Kill them all!' Gian Galeazzo demanded again.

He was not obeyed. And I'd had enough of his bravado and his vanity. I leant out, and dropped Ambrogio's sword point first into the dirt by the young man's head.

'Challenge us again when you've learnt to ride,' I said with all the contempt I could muster.

And then we turned and rode back over our bridge and into Asti.

When we were safe inside our own walls, with our well-paid crossbowmen covering us and Ewan leaning out from behind a merlon to wave, Richard glanced at me.

'I think you'd better pray that Robert of Geneva never allies with the Visconti,' he said.

In less than a week, the Visconti army broke up the siege and rode away to the south. There were loud recriminations among the enemy captains – so loud that we heard them.

We fetched our horse herd, ate some fresh meat, and waited for the army of Enguerrand de Coucy, which was coming over the passes behind us. Under the count's orders, my company probed south and west, looking for Bernabò, who was making another thrust for Bologna, this time at the head of his own forces.

We passed straight down the Via Francigena. This time, all our enemies were in front of us – Gian Galeazzo's army had splintered, with most of his forces going to join Bernabò. I stopped the night at the same monastery that I'd visited heading north. We didn't pretend to be Bernabò's men, but we still paid our bills, and we purchased the rest of their grain. Italy had monasteries as big as English towns – they were very rich.

It was simple service, and my archers and men-at-arms behaved well. We didn't pillage, we didn't rape, and we cleared Bernabò's pickets off the road. He was building up near Parma, with posts out towards Reggio Emilia and Rubiera. He had another ring of companies facing north, to watch us.

The only military feature of the campaign was when I realised that we needed a crossing of the Taro river, and that, as I was eighty Roman miles ahead of the Count of Savoy and de Coucy, I had the chance to perform one of those feats of arms that help make men famous.

About six miles west of Parma, the Ponte Taro had earthworks at either end, held by one of the Milanese companies. I had a look at the edge of darkness, wearing a carter's smock and a huge straw hat – I suspected it was Father Angelo's. I planned the operation in the same clothes, with Janet and l'Angars, and we tried it that same night. The plan was for my company to take the bridge, seizing it from both ends in our old accustomed way, as we had done in France. De la Motte led the men who crossed the river on a cattle ford, and sneaked through the darkness. Lapot led the escalade from our side. Janet led a dozen young men-at-arms dressed as women, including my new squire Roger, who made a most disconcertingly pretty woman, even with a misshapen gown over his breastplate.

I waited behind the nearest woods, about five hundred paces from the nearest earthwork, with de la Motte and the rest of the men-at-arms and archers, all mounted. Pilgrim lay at my feet, tongue lolling. Above me, in an old oak, Witkin watched the action at the bridge.

'There they go,' he said at last.

Everything seemed to be taking too long. The sun was rising – I wanted it to be over. I was beginning to regret the feeling of family I had about my little company – I couldn't abide losses. Ewan, there. Lapot? L'Angars? Janet? Pilgrim?

I couldn't lose any of them.

Sam Bibbo sat on his charger, as impassive as ever.

'Get ready!' Witkin called.

We *were* ready.

'Milady drew her sword!' Witkin called.

'Go!' I roared.

And we cantered down the road.

Sometimes a plan works. That day, Janet strolled in past two bored sentries at the near *bastide* and found the earthwork almost empty. The rest of the garrison was sitting in a wattle shack, playing dice and trying to stay warm in the chilly early autumn air.

Janet took them all.

Perhaps three hundred heartbeats later, we cantered through the outer ward and I flipped my visor down and rode for the bridge itself. It was a big bridge that crossed not just the channel of the river but the mudflats on either side – the Taro ran much bigger in spring.

The problem, for whoever was holding the bridge, was that the length of the structure meant that the two ends could not support each other – they were just two isolated outposts. De la Motte had gone up his ladders as soon as he saw Janet on the far bank. He held one gate tower and about thirty feet of wall, and the Milanese might have made a fight of it, except that fifty armoured men rode across the bridge and their resistance collapsed. Just like that. No men died – a few had cuts – and we had the key to Bernabò's route back to Milan.

The next day, Ambrogio made an attack on the south end of the bridge, but Ewan and Christopher alerted us an hour before the attack rolled in, and we had eighty good archers. The attack didn't last very long, and the attackers, when they fled, left a petard like the one we'd used at Corinth and several barrels of powder on the ground. I sent young Roger to Ambrogio with an offer to hand over his wounded, and Roger came back saying that Messire Ambrogio was 'wondrous abusive'.

On the fourteenth day of September, which was the next day but one, Messire Bernabò Visconti came in person to look at my defences. I knew his banner, and I knew him by his size and the size of his horse. He had a long look, waved his arm a number of times, and rode away.

The next morning, Ewan and Lazarus the Greek and Beppo took a scout to the north, behind us, and came back to say that there was no one moving between us and Piacenza, but Christopher, who went up the river, caught Ambrogio crossing with two hundred lances. That evening, Antonio's company rode into the south side and began to dig in.

'This could get warm,' Janet said. 'You might want to grab one of the local boats, before they do.'

'Whatever for?' I asked.

'If Savoy and de Coucy take their time,' she said, 'you need to get out. The rest of us can always surrender. They'll kill you.'

My little piece of bravado in grabbing the bridge was now appearing as arrogant as anything Gian Galeazzo had ever done, and when Ambrogio's crossbowmen put a barricade across the road north, I grew concerned. I had Beppo take a dozen local boats.

'Three days' food,' Janet said. 'And only two days' forage for the horses.'

She looked around, decided we were alone on our earthwork wall, and brushed her lips on mine.

'Mmm,' I said.

'I know,' she said. She shook herself. 'No,' she said, and walked off quickly.

I didn't sleep well that night, and Ambrogio was only part of the problem.

I woke with the decision made. I looked at it, lying on my pallet of straw inside a canvas forage bag, and the more I thought about it, the better I liked it.

We'd assault Ambrogio's camp. I was only outnumbered by about one third, and I had the better people. I smiled, because I knew it was the right answer, and I slept for another hour in celebration.

And woke to find that he'd abandoned both his barricade and his camp. I got a new pavilion.

Enguerrand de Coucy rode across my bridge before Sext, and took my hand with a broad smile.

'Why am I not surprised to find you here, Sir William?' he said in excellent Norman English-French. 'Here, I was concerned about how we would make it across the Taro, and the Count of Savoy smiles and says he is sure that it is all arranged.' He bowed. 'My lady wife sends her greetings. And her thanks.'

'Thanks?' I asked.

He leant close. 'You shook the tree,' he said. 'She intends to cut it down.'

We pulled apart our barricades at the far end of the bridge, and Antonio's light horse retired before us as we moved south towards Parma. Coucy had a cadre of Breton adventurers, but he also had bought a company of Hungarians – men I knew, at least a little. I sent my own outriders with the Hungarians in a broad sweep, south to Parma and west.

Coucy was an able captain. He had an odd temperament, as I'm sure you'll recognise. He seemed lethargic, but it was only his idea of how a great noble should behave. His languid disinterest hid a keen mind and a quick hand. And for the next few days, I was his lieutenant as we turned Bernabò out of Parma and denied him access to Milan. I spent a day cutting the road to Mantua, flagrantly violating Mantua's supposed neutrality. I sent a polite note to the Lord Gonzaga, apologising for my intrusion, and suggesting, in the language of chivalry, how it might not go well if he allowed Bernabò to have supplies from Milan.

Sam Bibbo was sitting on his riding horse, eating a roast chicken, as we withdrew from Mantuan territory, richer in pocket and in body.

'I do love visiting Mantua,' he said. 'Better 'an France in the old days. Richer.'

'Softer,' said Ewan.

'Bra,' Thorald said, laughing.

By the end of September, we'd moved past Parma. De Coucy chose to build a fortified camp at Novellara and gave me the honour and duty of holding the forward posts near the Abbey of Campagnola, which I occupied. Father Angelo promised the monks that we wouldn't loot the place to the ground, and then we shooed them out and we rendered the place impregnable – if a little ugly – over the next week. Ambrogio tried an assault at midweek, but my well-paid peasant guides gave him away and he retreated after the first shower of war bow arrows.

And the next afternoon, the entirety of Hawkwood's two hundred lances rode up in broad daylight. They made a camp well beyond extreme bowshot.

That night, I escorted a cloaked man through my lines, and all the way to Hawkwood's pickets. I waited with a dozen lances to escort him back, but instead of my masked and cloaked friend, I saw John Hawkwood in full armour.

'Well?' I asked.

He laughed. 'We have a truce. The Pope and the Visconti are in peace negotiations.'

'Good God,' I said.

'Don't worry,' he said. 'They won't last a week. In the meantime, I'm done with him. The fool.' He looked back over his shoulder. 'Tomorrow.'

'Tomorrow?' I asked.

'We're coming over to the Pope. I'm allowed five hundred lances and an independent command.'

I grinned.

'Are you with me, William?' he asked.

As an answer, I embraced him, and he laughed.

'I'm going to need your secret,' he said.

'It's not mine any more,' I said. 'Isabella of England has it all.'

He smiled his fox's smile.

'I'll just borrow it for a while,' he said. 'And then we'll raise a little hell.'

EPILOGUE

I t was very late, but no one had left. Froissart was still writing by the light of a candle that Aemilie had brought him. Chaucer was looking at the dregs in his wine cup and obviously considering more. The men-at-arms and archers were smiling. Some had been mentioned by name, and they grinned sheepishly and elbowed each other.

'It's a very good story,' Chaucer said. 'Is it true? About the Visconti and Prince Lionel?'

'You know it is,' the big knight said.

One of their long looks passed between them.

Chaucer smiled slowly. 'I can neither confirm nor deny,' he said. 'And the Visconti are as powerful today as they ever were.'

'They never took Bologna,' Sir William said. 'They lost everything in the Emilia.'

'Until Florence changed sides,' Chaucer said.

The two men nodded, the weight of shared and hidden knowledge obviously heavy on both.

'But ...' Aemile spoke from the fireside. 'But, did you love this lady-knight? I like her. I didn't know there even *were* lady-knights.'

Froissart looked up. 'I cannot write this,' he said. 'No one would believe these things of seigneurs so very powerful and famous.'

Again, Chaucer and Gold exchanged looks.

'As for the lady, that's for another day,' Gold said.

'And are you not the Captain of Venice? How did that happen? What of the Great Raid? What of ...?' Froissart was leaning forward.

Sir William got to his feet. 'I'm for a walk on the walls with Master Chaucer,' he said. 'And then bed. Perhaps tomorrow, Master Froissart. Perhaps tomorrow we'll talk about the great raid, and the Chioggia War.'

He got up, and most of his company rose, some unsteadily.

'Don't give these good people any trouble,' he said to a big archer. The man smiled back.

'Na' trouble, Sir William.'

Chaucer followed the knight out into the darkness, and they heard him say something about 'Clarence', and Sir William's booming laugh.

'I liked the bit about you and your sister riding to Canterbury,' Chaucer said, and then the closing door cut off the sound.

CREDITS

Christian Cameron and Orion Fiction would like to thank everyone at Orion who worked on the publication of *Hawkwood's Sword* in the UK.

Editorial
Lucy Frederick
Celia Killen

Copy editor
Steve O'Gorman

Proof reader
Clare Wallis

Contracts
Anne Goddard
Jake Alderson

Design
Rabab Adams
Tomas Almeida
Joanna Ridley
Nick May

Editorial Management
Charlie Panayiotou
Jane Hughes
Alice Davis

Production
Ruth Sharvell

Publicity
Will O'Mullane

Finance
Jasdip Nandra
Afeera Ahmed
Elizabeth Beaumont
Sue Baker

Audio
Paul Stark

Rights
Susan Howe
Krystyna Kujawinska
Jessica Purdue
Louise Henderson

Sales
Jen Wilson
Esther Waters

Victoria Laws
Rachael Hum
Ellie Kyrke-Smith
Frances Doyle
Georgina Cutler

Operations
Jo Jacobs
Sharon Willis
Lisa Pryde